CATAN

KLAUS TEUBER

CATAN

THE NOVEL

BLACK STONE PUBLISHING

Published in 2025 by Blackstone Publishing
Cover and book design by Candice Edwards

Printed in the United States of America
Originally published in hardcover by Blackstone Publishing in 2024

First paperback edition: 2025
ISBN 979-8-228-39625-8
Fiction / Historical / General

Version 1

Blackstone Publishing
31 Mistletoe Rd.
Ashland, OR 97520

www.BlackstonePublishing.com

CONTENTS

Prologue....1

PART 1: (WINTER, AD 860)....5
- Chapter 1: Over the Mountains....7
- Chapter 2: The Homecoming....53
- Chapter 3: Halldor's Revenge....71

PART 2: (SPRING, AD 860)....103
- Chapter 4: The Decision....105
- Chapter 5: The Hunt....113
- Chapter 6: Preparations....132

PART 3: (EARLY SUMMER, AD 860)....175
- Chapter 7: Carla....177
- Chapter 8: Frida....197
- Chapter 9: Coronium....219
- Chapter 10: On the Open Sea....228

PART 4: (SUMMER, AD 860)....267
- Chapter 11: Hunger....269
- Chapter 12: The Chain Wielders....286
- Chapter 13: Woodhaven....304

PART 5: (FALL, AD 860)....331
- Chapter 14: Harvest Feast....333
- Chapter 15: The Murder....351
- Chapter 16: Ryan....405

PART 6: (SUMMER, AD 861)....433
- Chapter 17: Infidelity....435
- Chapter 18: Parchment....446
- Chapter 19: Wolfhounds....479

PART 7: (FALL, AD 861)....507
- Chapter 20: The Feud....509
- Chapter 21: Ox Gall....526
- Chapter 22: The Jarl....541

Afterword....571

Acknowledgments....577

the settlers' Journey
N
100 km
Flight
Strong Winds/Storm
Calm
Knarr
Yellow beak
Catan
Terra
Incognita
Buzzard

Northland
North Atlantic right whale
Denmark
Ireland
HEDEBY
Britain
Francia
Land of
the Bretons
ORUNIUM
Galicia
Asturias
Emirate
of Cōrdoba
Dau
Hot Land

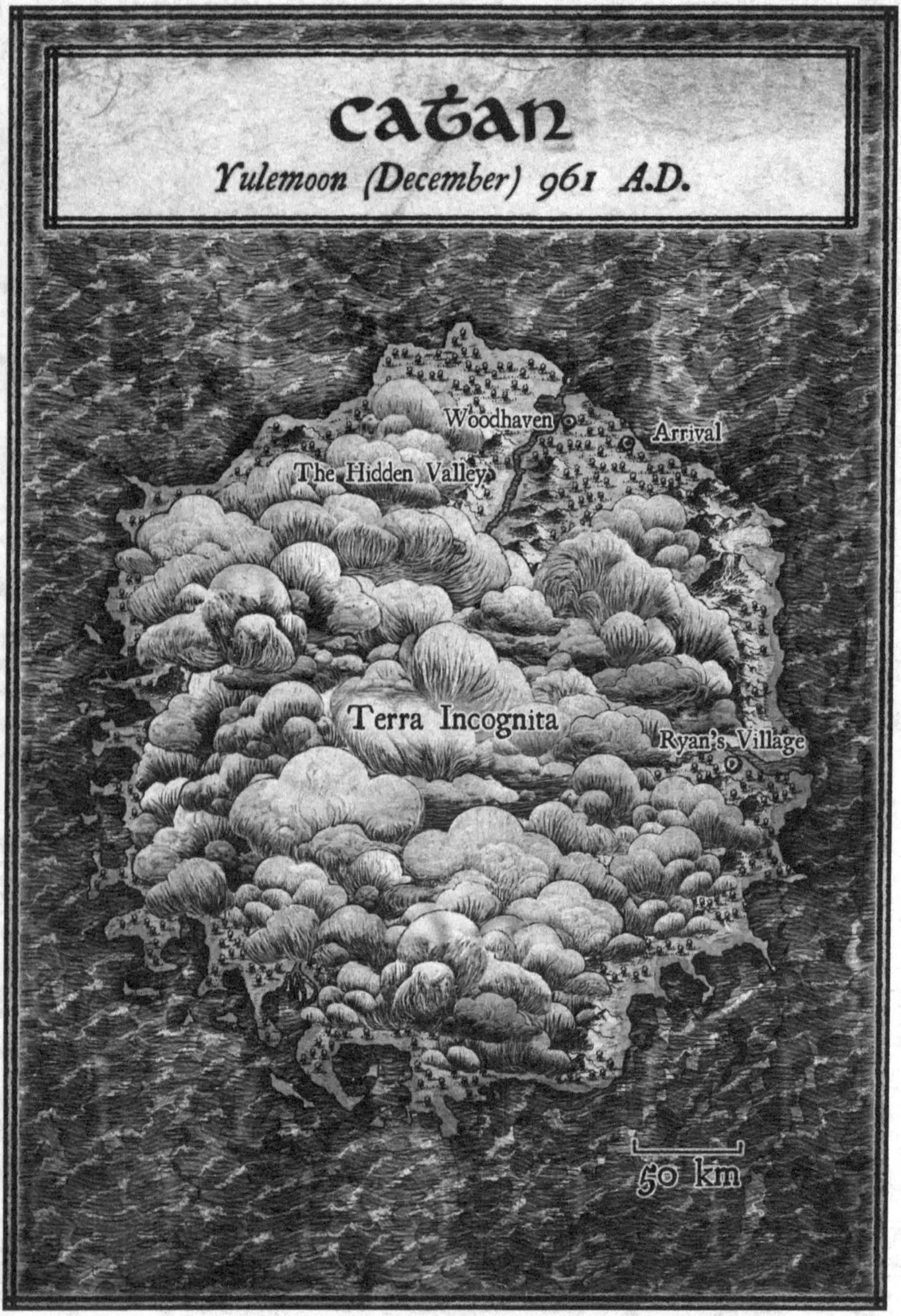
Catan
Yulemoon (December) 961 A.D.
Woodhaven
Arrival
The Hidden Valley
Terra Incognita
Ryan's Village
50 km

Woodhaven and Surroundings
10 km
Arrival
Woodhaven
100
Saltmarsh River
200
200
500
Guardian
of the Portal
200
200
500
500
The
Hidden Valley
1000
1000

PROLOGUE

My name is Björn Einarson. I live on Catan, an island blessed by God with fertile ground. The vast ocean surrounding our island determines the weather on our shores. Mostly, its winds are kind to us, ensuring a harmonious balance between fair days that bestow golden ripeness upon our grain in the fields, and dull days with heavy, dark clouds that bring abundant rain to saturate our soil and allow lush greenery to thrive.

However, sometimes the ocean rages, sending us tempestuous storms. Then, mighty waves eat into our coastline and blinding flashes of lightning followed by booming thunderclaps instill fear, and not only in the children and dogs.

When I was little, those thunderstorms used to frighten me. Seeking shelter, I would crawl under a bench and recall an eerie tale the old folks told us. It was the tale of a huge serpent that spells the end of the world. In my childhood imagination, I feared the storms as the harbingers of this powerful monster whose wide-open jaws would greedily devour not only house and farm but our entire island.

My mother, aware of my fears, one day pointed at a small globule of fat floating on the surface of my broth, saying this was an island in the sea of my soup. Just like the fat, a real island cannot go under—least of all Catan, she emphasized with a smile. The island was much too big for that.

From then on, I found the storms a little less intimidating.

When I turned thirteen, my father told me Catan had not always been inhabited. Many winters ago, the generation of my grandmothers and grandfathers sailed across the ocean in ships capable of navigating the deep seas and took possession of the island.

I struggled to imagine such a voyage, and, scarcely believing what I'd heard, I begged him to tell me more about our forefathers—who they were and where they had come from. Father laughed and placed a calloused hand on my shoulder. He told me there was a man who was one of the first settlers and who was better suited to satisfying my thirst for knowledge. The time was ripe for me to meet this man.

One week later, my father took me to a ship bound for a village that lay four days' sailing down the coast. My great-uncle lived there, and with his nearly seventy winters, he was likely the oldest inhabitant of Catan. At least that was how he struck me when I met him for the first time.

I can still see him standing outside his house. He leaned heavily on a gnarled stick when I greeted him and explained who I was and what I wanted. The many years my great-uncle had seen shrank his bones, took almost all his hair, and furrowed his skin with deep lines, but time conceded defeat before his eyes. Their blue was of a clarity usually possessed only by the young. They were intelligent eyes, eyes that were home to a merry fellow named mischief who twinkled as he took my shyness with a small jest and led me into the house.

On that day, a deep friendship began between him and me, a friendship that would last almost three years—until his death. I visited him regularly during that time, and he answered all my questions, satisfied my longing for knowledge, and more: he deepened my skills in the arts of reading and writing. This, in particular, seemed to bring him joy.

On the very first day of our acquaintance, he addressed my most pressing question: that of the origin of my ancestors. The rusty hinges creaked pitifully when he opened the lid of a scuffed old chest, lifting out a piece of parchment with torn edges. Upon it, so he explained, he had sketched when he was younger all the lands of the old world known to him. He tapped a gouty finger on a jagged coastline. This was the Northland, his former home. It was from there that he, his brothers, and many settler families had set off on their long journey. The Northland, he taught me, was a barren land, bitter cold in the winter and inhabited by farmers, shepherds, and fishermen, as well as chieftains who took their longships, laden with warriors hungry for loot, on viking raids. Noticing my puzzled look, he added that "viking" meant simply "pirate" or "raider."

He squinted at the map, his finger traveling farther west to a larger and a smaller island, and finally coming to rest on a landmass to the south. The Vikings as a people had sailed to all those places. Along the coasts of the Irish, the Anglo-Saxons, and the Franks, they raided monasteries and homes, enslaving the inhabitants and filling their chests with gold and silver. When I asked if he went on such raids, he shook his head, professing with a small smile that he preferred trading with goods to stealing them; however, his father had been a Viking lord of great reputation.

My ancestry, he said, consisted of Irishmen, as well as Northmen. Even the blood of a woman from the Hot Land flowed through my veins. To her, I owed my bronze complexion and my black curls. As if to assure himself of those curls, he tousled my hair with his crooked fingers.

My great-uncle's vivid narrative conjured images in my mind that grew in number over the years and finally merged into one complete picture.

On the day of his death, he sent away all the visitors who had come to pay their final respects. His daughter and I alone were permitted to stay.

Before drawing his last breath, he whispered, scarcely audible, "Carla"—the name of his wife, who had passed several years earlier. The light went from his eyes, but his lips were smiling as they must have done often during his full life. Weeping, his daughter closed his lids.

In that moment, I decided that one day I would set down his story, which is also the story of his two brothers and many brave women and men, and so preserve it from falling into oblivion. I would have liked to start right away, but my duties—first on the farm of my father and later on my own—seemed jealously eager to steal any spare time that such an endeavor would require.

Only now, twenty-five winters later, with the children my wife gave me nearly grown and able to support me in our work on the fields, I finally find the time to pick up my quill. Some details my great-uncle told me I remember quite vividly, while others I may have added as a boy, and for others again, I must rely on my adult powers of imagination.

The story of my great-uncle begins with a dramatic escape in the wintery Northland.

PART 1
THE ESCAPE

(WINTER, AD 860)

CHAPTER 1
OVER THE MOUNTAINS

Asla lay in bed with her eyes wide open. She was staring at the hearth, whose embers painted its surroundings in a pale-red glow. Every now and then, a yellow flame would flare up from the glowing coals, for a brief moment, bathing the whole room in a dim light. Then the wooden pillars carrying the roof of the large, three-aisled hall would cast long and pale shadows against the wall.

No falling asleep, Asla reminded herself.

Her parents were still awake. She could tell by the hushed whispering and the occasional stifled snort of laughter from her mother behind the curtain, which shielded her parents' bed from prying eyes. Most likely, her parents were wagging tongues about some guest or another who'd attended the Yule celebrations a few days ago and made a fool of themselves.

She needed to be patient. Only once her parents began to snore evenly would Asla be able to attempt her escape.

She snuggled deeper into her fur blanket. Despite the warmth from the hearth, it was cold in the great hall of Halldor, her father, who liked to style himself as king of the Northland. It was a title he claimed even if few chieftains and jarls pledged allegiance to him thus far. Many powerful leaders of the North refused to acknowledge him.

Halldor was an imposing man and a feared, battle-hardened warrior. Her mother loved and his followers worshipped him. Many of his free farmers and those of his allied chieftains readily picked up their weapons when he called upon them. But even though Halldor was capable of summoning an impressive army, numerous energy-sapping conflicts had not been enough to vanquish his greatest enemies.

Since his warriors had grown tired of fighting, increasingly reluctant to leave their farms and follow him into battle, Halldor had changed his strategy. Instead of swords, he now planned to utilize his four daughters, who were growing into extraordinary beauties, just like their mother, to help him become king of the entire Northland.

With her seventeen winters, Asla was the eldest of them. She'd been the first of the pretty pawns Halldor had thought to use in his game for power and glory, delivering her into an uncertain fate. The husband he had chosen for her was called Hafur and had, until then, been one of the most powerful jarls to refuse his allegiance to Halldor.

Several weeks before the Yule fest, while Halldor was negotiating with his rival over an alliance, he introduced Hafur to his two eldest daughters, Asla and Stina. The sisters had each felt like mere husks filled with flesh when Hafur examined their bodies thoroughly and wolfishly. Their faces he had only glanced at with little interest.

From Hafur's servants, Asla learned that he had outlived his first two wives and counted nearly fifty winters by now. They described how Hafur had treated his spouses brutishly, never sparing with thrashings. There was even a rumor he had drunkenly beaten one of them to death.

Asla now shuddered and pulled her blanket more tightly around herself as she thought about the burly, bald-headed chieftain with his rotten teeth and repulsive breath, as well as her imminent espousal to the same. Halldor and Hafur had set the date of the wedding for the day in spring when the light of the sun reigned just as long as the dark of night, and they'd sealed their alliance with a handshake.

She sighed softly and allowed her thoughts to roam to Thorolf, who was waiting out there in the night for her. In her mind's eye, she could see his face, as if he were standing in front of her. His black hair formed an exciting contrast to his luscious blue eyes in whose depths she liked to lose herself. His distinctive chin, which he would jut out when he was tense or trying to win an argument, gave him the appearance of possessing an inherent, elemental strength. Most of all, she loved the dimple in its center.

Asla had known the son of Jarl Ulrik since childhood. Their families had come together during many celebrations, and for as long as she remembered, she had spent the carefree holiday seasons seeking out the company of her brother, Hilmar, and his friend Thorolf, who were inseparable.

In the early days, the two older boys had successfully escaped from her, the annoying little sister—an easy feat on account of Hilmar's and Thorolf's longer legs. As Asla grew older, the boys began to accept her presence while they bashed each other with wooden swords, played small tricks on the slaves, or took their bows and arrows on the hunt for hares and ducks. When she turned fourteen, Hilmar had presented her with her first bow. During the same summer, she noticed several times, to her amusement, that Thorolf no longer looked at her as if she were a girl, but as the woman she was growing into.

Finally. Her parents snored in unison.

Asla rose slowly. She tried to move silently so that she would not wake Stina, who shared her sleeping place, and her two younger sisters, Hoffa and Njala, on the neighboring bed. She draped her fur blanket around her shoulders and reached for her leather shoes. Carefully placing one foot in front of the other upon the cool pounded-dirt floor, she arrived at the entrance to the hall almost soundlessly, thanks to her woolen socks.

Beside the door, she discerned the silhouette of Loki, her father's two-year-old medium-sized hunting dog, who enjoyed the privilege of being allowed indoors, unlike his canine friends. When Asla bent down to pat his head, Loki lovingly licked her hand. She would miss the loyal dog and all the times they had explored the meadows and woods together.

Even more she would miss her mother and her siblings, but not her powerful father, whom, as a child, she used to worship almost as a god. She could not forgive him. He had turned a deaf ear to all her begging, had not yielded to her pleas to give her to any other man but Hafur. Eventually she was forced to realize that her father regarded her as little more than precious goods to be traded without any qualms if it served his hunger for power. When her final desperate appeals to him proved ineffectual, she began to hate him. She decided to flee and spend her future with Thorolf, who had professed his love for her three moons ago. She felt no remorse at thwarting her father's selfish, coldhearted plans.

She cast one last glance at her bed and the sleeping Stina, the sister Asla was closest to. She would likely never see her again. But melancholy wasn't getting her anywhere right now. It couldn't be helped—her days at her childhood home were over, one way or the other. Carefully Asla pushed back the bolt and opened the heavy wooden door almost soundlessly. Her mother couldn't stand to hear the door creak constantly whenever someone opened or closed it, and instead of complaining, she smeared the bolt and hinges with tallow each week.

Asla stepped across the threshold and slowly shut the door behind her. With relief, she inhaled the clean air, which was relatively mild for this time of the year. The first step of her escape was complete.

In the darkness of the night, the light from the clear, star-spangled sky and the crescent of the moon accentuated the outlines of the houses belonging to her father's hall. To her right were the livestock stables, and to her left lay the lodgings of the servants and maids and her father's closest followers. In front of her stood the longhouse of her brother Hilmar, who had recently married, founding his own household.

All was silent aside from the hooting and warbling of an owlet. Asla pulled on her shoes and sneaked, hunched over, past her brother's house. Over her shoulder, she thought she glimpsed a dark figure disappearing into the servants' quarters. She froze for a moment but couldn't detect any further suspicious movements.

Soon she reached the place along the man-high palisade that lay in the shade of a tall oak tree. The enclosure around her parents' estate served mainly to protect the livestock, especially the chickens, from the hungry fangs of wolves and foxes. Human predators were deterred in other ways: since they would have to row their longships up the fjord to reach Halldor's hall at the end of it, the sentries positioned along the fjord could light warning fires to alert the village of an attack in time.

Asla fished her knapsack out of the bushes at the foot of the oak. She had hidden it there the previous day, having packed it with important items for her escape: a clean linen undergarment, a longish woolen cloth, wooden sticks to clean her teeth, various satchels with healing herbs, and some rope. She felt inside the bag for the beautifully worked comb of whalebone to make sure it was still there.

She had received the comb as a gift three moons ago when she and her family were guests at the hall of Thorolf's father, the jarl Ulrik. While the men of both families caroused, celebrating the harvest feast, Thorolf had led Asla to a remote spot by the fjord. There, he had placed the comb, masterfully crafted and studded with small gemstones, into her hands and asked her to be his wife.

Without hesitating, she had risen to the tips of her toes and planted a quick, cheeky kiss on the dimple in his chin. She couldn't reach any higher, and both of them laughed. When she assured him that she had loved him ever since she could remember, Thorolf pulled her down upon his coat which he'd laid out on the soft grass . . .

Asla pulled herself together. She knew she mustn't dream now but had to get on with her escape. Hastily she draped around herself the long, sleeveless woolen coat that she'd also hidden in the bush, then placed the fur blanket around her shoulders once more. Using the rope, she swiftly scaled the palisade and soon landed in the meadow on the other side. With quick strides, she headed for the path that led toward the forest.

Again and again, Asla anxiously glanced across her shoulder, but no one pursued her. Only once she thought one of the shadows moved, but on closer inspection, it was just a bush swaying in the breeze. Her heart leapt when she thought of her imminent reunion with Thorolf.

Thorolf and his brothers, Yngvi and Digur, set up camp on a small clearing in the woods, where the womenfolk of Halldor's village picked berries, herbs, and mushrooms in the summer and fall. Even though now, during winter, chance visitors were unlikely, one of the three brothers kept watch at all times.

That night, Thorolf had taken the first watch, guarding his brothers' rest. To pass the time, he worked a large piece of oakwood with his knife. In the three days they had been waiting for Asla on the clearing, his work had come along nicely. The shape of an eagle with spread wings was clearly recognizable.

Often while he whittled, Thorolf thought with longing of the night of love three moons ago when he and Asla had held each other, painting colorful pictures of their future together. Rather less pleasant was the sobering memory of the following morning. He had come before Halldor with Asla and asked his permission to take the king's daughter for a wife. His plea was unseemly since his own father, Ulrik, ought to have led negotiations with Halldor about a marriage with Asla, but Thorolf, in spite of his young years, was a successful trader in his own right and had saved up enough to be able to offer a generous bride-price. However, Halldor's reaction had been unmistakable: first he had gawked at the young lovers in disbelief, then his face had turned red, and finally, waving an angry finger at Thorolf, he had told the young man to get out. Shortly thereafter Halldor had departed, earlier than originally planned, with his family and men.

Thorolf had not seen his beloved since then. Not even seven days ago, when his father and the other allied chieftains and their families had arrived with their ships at the harbor, following Halldor's invitation to the Yule celebrations. The self-proclaimed king of the Northland and his family had welcomed their guests. Next to Halldor's wife stood their daughters Stina, Hoffa, and Njala, but Asla had been nowhere in sight.

The same evening, the chieftains and their warriors had

started feasting in Halldor's great hall. Halldor showed himself to be generous: mead, wine from the south, and ale flowed freely. Spirits mostly ran high and cheerful; skalds sang songs of heroes and told stories of the gods. Warriors boasted vociferously of their deeds, and occasionally a heated discussion would lead to bloody fights which, spurred on by the drunken onlookers, were carried out outside the hall. The following day, the men celebrated—just like in Valhalla—their resurrection from a deathlike sleep and merrily boozed into the next night.

When Thorolf wasn't at the feast, he would wander Halldor's village in the hope of finding Asla or at least some clue as to her whereabouts. At last, Stina, Asla's next-younger sister, had pulled him aside and whispered to him that Halldor had locked his eldest daughter in a hut for the duration of the festivities and forbidden her from leaving it. Guards conscientiously took care this command was obeyed and that he, the unwelcome suitor, came nowhere near the hut. But Halldor had not reckoned with Stina, who loved her sister and supported her loyally. During the final two days of the feast, Stina played messenger between Thorolf and Asla. The younger sister had seemed pleased to be able to help Asla and to be at the center of an exciting adventure of the kind she didn't get to experience every day.

That was how he had been able to arrange meeting Asla at the clearing, promising to await her there.

Thorolf studied the half-finished eagle. He would gift it to Asla, and she would proudly hang it above the door of their future home.

After the Yule festivities, many guests had left the harbor beneath Halldor's hall on their ships. Thorolf, too, had ordered his men to row the *Goldeagle* out of the harbor. As he stood in the stern of his wide-bellied, spacious knarr, he saw Halldor, tall and broad-legged, raising his hand from the shore in a frosty farewell. Thorolf read no friendship in the eyes of the king, only triumph and smugness at having prevented the would-be suitor's possible tryst with Asla.

But Thorolf had not sailed home. Once the *Goldeagle* was about halfway down the fjord, his men lowered a small boat into the water and rowed Thorolf and his brothers ashore. Under the cover of night, they rowed to the shore and concealed the vessel. While his followers sailed the *Goldeagle* homeward, Thorolf, Yngvi, and Digur struggled up a narrow and steep path that led them along the mountain range framing the fjord on one side, and past Halldor's village to the small clearing where he had arranged to meet Asla.

Thorolf paused, lowering his knife. *Was that a sound?* Did he hear fallen leaves rustle at the edge of the clearing? He listened. The rustling grew louder; twigs cracked.

He hissed at Yngvi and Digur to wake up, and they instantly grasped the swords at their sides and sprang to their feet. Thorolf, too, drew his sword and rose. A figure peeled from the darkness of the forest and emerged onto the starlit clearing.

"Thorolf. Yngvi, Digur! What are you standing around with your big knives for? Is that what you call an appropriate greeting for a king's daughter?"

When Thorolf heard the familiar voice, he dropped his sword and ran toward Asla, who shrugged off her heavy fur blanket and laughed as she threw her arms around him. For a long moment, Thorolf rocked his beloved in his arms, speechless, kissing her warmly and inhaling her scent, squeezing her again and again as if he would never let go.

It all took too long for Yngvi. "Dear brother, if you carry on thus, there soon will be nothing left of Asla. Digur and I would like to welcome your beautiful bride too. Perhaps she has a kiss of greeting for us also?"

Digur nodded in agreement.

Asla gently freed herself from Thorolf's embrace and stepped toward the two men, her eyes sparkling with mirth. "You shall have your kiss, brave warriors, as thanks for standing by Thorolf's side during my escape. And I'll even give you a second kiss, just because I like you both."

Yngvi scarcely needed to lower his face to receive a kiss on each cheek from his future sister-in-law, while Digur, a hulking, powerful warrior, was forced to bend his broad back a fair way to accept his reward.

"Don't be frightened! It's me, Stina."

Unnoticed, Stina had stepped into the glow of the few flames from the fire and now stood shivering with her arms crossed on her chest. She wore only her long undergarment and a light woolen cloak. Her feet were clad in simple leather shoes.

Asla was the first to regain her composure. "What are you doing here, Stina? I thought you were asleep when I left the hall."

"No, I was wide awake. As your messenger, I knew where you were going."

"Are you alone? Were you followed?" asked Thorolf harshly, eyeing the dark forest edge distrustfully.

Stina shook her head. "I was careful. Nobody saw me when I left the village."

"Don't tell me you want to come with us?" asked Asla in disbelief.

"I do!" her sister replied defiantly. "Who do you think would have to fill your shoes when you're gone? Me! Our sisters are too young to carry your burden. I would be the one who'd have to marry disgusting old Hafur in your stead." Stina grimaced as if she had bitten into some bitter fruit. "I feel sick at the thought of even being touched by him. That's why I followed you, Asla." She turned to Thorolf, her eyes pleading. "Please, take me with you."

Ashamed, Asla was forced to admit that she'd thought only of herself, ignoring the consequences her escape would mean for Stina.

Thorolf looked from one sister to the other. At first glance, the two of them looked very much alike. Both were slim and of average height, and their luscious hair framed oval, harmonious faces in blonde waves. Both girls had large, speckled hazel eyes shaded by long lashes. But a closer inspection revealed small differences: Asla's lips were fuller and her forehead higher, giving her an air of serenity and elegance. Stina, on the other hand, appeared somewhat pert and defiant on account of her slightly upturned snub nose and her freckles, which now, in the winter, were rather pale.

Yngvi broke the baffled silence. "Why are you hesitating, Thorolf? Once Halldor finds out that Asla, his most precious belonging, has vanished, he's going to thrash the furnishings of his hall in one of his notorious tantrums. Stina's flight is merely an additional nuisance that might cost the life of one or two chickens unfortunate enough to cross his path. One abducted daughter more or less won't matter. Halldor will be furious either way and try to hold us accountable. What of it? I am in favor of taking Stina along."

Digur nodded his assent.

Stina gazed in gratitude at the two brothers.

Thorolf, however, shook his head gravely. "We cannot take Stina with us. If I send Halldor the greater part of my fortune as bride-price, he might accept the loss of Asla. The more so if he is wise enough not to jeopardize the alliance with our father. But he is going to demand the return of Stina in any case." He looked into his younger brother's eyes with urgency. "Yngvi, you must understand that, if we do not send Stina back to him, he will not accept my offer and will instead reclaim Stina as well as Asla by force."

"That may be, Thorolf," replied Stina softly in a voice that was laced with despair. "Though I had hoped you would find a way to take me nonetheless." Stina hung her head, dejectedly staring at an imaginary spot by her feet. "If you don't, you will have no choice but to tie me up and carry me back. Or leave me standing here by myself. I will never return freely."

Asla took the hand of her younger sister, who was bravely fighting back her tears, and squeezed it gently. She had reached a decision. "Thorolf, I cannot leave here with you if you send Stina back. If I did, my conscience would forever haunt me for having built my happiness upon the unhappiness of my sister. Such guilt would, in time, poison my love for you."

Stina pressed herself against her sister. She was shivering, and not just from the chill of the night. Asla wrapped her arms around her sister protectively.

"So, take us both or none at all. It's probably not yet too late for Stina and me to return unnoticed. Should you decide to take us, we will find a way to appease my father with the help of yours. And if we don't, we can always board your ship and seek a new home on the Faroe Islands or Hjaltland."

Thorolf would, in truth, be sending back three people, thought Asla—for she carried his child beneath her heart. But she did not wish to tell Thorolf under these conditions; he should decide freely and without any sense of obligation, either for her and Stina or against them.

While Thorolf, visibly surprised, digested Asla's serious declaration, Yngvi spoke again. "What's the problem? We can hide Stina from Halldor's spies, claiming we knew nothing of her whereabouts. Maybe she was eaten by wolves or raped and murdered by a follower or slave of Halldor's while she tried to follow her sister."

Digur had scarcely taken his eyes off Stina since her arrival—something about her seemed to fascinate the placid warrior, who was feared among his enemies on account of his size and strength. He suddenly spoke up: "Where do you suggest we hide her?"

"I know the charcoal burner near our village. He and his wife still owe me a favor." Yngvi grinned mischievously. "We'll dress Stina up as a boy and home her at the charcoal burners' as a helper. If we crop her hair and smear her with a good portion of coal, no one is going to suspect a girl behind the charade. Then, in the spring, when we set sail for our next trade voyage, we can take her to our uncle on the Faroe Islands. What do you think?"

"Sounds good," said Digur. "It might just work."

Thorolf wondered at his older brother. Normally Digur preferred to let others do the talking. For his standards, he was being markedly communicative.

"Evidently you are all in favor of taking Stina with us." Thorolf cleared his throat and tried to sort his thoughts. "Then that is how it shall be. We will do as Yngvi suggests." He gave each of them a serious look in turns. "May the gods be on our side."

Asla thanked Thorolf with a kiss and whispered something in his ear. He hugged her against his chest, a thoughtful expression on his face.

Stina felt endlessly relieved. Like Asla, she would receive the chance to escape marriage to Hafur, and maybe she would one day be granted the opportunity to take her fate into her own hands. Who could tell how the Norns would spin their threads? She was eternally grateful to Asla. Her elder sister had tied her own fate to hers and therewith smoothed the path for Thorolf's decision. As Stina gazed at her affectionately, Asla gave her an encouraging smile. Yngvi and Digur, too, had spoken in her support. To show her appreciation, she slowly pulled the two silver rings her grandmother had given her from her fingers, walked a few steps, and stopped before Yngvi.

"This ring is for you, Yngvi. May it bring you luck, protect you, and preserve your wit."

Yngvi reacted in his typical manner: he grinned. "Was that all, dearest Stina?" he asked, brazenly holding out his left cheek.

Stina breathed a kiss upon it. Then she turned to Digur, offering her second ring to him.

"This ring is for you. May it bring you luck, protect you, and preserve your strength."

Digur stood like a rock with his back to the fire, pondering what it was about that girl that unsettled him so. He hoped this uncomfortable situation would pass swiftly. He grasped the proffered ring before his hesitation became obvious. Stina's slender hands enclosed his calloused paw, and then she looked up at him. Digur gazed into her striking green-speckled eyes and gave a start: it seemed as if suddenly a different girl were standing before him, a girl from his past, staring at him reproachfully and accusing. Digur shuddered and looked away from Stina.

Finally, Stina turned to Thorolf. "Unfortunately I do not own a third ring with which to show you my gratitude, dear future brother-in-law. But with my help, you now hold my dear sister in your arms. I ask the gods to smile upon your union and keep harm from you."

Uncertainly, Stina stepped back. Up until the last few days, when she'd become Thorolf's messenger, she'd known the three brothers—who were in fact half-brothers—by reputation alone, having met them only briefly at feasts their families had celebrated together over the years. She hoped her decision to entrust her life and future to them was the right one.

Thorolf sighed. "Let us pack up and leave," he said to his

companions. "I have a bad feeling as long as we are this close to Halldor's village. Who knows, perhaps someone noticed your escape."

A hike of several days lay ahead of them. It would lead them across the heights of the mountains and through low valleys that lay between the fjords belonging to the realms of Halldor and of Ulrik, Thorolf's father. Frost and snow would challenge them up in the mountains, so the brothers had packed warm clothing and fur-lined shoes for themselves and Asla. There was enough clothing to protect Stina from the cold, too, but there was not a spare pair of warm and comfortable shoes for her.

When Thorolf handed Asla a coat, she seemed puzzled. "I thank you for your kind concern, dearest, but it isn't far to your ship, and the night is mild. What in Odin's name are we supposed to do with all these fur coats?"

"We are not going to my ship, Asla. It would have been too dangerous to keep the *Goldeagle* at anchor for several days in the fjord. Your father's guards would have noticed her sooner or later, and Halldor would have grown suspicious and kept you prisoner for longer. That is why we are taking the route across the mountains. My guess is that we will reach my father's hall in three days."

Asla and Stina did not appear thrilled at the prospect of hiking for several days, but they had no choice.

When everyone in their small troupe was ready, Thorolf lit a torch and led the way. Asla, Yngvi, and Stina followed him into the night, and Digur secured the group's rear.

By morning, they had made good progress, the path first gently sloping upward through the forest before zigzagging in serpentines to a treeless plateau with brownish-green vegetation.

Melting islands of snow testified, even at this higher altitude, to the uncommonly mild winter for the time of the Yule fest.

Asla and Stina were unaccustomed to long walks, and around the middle of the day their legs and feet began to ache, exhaustion showing on their faces. Thorolf couldn't blame the young women for the occasional groan. After all, they had been marching for half a night and half a day almost without stopping.

When they reached the shelter of the woods following a descent into a valley during the early afternoon, Thorolf and his brothers decided to rest there until around midnight. They would be able to replenish their waterskins from a babbling creek nearby.

The sisters breathed sighs of relief, and their expressions relaxed as they slumped down on the trunk of an uprooted tree. Thorolf and Digur left to gather dry wood in the forest, while Yngvi searched for tinder nearby.

Asla pulled off the fur boots Thorolf had given her, massaging her aching feet with both hands. "Oh, that feels good."

Stina sat beside her, unmoving and quiet.

After a while Asla asked, "How are your feet and calves? Would you like me to give them a kneading?"

Her sister shook her head. "Thank you, that won't be necessary. Your leather shoes serve me well."

Stina did not hesitate to utter this lie. Asla's sturdy footwear was indeed far better suited for a longer walk than the thin leather slippers Stina had worn when she'd left home, expecting Thorolf to take her and Asla to his ship and continue their escape via the sea route. For a longer hike, however, the shoes were pinching, and so blisters had formed on her feet that she did not want to see and the sight of which she wished to spare Asla.

Stina changed the subject by pointing at blond Yngvi, the youngest of the three half-brothers, who was busy scraping a large mushroom off a tree. "People say all sorts of things about him. Apparently, he's had more women than he has seen winters, and that can't be fewer than twenty."

"No wonder," replied Asla, smiling. "With his charm, his looks, and his radiant liveliness, he is bound to arouse the interest of many women."

"Including you?"

Asla gave a quick laugh. "No, certainly not. I like Yngvi. But he is not a man I would wish to share my bed with. He is too fickle for my taste, too giddy. But I welcome him gladly as a friend and future brother-in-law. And you? Are you interested?"

Stina looked down, her long blonde hair hiding her face. "I like Yngvi too. But he does not touch my heart like Thorolf touches yours. If my escape is successful, I hope I may someday meet a man I would like to spend my life with. One that I chose myself, and not one like that disgusting Hafur that Father wanted to force upon you."

"Why did you not mention your fears to me before I ran away?"

"Would it have helped?" Stina tossed back her hair, glancing at Asla skeptically. "You never would have taken me with you and risked making trouble for Thorolf. But had I told you, you would not have wanted to flee. You would have stayed out of love for me, and you would have been forced to marry Hafur. For me, nothing much would have changed: I might have been spared from marrying him, but, according to Father's plans, I would have been forced to bear the children of the next chief or jarl—perhaps even as a second wife, if his legitimate wife were still alive. We, both of us, would have lost." Stina paused for a moment, rubbing her nose. "My—no, *our* only chance was for me to follow you secretly and confront Thorolf with done deeds." She gave her sister an apologetic look. "I know this wasn't fair. But I did not know what else to do."

Asla placed a hand on her arm. "It is good just the way it is now, and I'm glad. We are together, and my heart is so much lighter than if you were still at home. Let us have faith in the support of the gods and a happy ending to our flight."

Asla pulled her boots back on and rose to her feet. "I want to wash a little. And I need to relieve myself. Are you coming?"

They found a good spot near the creek to see to their needs.

"Did you hear that, Asla?"

"What?"

"Sounded like a dog."

Asla, squatting, stopped peeing and listened. For a while, all she heard was the soft rustling of dried leaves in the wind and the murmur of the creek. But then she heard it too: distant still, but unmistakably the barking of a dog.

She quickly stood up and smoothed down her clothes. "They are on our heels. If I'm not mistaken, it is Loki following our trail. He won't be on his own. Father might have come personally to fetch us back."

Stina blanched, staring at her sister with fright. "What do we do now?"

Asla thought. "There is no point in running. They will catch up with us sooner or later. I don't think Thorolf and I have a choice but to confront them here and now. Maybe we will reach a peaceful agreement—but only if they don't find you with us. You must hide, Stina." Asla looked around. "You best follow the course of the creek and hide somewhere nearby. If you wade in the water for the first while, Loki will find it harder to pick up your trail should they search for you."

Stina stared at her fearfully. "And then?"

"Then you wait in your hiding spot until I come to get you. Should I not return by moonrise, my escape most likely failed and I must return to the village. But then perhaps at least you might escape our father's clutches together with Thorolf and his brothers. Promise me to wait for one of us—don't show yourself any sooner!"

"I promise."

Stina cried as she hugged her sister farewell, and Asla struggled to hold back her own tears. She knew she might never see Stina again.

When Asla arrived back at camp, Thorolf received her with a serious face, gesturing at a group of four climbing down the same path they had used to reach the valley. She leaned against his shoulder. "I recognize Hilmar by his blond head of hair. He is coming to take me back."

Thorolf, concerned, asked, "Where is Stina?"

"She will follow the creek in the woods and find a hiding place nearby. She is going to remain there until we come to get her," replied Asla. "She promised."

Thorolf nodded. "Very well. If the encounter ahead is to stand any chance of passing without bloodshed, it's only if they don't find Stina with us."

When their pursuers caught up with them, the sun was already nearing the mountain ridge to the southwest. A brisk wind and gray clouds pushing unstoppably into the blue sky announced a change in the weather.

The first to reach them was Loki. Panting and barking, he jumped up at Asla, licking her hands, whimpering, and spinning in circles to express his joy at having found her.

Asla crouched down, wrapping her arms around him, caressing his thick gray-white fur and whispering words in his ear that the dog seemed to understand, answering her back with happy yelps.

Shortly thereafter arrived Hilmar, the brother of Asla and Stina, along with three warriors. Asla recognized Knut among them. The long-standing follower of her father had not long stood in Hilmar's service, and he was glaring at her grimly.

"Greetings to you, Thorolf, my friend." Hilmar grasped Thorolf's forearms and gave him a tight smile. "You know why I'm here?"

Thorolf nodded. "Yes, and I hope that we will part ways in the same manner as we greet one another: in friendship."

Asla gave Hilmar a thin smile, reaching for Thorolf's hand to underline who she belonged to. Loki, having calmed down, was sitting beside her with his tongue lolling out the side of his muzzle. The dog turned his wolflike head from Hilmar to Asla and back, as if sensing the underlying tension between the siblings.

"You found us fast," Asla said.

"Njala had a nightmare and went to snuggle up between you and Stina. When she found your bed empty, she cried and woke our parents. Father first searched for you by himself, then with me and several of our men in the village and its surrounds. A servant told Father that he'd seen you walk toward the palisade by the great oak tree when he'd needed to step outside. It was a mistake not to wake Father right away. Tomorrow the man is going to get whipped."

"I bet," Asla remarked drily, "had he woken Father, he still would have been whipped."

Hilmar ignored his sister's disrespectful comment. "We let Loki sniff one of your worn shifts and led him to the point where we assumed you crossed the palisade." There was a wry tone in his voice as he continued. "Loki adores you, and he immensely enjoyed following your trail. It was child's play, finding you."

Asla watched Hilmar as he talked. Standing in front of her wasn't the familiar and beloved brother, her childhood playmate and protector in whom she confided all her fears. Not the sensitive, mature, handsome Hilmar who valued honor and justice above all else. Standing before her was the heir, the extension of Halldor, who was by no means unconditionally well-disposed toward her and Thorolf.

Hilmar glanced about. “Where is Stina? I don’t see her.”

Yngvi rubbed the stubble on his chin, replying innocently: “Are you talking about the same desirable Stina I had the pleasure of dancing with a few days ago? Sadly, I have not seen that Stina ever since.”

Yngvi had no qualms about this lie. To him, honesty and honor weren’t virtues to be practiced too slavishly. To attain a noble and important goal, he was prepared to stretch the truth or even twist it.

Digur, his hand on the hilt of his sword, confirmed his brother’s statement. “I know of no Stina.”

Asla, hoping her acting skills appeared believable, donned an expression of concern. “Are you suggesting Stina followed us? She did not flee with me. The servant that Father is having whipped tomorrow should be able to attest as much. Poor Stina—what might have befallen her?”

Sobbing, Asla buried her face against Thorolf’s shoulder, not so much for consolation but for fear her put-on despair for Stina wasn’t showing convincingly on her face.

Thorolf placed a soothing hand on the head of his beloved. “Hilmar, what do you want? Asla and I are destined for one another, and I will not allow you to lead my bride, your sister, into the arms of this Hafur. You and I have always been friends and spent many good and exciting times together in our youth.” With his free hand, he gestured toward the path Hilmar had come down with his followers and Loki. “In the name of our friendship, turn back and tell Halldor I will pay a high bride-price for Asla. You know I am able to.”

Hilmar had listened to his friend's words with a stony expression. "Thorolf," he said, sighing. "You know Halldor will hardly be interested in your bride-price. He wants to forge alliances to gain recognition as king of the North. And for that, he needs Asla and Stina." He took one step toward Thorolf, fixing him with his eyes and grasping his friend's sword arm with his right hand, shaking it gently. "Thorolf, wake up! In the name of our friendship, won't you see reason? Since ancient times, we sons have fought with our swords for the future of our families, and our sisters are bound by duty to yield to our fathers' marriage plans and ensure the success of their alliances. You know that as well as I do."

Hilmar let go of Thorolf's arm, stepped back, and continued speaking. "As far as I know, the marriage of your father, Ulrik, and your late mother was not the result of the volatile flame of love, but of hard negotiations by your grandfathers. So leave this silly dalliance be and hand over Asla. And should Stina be nearby after all, you'd best hand her over right away, too. You will not be able to conceal my sister from my father's spies. You know Halldor. If he learns that you abducted Stina also, there will be war between our tribes. None of us wishes for that."

To avoid being overheard by his followers, who were waiting five paces behind him, Hilmar once more stepped toward Thorolf and Asla, whispering imploringly. "I will tell my father that I found my sisters alone and helpless in the woods. Then he can't accuse you, and the matter is done."

Hilmar's speech and his appeal to their friendship touched Thorolf. The customs and laws of his people were deeply ingrained in him, too, and he knew he would break them, turning himself into an outlaw, if he did not comply with Hilmar's demand. He jutted out his chin, grinding his teeth as he pondered the matter.

Hilmar evidently interpreted his friend's hesitation as an indication of victory. "No harm will come to Asla as Hafur's wife. Should Hafur chastise her, it would be as if he struck and insulted our whole tribe. He will have to fear our revenge. He knows that. And besides, Hafur is old. Asla will survive him by many years and, as a jarl's widow, lead a good and respectful life."

Asla could almost feel the inner struggle Thorolf was fighting with himself, and as a woman of the North, she understood. When she began to fear that Thorolf would give in to Hilmar's coaxing, it was time for a confession.

She spoke in a low voice so that only Thorolf and Hilmar made out her words: "I am with child. If the wise Oda is right and if the gods are with us, then I will give birth to Thorolf's son around midsummer."

Thorolf stared at Asla in surprise. Hilmar, too, took a few moments to digest this news, but he collected himself more quickly than his friend. Squinting, he scrutinized his sister and eventually said coldly: "The wise Oda you visited so often is bound to know means and ways to end your pregnancy."

Asla felt anger well up in her in the face of her brother's coldhearted suggestion. Her eyes blazed as she hissed at him, "Guess what—she shared her vast knowledge with me. She taught me much—so much that I even know how to take care of it myself, should I wish to!"

"Then do it," he said, unblinking.

Asla's skin reddened with fury, and she raised her voice angrily: "I will carry Thorolf's child to the end! You will not stop me from giving your nephew the gift of life."

Yngvi and Digur exchanged an astonished look, and Hilmar's followers, too, showed surprise at the unexpected news.

Finally, Thorolf recovered from the shock. He proclaimed his decision loudly and clearly: "Asla carries my son—my heir—beneath her heart. That changes everything. I would never allow his life to be taken, or for him to grow up as an unwelcome bastard in the hall of Hafur. I ask you again, Hilmar: leave in peace. I will not hand over Asla and my son. Never!"

For a moment, then, Hilmar dropped his standoffish mask, and deep regret filled his eyes as he spoke quietly to Asla. "I swore to Father with my blood on my sword to search and find you and Stina so that you can fulfill your duty. If I do not fulfill this oath, I cannot return home alive."

Asla's anger evaporated. The life of her brother for that of her unborn son? It was an impossible choice. Desperately she searched for a way out.

"What if you tell Father you found our dead bodies, mangled by the wolves?" she suggested in a whisper.

"And my men? Do you think they would keep quiet? No, sooner or later, they would tell Father the truth. Besides, an oath is sacred—I cannot break it either way. I had hoped to persuade you to heed the will of our father and king. I had not reckoned with your child. Even if I understand you, I cannot let you go. There is only one way this can end for me."

Hilmar seemed cool and distant once more as he took a few steps back, announcing loudly: "Thorolf and I were unable to reach an agreement. To fulfill my pledge, we must fight."

Yngvi took a knife in each hand. He carried several on his belt, and he was deft at throwing them, usually hitting his target. Digur reached for his axe with his right hand and drew his sword with his left.

With a metallic hiss, Hilmar's men also drew their swords, fixing their eyes fearfully on the hulking Digur, who was most likely capable of tackling two or even three opponents at once.

Thorolf and Hilmar faced each other in silence, their eyes locked.

Eventually, Thorolf spoke. "Let us avoid unnecessary bloodshed, Hilmar. Allow the gods to decide the outcome of our quarrel. The loser is whose blood is drawn first. If you win, Asla will go with you. If I win, she will stay with me, and you and your men will let us go in peace."

Hilmar shook his head, his voice rough but steady: "As I explained to you, I cannot return home without my sister—not alive, in any case. If we are to agree, then our fight must be to the death."

A few snowflakes tumbled from the sky, chased by a wind that grew stronger and colder.

Asla watched the events unfold in disbelief. This seemed surreal, incomprehensible. "No!" she shouted in despair. "You mustn't! Neither of you must die because of me. I love you both, and I could never bear it if you killed one another." Her breath came in gasps as she paused for a moment. Then she looked at her brother beseechingly. "Hilmar, I will go back with you. Take me and lead me to our father. I will submit to my fate and marry Hafur. But please, Hilmar, stop this madness!"

Hilmar gazed into Thorolf's eyes, silently asking for his assent, all the while knowing he would not receive it.

Thorolf returned his friend's look with woebegone regret. Then he said to Asla: "No, that is impossible. I cannot let you go. You carry my son under your heart. I must fight for him and for you. Gundahar, who knows how to read the runes, foretold me once that my firstborn would change the fate of my tribe significantly for the better. I cannot and will not abandon my son to an uncertain future."

"So be it," Hilmar replied calmly. "The Norns leave us no other choice. They have entwined our threads of fate, and today, they will cut one of them." He turned to his men. "Should you carry my dead body away from here this day, you will let Asla go with Thorolf. Swear on your swords that you will follow my demand."

Each of the two men Asla didn't know wrapped their hand around the blade of their sword and swore by their blood. Hilmar had to shoot Knut a sharp glance before the latter reluctantly grasped his blade and uttered the oath with a glum expression.

"Should I lose this fight," said Hilmar, "I will have done my utmost to fulfill my oath. This you must tell my father if you take home my dead body."

The men nodded.

Thorolf addressed his brothers. "If I die in this fight, you will let Asla go with Hilmar."

Their faces serious, Yngvi and Digur made the oath on their swords.

Loki sensed the menacing atmosphere. Whining softly, the dog looked up at Asla as if asking his mistress to dispel the tension. But Asla stood frozen between her lover and her brother.

Hilmar spoke once more. "Thorolf, choose one of your brothers to accompany us to our combat. I select Knut."

The chosen man stepped to Hilmar's side.

"I choose Yngvi," replied Thorolf.

"No!" screamed Asla. She turned to Thorolf and clasped his stubbled cheeks between her hands. "Please, let me go with Hilmar. In the name of our love, I beg you: do not fight my brother! If you die, I will hate Hilmar forever. If Hilmar dies, his blood would forever be between you and me." With tearful eyes, she gazed at the father of her unborn child imploringly.

But Thorolf wasn't swayed. His expression unmoving, he looked at Digur and spoke in a hoarse voice: "Take her away. Wait for Yngvi in the woods with her."

Digur grasped Asla by the arm and dragged her away from Thorolf. She wailed and struggled, which cost the mighty warrior no physical effort, but it touched his heart more than he cared to admit. Nonetheless he tightened his grip and pulled Asla relentlessly to the edge of the woods.

Asla eventually saw that she had lost. She did not possess the power to detain Thorolf and Hilmar from their deadly intentions. Sobbing and no longer resisting, she followed Digur like a sheep to its inevitable slaughter.

Hilmar ordered his other two men to leash Loki with a rope and follow Digur with the dog. "Keep an eye on the big man!" he called after them.

The wind had dropped. Thick snowflakes twirled to the ground, over winter-pale grass and rocks, covering it all in a blanket of innocent white. Yngvi and Knut used torches to stake out a square fighting area; they would light the torches once the darkness became impenetrable.

"No shield?" asked Thorolf.

"No shield, just our swords," Hilmar replied decidedly. "Let us get it done and over with."

The two friends grasped each other by their forearms one last time and exchanged a nod. Both were excellent swordfighters and each other's equal. Hilmar expressed what both of them were thinking: "May the gods be with the luckier one."

Before they released one another, Thorolf asked: "If I die, will you care for my son?"

Hilmar nodded. "As well as I can."

They each took three steps back, planted their feet firmly apart, and drew their swords. Now they were mortal enemies.

Yngvi whispered in his brother's ear, "May your unborn son bring you luck."

Knut wished his master that Odin himself may guide his arm. Then the two witnesses retreated from the fighting arena, declaring almost simultaneously: "Ready!"

Thorolf focused as he waited for Hilmar to attack. From the countless battles they'd fought in their youth with their blunt wooden swords, he knew that his impatient friend preferred to seek advantage in the attack, while he himself waited for opportunities to counter. Hilmar had caught many a bruise from him this way.

The pale, grassy ground still held the mildness of the last few days. The snow landing upon it melted, rendering it wet and slippery. Thorolf took note of that and made sure his boots found firm footing.

As he had expected, Hilmar opened the duel, storming toward him with his sword raised. Thorolf blocked the blow and shifted to the side. Hilmar slid past him and quickly spun around, in his turn parrying Thorolf's blow.

Attack, parry, counter, feint, attack—that was how it went for a while in swift succession, back and forth, without either opponent receiving serious injury. The hard metallic clanking when the blades crashed together, the bright whirring and singing as they scraped along each other, and the grunting and gasping of the combatants filled the air of the waning day.

Despite his fear for his brother, Yngvi could not help but admire the swordsmanship of both warriors. He himself was far from such a level of skill.

Dusk seeped quietly into the valley. Knut lit the torches, but the snow was falling so thickly now that the flickering light scarcely helped improve the men's vision. Breathing hard, the two friends whom fate had turned into foes paused exhaustedly, trying to summon new strength, a distance of about seven feet between their sword arms.

Thorolf was barely able to make out Hilmar, but he heard his words clearly. "Will you do me the final honor of placing my sword in my hand if I die?"

"Why do you ask? Was I such a poor friend to you to make you doubt my loyalty? I will send you to Valhalla as the brave warrior that you are, and I know you would do the same for me."

This time it was Thorolf who attacked. As he stormed at the shadow in front of him, he feinted an upward stroke with his sword arm, as if he wanted to hit Hilmar vertically, but then, halfway up, redirected his sword's momentum to a horizontal swing.

Taken by surprise, Hilmar managed to parry the blow in the last moment, protecting the side of his body with both his hands holding his sword. But he was too late to fend off the fist Thorolf threw out at full speed, landing it on his chest. Hilmar staggered backward, losing control, one foot slipping on the slick, wet slush, sending him sprawling to the ground. Thorolf felt the earth shudder beneath his boots.

His opponent did not move. The sword had slipped from his hand.

"Get up. Are you trying to trick me, like you always used to do?" Thorolf said, breathing heavily.

Hilmar did not stir.

"Do you think I'm going to strike a man when he's down, defenseless? Get up and fight already!"

While Thorolf waited for a reaction, alert, sword in hand, Knut walked to his master and leaned over him. Yngvi stepped beside his brother, placing a hand on his shoulder.

Knut rose. "Hilmar is dead."

Thorolf approached his friend's lifeless body, kneeled down, and set aside his sword. He noticed blood melting the snow around Hilmar's head, and he lifted it. Hilmar had landed on a rock with the back of his head, shattering his skull. No man survived such an injury, Thorolf knew.

The fight for Asla and his son was decided. Thorolf ought

to have shouted his triumph into the night—but he could not. Too bitter was the taste of victory, and too much tied him to Hilmar, too many happy memories from their youth.

Gently, Thorolf closed his friend's eyes, which seemed to gaze with surprise into the snowy heavens. He grasped his right hand and squeezed it in farewell. After a few moments, he picked up Hilmar's sword and placed it into his friend's hand, gently closing the dead man's fingers around the hilt.

He spoke a low, halting farewell to his friend. "You fell bravely in battle, with your sword in hand. Now the Valkyries will fetch you and carry you to Valhalla. You will feast at Odin's table and take your pleasure with the most beautiful women. When I follow you one day, we will be reunited. Then we fight with swords that cannot kill, and then we feast in Odin's great hall with all the other fearless warriors."

Thorolf reached for his sword and stood up. His eyes still on Hilmar, he turned to his brother. "Yngvi, go fetch Digur and Asla."

Yngvi nodded, picking up a torch and leaving in silence. In this sad moment, even he appeared lost for words.

No sooner had Yngvi vanished in the thickly falling snow than Thorolf caught a movement in the glow of the torches to his right. He reacted instinctively, turning at lightning speed, ducking and raising his sword—just in time to shield his head from the deadly blow Knut swung at him.

In a flash, the grief that had filled Thorolf turned to boundless rage. Not only had Knut broken the oath he had given his master to keep the peace in the event of his death, but also he had attacked Thorolf in a cowardly manner. Thorolf roared his pain and his fury into the frosty air, clouds of steam rising from his mouth. In the same instant, he struck back.

The fight did not last long. Thorolf thrashed at Knut with

the force and anger of a berserk until his opponent sank to the ground with a split skull.

But Thorolf's anger was not yet satisfied. He scarcely felt the wound Knut had inflicted on his left thigh. Knut had disregarded Hilmar's wishes and betrayed his master. Again and again, Thorolf cut into the corpse of his adversary until finally growing aware of the senselessness of his doings, gasping for breath as he stopped.

He bent down, picked up the traitor's sword, and hurled it with a bestial scream into the darkness. With a dull thud, the weapon landed somewhere in the distance. The heavy snowfall would cover it under its blanket.

Exhausted, Thorolf dropped to his knees beside Hilmar, who looked as though he were sleeping peacefully, unaffected by the fate of his follower.

Asla sat in silence, withdrawn into herself, next to Digur on the trunk of an uprooted tree. She could not bear to contemplate what was happening just a few hundred paces away from her. Instead, she combed her memories for happy moments—like the one when she went hunting with Thorolf and Hilmar, her brother teaching her how to handle her new bow. Occasionally, she gave a start, when she thought she heard noises in the distance sounding like swords clashing or battle cries. But her hearing might have been playing tricks on her, fueled by her fears, and so she allowed her thoughts to roam back to the past.

When Yngvi, carrying a torch, stepped into the glow of the still young, flickering fire the small group had lit to warm themselves as they waited, Asla, Digur, and Hilmar's two followers rose, staring at him expectantly. Loki barked, tugging at the rope that tied him to a tree.

Asla rushed headlong at Yngvi, grasping his right arm with both hands. "What is it? Tell us!"

It made no difference to her grief which of the two men had won, but she was eager to receive certainty.

Yngvi looked at her with a grave expression. "Your brother lost the fight, Asla. But not through Thorolf's sword. Hilmar slipped and fell during the fight, and his head struck a rock. He died instantly."

Asla gave a hoarse cry, digging her fingernails into the sleeves of his coat. Yngvi wrapped his free arm around her shoulder. Reluctantly she loosened her grip. Grief over the death of her brother competed in her heart with relief at knowing Thorolf was alive. In the end, neither emotion won, and she felt a desolate emptiness spreading inside her, numbing her every thought, doubt, and question.

When they started to move, Asla followed the men with dull eyes. Loki, now free of his rope, jogged beside her. The dog glanced up at her now and then, giving small barks in the hope his mistress would pay him some attention. But Asla was oblivious to him and her surroundings.

The snowing had eased, and when the group arrived at the torchlit fighting ground, they saw Thorolf kneeling beside Hilmar's body with his head hung. It was clear that Asla's brother had departed this life honorably with his sword in hand, but a few steps to the side lay Knut's mangled body in his own blood. A thin layer of white covered the clothing of the dead bodies, while the remaining warmth in their hands and faces still warded off the snowflakes for now.

Before anyone asked, Thorolf lifted his head and shot a

contemptuous glare in Knut's direction. "The traitor broke his oath and attacked me cowardly."

Hilmar's two men looked around, and the taller one asked: "Where is Knut's sword?"

Thorolf replied grimly: "The earth kindly swallowed it up." When the warriors stared at him with blank expressions, he roared: "Do you think I would allow Hilmar to travel to Valhalla together with a cowardly traitor?"

"He was no traitor," the shorter one objected. "Halldor made Knut swear an oath that he would kill you if we found Asla with you. Hilmar knew nothing of this. The oath Knut gave the king weighed more heavily than the one Hilmar forced him to take today."

Thorolf understood. He rose, pointing into the darkness with one hand. "I tossed his sword somewhere in that direction. If you're lucky, you'll find it tomorrow."

He approached Asla with heavy steps. She was leaning against Yngvi's shoulder, staring at Loki who had lain down beside Hilmar's body. The loyal dog was whimpering and licking the dead man's left hand as if he might bring him back to life this way.

Thorolf cleared his throat. "Asla . . ." He couldn't find any other words.

She slowly turned her face to him. The light from one of the torches reflected in her eyes, and the emptiness inside them frightened Thorolf. Her gaze was directed at him, but it seemed as if she was looking right through him. He tried to hold her cold hand, but she pulled it away, turning her face back toward her dead brother.

Yngvi touched his arm. "Give her time."

Thorolf looked into his brother's sympathetic face and nodded. Then he made a decision.

"Digur, Yngvi, we will pack our things and make camp in the woods. You two," he said, turning to Hilmar's men. "It is your duty to return your master's body to his father. There is plenty of wood around to build a carry frame." Thorolf nodded at Knut's corpse. "Do with him as you please." Then he pointed his sword at both warriors. "And don't you dare follow us. Should we find you near us, we will take it for an attack and kill you without warning."

The two men nodded dejectedly. When they returned to Halldor, the king would vent his anger over the failed mission and his son's death on them. Thorolf didn't even want to think about what the king might do afterward to avenge Hilmar.

When the brothers set off together with an apathetic Asla, Hilmar's men had begun collecting wood for a fire. Thorolf shot one last bitter glance at them. The following morning, the two warriors would search for Knut's sword and place it in his hand. Once their fellow liege was thus prepared for his journey to Valhalla, they would cover him with loose rocks to protect him from scavengers.

Loki remained for a while longer beside the body of Hilmar, unsure what to do. Then he jumped up and followed the trail of his mistress.

Stina sat atop a pile of dried leaves that she had heaped up in a small hollow near the creek. She was shivering, despite the warm coat and the fur blanket she had wrapped around herself. It had grown colder, and an army of snowflakes danced down upon the earth. But she wasn't only shivering from the sudden return of winter; the eerie stillness of the forest stoked her fears. In her loneliness, she would have welcomed the ugly cawing of a raven. Stina sighed, pulling the fur tighter.

At some point, she must have nodded off. When she opened her eyes, she was enclosed by the impenetrable blackness of a moonless, starless night. She had lost all sense of time, her teeth chattering with cold. Despair opened up beneath her like a bottomless black pit at the thought that Asla, Thorolf, and his brothers might have been killed during an attack by Halldor. Then no one would come to fetch her, and without a warming fire, she would soon freeze to death.

The distant howl of a wolf startled her from her gloomy thoughts. She needed to get away from here, needed to find out what had become of the others. Anything was better than waiting in this hollow any longer, being tortured by the icy talons of frost and allowing them to rock her into eternal sleep.

She was about to get up when she thought she heard voices and noticed a pale glow scurrying across the tree trunks to her right. The light of a torch? Was her father coming to get her? The voices were coming closer. They were calling for her. When Stina recognized the low bass of Digur's voice and the bright tones of Asla's, all tension fell from her. Tears of relief and joy streamed down her cheeks.

"I'm here!" she called out and rose, clutching the fur tightly. And there was Loki, happily jumping up on her.

Soon her companions arrived at her hiding place, Thorolf's torch dispelling the darkness Stina had feared so.

Asla embraced her, whispering, as if she feared uttering the words out loud, "Hilmar is dead."

Stina was shocked. She and Hilmar had not been particularly close, but he had always been there in the course of her young life, and he had always been kind. The death of her brother pained her. But she wondered how it must be for Asla, who had worshipped Hilmar, loved him more than she loved anyone else in the family.

Asla sobbed, heavy tears rolling down her face. Stina held her tight and stroked her trembling back, crying with her, but Stina's tears flowed more for Asla's suffering than for Hilmar's death.

The brothers, abashed, stood for a while beside the sniffling, sobbing sisters.

Yngvi was the first to break the silence. "Hilmar wanted a fight to the death."

"It was a fair fight," added Digur.

Thorolf felt obliged to say something, too. "Hilmar did not die by my sword."

Asla loosened her embrace of Stina, gazing at Thorolf from red-rimmed eyes. "And yet you carry the guilt of his death," she said accusingly, her voice breaking. "If you had yielded to my request and allowed me to go with Hilmar, he'd still be alive. Do you deny it?"

"Asla, this was about our son. I could not abandon him to an uncertain future."

"Oh? And if the wise Oda had foretold us a daughter? Would you then have been prepared to let me go with Hilmar? I could feel your doubts when my brother reminded you of your friendship with him and of our Nordic customs." She wiped her nose on her sleeve. "But no. Your hope and your pride to become the father of the savior of your tribe brought death to Hilmar." Asla paused to catch her breath, her voice sharp when she continued. "Had your love for me been greater than your vanity and your selfishness, my despair would have touched you, and you would have yielded to my pleas. Yes, I am blaming you for Hilmar's death!"

She had almost screamed the final words. Softly, more to herself, she added: "But I also blame myself, for getting involved with you in the first place."

Stina listened to her sister's harsh accusation with horror. Was this the end of the great love for which Hilmar had died?

Thorolf made no reply to Asla's hard speech. It was clear that he felt convinced he'd done the right thing, but perhaps, somewhere in the depths of his heart, he was beginning to wonder whether there was some truth to her words.

Yngvi came to his brother's aid. "Asla, Thorolf only wanted the best for you and your son."

"No, he did not! He only wanted the best for himself," she replied defiantly. She again wrapped her arms around Stina, who was trembling from the cold.

Digur, pragmatically minded, was losing patience. "Quit whining already. I'm hungry. It's cold. We need a fire, or else we won't make it through the night. Thorolf, let's find wood. Yngvi, got any tinder left?"

Yngvi, appearing grateful for his brother's unusual outpouring of words, evidently thought to lighten the mood. "Sure, I always carry plenty of tinder in my pouch." Even as the words left his mouth, he seemed to realize how inappropriate and unoriginal his comment was. When no one reacted to his joke, he added sheepishly: "So, I can help you collect wood."

It had stopped snowing by the time the brothers managed to light a fire with the nearly spent torch. The sky cleared and the cold intensified. They huddled around the fire, and Thorolf handed out dried fish and sour-milk cheese from his carry sack. Loki, too, received a fish, gobbling it down hastily.

Thorolf tried now and again to make eye contact with Asla, who was kneeling opposite him. In vain. Asla stubbornly avoided gazing in his direction.

Tired from the exertions of the past day, they ate their rations in silence. Soon after, Asla and Stina lay down on the dry leaves and covered themselves with their furs, cuddling close together as they fell asleep. Thorolf and Yngvi followed suit a short while later. Digur sat on a rotting piece of wood at the edge of the hollow, taking the first watch. Their camp was a fair distance from the edge of the woods, and Digur did not really believe the two warriors would come to attack them, but it was no accident that he'd survived many wars: if at all possible, he left nothing to chance.

When morning dawned, the group carried on. Last night's snowfall had covered the ground with about two handsbreadths of fresh snow—not enough to seriously hamper their progress.

Around noontime, they left the valley and scaled the next mountain ridge. The low sun grazed the peaks to the south, its rays causing the crystals on the snow's surface to sparkle, the mountains' wintery robe shining in the purest of white.

As the short day neared its end, Digur, trudging through the snow at the rear of their group, noticed Stina's limp and unsteady footfall in front of him.

"Stina, what is it?"

The girl stopped, turning her pale face to Digur. She trembled. "My feet . . . I scarcely feel them."

Digur called out to Asla, cleared the snow off a boulder with one hand, and gestured for Stina to sit. "Check Stina's feet," he said.

Asla kneeled down and carefully freed her sister's right foot from its shoe and wet sock. She gasped. Several blisters had burst, and the bleeding wounds had begun to fester. The foot was reddish and felt icy to the touch. Asla pinched the cold skin. "Did you feel that?"

Her sister shook her head.

Asla cast a worried look at the brothers. "Stina's feet are bitten by frost, and she has open sores that I must treat. We have to rest. She cannot possibly keep going in this state."

Thorolf scanned the treeless, snow-covered plateau, then turned to Asla, unease in his voice. "We can't make camp here. We need to get down in the valley where there's wood for us to light a fire."

"I'll carry her," grunted Digur. "Take off her other shoe, too."

Asla did as he asked. The left foot looked no better than its twin.

Digur bent down and picked Stina up in his arms. Asla helped him bury Stina's naked, battered feet inside the thickly woven coat of wool he wore beneath his fur cloak. "Let's move," he said to the others, "or are you trying to grow roots?"

Stina felt as if she were a feather in Digur's strong arms. He seemed to barely notice her weight. He never looked at her, staring instead at the tracks left by Thorolf and Yngvi in the snow, or else at the rhythmic bobbing of Asla's woolen hat in front of him.

Stina studied Digur's profile. The lower half of his longish face was dominated by an angular chin and full lips. Then, above a straight nose, his high forehead ended in a mass of tight black curls. Digur's eyes shone in the pure blue of many people of the North, making for an impressive combination with his dark skin and hair.

Stina remembered hearing about Digur for the first time when she was still a child. Folks in the village spoke of his heroic deeds and his outstanding swordsmanship. He fought as swiftly and cleverly as the father of the gods himself, and was invincible, so they said. His presence alone inspired the warriors in his ranks to give it their all while petrifying his enemies. The people of their village sometimes reverently called him Thor's Black Hammer, a name bestowed upon him by his enemies.

It must have been around her fourteenth winter when a skald entertained at the hall of her father. Among others, the burly man recited verses that told of Digur's bravery. Once, when she found the poet on his own taking a meal in her father's hall, she sat down beside him and asked him questions about Digur. The skald seemed to like her, readily sharing his knowledge.

Apparently, Thorolf's grandfather had bought Digur's mother, Diara, at the slave market as a child. She served in his household, and when she reached the threshold of adolescence, Ulrik, Thorolf's father, cast a desirous eye upon the tall, beautiful, dark-skinned girl from the Hot Land. Soon after, Digur was born. Before his wedding to Thorolf's mother, Ulrik—with the assent of his father—gifted Diara and their son, Digur, their freedom. Digur grew into a promising youth who excelled at sword practice. He knew how to use his fists, too, allegedly, and he liked to use them often and effectively when his younger brothers, Thorolf and Yngvi, were in danger of being overpowered by a mob of rowdy boys.

During that time, so the skald told Stina, the three half-brothers grew into an inseparable unit that was tied together not only by their shared blood, but even more so by deep mutual respect, honesty, and unbreakable loyalty to one another.

Ever since he was old enough, Digur had accompanied his father to war whenever he was called upon by Halldor. Usually it was to put some unruly chieftain in his place for denying Halldor's claim to the crown of the North. In the course of the years, the hulking Digur gained the reputation of an invincible warrior. During the most recent summer, however, Digur apparently left Halldor's army with no advance warning. Several of his fellow warriors reported that he had practically fled—but from what, no one could say.

That was when Digur joined his brothers, journeying out to sea in Thorolf's broad-bellied knarr, *Goldeagle*. By that time, Thorolf was already established as a successful trader, but when Digur joined him, business went even better. Once or twice, when a trade partner thought to take the precious goods of the North by force to avoid paying for them, the brothers and their men soon disabused them of any such foolish notion. Then it would be the greedy merchant who lost his goods, adding to Thorolf's wealth instead.

Two years had passed since Stina's conversation with the skald, and as far as she knew, Digur was still accompanying his brothers on their trading voyages.

Her eyes rested on his face. His expression showed severity and a certain gloominess, and she marveled at the fact that such a merciless, battle-hardened warrior, who must have killed many men, was showing her such a gentle—yes, almost compassionate—side.

Thanks to the heat from Digur's body, she was beginning to feel her feet again. But with sensation came pain, forcing tears into her eyes. Stina gritted her teeth. She had no choice but to bear it bravely.

In the valley, they found enough wood to light a fire. Asla hung the small pot that Yngvi produced from his carry sack to a frame that Thorolf set up above the fire. Then, she filled it with snow. Once the water was boiling, she added herbs from one of her pouches, and then placed the pot into the snow to cool.

"Drink—it will do you good."

The brothers fetched wooden cups from their bags and scooped hot tea from the pot. Once everyone had helped themselves to a cupful, Asla used the remaining herb brew to clean dirt and pus from Stina's feet. Then she tore strips of her undergarment, wrapping them around her sister's feet.

When they set off the following morning, Digur lifted Stina into his arms matter-of-factly, as he had the day before. The winter sun shone, but it lacked the strength to dispel the frost and warm the hikers.

Around the middle of the day, they descended the final mountain along snowy, winding paths. Halfway down, a breathtaking view opened before them: in the center of snow-covered flats dotted with tiny farmhouses stretched the blue-gray, perfectly smooth waters of the fjord. Winding between mountain ranges, they knew, it met the sea about half a day's journey by boat. Directly beneath them, at the inlet's end, huddled the houses of Hellefjord, the village of Jarl Ulrik, along a small river whose waters lazily flowed into the fjord. A little off to the side, upon the flat crest of a hill, sat Ulrik's large, three-aisled hall. Built around it were stables, storehouses, and quarters for the servants.

Anchoring in the harbor were several smaller fishing boats and two larger vessels: Thorolf's *Goldeagle* and the longship Ulrik and his men had used to sail home. All the other ships belonging to the traders and raiders were stored in boathouses, awaiting their deployment in the coming spring.

They did not choose the direct route to Hellefjord, opting instead for a detour that led them into a large forest. In the fading light of dusk, they reached a clearing, in whose center stood a crooked, ramshackle hut. About one hundred paces to the right of the charcoal burner's hut were a shelter and several pits covered with slabs of turf, interrupting the monotony of the white snow cover. Thin lines of smoke rising into the air indicated that wood was smoldering into charcoal inside the pits.

Yngvi knocked against the hut's door. "It's me, Yngvi!"

A man of average height opened the door. His hair was sparse, and the soot in the countless lines of his weather-beaten face looked like they'd never encountered water, making the charcoal burner appear older than he was. Standing behind him was a plump woman who had probably seen a little over thirty winters. When she recognized Yngvi, a wide smile lit her round face and a warm glow in her eyes bid the visitors welcome.

"Hilda, Oddur, I am pleased to find you in good health," Yngvi said. "My companions and I ask admittance to your home. You promised me a favor once. Now I am here to claim it."

Oddur, who had gazed kindly at Yngvi until then, frowned, but Hilda pushed past her hesitant husband and clasped Yngvi's hands in hers. "You are always welcome here, as are your friends. Come inside where it's warm."

The hut consisted of one single room. It was cozy, thanks to a hearth full of glowing red coals in the center. The hut looked clean and tidy in the weak light of two tallow lamps. The travel companions were pleased to escape the merciless cold of the impending night.

Digur gently lowered Stina onto a bench.

Before he stepped away from her, Stina caught him by a sleeve. "You are a very strong man, but when the track led steeply uphill, I noticed your heavy breathing. You went to your limits to carry me along with your baggage. I thank you for it."

"It was nothing," he muttered, and it almost seemed as if he were fleeing from her when he dropped to the floor exhaustedly at the opposite wall of the hut.

Since there was only one bench there, and since the master

of the house claimed the free spot next to Stina, the remainder of his guests sat down on their rolled-up furs.

Hilda fetched a cauldron and hung it above the hearth. "I cooked a hearty stew for Oddur and me for the next few days. There's enough for all of us for tonight."

Oddur's eyes followed his wife's movements sullenly. He looked as if he feared he would have to go hungry for the foreseeable future. He cut to the chase. "Yngvi, what do you want from me?"

"Not much, my friend. Nothing more than for you to take in Stina as your helper and hide her here."

"Helper?" scoffed Oddur. "She is a girl."

"No one will notice. We will crop her hair, bind her chest, and blacken her with coal. Not even Odin will recognize her as a girl."

"And why?"

"I want to be honest with you, Oddur," said Yngvi. He told the couple the story of their escape.

When he finished, Oddur pensively twisted his mustache between his fingers. "As much as I would like to help . . . I know I am in your debt, but—"

"No 'but'!" Hilda said, cutting off her husband. Her kind face hardened. "Where were you when those scoundrels attacked me in the spring on my way to the village, trying to violate me? If Yngvi hadn't arrived just in time to chase the pair away, I might not be here now to cook your meals, patch your clothing, and warm your bed. The girl stays for as long as she needs to. That is the least we can do for Yngvi."

"Woman, we've scarcely enough supplies to make it through the winter. How are we supposed to feed another mouth?" replied the charcoal burner grumpily.

"Then we will just tighten our belts. It won't kill us. And

besides," she said, nodding at the paunch bulging beneath Oddur's robe, "you can feed off your own stores for a while."

Thorolf reached inside a pouch on his belt. "Here you go. This will help replenish your supplies."

Oddur stared at the coins and hacksilver Thorolf was holding out to him, and he grasped it greedily.

"If you take Stina in and treat her well, the rest of this pouch is yours, too."

Oddur's face lit up. The pouch the silver had come out of still seemed quite heavy.

"I will also stay for a few days, charcoal burner," said Digur. "I will pay for my meals and help you at work."

Hilda filled small wooden bowls with her stew of onions, turnips, cabbage, and hare meat, placed a piece of flatbread on top and handed them out to her husband and their guests.

Loki, having recognized the mistress of the house as the food giver, wagged his tail, attentively following each of her movements. When he yelped a few times, Hilda took pity on the hungry dog and fetched a leg of a skinned hare from the corner, patting his head as she placed it before his paws. With a grateful whimper, Loki sank his teeth into the raw meat. Hilda didn't appear perturbed by her husband's dark glare, for tonight she had won a new friend.

The soft clacking of wooden spoons in bowls was accompanied by contented slurping and smacking, adding to the coziness of the charcoal burners' small, warm hut.

Yngvi's spoon hovered above his bowl for a moment. "This is a truly delicious meal, dear Hilda. Thank you. Your husband is a lucky man to call such a remarkable cook his wife."

Thorolf and the two young women nodded in agreement. Digur burped with satisfaction, which was also a compliment of sorts.

Hilda beamed at Yngvi, her smile fading as she turned to her husband. Evidently, she had never received a word of praise from him for her accomplishments.

Hilda emptied the pot, succeeding in filling every bowl a second time. Her guests smiled at her in gratitude.

Once Digur polished off his second helping, he stared into his empty bowl with disappointment.

Yngvi smirked. "Look, Thorolf, our big brother gazes hungrily at his bowl as if he might devour it. No wonder, since he walked for two today."

His comment, humorously intended, ebbed away without response; only Digur shot him a sharp look.

"All right, I give up trying to cheer you up."

Stina rose and limped over to Digur, holding out her nearly full bowl. "Take it. I'm not hungry."

Digur shook his head. "You need to regain your strength. You eat it."

Stina braced her free hand on her hip, wrinkled her forehead, and stood a little taller. "I haven't moved the entire day. I have regained my strength."

Thorolf and Yngvi watched in amazement as their brother smirked—yes, almost smiled, even. Digur took the bowl from Stina's hand, holding her gaze for the duration of a few heartbeats. Hilda, having watched the scene with amusement, placed another piece of bread on Digur's third portion of stew.

When the charcoal burner carried a torch outside to check on his pits for the final time that evening, Hilda added some coal to the hearth. There was just enough room in the hut for the guests to spread out their furs and lie down upon them. That night, they would finally sleep once more around a warm hearth, sheltered from the icy winds whistling their monotonous song around the corners of the charcoal burner's hut.

CHAPTER 2
THE HOMECOMING

In the morning, Thorolf, Yngvi, and Asla packed up their belongings. Loki ran around Asla excitedly, as if telling her he was ready for new adventures.

But his mistress pointed at her sleeping sister, gazing deep into the dog's loyal eyes. "Loki, you stay here and watch over Stina."

The dog appeared to understand, barking briefly and dropping on his haunches beside Stina.

Thorolf, Yngvi, and Asla left the charcoal burner's hut, following the snow-covered path to the village in the first soft light of day. The wind was still icy. But the cold didn't annoy Yngvi nearly as much as the frosty silence between Asla and Thorolf. He hated the glum mood, but he wasn't about to make a fool of himself a third time with a jest.

When the small group emerged from the forest, the sun had come up behind the mountains, brightening the cloudless sky. The air was crisp, and they could clearly distinguish the hill with Ulrik's hall in the distance.

The gate in the palisade surrounding the village beneath the jarl's domicile stood open. The snow on the road was firm from foot traffic, and in some places, it was treacherously slippery. They moved carefully to avoid falling and becoming the laughingstock of the two small girls who, skipping and dancing lithely, accompanied them some of the way. Houses of craftsmen and traders lined the road to the left and right. The travelers could hear oinking, clucking, and mooing from stables. The heavy blows of a hammer on an anvil told them the blacksmith had begun his day's work. The tanner waved a friendly greeting as he slid past along a slippery stretch of the path. By the fork in the road that led to Ulrik's hall, a group of boys led a snowball fight, cheering when they struck their aim and yelping angrily when they themselves became the target.

Yngvi's cold, red nose was struck hard by a snowball. He drew two of his knives, hunched his back, and twisted his face into an ugly grimace. His arms spread wide, waving his knives menacingly, he staggered toward the culprits like an undead corpse freshly risen from the grave, letting out an unnatural, eerie cry. The children froze with fear, then scattered in all directions, shrieking in panic.

Yngvi straightened up and slid his knives back into his belt. He grinned at Thorolf and Asla, who each had a smile on their lips. *Well, better than nothing.*

At Ulrik's estate, the servants were busy completing the morning's tasks: a maid lowered a wooden pail down the well to fetch water, a stable hand led two horses to a paddock, and a boy scattered grain on a patch of ground that had been cleared from snow for the chickens, who raced hungrily for the seeds.

The door to Ulrik's longhouse was pushed open, and a small but sturdy girl stormed outside, wailing. She was barefooted and wore her flaxen hair unbound. An equally flaxen-haired middle-aged woman followed just a few steps behind, cursing. When the woman noticed the arrivals, she stopped, looking startled, while the girl continued to run, half-blind with tears.

"Yngvi, Thorolf, where is it you're coming from? Why were you not on your ship when it returned? Your men refused to utter a word regarding your whereabouts." Her eyes traveled to Asla, staring at her with puzzlement. "And you? What in Odin's name are you doing here?"

"Mother, it's a long story," Yngvi replied. "Let us go inside. I assume Father is in?"

Ulrik's large, three-aisled hall testified to his status as a chieftain and jarl. Most longhouses contained one central firepit enclosed by a stone wall, serving simultaneously for cooking and as a source of heat. Ulrik's longhouse had two. In the hall's central area, along the walls between the two fireplaces, stood low, wide benches that were cushioned with straw-filled linen sacks and furs, serving as the family's beds. The rear part held chests of clothes, weapons, and jewelry, two looms, and nonperishable provisions. The walls were hung with furs and trophies that Ulrik had collected during his Viking raids. In the hall's front part stood the raised seat of the master of the house. There, during times of festivities, Ulrik liked to carouse and feast with his guests at three long tables with benches.

On this morning, only Ulrik and six-year-old Erik, his youngest son, were sitting at the table, peaceably eating their salted porridge. Without lifting his eyes, the chieftain groused: "Shut the door already, woman, there's a cold draft."

Eventually the broad-shouldered jarl, who had gained a legendary reputation on his raiding voyages, noticed that he had visitors. He looked up, setting aside his wooden spoon. Gudrun, his wife, did as she was asked, shutting out the cold, as well as the daylight. Now, merely sparse amounts of light streamed in through small vents in the hall's roof.

"Sit—you must be hungry." Gudrun signaled to a maid, whereupon the girl readily scurried to the rear of the hall to fetch bowls and spoons for the guests.

The mistress of the house sat down beside her son, who grinned at his elder brothers Thorolf and Yngvi. Erik probably hoped to persuade them to play in the snow later on.

Gudrun was slim, almost gaunt. Her posture and the high cheekbones in her narrow face gave her a noble appearance. Crow's-feet around her pale-blue eyes and some first wrinkles around her mouth betrayed her age of almost forty winters.

If Gudrun lacked some meat on her ribs, her husband had plenty thereof, brimming with strength and vitality as he sat enthroned at the table. He scrutinized his sons and especially Asla, who silently sat down opposite him.

Asla's eyes gradually grew accustomed to the sparse light, and she noticed Ulrik's suspicious looks. Perhaps the jarl guessed at the misfortune she was bringing to his house. Like his son Thorolf, Ulrik had a face that was angular and longish with a prominent chin. He wore his silver-streaked hair plaited. Bushy black eyebrows and a jagged, poorly healed scar running from his right ear to his chin gave him a dauntless and dangerous aura. The appearance was not deceptive, Asla knew. Ulrik was known as unrelenting and merciless toward his enemies, and none of his free farmers and followers would ever dream of second-guessing his standing as their leader and jarl.

Young Erik, having finished his porridge, tugged at his father's sleeve, whispering something in his ear. Ulrik's gentle smile betrayed the good-natured, friendly side of his character, which he displayed to anyone he loved and who did not oppose him.

When his father nodded, the boy hooted with delight, fetched his woolen coat and stormed to the door, nearly crashing into Isold, who, shivering with cold in her undergarment, was returning from her flight from her mother. Once her younger brother happily pushed past her out the door, Isold noticed her older brothers and Asla. A shy smile spread on her round, puffy-cheeked face, only to vanish almost instantly as her mother greeted her with angrily knitted brows.

"Mother, I—"

"Close the door, get dressed, and fetch a bowl, Isold. We'll talk about your crime and your greediness later."

Isold, hanging her head, obeyed.

Thorolf, Yngvi, and Asla filled their hungry stomachs in silence with the tasty porridge the maid had ladled into their bowls. The soft sounds of eating and the cracking from charring logs on the fire stretched the time, everyone hoping the silence would soon be broken.

When Ulrik began to drum his fingers impatiently on the tabletop, Thorolf took a deep breath. "Father, Asla ran away from home. Digur, Yngvi, and I helped her escape across the mountains." Thorolf paused for a moment, as if he expected a reply from Ulrik. But his father nodded at him to continue. "According to her father's will, Asla was to marry Hafur. She was afraid of the chieftain's cruelty." Thorolf glanced at Asla, hoping she would support him in this speech. But she merely stared at her slender hands she held folded in her lap. "Further, Asla and I have been promised to one another since the fall. We wish to marry. I'm aware that to Halldor this will look as if I abducted Asla. He will be angry, and this might jeopardize your alliance. I want to avoid this at all costs. Therefore, I will give him the greater part of my wealth as a bride-price."

Ulrik did not appear surprised. He had probably pieced together what happened when he laid eyes on the beautiful Asla with his sons. He replied to his son composedly, but with severity in his voice. "You disregarded the customs of our people and broke our laws. Don't you think it should have been my task to negotiate your marriage with Halldor?"

"Yes, Father," replied Thorolf firmly. "But your negotiations would have been doomed from the outset. Halldor needs the connection between Asla and Hafur for his ambitious plans. I could not have acted differently. Especially once Asla confided that she is expecting our child in the summer. The wise woman at her village foretold her a son."

Ulrik's bushy eyebrows went up. "I see. My son heedlessly followed the urge inside his pants. I would have thought you more sensible."

Thorolf stifled a grin, despite his precarious situation. Upon close inspection, the faces of several children of maids bore an undeniable resemblance to Ulrik. Thorolf's father was not a man to resist the urge in his pants. But maids were not free; a dalliance with a maid had no consequences for a freeman. If he, however, impregnated a king's daughter without permission, foiling her father's plans, the situation was entirely different.

Gudrun, who loved Thorolf nearly as much as her own sons, Yngvi and Erik, shot her stepson an admonishing look. Isold gaped at her father and her half-brother as she listened to their conversation.

Yngvi alone seemed untouched by the tense atmosphere in the hall. Unperturbed, he gobbled up spoonful after spoonful of his porridge.

"That is not all," Asla declared quietly and without looking up. "Hilmar is dead. He was killed while fighting Thorolf when he came to take me back."

This time, Ulrik's eyebrows shot up in alarm. "What?" Glaring at Thorolf, his face turned red, angry veins throbbing in his temples. He slammed his fist hard on the table, so hard that the clay bowls upon it danced, one of them shimmying over the edge and shattering on the ground.

Isold sprang to her feet with fright, fleeing into the rear part of the longhouse. Asla winced, pressing one hand to her mouth.

Gudrun, evidently, was accustomed to her husband's fits of anger, which, as Yngvi liked to say, fizzled out almost as quickly as they arrived, and so she took this latest outburst as calmly as always. As did Thorolf, who held his father's furious gaze when Ulrik roared at him. "You killed Halldor's only legitimate son! Do you have any idea what that means, you fool?"

Yngvi, feeling obliged to defend his brother, explained to his father how the fight came about and that Hilmar did not die by Thorolf's sword but from an injury to the head sustained when he fell upon a rock protruding from the ground.

Ulrik jumped up from his bench and swiped his right arm across the table, sending all bowls and spoons within his reach flying to the ground. He leaned with both hands on the tabletop, lowering his bulky torso toward Yngvi.

He almost touched the tip of his son's nose when he snarled at him. "Do you seriously believe that makes any difference? If you do, then you are just as great a fool as your brother. Halldor loved his son. Hilmar was his heir, destined to follow him as king. Halldor will want to avenge his death and demand Thorolf's head. And yours too, you idiot. To Halldor, it is all the same whether the fight was fair, whether it was a stone or Thorolf's sword that killed his son. Hilmar died because he tried his utmost to fulfill his oath, according to the laws of our people. Hilmar was in the right—you acted wrongfully!"

Yngvi did not flinch during his father's angry speech, stoutly bearing the drops of saliva and porridge spattering his face.

Ulrik slumped back onto the bench, resting his head in his hands.

Thorolf cleared his throat. "Father, I want—"

"Silence!" snapped Ulrik without looking up. "I need to think."

Muttering a curse, he eventually stood up and walked over to his sleeping place. He slipped into his trousers, shrugged a thick fur coat over the top of his linen tunic, and pulled on his heavy boots. Without another word, he trudged to the door, yanked it open, and disappeared into the bright daylight.

"Fetch me my horse," those remaining in the hall heard him shout at a servant.

Gudrun closed the door. "When he returns, he will have calmed down. Then we can talk sensibly with him and discuss what to do."

While the brothers finished their porridge, Asla remained sitting with hunched shoulders, gazing into her lap and fighting back tears. Ulrik's hostile, cold stare had made it unmistakably clear that she was not welcome in his hall. But where was she supposed to turn? She could not go back to her family, and she did not want to go with Thorolf, the man who had killed her brother. She sniffled softly. Never before in her life had she felt as lost as in this moment.

A short while later, Thorolf and Yngvi rose to leave. As Thorolf walked out, his eyes begged Asla to come with him. Asla shook her head, instead shooting a pleading look at Gudrun, who indicated with a nod that she might stay.

No sooner had the brothers left than Gudrun asked her daughter and her guest to follow her to the looms at the back of the longhouse. With a jerk, she pulled a block of wood out of the wall, allowing daylight to stream in and illuminate the two upright looms.

With a sweeping gesture, the mistress of the house invited the two girls to help themselves to the looms, while she herself took a seat on a bench with a fur across her knees and picked up an embroidery frame.

Isold lowered herself onto one of the stools and continued to work on the woolen cloth she would soon finish. Asla took the other loom. She guessed that Gudrun had been the last person to work on the half-finished cloth woven in the threads.

"What's this going to be?" asked Asla with interest.

"The sail for Father's new longship," replied Isold proudly. "As soon as we and the other women have woven enough pieces, we sew them together to make one large cloth."

They worked in silence for a while. The maid quietly fed logs to the fire. The soft sliding sounds of the shuttles, binding together thread after thread, created a soothing, relaxed atmosphere.

When Gudrun began to ask Asla questions, the younger woman gave curt and rather standoffish replies at first. But gradually she opened up, and soon the words came gushing from her lips, describing the reason for and the course of her escape, albeit without mentioning Stina. Asla soon started to feel better, for Gudrun was kind and proved to be a sensitive, caring listener.

As dusk fell, the young women set down their work and took their evening meal with Gudrun. Shortly after the maid had cleared the table, Ulrik returned home. He removed his outerwear and sullenly sat at the table. The maid silently served him meat and bread. Gudrun stayed with her husband while the two young women retreated to the back of the hall. Ulrik's eyes followed Asla glumly.

"What is that woman doing here? Why isn't she with Thorolf?"

Gudrun told her husband what she had learned from Asla while they'd been working.

Ulrik cut off a piece of meat, stabbed it with his knife, and shoved it in his mouth. "Then it was no escape but an abduction," he grumbled with a full mouth. "That doesn't help things."

Gudrun had her elbow on the table, propping up her chin,

glancing at her husband sidelong. "What do you think Halldor will do? Do you truly believe he is going to demand Thorolf's life?"

"I fear he is. Especially since it is his right to do so."

Gudrun warmly placed her free hand atop his. "But you won't allow it."

"Of course not. But I do not yet know how I am supposed to protect Thorolf's life and satisfy Halldor's longing for revenge at the same time." Dejected, he tore off a piece of flatbread and chewed on it.

While her parents spoke in low voices on the other side of the fireplace, Isold picked up a stick, lighting it on the glowing embers. Concentrating, she lit two oil lamps and sat on a bench, setting down the two vessels with their merrily flickering wicks beside herself.

Then she waved at her new friend to sit. "Asla, if you like, I'll share my sleeping place with you."

"Thank you, Isold. I would like that." She was already fond of the girl. "Why was your mother so mad at you this morning?"

Softly and a little abashed, Isold replied, "I ate a whole pot of honey from mother's stores. I know that honey is difficult to make and precious. I didn't mean to do it. I only wanted to taste it, so I stuck my finger in the pot and sucked on it. The honey was so delicious that I couldn't help but stick my finger in again and again." Isold ran her small, pink tongue across her lips and closed her eyes as if she were reliving this wonderful moment of utter enjoyment. "At some point, I stopped caring whether my mother was going to be mad later on. And then, suddenly, the pot was empty."

Asla smiled at the childlike, almost comical way the girl described her crime.

Isold gave a heartfelt sigh. "As punishment, our maid can't give me any sweet porridge until the spring. My mother declared that until then I must make do with salted porridge, bread, dried fish, and stew. She says I am too fat in any case, and that no man Father picks for me shall want me." She paused for a moment, considering. "Do you think she's right?"

"Nonsense. She only says that to scare you, so that you won't touch the next pot of honey. There are plenty of men who prefer stronger women. Your golden hair and blue eyes are pleasing, too. But eating with a little more restraint wouldn't hurt you. You might not wish for those puffy cheeks to become much rounder."

"I know," groaned Isold. Then, she added stubbornly, "But I like eating so much."

For a while, the young women fell silent, each lost in her own world of thoughts. Then Isold restarted the conversation. "Tell me, why did you stay here instead of going with Thorolf? You love each other, and my brother is a great man."

Asla drew her feet up on the bench, hugging her shins, resting the side of her head on her knees, and gazing sadly at Isold. "Because whenever I'm with Thorolf, I think of my brother. I see his face in front of me. In the beginning, it looked peaceful—just like it did when Hilmar closed his eyes for good—but now his face is waxing more accusing and severe whenever I come near Thorolf, as if Hilmar were telling me: 'You have betrayed me and our father. My death is your fault.'" Asla breathed deeply, then exhaled with a small sigh. "And he is right. I defied my father and provoked terrible misfortune. If I returned to Thorolf now, I would condone my deeds. Hilmar's ghost in my head would torment me even worse. I love Thorolf as I always have, but his and my guilt forbid me from being with him."

Isold, seeing tears gleam in the eyes of her friend, folded her arms around her.

In the following days, the weather changed little. The clear nights were bitter cold, and even in the middle of the day, the low sun failed to warm the people. At least the cutting northeastern wind had dropped—a blessing to all those forced to work despite the cold.

Yngvi helped Thorolf and his servants bring the *Goldeagle* ashore to winterproof her. The evenings he often spent in Thorolf's longhouse. When they weren't discussing the events of the past few days, they would often strategize over a round of hnefatafl, a game with pretty playing pieces whittled from whalebone by Thorolf. In it, one player tried to bring his king to safety in a corner while the other was out to stop him, attempting to capture the king first. When playing against Thorolf, Yngvi frequently enjoyed the pleasures of winning, which was almost never the case when he played his servant Gregor. Most evenings they rounded off with a simple game of dice.

On the morning of the fifth day following the arrival of Thorolf, Yngvi, and Asla, a knarr flying Halldor's banner approached the mouth of the fjord leading to Ulrik's village. The sentries guarding the fjord's entrance from a boat counted a mere eight men at the oars, and since Halldor was an allied jarl, they saw no reason to signal to the guards on shore to warn the village with smoke signals.

When the knarr moored at the jetty in the harbor, the harbor guards questioned the ship's commander as to the reason for their visit. Then one of the guards hurried up to Ulrik to inform him.

Ulrik immediately sent for Thorolf, Yngvi, and Digur, the latter having returned to the village the previous evening.

Once his sons were gathered, Ulrik granted Halldor's men permission to leave the boat. Björn, Halldor's bastard son, and two of his followers climbed the hill to the longhouse escorted by Ulrik's men. However, Björn alone was granted entry to the hall.

Displaying his status, Ulrik was sitting upon his high seat clad in his best garments. His sons stood beside him with folded arms.

Björn, a battle-hardened hulk of a man like his father, bowed his head slightly. "Jarl Ulrik, King Halldor sends his greetings. I come at the behest of my father, who has acknowledged me as his rightful son and heir." Standing tall, he allowed his words to take effect for a moment before continuing. "Your son Thorolf abducted my sister. In addition, he slew Hilmar in one-on-one combat, preventing my brother from fulfilling his sacred oath of returning Asla home."

Ulrik nodded, cutting Björn off. "I know all that. What do you want?"

"During the assembly of his freemen, Halldor will pass judgment on Thorolf's wicked deed. My father demands Thorolf's presence during the assembly. There he shall receive my father's judgment and atone for his sins. I am here to collect your son."

Thorolf had been prepared for this. He knew offering a large amount of silver as a bride-price to Björn would be futile. For the self-proclaimed king, this was no longer about his pregnant daughter. This was about revenge for the death of Hilmar. Thorolf glanced at his father. How would he decide?

They had seen each other a few times since Thorolf's return, but every time he'd tried to ask Ulrik what he intended to do when Halldor demanded his head, his father had replied evasively, stating that he'd see when the time came.

Ulrik rose, hooking his thumbs on his belt. "Please carry the following message to my old friend, our king: my son Thorolf is in the wrong and carries the guilt for Hilmar's death. For this, I punish him with a banishment of seven winters. I am banishing Yngvi and Digur for the same amount of time, for they, too, are to blame. At the latest, my sons will depart the fjord in their ships on the day in the spring when the light of day is equal to the dark of night. From that day on, I declare them outlawed. Should they linger in the Northland past that point in time or return here before their time is up, any man may kill them and take their belongings without fear of punishment. Further, Thorolf will pay a wergild to the sum of the entire fortune he has accumulated in the course of his trade voyages."

Ulrik whistled, and two of his most trusted men emerged from the rear of the hall, lugging a heavy chest.

Thorolf turned pale at the sight of it. It was the chest holding all the gold and silver coins and hacksilver he possessed. He stared at Ulrik in disbelief. "You can't—" His words died under his father's furious glare.

"Oh yes, I can. As you probably remember, I helped you bury your hoard. I had it lifted when I suspected the kind of justified accusation that was coming our way."

Björn kneeled and opened the lid, its rusty hinges squeaking. He dug his right hand into the coins of gold and silver, then nodded appreciatively at the jarl. "This is a hoard deserving of a king. I believe my father will be satisfied with this richly filled chest, as well as the banishment of Thorolf and his brothers."

"If he is not, there will be war. Halldor must be aware of the fact that, if it came to that, some of our allies would take my side."

Björn closed the chest and rose, ignoring Ulrik's threat. "Where is my sister? I have a message for her, too."

"Asla has gone with my wife to see our healer, Alfhild."

"Then tell her that her father has cut her off and declared her an outlaw. He who kills her receives from Halldor a reward of twenty sheep. The words he gave me for her were as follows: 'May the Midgard serpent find you and tear the child from your womb!'"

Ulrik nodded, his expression unmoved. "I will pass it on."

Björn opened the door and ordered his men to carry the chest to the boat. Before leaving, he turned to the jarl once more. "One more thing, Ulrik. Stina has been missing since the night Asla fled. If we find out that Thorolf is responsible for Stina's disappearance as well, Halldor won't hesitate to fetch back his daughter. And he will not come alone. Bear that in mind and send Stina back to us should you see her."

"I know nothing of Stina's whereabouts," replied Ulrik truthfully. "She is not here. Now go and deliver my greetings to your father."

Once Björn and his men had left with the chest, Ulrik eased himself back into the high seat, gesturing for his sons to sit also. Upon his signal, a maid brought cups and a jug of ale.

The men sipped the flavorful brew, and Ulrik studied his sons, frowning. The brothers held their father's stern gaze, albeit with unhappy expressions.

Ulrik broke the silence. "I hope you aren't going to complain about my verdict." He glanced from man to man, daring them to object. "If you are, I will take you down to Björn's ship myself. Then you may continue to rail against your fate in the clutches of Halldor. If you are not, I may come to accept that you are growing up, learning to bear the responsibility for your actions."

When Thorolf, Yngvi, and Digur showed no immediate reaction, Ulrik continued in a slightly friendlier tone. "Because you are my sons, I pronounced the mildest verdict possible in this situation."

"You did what was necessary to save my neck and avoid a war with Halldor," Thorolf admitted, dejected. "But why didn't you warn me? I could have set aside a handful of coins and some hacksilver and wouldn't be left wholly without means now."

"Because you are a pitiful actor, son," said Ulrik with a mocking smile. "If I'd told you beforehand, you never would have reacted so convincingly upset and despairing at the sight of your hoard. Björn would have rightly guessed we were giving him but part of your treasure."

Ulrik pulled back his cloak and untied a plump pouch from his belt, tossing it at Thorolf. "Here is the—meager, admittedly—remainder of your treasure. It will suffice to acquire provisions for your voyage into exile."

Thorolf caught the pouch, registering with relief that it was quite heavy. "Thank you." After a few moments, he looked Ulrik straight in the eye. "I'm sorry I cause you trouble, Father."

Yngvi and Digur nodded in agreement.

"That's what I wanted to hear. I'm glad you can see the foolishness of your mistake. I, too, committed one or two missteps during my youth for which I paid dearly."

Ulrik grinned, turning once more into the good-humored father who raised his cup, asking his sons to do the same. "Let us drink to your safe return following the completion of your banishment. May you come home with all your limbs and heads intact."

Relieved, the brothers lifted their cups and touched them against their father's.

Ulrik tugged at his earlobe, as he always did when pondering or trying to sort his thoughts. "Björn mentioned that Stina might have fled along with Asla. Is there any truth to that?"

Yngvi spoke before Thorolf had a chance to reply. "No, Father, Asla came alone to the meeting place. Who knows where Stina is right now? Maybe she is hiding at some warm, comfortable hut, or maybe she is trudging through the snow somewhere, freezing, or maybe she fell victim to the wolves . . ."

Thorolf couldn't help but admire his brother's cunning. Yngvi had artfully succeeded in providing Ulrik with a satisfactory answer without directly lying to him.

The master of the house rose. "I must check on the servants.

Meet me back here the evening of the day after tomorrow. I am giving a feast to mark the safe return of Egil. I'm sure he'll have many a thrilling tale to tell."

Egil was the most successful trader in Ulrik's realm. Only the day before, his knarr had arrived in the harbor, though the other ships of his fleet had returned home several weeks ago. Now folk looked forward to hearing Egil and his men tell stories of adventures in exotic, faraway lands. People would tell and retell those stories of the well-traveled trader, sweetening the long, dark, and monotonous winter nights. Soon they would elaborate on this detail or that. The huge breaker that nearly overturned the ship might turn into a flick of the tail of an enormous sea serpent, or a smoking mountain might become a horde of fire-spitting dragons.

After Ulrik left the hall, Thorolf waved at the maid, ordering her to bring another jug of ale. When each cup was filled again, Thorolf cleared his throat and looked from brother to brother.

"I'm sorry I dragged you into this unfortunate situation. It was wrong of me to ask you to help me with Asla's escape. I should have done it on my own. Then you wouldn't be banished from your home for years."

Yngvi drank deeply from his ale and wiped his sleeve across his mouth. "Do you think we only follow you when there's gold and silver to be gained? We are your brothers, not some stinking rats. Would you reject me or Digur if we needed your help?"

Thorolf shook his head. "Of course not."

"There you go. If we stick together like we've always done, we are going to make it through the coming years just fine. Who knows—perhaps our banishment could be just the thread the Norns require to weave a destiny that allows us to return as filthy-rich merchants?" Yngvi left the question hanging between them, glancing at his brothers with confidence.

Digur twisted his mouth into a somewhat misshapen smile, nodding.

Thorolf knew how attached his elder brother was to his mother, Diara, and his other half-siblings. The thought of not seeing them for many years must have been hard on Digur—but he would never allow this weakness to show. Thorolf, too, struggled to share Yngvi's optimism. Though he had been away from home several moons at a time on trading voyages, he was always secure in the knowledge that he would return home to those he loved. But once he set off on this next journey, he would not be allowed to set foot on home land for a long time, and the thought pained him.

Yngvi seemed disappointed at his brothers' muted reaction to his hopefulness. "Come on, Thorolf, no point pulling such a sour face. At least we will keep you company, along with your lovely Asla."

"Yes, she will accompany me. She has no choice. The road home is closed to her, and she cannot stay here without living in danger of being killed for the reward of twenty sheep." Thorolf sipped on his ale, sighing. "I have serious doubts whether she will ever love me again the way she loved me before Hilmar's death. At the moment, she ignores me and avoids crossing my path." With his hands, he grasped one hand each of his brothers, squeezing them tightly. "But I am glad to know you'll be by my side in the coming years."

CHAPTER 3
HALLDOR'S REVENGE

Dusk was falling when Björn gave the order to set off. Once his men had rowed the knarr through the narrow passage separating the fjord into upper and lower channels, they dropped anchor at a shallow, concealed spot near the shore. Under the cover of darkness, twenty-one men crawled from the low spaces beneath the decks in the ship's bow and stern, where they had been lying on their stomachs in hiding, and gathered around Björn.

"Ulrik refused to deliver Thorolf. You know what to do."

The men nodded, but Björn, wishing to make absolutely certain, instructed them one more time. "Find a suitable hiding place and wait for two days. During the night of the second day, split into seven groups. Each group takes two outlying farmsteads. When you're done, take the quickest route back across the mountains. Be careful and don't get caught. Ulrik may guess who's behind the attack, but he shall not receive certainty. And keep your eyes peeled for Stina. He who returns her to Halldor will be richly rewarded."

The men nodded once more, then lowered themselves into the hip-deep, ice-cold water, balancing the bulging sacks their mates passed down to them on their shoulders. Cautiously they waded toward the shore, careful not to slip and get their load wet.

Later, when Björn and his men rowed out of the fjord, the crew of the local sentry boat counted eight men at the oars by the light of the moon, the same number that had entered the fjord that morning.

Ulrik had invited the heads of the most important families of his realm to his hall. For the most part, they were influential craftsmen and successful traders, but there were also some farmers who, with the help of thralls, ran large properties and thus ensured the provision of all people living in the area.

When Thorolf entered his father's hall, the feast was in full swing. Maids rushed back and forth between the large wine barrel and the tables, carrying jugs, refilling cups, and trying to evade groping hands. They deftly moved down the rows balancing bowls filled to the brim and planks holding pork, cheese, and bread, setting them down before the hungry guests.

Högni, the ship builder, climbed on a bench, his hair wild and his cheeks reddened, raising his cup. "Let us drink to the noble Egil and thank him for the delicious wine he brought us from the south."

Everyone raised their cup, stamped their feet, and drummed their free fists on the table, hooting and roaring thrice: "To the noble Egil!"

The man in question, sitting in the place of honor next to Ulrik, rose and lifted his cup to the men and women in the hall, smiling broadly. His tanned face, lined with countless furrows and tiny wrinkles, bore witness to his long journeys beneath the southern sun and made the wiry trader look older than the scarcely more than forty winters he had seen. When Egil sat back down, the cheering subsided, and the guests helped themselves to meat and bread, rekindling their conversations.

Thorolf spotted a small gap between Digur and Yngvi, who readily shuffled to the side so that he could squeeze in on their bench. To Digur's right sat his mother, Diara.

Following Diara's release from thralldom, Högni had fallen in love with her cheerful nature, her immaculate dark skin, and her tightly coiled hair, and married her. Over the years of their marriage, she had given him eight children, five of whom survived past infancy. Högni accepted little Digur, the bastard son of Ulrik. Even though the shipwright looked somewhat coarse and seemed like someone who might on occasion lose his temper, he had always treated his wife with respect and raised his stepson, as well as his own children, with strictness but fairness and not without warmth. Whenever Digur spoke of his stepfather, his words were filled with regard.

Thorolf drained his cup of wine in one gulp. He couldn't see Asla anywhere, nor his half-sister Isold. Digur, noticing his searching gaze, told him the two young women had sought shelter in his house, where it was quieter. Thorolf nodded, grimly knocking back a second cup of wine. He missed being near Asla.

Yngvi shared a joke that caused Diara's eyes to sparkle with mirth. She opened her full lips in a low, hearty laugh, revealing rows of white teeth. Högni and even Digur became infected by the spirited woman's laughter. Only Thorolf remained untouched by his brother's jest. Sullenly, he stared into his cup, which, much to his chagrin, had not yet been refilled, his thoughts wallowing in a past where he still believed in a promising future with Asla.

Harald awoke. The dog was barking. But not for long; it soon fell quiet. Most likely, thought Harald, a cat had teased the dog on its rope. It must have been past midnight, he guessed. He turned onto his other side and tried to go back to sleep. In vain.

When he heard low, irregular noises outside that he could not place, he sat up.

Harald's smithy lay remotely at the foot of a mountain blessed with a vein of ore. His nearest neighbor's homestead was about as far away as the time it took his slave to milk his five cows.

Maybe they were robbers, taking advantage of his home's isolated location to steal finished and half-finished tools and weapons from his workshop? But then the dog would have barked for longer. The noise outside had ceased, so Harald lay back down.

The moment he closed his eyes, he heard a soft, dull sound on the other side of the wall. Someone was there! Nothing kept him in bed this time. He quickly got up and slipped into his shoes. Then he woke Abena, the pregnant maid he shared his bed with, pressing a finger to her mouth.

"Ssh, someone's outside. Get up. When I nod at you, open the door, quietly. Lock it as soon as I'm outside. Stay with the children and wait till I'm back."

Harald wrapped a coat around his shoulders and picked up his sword with one hand and a torch with the other, lighting it on the embers of the fire. He nodded at Abena, who opened the door for him.

Five paces from the doorstep, his guard dog lay dead in the snow, an arrow protruding from its body. Harald cautiously stepped outside, glancing in both directions. Behind him, Abena barred the door. He saw no one, but there was a smell of burning whale oil and smoke. In the glow of his torch, he noticed some gray plumes speckled with sparks that the wind carried from around the back of the house. Firmly gripping the hilt of his sword, he sneaked toward the left corner. Harald feared a potential fight. As a blacksmith, his muscles were steeled, but he had never been a deft swordsman. He would struggle if faced with more than one opponent.

Harald peered around the corner and froze when he beheld the flames that hungrily ate into the timbers of the long side of his house. Filled with terror, he saw that his servants' quarters, about fifty paces away, were also ablaze, and just a moment later, flames climbed up the entrance to his stables as if lit by the hand of a ghost. He wanted to scream, to utter a cry of warning. But he never got the chance. Something struck him hard on the back of his head, and he slumped to the ground.

Abena sat on her bed, afraid. She feared the worst. Something thudded heavily to the ground outside. She listened for sounds of fighting, but there were none—only the sound of soft crackling, like flames eating into wood. Then she smelled the smoke. Startled by the sudden realization, she screamed, "Fire!"

Abena jumped up and woke the children. They rubbed their eyes sleepily, asking what was the matter.

"There's no time," she replied, her voice breaking. "Get dressed. Quickly now! There is a fire!"

Erratically, she helped her six-year-old son, Caven, into his shoes and thick fur coat. Then she hastily pulled on her own winter clothes. Harald's two elder sons, Runar and Knut, could cope on their own. "Come on, we need to get out of here!" she shouted, her voice filled with fear. She grasped Caven by the hand.

Abena pulled back the bolt and pushed on the iron knob. Nothing happened. She pushed harder. Panic crept up inside her like an evil creature. The door wouldn't open.

Screaming for help, she desperately drummed her fists against the door's timbers. The children cried, clinging to her coat in search of comfort. Now the fire was eating its way inside in two places along the longer side of the house. Frenzied, Abena threw herself against the door again and again. In vain.

Most of the smoke left the house through the gap in the roof above the fireplace, but the room grew smokier by the moment nonetheless, and the maid's and children's panicked screams were increasingly interrupted by fits of coughing. In the room's center, flames already licked at the rafters. The dry thatch immediately caught fire. The melting snow on the roof did nothing to stop the hungry flames.

The other maid and Harald's two laborers sleeping in the servants' quarters had noticed the fire in time, thrown their coats around their shoulders, and fled outside unscathed.

Now Rutger, the older servant, pointed at Harald's longhouse, which, aside from its gable ends, was fully ablaze. The servants raced toward the house and, moments later, found their unconscious master.

While Rutger dragged Harald out of the danger zone, Lars, the younger servant, spotted the wedges that had been pushed under the door to Harald's home, blocking it. Together with the maid, he removed them and tore open the door. Coughing, Abena staggered across the threshold with her son Caven in her arms. Runar and Knut, still clinging to their stepmother's coat, stumbled after her. Lars helped them to safety.

Abena sank to the ground. She felt nauseated, and her head ached as if Harald's hammer were pounding his anvil behind her forehead. She coughed, vomited, began to feel a little better before vomiting once more. Then she glanced at her son.

Caven was lying next to her. His face was as pale as wax, and he did not seem to breathe. It couldn't be! Abena shook her son, desperately smacking his narrow chest, then shaking his small body again, begging him in a hoarse voice: "Come back to me!" In her panic she drummed her fist on the boy's chest again, as if she might fix something inside him that had broken and was blocking his breath.

At last Caven thirstily inhaled the crisp winter air, breathing, coughing, and throwing up in turns, until his ribcage finally rose and fell evenly. Abena, endlessly relieved, gazed lovingly into her child's large eyes, which were reddened from the smoke and staring back at her in bewilderment. As if only just remembering what had happened, Caven began to cry pitifully, clinging to his mother's neck.

Abena rocked him tenderly in her arms, whispering to him in a husky voice: "All is well, my darling, all is well."

She turned to look at Runar and Knut, who sat at her right side with exhausted, pale faces and red, watery eyes. Knut still clutched a fistful of her coat. They, too, had vomited, but they appeared otherwise fine, Abena saw to her relief.

"Come," she said to the two boys, holding them tight with her free arm.

Harald was lying a few steps away. His second maid was about to bandage a bleeding head wound with a strip of linen from her undergarment, while Rutger rubbed snow on Harald's cheeks and forehead.

The blacksmith slowly came to. His head was thumping, and he tried in vain to recall what had happened before the blackness had swallowed him.

He propped himself up and spotted Abena with his sons sitting on the ground nearby. He started to smile, but his smile was wiped off when the meaning of the yellowish flickering dawned on him, illuminating the people and objects around him.

Still feeling dazed, Harald pulled himself to his feet with the help of Rutger and looked around. The sight sent cold shivers down his spine and tripped his heartbeat. Not only his house was engulfed by flames but also the smithy, the servants' quarters, the barn, and the stables. His entire property was falling victim to the hungry flames.

"What about the animals?" Harald tiredly asked the servant, already suspecting the answer.

Rutger shook his head sadly. "We couldn't save them. The stable was burning on all sides by the time we noticed the fire and came outside. And we first needed to look after you, Abena, and the children."

Harald nodded, placing a resigned hand upon the loyal servant's shoulder. Aside from the anvil and a handful of tools that might survive the inferno in the workshop, he and his children and slaves had lost everything but the clothes they were wearing.

He cast a glum look at Abena and his sons, who stood shivering beside the younger servant. "We must go to the village. Ulrik will help us."

As the small group set off, the blacksmith noticed the glow of fire on the horizon. It would seem he wasn't the only one to lose his worldly goods that night.

The feast in Ulrik's hall neared its end. Some of the guests had already left, while others who, like Thorolf, had overindulged on wine, had passed out, slumped over the tabletops, or else slid off the benches, as helpless as game shot on the hunt, sleeping off the booze on the hard dirt floor.

Aside from the chorus of snores, the hall had grown still, and in this quiet atmosphere, Egil was at his best. His eyes sparkled as he spoke of his adventures in distant lands. Mesmerized by the seafarer's words, Yngvi, Digur, and Ulrik had stopped drinking a while ago so as to not miss any details.

"Once we passed the strait between the realm of the Moors to the north and the Hot Land to the south, sailing westward, I advised my son to sail our ships home. I myself wanted to take the *Seaserpent* south once more, exploring the coast. This time we chose a course so far from land that, at times, we barely saw the shore."

"Why did you take the risk of sailing away from the coast?" asked Ulrik, curious.

"Risk? It was no risk," Egil replied firmly. "I know those waters, and never before have I experienced foul weather there during the fall. And the sun and the stars never abandoned me. No, I was longing to find out if there is more land in the sea to the west of the Hot Land." He gave a meaningful grin. "Perhaps a land with mountains of gold and silver?" He lifted his brows and held up a forefinger. Once he was certain he had his audience's undivided attention, he went on in a conspiratorial voice. "And indeed, one exceptionally clear day, when the wind blew from the west and not a single speck of dust from the deserts of the Hot Land clouded our sight, we espied gentle slopes of land on the western horizon. We made course for those hills and reached an island covered in low shrub, rising wonderfully green from the ocean's blue expanse. We dropped the anchor, and when I went ashore with some of my men, a group of people emerged from the woods. They were unarmed, and there were women and children among them. And so we left our swords sheathed. They stopped about fifteen paces from us, their faces open and friendly. Their skin was the color of light bronze and their smooth hair was pitch-black. They were clad in nothing but loincloths. The women wore their breasts uncovered with no shame, and my boys eyed them lustfully. I glared at the lads, and they soon understood what not to do."

Egil laughed, looking around at his audience. "You know what men are like when they haven't lain between a woman's thighs for weeks. I ordered my men to stay put, and then I approached the islanders with open hands and the friendliest face I am capable of. When I stopped, some of the women stepped forward and touched my fair hair, smiling dreamily. Believe me—I understood the cravings of my men all too well." Egil chuckled. "But there were the children, staring at me reverently, and the men, their faces free from any suspicion. I think they considered me and my men something halfway to gods. I did not wish to destroy this illusion. Least of all because I quite liked the role of a half-god." Egil chuckled again.

"Our restraint would pay off. When the islanders led me and my men to their village, inviting us to a sumptuous meal of lamb, seal, fish, and other foods of the sea—served with an admittedly rather sour wine they produced from the fruits of a palm tree—the world seemed a lovely place to us. As soon as we'd filled our bellies, the women led us to bathe on the beach." Egil smiled at his listeners, who were hanging on his every word. "Of course, bathing is not all we did, and now we truly felt like gods."

Egil sighed wistfully, sipping on his wine. "Believe me, my men and I deemed ourselves in the paradise praised by the Christians and Muslims in their tales." He gave a laugh. "When death comes to fetch me one day, I would rather dwell there than fight my comrades day in, day out in Valhalla and get drunk every night."

Egil's face turned serious. "We stayed for two weeks with the Majo, as they called themselves, and learned to communicate in a basic way. They called their island Cat-An, which in their language means 'land of the sun.' They mostly live off fishing, and off their sheep and goats. But I also saw a few fields of barley. If I understood the Majo correctly, it seldom rains on Catan, and it is always warm and rarely hot. Before we set off, we thanked the Majo men with bronze arm rings and daggers, and the women with colorful scarves, for their hospitality. We found it difficult to say farewell to that peaceful, almost perfect island."

Egil's eyes gleamed happily as he paused, reveling in his memories of Catan and its hospitable inhabitants. He sipped from his wine again to wet his throat, which was parched from all the talking.

Yngvi used the pause to nip outside and relieve his urgent need. Hastily he lifted his tunic and pulled down his pants, and at almost the same moment, a hot stream spurted into the snow, steaming. He sighed, lifted his head, and, relaxing, gazed out at the fjord whose ripples glistened in the light of the moon.

Something unexpected caught his attention. He looked more closely, discerning yellow lights on the water's left shore, flickering and wavering in the darkness. Those lights were fires, he realized with shock. They were no signals from the sentries, but flames of destruction that were probably turning farmsteads to ash.

Quickly pulling up his pants, he ran back into Ulrik's hall, where Egil had relaunched his imaginative descriptions.

"Fire—there are homesteads on fire!"

At first the men cast reproachful looks at him for having interrupted Egil's riveting tale, but when the meaning of Yngvi's words sank in, they leaped to their feet, sending cups flying off the table and toppling the bench upon which Digur and Ulrik had been sitting. Worried, they scrambled outside, gaping at the fires flickering in the distance like small, harmless oil lamps.

Digur froze, his thoughts spinning. On the fjord's left shore lay the charcoal burner's hut. Stina was in danger! He was already running toward his house when he heard Ulrik's order: "Yngvi, wake my men. Tell the servants to saddle our horses."

Digur tore open the door to his hall and stormed into the room. His servants sprang up from their beds, staring at their master with alarm from eyes still puffy with sleep. "You," he said, pointing at one of them, "saddle my horse and bring it to me. You"—he pointed at the second man—"help me dress. And you," he said to the third man, "help him with it."

While Otto ran off toward the stable, the other two, Enno and Kilian, lit the whale-oil lamps and opened chests, lifting out Digur's chain mail, helmet, weapons, and battle shoes.

Asla, having woken up, looked at Digur with a frown. "What is it?"

While his servants helped him with his war gear, he waved her closer and spoke in a low voice. "On the fjord's left shore, several homesteads are burning. Halldor, evidently. Your sister is in danger. Don't ask—I'll explain everything later."

Fear for Stina clasped Asla's heart with icy claws. She rushed to her sleeping place, where Isold still lay slumbering peacefully, and reached for her clothing. "I'm coming with you!"

"You stay here and wait," Digur ordered in a tone that allowed no objections. "Kaja, look after her."

The maid, who not only took care of his household but also occasionally relieved his manly needs, grasped Asla's arm hard, dragging her back to her bed. Asla knew she stood no chance against the strong maidservant, who towered over her by half a head but whose slanted dark eyes gazed at her not without warmth. "It's all right. I will not resist."

The maid loosened her grip but remained beside her. "For the best. Digur won't tolerate nonsense right now," replied Kaja in an unusually low but pleasantly full voice.

Asla knew that Digur had bought the attractive maid at a slave market. Like some other enslaved servants in Ulrik's area, she came from the endless plains of the steppes in the Far East. She was a loyal and conscientious maid to her master, and he treated her well.

When Digur snapped at Enno to hurry up, Isold started from her sleep. Asla filled her in briefly, but without mentioning Stina.

Digur slid on his helmet and looked into the faces of the three women, pale in the yellowish light of the oil lamps. He gave them a nod of farewell and, outside, mounted his powerful dun stallion, who greeted his master with a happy snort. Digur thanked the gods for the almost-full moon that would allow him to reach his destination faster.

"We should get started," the bald one said impatiently. "They're all asleep."

"Missing your old lady, are you? Can't wait to get back to her apron strings?" jested the gray-bearded one, receiving a dark look in reply.

Their leader was about to give the signal to leave the shelter of the wood stack to smear the long sides of the hut with whale oil before setting fire to it, when the door opened. So instead he placed a finger on his lips, and they remained in their hiding place.

A medium-sized dog leaped out the door, barking happily, and lifted its leg against a corner of the hut. A dainty boy followed the dog.

"The dog reminds me of Halldor's young hound. Sounds just as pathetic," the gray-bearded one remarked.

"True," said the bald one. "And it's got the same bushy tail."

"And the boy is a girl," stated the leader when the ostensible boy gathered his tunic and peed crouching down. Then the boy-girl and dog disappeared back into the hut.

The men exchanged a look, almost simultaneously arriving at the conclusion which Gray Beard put into words. "If that isn't Stina, may the earth swallow me up right now." The earth did not.

"The old fellow's going to reward us handsomely if we return his little girl to him," the bald one said cheerfully, his eyes gleaming with greed.

"You can wager that," Gray Beard replied. "A golden arm ring each is the least he'll owe us."

"We haven't got the lass in a bag yet," observed their leader, dampening their glee. "We don't know who else is inside the house."

The bald one wiped the snot running from his cold nose with his sleeve. "Why don't we set fire to the hut? Like the one earlier? Then we'll soon see who comes out."

"No, the stupid mutt's inside, where we can't kill him. He will bark the moment we touch the walls, and then they are warned." The leader scratched his head, and then he had an idea.

Even though Stina had gone outside for only a moment, the cold of the night had crept deep into her limbs. Shivering, she lay back down on her sleeping place, wrapping her fur blanket tightly around her. "We both had the same urge," she said sleepily to Loki, who curled up contentedly by her bed.

Stina had just drifted back off when someone hammered on the door, tearing her from her sleep. Loki growled. There was more hammering. "Open up. Thorolf sent me. I have an important message for Stina."

Oddur rose laboriously. His joints creaked. "Hold on, I'm coming," he said hoarsely.

While the charcoal burner wrapped his coat around his shoulders, shuffling sleepily toward the door by the glow of the embers in the cooking fire, Hilda lit two tallow lamps using a wood shaving she briefly held into the hearth. Stina, too, had risen, and while she slipped into her men's trousers, she wondered what news the messenger might have for her. Loki, beside her, growled once more, a low, menacing growl this time.

"Settle, Loki. It's just a friend of Thorolf's."

Oddur lifted the horizontal bar out of its brackets and opened the door. A man he did not know stared at him. Before he had a chance to say anything, the man rammed a knife into Oddur's throat. Warm, steaming blood streamed onto the doorstep as the charcoal burner collapsed upon it with a helpless wheeze.

Hilda gave a piercing scream and tried to rush to her husband, but the leader, having stepped into the hut, shoved her back to see if there were more men in the room. Undeterred, Hilda wailed as she tried again to reach Oddur. When Loki sank his teeth into the warrior's leg wraps, the man had enough. Uttering a curse, he slammed his gloved fist into Hilda's face. Blood splattered. Hilda tumbled backward with a gargling sound, her head hitting the bench's edge hard. Then he kicked with all his might at Loki. The dog let go of him and, with a yelp, collapsed beside the charcoal burner's wife. Neither of them stirred.

Stina had watched the brutal scene in shock. It all happened so quickly. Unable to utter a word, her entire body started to shake. She knew the warrior who, followed by two men, strode toward her, stopping with his fists on his hips. It was Hakon, a respected follower of her father's. She had seen his companions before but did not know their names.

Hakon grinned. "Have we found the little dove that flew away from home?" His voice sounded frightfully gentle, causing Stina to shake even harder. "Go on—get dressed! We have a long way ahead of us."

Incapable of stirring, she stared at the men.

Hakon raised one hand and slapped her face, not as brutally as he would have struck a man—after all, he wanted to return Halldor's daughter unblemished—but it was nevertheless a hard blow. Stina held her burning cheek, waking from her state of shock. Still trembling, she pulled on her shoes and slipped into her coat.

"Tie her and bring her outside," Hakon ordered his men. "Hurry, we aren't done here yet." He dragged the dead charcoal burner into the hut and, with an expression of contempt, dropped the slack body next to the unconscious Hilda. Then he rummaged through the couple's chests, finding nothing worth taking.

Meanwhile, the two other warriors had tied Stina's hands and feet, carried her a few steps outside the hut, and then dropped her harshly like a sack onto the cold, snowy ground. She lifted her head and watched by the light of the moon as Hakon blocked the door to the hut with wedges while his men smeared a wall with something from a skin, something that smelled of whale oil. When the bald-headed warrior used firestones and tinder to light a torch, she realized what he intended.

"No!" she shouted, horrified. "You mustn't! I swear I will go with you willingly, and I will not try to run. But get Hilda and the dog out of there! Please!"

Hakon shook his head. Stina thought she saw a hint of regret in his shuttered expression. "You won't run, little dove. We'll make sure of that. And you can spare yourself the begging. The woman must die. She saw us, and your father wants no witnesses." He nodded at the bald one with approval.

Just as he turned toward the oil-smeared wall with his torch, the night was pierced by a battle cry so powerful that even Halldor's seasoned warriors jumped with fright.

The men saw a giant leap out from behind a stack of timber, swinging an axe. His mail shirt sparkled, and his eyes seemed to shine in the light of the moon. The face alone remained dark.

"By the gods, it is Thor's Black Hammer!" called out the bald man, his eyes wide with fear. Hakon and Gray Beard drew their swords. The bald one never got that far, the sharp edge of Digur's axe splitting his skull first. His dying body dropped on the torch, extinguishing its flame.

Stina felt endlessly relieved as she watched Digur, having drawn his sword with his right hand, attack her father's men. But at the same time, she felt a stab of fear in her heart. Was he a match for two experienced warriors at once?

She soon saw that her fear was unfounded. Digur did not fight his opponents—he danced with them. Light-footed, nimble, and focused, he parried their attacks with his shield and his sword, forcing his choreography upon them, then spun around and swung his weapon to strike. His movements seemed effortless and perfect, and so fast that Stina struggled to follow them. His body seemed to have become one with his sword and shield, woven together to form a deadly, supernatural being that first felled Gray Beard and, a short while later, gave Hakon the death blow.

Digur checked that Gray Beard was, in fact, dead, then picked up a lump of snow, cleaning the dead men's blood off his blade as best as he could before sheathing his sword. He walked over to Stina and freed her from her bonds.

Instinctively, she clasped the tall warrior's neck and drew

down his head. “Thank you,” she whispered in his ear, kissing him on the cheek. He looked to the side.

“Who or what are you, Digur? I did not know that a man could fight like that.”

“I learned to fight. No more, no less. I do what I know,” he said gruffly.

Stina loosened her grip. “We must see to Hilda and Loki.”

Loki limped toward them on three legs when they entered the hut. He held his left foreleg in the air, and on his head, there was a patch of crusted blood. He greeted Stina with a whimper that was filled equally with joy and pain.

Stina stroked the head of the injured dog, and he thanked her by licking her hand. Then she bent over Hilda. With relief she found that the charcoal burner’s wife still breathed. But Hakon’s brutal fist had done thorough work. The right side of Hilda’s face was bloodied, her eye swollen shut, the nose apparently broken. Carefully Stina turned Hilda’s head to the side and discovered a long, gaping wound at the back of her head that was still bleeding and concerned Stina much more than the injuries in Hilda’s face.

“Hilda needs help, urgently. You’d best fetch Asla. She will know what to do.”

Digur lingered, indecisive. “What if there are more warriors nearby?”

“I don’t believe there are,” she replied impatiently. “Go!”

He nodded and strode out of the hut and over to his horse, tied to a tree in the woods.

Stina filled a pot with snow and hung it above the fire, reviving its weak embers with fresh coals. She knew her sister would need hot water to treat the injuries. Then she dragged Oddur’s corpse into a dark corner of the hut; she did not want Hilda to behold her husband’s white face and the fatal wound on his throat when she awoke.

After a while, Hilda came to, groaning as she touched her forehead with one hand. Stina rolled up some bed linen and placed it beneath the woman's neck. "Hold still. Help is on the way."

It wasn't long before Asla came through the door. Loki barked happily, hobbling toward his mistress on three legs.

Stina greeted her sister with a warm embrace, then took the carry sack off her and helped her out of the heavy coat.

"Where is Digur?"

"He dropped me in front of the hut. He wants to ensure there are no more enemies lurking nearby," Asla said, opening the sack in which she kept herbs and supplies to care for the sick and injured. When she took out some utensils, placing them upon a small table, Loki gave a quick bark. The dog gazed at her attentively and held up his hurt paw, as if putting himself forward for the first treatment.

Asla couldn't help but smile. "It's your turn soon, Loki. First I need to look after Hilda."

With Stina's help, Asla gently lifted the woman's upper body and examined the wound on the back of her head. Hilda moaned, inquiring after her husband.

Asla, having been informed of the events by Digur, spoke softly. "I am so sorry, Hilda. I cannot help Oddur—he is dead."

A sob of resignation mixed into Hilda's moaning. "I feared as much."

Asla drew a handful of herbs from a pouch and tossed it into the boiling water, together with some linen cloth and a needle threaded with a horsehair. Then she asked Stina to take the pot off the fire and place it into the snow outside to cool off.

"Why do you put the linen and the needle into the boiling water?" asked Stina, frowning, as she wrapped a cloth around her hand and reached for the pot handle. "Does the spirit of the herbs enter those items, helping them to heal?"

"Yes, Oda explained it to me something like that. She said, since she has been practicing this habit, the wounds she treats heal better and fester less often."

Asla now examined Loki. When she gently felt his left leg, the dog yelped with pain and snapped at her hand, but without hurting her.

"Nothing is broken, but there is a swelling in his shoulder that pains him. The wound on his head looks worse than it is. He'll be fine."

When the pot had cooled sufficiently, Stina fetched it back into the house. Asla poured part of the herbal infusion into a bowl, washing her hands carefully with the warm brew.

Her sister watched with interest. "Why do you do that?"

"The spirit of the herbs helps my hands to heal. Or at least that's what Oda thinks."

Just as she puzzled over the question of how to keep Hilda still, Digur returned. "The gods sent you," she said. "I need you to hold Hilda's head while I sew up her wound."

The tall, powerful man nodded and then knelt before Hilda, who was sitting upright. He took her legs between his and pushed a stick of wood between her teeth, clamping her injured skull between his large hands so that Hilda could scarcely move her head.

"This is going to hurt," said Asla in warning, using a sharp knife to saw off the hair around the edges of the wound.

Hilda bit down hard on the wood between her teeth, gasping. Asla dipped the linen into the pot and used it to wash the wound thoroughly. Then she picked up needle and horsehair and placed the first stitch to sew the wound's edges together. Hilda stifled a scream, her eyes welling up from the pain.

Stina admired her sister—how steadily she moved the needle and how confidently she treated Hilda. Against her will she felt envy grow inside her, wishing she possessed some similar skill.

But she knew that the art of healing had not merely dropped into her elder sister's lap. Since Asla's twelfth year, she had spent much of her free time with Oda, absorbing everything the wise woman knew about the uses and effects of herbs. With great dedication and passion, she had learned how to produce ointments and herbal infusions, treat wounds, and bring babies into the world.

Once Asla had stitched up the wound, she washed the swollen half of Hilda's face, cleaning away the blood from her wounds and broken nose.

"Your nose will probably never be straight again, Hilda," said Asla.

"If that were all," sobbed the charcoal burner's wife, glancing at her husband's corpse, which she had spotted in the opposite corner. Slowly, she pulled herself onto the bench, her stiff movements showing that she did not feel steady enough to stand. Now she stared at Digur reproachfully from the eye that was not swollen shut. "You brothers carry both good and bad luck in your bags. If you had not hidden Stina here, Oddur would still be alive."

Digur took Hilda's strong hand into his own, and she let him. "I am sorry for the death of your husband. But many houses and farms burn this night."

Stina flinched at this news.

Digur let go of Hilda's hand, turning to the sisters. "Hakon was your father's man. Halldor did not want to go without his revenge, even if he had to conduct it in secret. If Ulrik finds proof that your father is behind this attack, there will be war."

As Asla returned the utensils she'd used to treat Hilda to her carry sack, she continued Digur's thought. "If we want to avoid war and even more suffering, we must hide the bodies of Halldor's men. Am I right?" She wrinkled her forehead. "But where? The ground is frozen—we cannot bury them."

"I know a place that could work," Hilda said quietly. "Oddur was planning to start another pile soon. He had already dug the pit."

Digur understood. "Very well. I will toss the bodies in the pit and cover them with a first layer of wood."

"But not Oddur!" Hilda's good eye gazed at Digur with fright. "I don't want him to travel to the realm of the dead together with his murderers."

"Of course not," said Asla soothingly. "We'll bury Oddur as soon as the ground has thawed."

"What am I supposed to do now?" wailed Hilda. "Oddur may not have been an easy man, and sometimes I even wished he'd never come back from the forest. But he ensured our livelihood through his work, and I wasn't alone. Who is supposed to keep the piles burning now, build new ones, and sell the coal? I can't possibly do it without him." She stared at Digur with despair.

"I will send you one of my servants. He's trustworthy and reliable. Under your guidance, he'll keep the piles running. And besides, you still have a young helper," Digur said cheerfully with a look at Stina, who met his gaze with a cheeky grimace.

Someone shook his shoulder and called his name. Thorolf awoke with a stale taste in his mouth. He found himself atop a hard bench. At least better, his foggy brain thought, than the cold dirt floor upon which one of his drinking companions lay snoring and making smacking sounds with his mouth. It sounded as if the sleeping man were chewing on his own tongue, about to swallow it up.

In the background, he heard Gudrun issuing orders, the busy footsteps of maids, and the clanking of cookware. Evidently they were preparing a meal. The thought made Thorolf feel even more sick. Slowly he straightened up. His nausea abated somewhat; however, the hammer in his head gained momentum. Once he had successfully made it into an upright position and decided he was sitting stably enough, he found himself looking straight into the pale-blue eyes of Yngvi, who gazed at him with mirth, as if Thorolf wore antlers on his head.

"You do not look well at all, brother. Your eyes are red-rimmed and swollen, your skin deathly pale, your hair tousled. I'm sure you're about to spew onto the table. Show us your tongue, if you're able to. I bet it's all dried up and furry."

"I'm thirsty," said Thorolf hoarsely, confirming his brother's suspicion. "Fetch me something to drink!"

"Mother, your stepson is thirsty. Is there still some wine in the barrel?"

Thorolf groaned. "No, not wine, you ass. Water!"

Gudrun winked at the thirsty man as she brought him a jug of water, filling a cup for him. Thorolf nodded his thanks at her and emptied the cup in one go.

On her way back to the fireplace, Gudrun kicked the last drunkard sleeping on the floor in the side, ordering him to shove off. Two maids helped the pale man out of the house and began to clear off the dishes, cleaning tables and benches from the remains of the nightly revels.

Thorolf watched the hustle and bustle in the gloomy hall from under heavy, half-closed lids. "What is going on? Will the feast continue this evening?"

Yngvi's face turned serious. "No, sadly not. Much happened last night that you don't know of." He told his brother about the arson attacks on the fjord's left shore. "The affected farmers, their families, and thralls have lost everything. They do not know where else to turn in this cold weather but to come here and ask for our help. Ulrik has ridden out with his men, scouring the area for the fire starters."

Trying to sort his muddled thoughts, Thorolf ran his hand through his tousled hair. "Do you think Halldor is behind the attacks?"

"Probably," said Yngvi. "A band of robbers would proceed differently, and I struggle to believe in a cowardly attack from an enemy tribe. They would not break the truce of winter. Maybe Father will catch one of the culprits. Then we'll know more."

Thorolf drained a second cup of water. "What are we going to do with the folk whose houses have burned down?"

"Högni and I are making sure they are looked after and will find a warm roof over their heads. Digur and you, I'm sure you don't mind that I ordered your servants to prepare your houses to take in homeless folk. After all, you were . . . er, indisposed." Despite the gravity of the situation, Yngvi couldn't suppress a grin.

"And Digur?"

"He rode out. I have an inkling where he might be. Egil and a few local farmers have taken in families. The next people Högni sends up the hill will be housed in Father's hall. Gudrun has given her assent."

"I need to get some fresh air," groaned Thorolf. "My head feels as if it's going to burst."

Yngvi helped his brother put on his coat and walked outside with him. Thorolf welcomed the crisp winter air that cooled his brow and quickened his spirits. His bladder ached. He hurriedly turned to some leafless bushes and relieved himself with a deep sigh.

In the first light of the day, Yngvi saw a group of people, visibly exhausted, climbing up toward them. He recognized Harald, the smith, leading the way with his two sons at his hands. Behind him followed two servants and two maids, one of whom carried a child in her arms.

Yngvi and Thorolf, who had reemerged from the bushes, studied the exhausted faces, blue with cold. The new arrivals were inadequately dressed for the bitter cold of the night, and it would seem that only the constant movement had preserved them from freezing to death. Yngvi greeted them briefly, then, without much further ado, opened the door for them and invited them into the warm hall.

Harald and his companions nodded gratefully, crowding around the warming firepit, their teeth chattering. Gudrun greeted the smith cordially and advised her maid to bring a mug of warm ale for each guest. Harald's sons had hiked through the snow bravely and without complaining. Now, though, with the warmth biting into their fingers and toes, they did not quite manage to stifle the occasional sob.

Gudrun placed a hand on Harald's shoulder. "We prepared two benches for you and your sons here in the hall. Your servants and maids may sleep in the servant quarters."

"I thank you, Gudrun. But my maid Abena shares my bed; she will warm me. Her son can sleep with my sons." Harald gestured at the young woman, who still clutched her sleeping child tightly, as if he might freeze to death even inside the warm hall.

Gudrun nodded. She knew the smith had bought Abena at a slave market and that she had become his lover following the death of his wife. She gazed at the maid, whose bronze-colored skin indicated that she came from the land of the Moors.

Abena appeared to sense her interest, raising her chin and meeting Gudrun's eyes warmly. When a maid offered her a cup of warm ale, Abena woke her son and gently set him down on his feet, gratefully accepting the brew. The child looked about sleepily, rubbing his eyes. Gudrun gave a little smile when she compared the little boy's profile to that of Harald. Both possessed the same high forehead and a strong, determined chin. From his mother, the boy had inherited his curved nose, dark-brown eyes, and curly black hair.

Harald asked Gudrun for another cup of warm ale before turning to Thorolf. "What is going on here? Are we at war with someone? Apparently my homestead wasn't the only one to burn—I saw more fires in the distance on our way here."

Yngvi answered in the place of his brother, who was still a little unwell. "We don't know, Harald. Ulrik is searching for the culprits with his men. We will know more once he gets back."

The blacksmith cursed. "I have lost everything: my livestock, my stores, my smithy. Am I supposed to spend the winter at Ulrik's hall as a supplicant?"

The question was left hanging in the room.

Around noontime, Ulrik returned with his horsemen. On the village square, he found Yngvi, who waved his arms as he debated with a farmer. Ulrik brashly cut off the man's outpouring of complaints about a homeless family being quartered at his house. "Yngvi, fetch your brothers and bring them to the assembly place."

Yngvi nodded and rushed off, leaving behind the unhappy farmer who continued to mutter curses.

Shortly after the sun had passed its low wintertime zenith, Thorolf and Yngvi arrived at the assembly place, a little way outside the village. Ulrik was already expecting them beneath the tribe's sacred tree, a mighty ash more than ninety feet tall.

"We can speak openly here. Where is Digur?"

"Still out," replied Yngvi. "We assume he, too, is searching for the fire starters. According to his servants, he rode off in full war attire."

Ulrik grumbled something indistinguishable, grouchily spitting a splat of saliva into the snow. "We rode past more than a dozen burnt-down farms. No trace of the fire starters. Perhaps Digur will be luckier."

Thorolf rubbed his hands. Even now, around the middle of the day, the air was freezing. "Do you believe Halldor is behind the attacks?"

"Of course! Who else?" thundered Ulrik. "It is like him—not declaring war openly but instead satisfying his lust for revenge in this cowardly fashion. The next time I come before him, he'll wink at me and speak warmly while he lies to my face about his men not being the fire starters—knowing all the while that I must keep up the pretense and swallow his lies. For I have no proof."

"Folk in the village are talking." Yngvi looked at Thorolf. "They believe our arrival with Asla is connected to Björn's visit as well as to the attacks. And the farmers who've been ordered to accommodate the victims are grumbling. They demand that we take in and feed the families ourselves. After last year's poor harvest, they've scarcely enough to make it through the winter themselves. The affected farmers and fishermen are lapping up the rumors around Asla's flight, since they need someone to blame for their misfortune." Yngvi's unusually serious gaze turned to his father. "There is a dangerous tide rising against us which we must stem urgently."

Ulrik nodded sourly. "We will have to share our stores with them and recompense the hosts with silver."

"I would love to," said Thorolf bitterly, "only I don't have anything left to share."

"But I do." Ulrik looked at his son without any trace of

reproach. To him, his sons' irresponsible deed had been atoned for by the verdict he'd pronounced. To him, the one had nothing to do with the other.

"The people expect an explanation from me. Yngvi, send messengers to every homestead. All heads of households are to gather here in two days' time."

As the last light of day faded, Digur rode into the village. Asla sat behind him, holding onto his waist. When they came to the fork in the road that led them up the hill, several freemen and women stared after them coldly. A stone struck Asla on the back of her head, her knitted headscarf scarcely dampening the impact. She winced but made no sound. She did not want to tempt Digur to turn around to hold the culprit accountable.

Digur left his horse with a servant and entered his hall, followed by Asla. Then he stopped with surprise. A farmer, Hafdan, and his wife, Britta, and their two small sons were seated at his table, helping themselves to bread and dried fish. Britta was nursing her youngest. She bore a bruise on her face, and her left eye was swollen shut. Kaja was pouring thinned ale into the family's cups.

When the maid noticed her master, she scurried over to him and explained that Yngvi had ordered her to take in and feed the farmer and his family.

Digur nodded, striding toward his guests to greet them.

Hafdan rose, thumped his right fist against his chest, and thanked the warrior, who towered over him by more than a head, for his hospitality. But when his eyes beheld Asla, his face darkened. "Aren't you that accursed witch who led Thorolf astray?"

Digur understood the farmer's hostile reaction. Hafdan had

lost his house and home, and now the unhappy man needed a target for his anger. Asla's arrival suited him perfectly. But Digur was not going to let Hafdan get away with his insulting behavior toward his brother's bride. Not in his house.

He stood with his fists on his hips, still impressively clad in his war splendor, glaring down at the shorter, haggard farmer. "Do not be too quick to judge, Hafdan. There is no proof that Halldor is behind the fires. But whatever it is you believe—under my roof, no one belonging to my family will be insulted. Stick to it or get out!" The final words Digur had spoken loudly and menacingly while pointing one finger at the door.

The farmer nodded obsequiously, but there was no agreement in his eyes. Coldly he stared at the young woman.

Asla tightened the woolen coat around her, as if trying to shield herself from Hafdan's hostile glare. The stone that was thrown at her and the farmer's unconcealed hatred had made her realize the peril she was in. All that was stopping people from killing her to secure the reward of twenty sheep was that she was a guest of Ulrik's and therefore under the chieftain's protection. Instinctively, she brought her hand to her upper thigh to feel for the knife hidden there in a leather holster. The concealed weapon gave her hope that she could defend herself should she find herself in distress with neither of the brothers near to protect her. Asla squared her shoulders and addressed Digur in a firm, clear voice. "I thank you for your hospitality and your assistance. But it is for the best if I return to Gudrun now."

Two days later, nearly all heads of families came to the assembly. It had snowed heavily during the night, and the cold had eased. Fresh white covered the ground of the assembly place and the roofs of nearby houses. The men debated, gesticulating wildly. Ulrik positioned himself with his sons and his followers upon the rise beneath the bare old ash tree. Floating up through the noise were names and words like "Thorolf," "Asla," "Halldor," "abduction," "flight," and "revenge."

"Quiet!" thundered the jarl, raising his arms, but the men were too engrossed in their conversations to care. Only when his warriors began drumming their swords against their shields in the rhythm of the heartbeat, and Ulrik roared "Quiet!" for the third time with all his might, did the men's clamor and fuss subside to a muted grumbling.

"Men, I know you are angered by the flight of Halldor's daughter Asla, which she achieved with the help of Thorolf. You believe Halldor took revenge by burning down your homesteads. But there is no proof. The miscreants responsible for the fires escaped." Ulrik paused for a moment, casting a disdainful glance around the freemen of his realm. "I ask you, could not one of our enemies, too, seek an advantage in weakening us, loyal allies to King Halldor?"

Aside from hushed whispers here and there, only Ulrik's clear, powerful voice filled the air above the assembly place now. The men listened to their lord attentively.

Ulrik gestured toward Thorolf. "My son knows that he acted wrongly, and he has accepted the punishment I imposed upon him. In the spring, he will leave for a seven-year exile."

A murmur went through the crowd. Seven years of banishment was a harsh penalty.

"Digur and Yngvi, who also loaded guilt upon themselves, will accompany him," went on Ulrik. "In addition, Thorolf paid for the death of Hilmar with his entire fortune. Björn, the son of Halldor, accepted the wergild and thus acknowledged the compensation in the name of his father. Therefore, Halldor has no reason to take his revenge on us, and there is no reason for you to lay the blame for the attacks at the feet of Thorolf or Asla." A threatening undertone seeped into Ulrik's voice. "He who believes he must seek vengeance on my son or his bride regardless better consider it well. For I will slay anyone who is foolish enough to do so." Emphasizing his words, Ulrik drew his sword, rammed its tip into the snow, and rested on its hilt.

The men stood silently as if they'd turned to stone. A light breeze tugged at their coats and furs. No one wanted to challenge the jarl who, until now, had led them wisely and whom they trusted. Ulrik sensed that he had convinced most of the men.

After a few moments of scanning the crowd with his eyes, he spoke the names of thirteen men. He nodded at each of them. "You lost your homes and your provisions. You are afraid that you will not make it through the winter with your families. You feel uncomfortable about living like thralls in the house of another, depending on another's hospitality. I understand your unhappiness. But you are not alone. I will share my stores with all freemen who took you in, and I will pay them from my silver. So you are not supplicants but my guests, guests of your jarl." Ulrik paused for a moment, allowing his words to sink in. "In the spring, we will rebuild your halls together, and in the summer, you come with me on viking trips. There are still plenty of monasteries and halls along the Anglo-Saxon and Irish coasts bursting with golden cups and precious ornaments, waiting for us to plunder them. With your share of the loot, you can buy livestock and seeds."

The gathered heads of families—farmers, fishermen, craftsmen, and traders—barely believed their ears. A jarl stepping in so generously for members of his tribe stricken by misfortune was rare.

Harald was the first to stamp the ground with one foot and

pound his right fist against his chest. Högni followed his example, then others. Soon, more than three hundred feet shook the ground in the same rhythm, and just as many fists accompanied the resounding stamps with their dull hammering.

"Honor to our Jarl Ulrik!" shouted Högni, and soon all men echoed the call, in praise of their chieftain.

One man alone remained silent; one among the many chanting men gathered continued to display a grim expression. As the crowd dispersed, Hafdan left the assembly place disappointed and bitter.

PART 2
FAREWELL

(SPRING, AD 860)

CHAPTER 4
THE DECISION

Two weeks later, life in the village and on the surrounding farms had returned largely to normal. It had snowed heavily several times, and it seemed as if winter wished to bury the tribe's entire territory under a thick white blanket. The men strapped on their snowshoes and went hunting with their servants in the mountains, or they fished the fjord with their nets. The women tended livestock together with their maids and looked after the households. Those who had taken in families who'd lost their homes to the fires received the provisions Ulrik had promised them. It did not strike them as enough to make it through the winter without suffering hunger, but since their guests helped as best as they could, topping up the food store now and then with freshly caught fish or game, they did not complain much.

Asla spent her days in the hut of Alfhild, the healer of Hellefjord. The gaunt, taciturn old woman had been dismissive of her at first. But when the wise woman found that Asla already possessed vast knowledge in the fields of herbs and healing and that she thirsted for more knowledge to the point of obsession, Alfhild had become more approachable, sharing her experience with Asla. And so each morning, Asla looked forward to visiting the old woman, producing creams and tinctures alongside her and healing the ailments of the ill or at least easing their pain. The time she spent with Alfhild seemed to her like rays of sunlight breaking through dark clouds, helping her bear her desolate situation and the uncertainty of her future.

She avoided Thorolf as much as she could. One time, when she ran into him by accident and he addressed her, she looked away and asked him to leave her alone and give her more time.

Thorolf had been reluctant to let her go, probably hoping that the time she required would measure in days, instead of moons or even winters.

Digur would often go hunting in the woods and there visit the charcoal burner's hut to see if all was in order and to supply its inhabitants with fresh meat. So he did today, having been fortunate enough to kill a deer on his hunt.

Hilda, who had recovered well from her injuries, welcomed him warmly and thanked him for the game. Then she praised Stina's quickness of mind. Over the past two weeks, the young woman had learned several basic skills of the charcoal-burning trade and was proving a big help. The servant Digur had lent Hilda also received some words of praise. Under Hilda's guidance, the strong lad kept the smoldering piles running to her satisfaction, and he had even started the new pile, where the corpses of Halldor's warriors smoldered beneath its timbers.

Stina was glad about the tall warrior's visit. Not only because it brought some change into her rather uneventful days, but also because she liked him and felt drawn to him. As soon as she spotted him outside, she rushed into the hut and, with the help of Hilda's soap, washed the grease and coal out of her short hair over a bowl of water, trying to make herself as presentable as she might. Then she awaited him in the unhappy knowledge that following his visit, Hilda would return her hair to the previous state.

Stina hated her disguise. It wasn't so much the large trousers and the tight cloth wound around her chest that bothered her, but the coal and the fat Hilda used to blacken her cropped hair. After a few days, her head exuded an unpleasant, rancid smell. And that, she did not wish Digur to experience.

Her camouflage was for her own safety, Hilda had scolded her when she complained. "What if men come from the village to fetch coal?" she had lectured. "Do you wish them to wonder what a blonde girl is doing at the charcoal burner's hut? Do you want them to guess that you might be the daughter of Halldor upon whose capture lies a hefty reward? Not even Digur's servant must find out."

Stina accepted that her disguise was necessary to secure her future, but she longed for the day when she could be Stina once more and would no longer have to pose as Hilda's nephew. Then she would at last be free to govern her own life. She hoped fervently that she would soon sail away from her Nordic home together with Thorolf, his brothers, and Asla.

When Digur entered the charcoal burner's hut, Stina greeted him with a merry smile. He leaned down to receive her kiss of welcome on his cheek, knowing the young woman expected this. He did not mind this familiar gesture.

Digur wasn't sure quite what he felt for this young girl, almost ten years his junior. He felt comfortable when he was near her and liked to watch her when, radiating with natural elegance, she brought order into Hilda's household or when she frolicked outside with Loki. Her girlish innocence, her unspoiled nature, and her kind treatment of others mesmerized him. In his world of battles, of blood and cruelties, she appeared to him the embodiment of the pure and beautiful. But every time he beheld her, he was also reminded of the girl that looked so like Stina—the girl whose life he had ended with one strike, years ago.

While Thorolf, as his older brother, preferred the hunt, Yngvi would rather go fishing with two of Ulrik's servants. Like many freemen on the fjord, he owned a boat with four oars. The fish in the fjord were bountiful, but during the winter, they were often sluggish, remaining in the depths and rarely swimming into the nets. This time of year, the fish even spurned the flesh of mussels pierced onto hooks, and so, on many days, the servants rowed the boat back to the shore without a single sea creature aboard.

But today had been Yngvi's lucky day. By noontime already six splendid cod stared back at him from the bottom of his boat with their cold, dead eyes. He delivered them to Gudrun, who turned them into an excellent meal for the evening.

"This tastes delicious, Gudrun." Egil picked a fishbone from between his teeth with his left hand, then used his right to fill his mouth with another piece of the juicy fish.

Ulrik nodded. "A pleasant change, tasting a bit of fresh fish, instead of forever chewing on dried ones."

A colorful mix had gathered around the table, including Harald the smith and Högni the ship builder. Those two as well as Thorolf, Yngvi, and Digur also nodded appreciatively at the cook. Diara clapped her hands and raised her cup, honoring Gudrun's skill. Ulrik's wife was visibly pleased with the praise.

Since Thorolf had paid for the last merry evening with a severe hangover, he had pledged to himself that this would not happen again. So he merely sipped on his cup filled with Egil's delectable wine every now and then. Wiping his greasy hands on his tunic, Thorolf used a moment of silence to ask the roving merchant to once more recount his discovery of Catan, which Yngvi had told him about.

Egil did not need to be asked twice. He was a gifted storyteller who knew how to win the undivided attention of his listeners, and no one took offense when, having fulfilled all their duties and standing at a respectful distance, the maids of Ulrik and Harald began to listen with awe to the tales of the eloquent, widely traveled trader.

When Egil reached the end of his report, each person could see an image of a paradisiacal island in their mind's eye, a place that promised a carefree life of plenty in contrast to their meager existence here in the North, where there was too little fertile land for later-born sons and occasionally famine. For a while, everyone dwelled on their thoughts in silence.

It was Thorolf who broke the silence eventually. "Do you believe there is sufficient fertile ground to grow grain and enough pastureland for sheep?"

"Yes, the islanders keep sheep, even if the grass isn't as plentiful as here. It does not rain often enough. But I did see some barley fields."

In Diara, Egil's descriptions roused memories of her childhood village in the Hot Land beyond the southern sea, from where she had been carried off by enemy soldiers. She hated the darkness, the wetness, and the cold of the long Nordic winters, and she often longed for the warmth of her home. Her dark-brown eyes shone warmly in the yellowish light of the oil lamps when she asked, "Is there no winter on Catan? No ice, no snow?"

Fascinated, Egil watched the spirited woman as she accentuated almost every word with gestures—a habit probably left over from the time when she learned the tongue of the North. "If I understood the Majo correctly, it is almost always sunny on their isle, and it never gets properly cold."

A soft, wistful sigh escaped Diara.

Högni appeared to guess what kind of thoughts were floating 'round his wife's mind. He winked at her as he, too, asked a question of the merchant. "What kind of trees grow in their forests? Tall and strong ones to shape into keels and planks?"

"No. The trees there are rather low and their trunks crooked. If a shipwright like yourself were to settle there, he would have to bring seeds of oak, beech, and ash with him and create his own woodland," replied Egil with a smile. The thought of a shipbuilder planting his own forest amused him. Högni would long be in the ground by the time the trees were tall enough to fell.

Sated, Digur stroked his stomach contentedly, though he would not turn down a small bowl of sweetened porridge to round off the meal. The thought led him to ask Egil, "Is there honey on the island?"

"I did not see bees, and aside from fruit, the Majo did not serve any sweets." Egil gazed around with wonder. "Are you toying with the thought of sailing to Catan to settle there?"

"Who wouldn't wish to find and live on the island you describe so colorfully?" replied Thorolf. "The more so since Digur, Yngvi, and I will have to find a place to bridge the time of our banishment without great hardship."

"And that appears to be possible in a most pleasant way on Catan," added Yngvi with a grin. "If we are considered half-gods upon the isle, revered by pretty, bare-breasted women, I might just spend the rest of my life there."

Gudrun raised an eyebrow. "Methinks you lack respect for women, dear son. We were not born merely to satisfy the needs of menfolk," she said mockingly.

Yngvi knew his mother's thoughts, the ones she had not spoken out loud. She would prefer him to find a wife to lead his household and raise his children, instead of happily chasing after every halfway-pretty maid.

"When will you leave on your next trading journey, Egil?" asked Thorolf.

"Around the same time that you must leave the Northland."

"What would you say if I asked to sail with you as far as the strait between the land of the Moors and the Hot Land? The rest of the way to Catan we'd manage on our own."

Egil did not consider for long. "Of course. I can't think of any reason why not. The larger the fleet, the safer it is from attacks."

Thorolf grinned at his brothers conspiratorially. "Yngvi, Digur, what do you say? Shall we?"

Both nodded without hesitation.

Högni sipped his wine and grasped Diara's hand. "Why not? Why shouldn't we start afresh once more? Ever since Egil told us about Catan for the first time, I cannot get the island out of my head. I may no longer be young, but I don't feel too old to dare something new. My eldest knows all about building ships, and when I leave this place, I'll not leave a large gap." His last words had been directed at Ulrik, who was eyeing him critically. Then Högni looked at the brother. "We will join you with my ship, if you'll have us."

Thorolf beamed at Högni. "Certainly. How fortunate we are to have an experienced shipwright at our side on such a long sea voyage."

Diara's mouth, smiling shyly at first, had begun to open as she listened to her Högni's words, and now she beamed with pure joy at her husband, who looked pleased to see his wife so radiantly happy. She waved her hands excitedly, fanning herself, and then she grasped Högni's head, planting a smacking kiss on his lips.

Digur smiled at his mother's joy. So she and Högni would join them on their voyage—and Stina would come, too. The years of banishment suddenly appeared less gloomy. Some of those who were important to him would accompany him into the unknown.

Harald, who had said nothing until then, cleared his throat and gazed at Egil. "Your descriptions of Catan lead me, too, to consider leaving my homeland. I can rebuild my hall elsewhere just as well." The smith hesitated a moment. "Thorolf, would you take me, my sons, and my thralls on the *Goldeagle*?"

"The *Goldeagle* offers enough room for more than forty people and their supplies. My brothers and I would welcome a skilled smith in our ranks." Thorolf held out his hand to Harald, who clasped it happily.

Ulrik, however, knitted his bushy eyebrows—an unmistakable sign of imminent trouble. "And your smithy, Harald? Are you simply going to leave it behind? You know that we need a second smith, one like you, who not only knows the craft of producing everyday tools but also forges good swords. I expect you to stay."

Harald was a freeman, and not even his jarl had the power to force him to stay at a place that he wished to leave. Instead of sharply pointing this out to Ulrik, Harald replied respectfully in a firm, calm voice. "The tool smith's second eldest son has been learning the forging of weapons from me for three years. He knows all that I know, and he can take over what is left of my workshop."

Ulrik, forced to accept that Harald's decision was final, nodded slowly. "Sounds like it might work." He raised his cup sympathetically. "Then let us drink to Catan and to a successful time in your exile!"

Now Thorolf allowed himself a longer sip of his wine after all. At last, the future he would be forced to spend abroad was taking shape.

CHAPTER 5
THE HUNT

Two weeks after the brothers had decided to sail for Catan, a fisherman came running into the village around the middle of the day, shouting with excitement. "A whale, a whale in the fjord!"

Those who heard him rushed over to him, and soon the bearer of the happy news was encircled by villagers. The fisherman freed himself from the grasp of the people who showered him with questions, and he ran up the hill to the hall of the jarl. Ulrik, supervising his servants' work outside his house, watched the man run toward him with his billowing cloak.

The corpulent man was out of breath, his message leaving his lips in gasps. "Ulrik, a whale . . . a big whale . . . swimming in the fjord. I saw it . . . with my own eyes."

The chieftain raised his eyebrows in surprise. This was good news indeed. The whale's meat would eliminate the threat of an impending famine. He gave the fisherman a cheerful slap on the shoulder. "You're a fortune bringer. I think you could probably use some refreshment, having run all this way. Go inside and tell my maids to bring you ale."

The man nodded gratefully and turned to the hall.

Ulrik sent for one of his men, ordering him to ride to the outlying steadings and inform the families of the whale sighting. "Tell them each man who possesses a fishing boat and some experience in the hunt of a whale should gather at the tavern just after sunset."

If there truly was one of the ocean's giants in the fjord, and if it remained there until the following morning, Ulrik thought, it would be a stroke of luck indeed. Only every two to three years did one of those creatures lose its way up their long arm of the sea, and often such animals would be sick or deathly exhausted. Then they would float apathetically to the shore, and killing them was an easy feat. If, on the other hand, the whale was healthy and strong, preventing it from escaping back into the open sea and killing it was a mortally dangerous endeavor for the hunters. Ulrik hoped the whale sighted in the fjord today belonged to the first category.

He ordered a servant to fetch his sons. Digur was hunting in the woods, but Yngvi and Thorolf were nearby and arrived shortly thereafter. Ulrik told them the news.

The brothers exchanged a look, each thinking the same thought: they would partake in the hunt for the colossal creature. The fever of the hunt and the prospect of a share of the catch made their eyes shine and painted adventurous smiles on their faces.

Two years prior, they had partaken in a whale hunt for the first time, and they remembered with pleasure the thrilling chase which, thanks to the smooth collaboration of the hunters, had been crowned by success. Högni had given the whale the death blow, and even though it was a smaller animal, it had supplied the people in the village and surrounding homes with meat and oil for half a year.

But there had also been fierce arguing over the prize. According to the tribe's ancient law, the flesh of a whale killed in the fjord was divided among all freemen and their families, and everyone accepted this law. The fight, however, was over the remaining parts like bones, baleen, and blubber, from which the precious whale oil was won. Several hunters had questioned the laws that had been passed up through the generations, demanding a larger share of the spoils. In the end, Ulrik decreed that a tenth was due to him as the jarl, another tenth to the leader of the hunting party, and yet another to the man who placed the death blow. Three tenths ought to be divided among all freemen who participated in the hunt with their boats, and the rest was to be shared among everyone else living on the fjord.

Ulrik had the runes documenting this law chiseled into a rock, and the rock was erected at the edge of the village square.

In the early evening, Ulrik entered the tavern with his grown sons and Högni, who was to lead the hunting party. Fifteen freemen who owned boats suitable for the hunt had shown up. They were sitting in small groups, leading lively discussions about the most promising hunting techniques.

When Ulrik shouted at the tavern keeper, "Ale for everyone!" the men looked up, thumping their fists on the tables to greet their lord and demonstrate their respect and gratitude.

When each man held a large cup of ale in his hands, Ulrik raised his and shouted, "If the whale is still in the fjord in the morning, it is ours!"

The men howled, stamped their feet and drank, some of them draining their cups in one swig.

"Another round for the men!" ordered Ulrik.

As uppermost lord of the hunt, Ulrik was responsible for dividing the boats into beaters—those who would drive the whale as required—and hunters, who would wound the animal until it became exhausted and ready for the final blow. He tried to accommodate the men's preferences, giving in to Yngvi and Thorolf's request to assign them and their boat to the hunters. The men listened eagerly to their jarl's instructions while knocking back a third tankard of ale. Then Ulrik gave the floor to Högni, who prepared the men for the hunt.

After the fourth ale, they all went home. Each man knew the following day would be for life or death, for rich booty or for wasted efforts. For this, they needed to sleep and be in full command of their strength.

When morning dawned, Thorolf and Yngvi took four servants down to the water's edge where Yngvi's boat lay moored. A gentle breeze blew from the south, dispelling the worst of the chill from the fjord but not quite strong enough to tempt the icicles hanging all about to drip.

Every man was clad in pants, leg wraps, and two layers of tunics. Yngvi and Thorolf wore fur coats on top, while the servants carried plainer coats from tanned animal hides. The men would take off their coats at the beginning of the hunt to be more agile during the battle with the giant of the sea. The servants carried the heavy gear needed aboard a hunting vessel: barbed harpoons, spears with razor-sharp heads of steel, and a long rope made of knotted whale skin.

The hazy light of the sun behind the mountains was slow to dispel the drab gray of dawn. While the servants fastened the rope on a bollard in the ship's bow, tying the other end to the shaft of a harpoon, Yngvi inspected the eighteen-foot-long fishing boat, the rowing oars, and the steering oar.

Thorolf gazed out across the fjord but could not see the whale's blow anywhere. This did not concern him greatly; the fjord was large and the light of the rising sun was still weak. The sensation of being watched caused him to turn. About thirty paces up the bank stood Asla, gazing down at him. Thorolf's heart skipped a beat, and without thinking, he ran up the shore.

"What are you doing here?" he asked her, knowing in the same instant how foolish his question sounded. Why, if not for his sake, should she linger here this early in the morning?

Asla smiled sadly. "Because I am afraid for you and because I want to wish you luck." She handed Thorolf a longish, light-gray woolen cloth and a beautifully wrought silver brooch. "Take it and wear it around your neck. I wove the cloth for you. May it bring you luck, protect you during the hunt, and keep you from death."

She spun around and, without glancing back, rushed up the well-trodden path through the snow to the village. Thorolf stood speechlessly, feeling like a man dying of thirst who was handed a cup of water—enough to ease the torment, too little to quench the thirst.

He smelled the cloth, inhaling Asla's beloved scent, drinking it in. With a sigh, he wrapped the cloth around his neck, fastened the two ends with the brooch and returned to the water's edge.

There wasn't enough wind to make use of the boat's sail. Yngvi was sitting in the back at the rudder, steering his boat which, thanks to the efforts of the four servants at the oars, swiftly glided through the gentle waves to the meeting point of the hunting party. Thorolf stood tall in the bow, keeping watch for the whale.

The fifteen vessels lay still in the fjord's center as the skippers peered in all directions, searching for a sign of life from the large ocean dweller.

Högni was the first to spot the narrow flare of a fountain of spray in the distance. "There, there he is!" he shouted excitedly, waving his arm in the direction of the fjord's narrow passage separating it into the upper fjord, where the boats currently drifted, and the lower fjord.

Those men whose eyesight was similarly good as Högni's saw the whale's blow too and cheered. "There!" shouted one of them. "It's blowing again." The rest of the men, not as blessed with keen eyesight but trusting in their leader and their mates, joined in the jubilations.

Högni barked an order, ending the cheerful hubbub. The fifteen boats set course for the neck right away—they had to urgently prevent the animal from escaping out the upper fjord. If the whale succeeded in slipping through to the lower fjord, hunting it would become much more difficult, and there was a risk that it might reach the open sea.

Despite the cold, the servants were sweating heavily by the time the boats reached their destination. The whale ambled along lazily in its wet element about six hundred feet away. It was the kind they called a right whale, for it was considered the best kind of whale to hunt, and this particular one was a very large one at that, Thorolf observed with mixed feelings. He estimated the beast's length to be almost sixty feet.

"Compared to this one, the whale Högni slayed two years ago was a runt," he said across his shoulder. "This is going to be a tough piece of work, Yngvi. Let us hope that he is weakened."

Upon Högni's command, the ten boats of the beaters spread evenly in front of the passage, which was about two hundred feet wide and bordered by tall cliffs, which separated the upper and the lower fjord. The servants slapped the water's surface with their oars and shouted insults at the creature. The giant responded by slowly moving away from the source of the noise, and the five hunting boats rowed after it.

When the whale turned to swim a gentle curve, Högni saw

his chance. The huge animal had slowed, and the shipwright's servants had only to pull on the oars a handful of times to get close to the massive body.

Thorolf and Yngvi commanded their men to cease rowing, and they watched as Högni rose in the bow of his boat, picking up a harpoon by its shaft. With a battle cry, he thrust the weapon deep into the fat beneath the skin on the beast's back. The whale shuddered. Then it dived. Underwater, it gained speed, and the rope that was tied to the harpoon's end whirred, loop by loop, into the water. The servants rowed toward the fleeing ocean giant to avoid putting too much strain on the rope when it stretched between the boat and the whale. Suddenly, the rope jerked out from the water, and Högni's boat leaped forward. Thanks to the barbed hook, the harpoon remained firmly lodged in the whale's back. The rope, knotted from elastic whale skin, also held as Högni's boat sped after the injured animal at twice the speed of rowing.

Thorolf's and Yngvi's servants and those of the other three hunting boats beside them pulled at their oars as fast as they might, but they stood no chance of catching up with Högni. When their leader's boat came to a halt not far from the harbor, the men in charge once again gave the order to stop rowing. Where was the whale?

They did not have to wait long for the answer, for Högni's boat began to move once more. The giant had turned, now heading in the direction of the neck of land. Toward them!

After a few moments of anxious waiting, they saw the colossus emerge scarcely three hundred feet in front of them, spouting a cloud of spray and then vanishing back under the water's gray surface, white foam swirling above the animal's back.

The many white barnacles on the enormous head of the whale told of its age. It almost looked as if the whale wore a white hat. Yngvi would surely have joked about it had they not been in imminent danger of being rammed by the burly head.

Ferociously the whale shot out of the water, leaping into the air. Its mouth was opened slightly, seeming almost as if the beast were grinning maliciously. With horror the brothers watched as the animal buried the boat beneath its enormous trunk not fifteen paces from them. Men screamed; the waters raged. Timbers burst apart, cracking into splinters. The men in the neighboring crafts ducked, clinging onto the rowers' benches as a tall wave rushed toward their small vessels, lifting them onto its crest.

When the huge animal had vanished beneath the surface once more, the target of its attack was gone too. Only a few bigger and smaller planks dancing in the ripples testified to its former existence. The skipper and one servant, who'd managed to survive by leaping into the frosty waters, flailed their arms about frantically to stay afloat. Blood spreading in the water around them suggested they were hurt. Three servants and the steersman had not survived the ocean giant's sudden attack. Their shattered bodies sank toward the bottom of the fjord. Högni and his men, whooshing past them in the whale's tow, stared in shock at the site of the accident.

The crew of one of the hunting boats took the injured survivors on board and rowed back to the harbor with them. Perhaps, thought Thorolf, that boat's captain was glad to escape the giant's murderous attacks. Should the others succeed in slaying the whale, he would still receive his share of the prize.

The beaters served their purpose. Their clamor irritated the whale, preventing him from escaping into the lower fjord. Yngvi and the second remaining skipper bid their servants to row back toward the passage. The enormous beast appeared to take a break, floating sluggishly at the surface.

Högni used the opportunity to make his rowers bring in the rope attached to the harpoon, drawing the boat toward the whale slowly but steadily. Högni reached for a spear, its steel head gleaming in the rays of the sun rising above the mountain-tops. Another ten feet and he would be near enough to ram the sharp blade into the animal's side beneath the two blowholes.

But the giant seemed to sense the approaching danger: with a flick of its powerful tail fluke, it sped forward, twisted slightly to the side, and, with a second flick of its tail, struck the rear of Högni's vessel.

The wood seemed to explode. Large and small pieces of planks, nails, and blood sprayed into the air and rained down on the water. The man at the steering oar and two servants stood no chance—they died instantly.

Högni and the two servants in the bow were catapulted from the boat, and in the process, Högni injured his throwing arm. Helplessly he paddled in the icy water with his left arm.

The whale spouted a mighty fountain as if in triumph, then dived under, dragging the boat's remains behind him like a drift anchor.

Yngvi steered his boat to the desperately kicking shipbuilder. Högni cursed and groaned in turns when the two brothers heaved his weighty body on board. The other two men were rescued by the crew of the second hunting boat.

Högni breathed heavily, clutching his right upper arm. "I think it's broken. The hunt is over for me. Thorolf, you take the command. You've got what it takes to finish the monster."

Högni called out to the second boat's skipper to row over and fetch him to take him back to land. He climbed into the other boat, trembling violently with cold and dampness, joining his servants who were equally freezing.

As the skipper of the other boat set off toward the village, he shouted at the brothers: "Leave it be. It's a murder whale. It's going to kill you all!"

Yngvi raised an eyebrow at Thorolf. "Shall we turn back?"

"No. The monster has sent seven of our men to a cold, wet grave. It must pay," replied Thorolf grimly.

Yngvi nodded. "Very well. The whale is injured and should be tiring. I believe we have a chance. Should it kill me after all, order a skald to rhyme a few verses about my heroic deed. And if he doesn't rhyme well, cut off his head, won't you?"

Yngvi would not be Yngvi, thought Thorolf, if he lost his sense of humor in the face of his possible death. He gazed into his brother's mischievous face and returned his grin. "Agreed. Let's go get the stinking mutt!"

The sun had reached the end of its brief appearance above the ridges, leaving the fjord to its shadows. The whale had turned once more, idling toward them.

Yngvi steered the boat to the beast's left side. As Högni had earlier, Thorolf also succeeded in lodging a harpoon firmly in the prey's fat and flesh. The pain sent the black giant into a panic, and with one powerful stroke of its tail, it dived under, dragging behind it the remains of Högni's boat on the one side and that of the brothers on the other.

Again the whale headed toward the harbor at great speed, then slowed as it came closer to the shore, as if searching for a way out. It swam in a curve before racing toward the passage again. When the beaters saw the whale chasing toward them, they resumed slapping their oars against the water and yelling coarse abuse at the animal.

But this time, the ocean giant was unperturbed by the menacing sounds. Without slowing, and towing its load behind, it rushed toward the passage, surfaced, and pumped out several spray fountains in a row before vanishing back under. The men in charge of the beaters recognized with shock the danger that was swimming toward them. Terrified, they shouted their orders, whereupon the servants pulled frantically on their oars to get out the way of the approaching beast. One boat was too slow. The whale surfaced, ramming the vessel with its massive head, sending it flying into the air, where it shattered into its components. None of the crew survived.

Following the collision, the whale appeared dazed, the movements of its tail fluke slowing and becoming erratic, and the giant drifted slowly toward the passage. Thorolf was starting to believe the moment had come to attack it with the spear when the mighty animal sped up once more with powerful strokes of its tail. Aghast, Yngvi, Thorolf, and the oarsmen watched as the whale escaped from the upper fjord. Hunching down, they clung to the benches to avoid being thrown out of the boat while it skipped across the waves created by the giant's tail. Without slowing, the fleeing whale followed the long lower fjord's winding course just beneath the surface, heading toward the open sea. It increasingly emerged to spout the typical fan-shaped fountain. It was evident that the creature was growing tired, and the brothers urgently hoped that its strength would fail before reaching the mouth of the fjord.

But the black monster did not oblige. While it did slow down, and the intervals between drawing breath shortened, the beast appeared to possess an iron determination as it pulled past the sentry boat guarding the area where the fjord met the sea. The two watchmen, having seen nothing of the hunt from their outlying post, gaped in astonishment as they watched the whale cruise past with Yngvi and Thorolf in tow.

Once the giant of the sea left the fjord's mouth, it appeared to have reached the end of its strength, ceasing all movement and floating apathetically on the surface.

"Now or never!" shouted Thorolf to his brother and servants.

The latter pulled the boat closer to the animal by the rope

tied to the harpoon still lodged in the whale's back, while Thorolf picked up a twelve-foot-long spear, positioning himself in the bow. Here, outside the fjord, the swell was bigger, and it took a great effort to balance out the boat's pitching. When the giant came within reach of the spear, Thorolf struck, thrusting the steel point into the whale's flesh a little to the side of and below the blowholes. The massive body shuddered.

Thorolf yanked the spear back out of the beast. When but a thin rivulet of blood ran from the wound, he knew that he had not struck a vital organ, and so he rammed the spear into the animal's side for a second time. His strike was good: when he withdrew the spear this time, a stream of blood spouted from the wound, dyeing the water red. The exhausted whale reacted with a weak flap of its tail, drifting forward by some distance. A wave struck the boat from the side, and Thorolf would have tumbled into the sea had he not ducked down in time.

When the servants pulled on the rope again to bring their vessel nearer to their victim, Thorolf stood with his feet firmly planted in the bow once more, nimbly riding out the boat's rocking motion.

He heard Yngvi, sitting in the stern and shifting his weight to counteract the boat's swaying, cheer him on: "Now, brother, finish the dirty mongrel!"

Thorolf threw his spear for the third time. With all his might, he buried it several feet deep inside the creature, levering hard on the shaft to cause as much damage as possible on the beast's innards. This time, a thick fountain of hot blood spurted from the leathery skin, pouring over the servants in the boat and past it. Thorolf knew that he had given the whale its death blow, and he roared his triumph across the sea. Yngvi and the oarsmen joined in with cries of victory.

But the wounded giant, too, sensed that its end was nigh,

and it gathered its very last reserves of strength. With a powerful stroke of its fluke, it darted forward, sending a tall wave slamming into the boat's left side. Yngvi cried out fearfully when their vessel pitched precipitously to the side. The rope the servants had been using to tie the boat to the whale slipped hotly through their fingers. In their need to cling onto something, they dropped it. Thorolf tried to hold on to the spear's shaft, but when the boat's solid timbers vanished from beneath his feet, the spear, unable to support all his weight, slid out of the heavily bleeding wound and sank to the bottom of the sea.

Ice-cold water enveloped Thorolf, taking his breath away for a moment. And yet he managed to grasp the rope that was still attached to the harpoon, pulling himself close to the beast's side in the rushing waters. It was his only way to steer clear of the deathly tail. The whale picked up speed. The rope jerked tight as the whale towed Yngvi's boat behind him once more.

The fatally wounded animal sprayed a fountain that glistened red with blood. Then it dived.

Thorolf just managed to fill his lungs with air before he was dragged into the depths. Desperately he clung to the rope, and when he thought his ears were going to burst and he would have to draw a breath, no matter whether air or water, the exhausted creature surfaced with him once more, pumping several red clouds from its blowholes. Thorolf thirstily sucked air into his lungs, his victim's blood raining down upon him, and the whale slowed. Thorolf hoped desperately that his opponent would finally give up and submit to its fate, but it seemed the animal's will to live had not yet died. Again it dived, and this time, Thorolf had no opportunity to draw breath. But the dying giant, having at last reached the end of its tether, quickly returned to the surface and blew out another red cloud. Sluggish, continuously struggling for air and spouting blood, the whale swam on.

Thorolf felt the cold creeping mercilessly into his limbs. He could not accompany the death throes of his victim any longer—or else death would claim him too. Since the tail moved only very slowly now, he risked climbing hand over hand along the taut rope running from the harpoon to Yngvi's boat.

Once he made it out of reach of the destructive tail fluke, he felt for the knife in his belt, his fingers stiff with cold. The chill was sapping his strength, and it cost him a great deal of effort and time to saw through the tough line. Succeeding at last, he was able to tie the loose end of the rope around his right hand while waving at his brother with his left.

Yngvi hauled in the rope and heaved Thorolf on board with the help of a servant. Thorolf, shaking all over, leaned heavily on Yngvi as they made their way to the bow, where Thorolf collapsed with a groan. Yngvi was concerned about his condition: Thorolf's skin was pale and felt ice-cold to the touch. Small clouds of steam rising from his mouth in quick succession told Yngvi that his brother was breathing much faster than he should. "Fetch our coats!" barked Yngvi at one of the men.

Yngvi covered his brother's shivering body with their warm coats as best as he could. Relieved at Thorolf's rescue, he sank down next to him, gazing at him with awe. "Man, that was some feat. The people will call you 'the whale slayer.'" He pointed a finger at the spectacle unfolding beyond the stern. "There, take a look!"

Surrounded by blood and vomit, the dying giant of the sea swam in circles that grew smaller and smaller. Dusk was setting when it spouted a meager fountain of blood for the final time. The huge body twitched; then it lay still in the water.

"We slayed the whale. We together," mumbled Thorolf almost unintelligibly.

But Yngvi understood, laughed, and gave his brother a friendly slap on the shoulder.

Thorolf reached for Asla's cloth, hanging wet around his neck, and pulled one end out from beneath the fur coats. "This brought us luck and gave me courage," he croaked softly.

One after the other, the beater boats and the sentry boat emerged from the end of the fjord, where their crews, awestruck, had watched the whale's death battle. It wasn't every day the men witnessed such an impressive spectacle.

As darkness settled, an icy cold descended from the starry sky upon the sea, creeping into Yngvi's bones. He missed his fur coat, but he certainly would not take it away from his sleeping brother. Instead he asked one of his servants to take the steering oar while he himself took up one of the rowing oars. The exercise would warm him.

"Let us row, men. We must hurry to get Thorolf to a warm hearth, or else our brave whale slayer might follow his prey to the realm of the dead." His words were supposed to sound cheerful, but he failed miserably. His voice was filled with fear for his brother's life.

There still was no wind to set the sail, and so Yngvi and the three men made their oars bite the water hard to pull their boat back toward the fjord's mouth. Behind them, the men from the beater boats secured the whale, which would not sink, thanks to its thick layer of fat, but which might be carried off by the currents, getting lost in the expanse of the sea.

Once the men had sunk hooks into the giant's corpse and attached those with ropes to four boats, the servants began to pull on the oars. The animal's bulk and the unfavorable current was against them, and their progress went haltingly. Once they reached the fjord, the current would no longer hinder them. Then, the other five beater boats would be able to take over the kill and, with fresh energy, transport it back to the village.

Yngvi cussed. When they reached the middle of the lower fjord, fog thickened around them, swallowing up the stars and thus the last remaining lights of the night. Yngvi told the men to cease rowing. When the boat lay still in the water, the men were enclosed by an impenetrable blackness and a ghostly silence. Yngvi felt as though he had lost his eyes and ears. One of the servants cleared his throat, as if he wished to dispel the eerie stillness. Another began to hum a low, melancholy melody.

When Thorolf moaned, Yngvi felt his way through the darkness to him, groping at benches and servants. He called his brother by his name. No reaction. He felt for Thorolf's face and slapped his cheek. Thorolf muttered, "Asla," but his other words were unintelligible. He was no longer responsive.

Worried, Yngvi called two of his servants to the bow and ordered them to take off their coats. Depending entirely on their sense of touch, the men bedded Thorolf on their garments and then covered him again with the fur coats. Yngvi sighed. Now his brother's back, too, was protected from the worst of the cold, but he nonetheless doubted whether Thorolf would survive this frigid, foggy night.

Yngvi gave the order to dip the oars in a slow rhythm. He had no idea where they were, but he and the men were growing more chilled by the moment. The movement would prevent their blood from turning sluggish and help them resist the cold. Only the man at the steering oar and the one who shivered the worst might wear one of the two remaining coats.

A rock crossed their path in the blackness. The boat's right side screeched along the hard, ragged obstacle, and the keel, too, scrunched across rock. The two starboard oars splintered.

Yngvi held his breath, sitting frozen on his rowing bench and waiting for the sound of gargling water bubbling through a leak in the boat, announcing their vessel's sinking. But nothing happened. Yngvi thanked the gods and ordered the men to insert one of the intact portside oars in the rowlock on the right. Now, just two of his servants rowed the boat away from the fjord's bank, which they had evidently come too near.

When Yngvi felt like the boat was roughly back in the middle of the fjord, he asked the servants to stop rowing once more. He did not want to risk another life-threatening encounter with the rocky shore. The servants swapped coats and huddled close. But they still suffered from the chill, gazing longingly in the direction of Thorolf lying upon the two other coats.

Yngvi had abandoned hope of reaching the village before Thorolf froze to death. His brother needed warmth. He needed it right now! Yngvi felt his way to the bow and crawled under the fur coats. Thorolf's body felt cold, his heart beating slowly. Yngvi pressed his body against his brother's, sharing his own warmth with Thorolf. Yngvi was exhausted. The boat rocked gently on the waves, and the servants argued in low voices over the remaining coats. Every now and then, his brother drew a rattling breath.

To stop himself from falling asleep, Yngvi kept his thoughts busy. He had been touched when his brother, confused and almost unconscious, whispered the name of his beloved, clutching her scarf as if doing so brought him closer to her. His brother seemed to have found something in Asla that Yngvi had not yet experienced.

He thought of the many women who had shared his bed.

With each one he had started the lovemaking gently, then proceeded passionately before finally spilling into her womb, moaning with delight. Afterward, however, his feelings invariably burst like a bubble of air on the water's surface, leaving behind nothing but a vague ripple. Rarely did he lust for a repetition of a union once it was consummated. If, like with Thorolf and Asla, there was something more than physical attraction, he had not yet found it. He could merely hope to one day meet a woman who would be more to him than a plaything for a few nights. Pondering over this thought, sleep finally overcame him.

A wind picked up. A short while later, lightning illuminated the thinning fog, followed by a grumbling in the distance. Yngvi awoke. There was a storm coming. Lightning storms in winter were rare in the North, but when they did occur, they were ferocious.

A wind gust swept through the fjord, and the air became milder. Lightning flashed more frequently, and the thunder moved closer. The fog dissipated, and the next time, a bolt of lightning drove into a mountaintop, Yngvi beheld a bizarre rock formation that he knew well from his many boat trips on the fjord. At last he knew where they were. With trepidation, he placed one ear against his brother's chest, making out a weak, slow heartbeat. Yngvi sighed with relief. Thorolf lived still.

Swiftly he disentangled himself from the coats and ordered his men to raise the sail. The southwest wind would carry them straight to the village.

Yngvi took the steering oar, and his servants set the sail. Then the fishing boat gathered speed swiftly. The rain set in—an icy rain, mercilessly drenching the men's clothes. The storm was above them, flashes of lightning dispersing the darkness for brief moments at a time, illuminating the banks and their steeps and helping Yngvi steer the boat around the bends of the lower fjord. Soon they passed the neck of land, reaching the upper fjord.

When the rain eased and visibility improved, Yngvi felt like screaming out with joy. Two small dots of light glowed in the distance—fires probably lit by Ulrik to light the hunters' way home.

CHAPTER 6
PREPARATIONS

The storm had passed completely by the time the shivering, weary servants fastened the boat to a jetty. The servant who'd been feeding the fires ran into the village to announce their arrival.

Yngvi bid his men to cut the sail off its ropes, lift Thorolf out of the bow, and lay him on the sailcloth, where they covered him with the furs once more. Yngvi and three servants carried his brother up the track to Thorolf's house.

Several curious onlookers approached them with torches. "Have you got the whale?" they asked with hopeful eyes.

Yngvi gasped from his brother's weight and the steep incline. "The whale is ours. It will be here tomorrow," he said between clenched teeth.

The sleepy faces filled with pure joy. The villagers slapped Yngvi's shoulder as well as those of the servants in appreciation. The people felt deeply fortunate—this winter, there would be no famine! More and more villagers crowded around them, slowing Yngvi's progress.

"Make way!" he shouted with agitation. "Thorolf lies in

this cloth, he who vanquished the mighty whale. He is fighting death. Make way, I said! Run to Ulrik's house and call for Asla. If anyone can help him, it is she."

Disconcerted, the villagers cleared the road. Some of them ran as if Fenrir the wolf were after them, racing to Ulrik's hall to notify him and Asla. Others walked alongside the carriers, lighting their way with torches.

Asla hastily slipped into her tunic and coat, grabbed her sack of herbs, and ran, her heart thumping heavily, to the house of Thorolf. Ulrik, Gudrun, and Isold followed her.

The messengers had reported that Thorolf, the whale slayer, was dying and she needed to come quickly. This could not and must not be true, she thought with desperation. Thorolf must not die!

The door to his house was left ajar. When she stormed inside, she saw Yngvi removing fur coats from Thorolf's body. The face of the unconscious man was bluish gray, and he appeared to be closer to the realm of the dead than the world of the living. He was clutching her cloth with one fist as if it were the anchor still tying him to life.

Yngvi briefly told her what had happened, and Asla bent down to listen to her betrothed's chest. Thorolf's heart beat slowly and irregularly, his breathing shallow. She rose, ordering Thorolf's maid Ilka, a mousy young woman, to stack more wood onto the fire and prepare a bed with many furs. Yngvi and Ulrik pulled the wet clothes off Thorolf's body.

Gudrun watched with distress as Ulrik and Yngvi lifted her stepson's pale, lifeless body onto the furs.

"Turn him on his side," directed Asla.

With a dark face, Ulrik stood next to his wife and placed an arm around her shoulder. Isold anxiously stood next to her parents. The sight of her strong brother looking so helpless and weak clearly frightened her.

When Asla turned to her and asked, "Will you help me warm Thorolf?" she nodded eagerly, glad to be of help.

Asla undressed down to her undergarment and asked the girl to do the same. Isold lay down at Thorolf's front, pressing her warm back against his chest, and Asla snuggled against his back, slipping one arm under his head and slinging the other across his chest. Ilka covered Thorolf and the two young women up to their necks with almost every cloth and fur blanket she could find in her master's household. Then she filled a small kettle with water. When the water boiled, she would add herbs from Asla's sack.

Gudrun and Ulrik saw there was nothing more they could do for their son. They took their leave in the hope that the young women's efforts would bear fruit. Yngvi wrapped himself up in a blanket on a bench. Even if there wasn't anything he could do for his brother right now, he felt certain that Thorolf could sense his closeness and his support.

Asla shivered. Even under all the warm blankets and furs, Thorolf's cold body drew more warmth from her than she herself produced. She could feel his struggle with death. Desperately she dug her fingernails into the skin of his chest to show him that she was there, that she was fighting for him. Tears streamed from her eyes and a helpless sob escaped her throat.

"Are you seeing Hilmar's face again? Is he looking at you angrily because you're lying by Thorolf's side?" asked Isold softly.

Asla realized that she had not thought of Hilmar since she'd been woken by the messengers. She imagined her dead brother's face. He no longer looked as glum, but nor did he carry the smile she had loved so much.

Asla nestled even closer to Thorolf, stroking his full black hair lovingly and answering Isold quietly: "My brother's ghost no longer looks angry. Believe me, I will never forgive myself for Thorolf's and my own guilt in Hilmar's death—but are we undoing our deeds by denying our love? Wouldn't my brother's death have been entirely in vain, then?"

Ilka filled three cups with the tea she had made with Asla's herbs. Yngvi accepted the drink gratefully. He, too, was suffering from the cold, and he relished the warming and reviving brew. The two young women sat up, drinking their tea in small sips. The warmth spreading inside them felt good. Once they had drained their cups, they pressed themselves against Thorolf once more.

Asla couldn't go to sleep. Terrible images and gloomy thoughts held her mind captive. She saw herself waking up in despair beside Thorolf's dead body, not knowing how she was supposed to carry on without him, endlessly alone without his support and his love. Perhaps that would be the just punishment for her part in Hilmar's death? She remembered staring down at Hilmar's body in disbelief—her dead brother, who seemed peacefully asleep. By now, she suspected, he was likely in Valhalla and glad to be feasting and fighting, day in and day out. The thought eased her mind, and maybe, she hoped, he no longer cared about the fault she carried in his demise. Her thoughts turned back to the future. Would Thorolf survive? And if so, would they ever reach Catan safely? Or would a vicious storm put a terrible end to their journey? Horrible images rose before her mind's eye. She saw Thorolf's ship go down in a merciless storm, watched her own and Thorolf's lifeless bodies sink toward the bottom of the sea until the eternal blackness of the ocean swallowed them up. Perhaps Hilmar had not forgiven her after all and was asking the father of the gods and the Norns to avenge him?

Asla softly cried herself to sleep.

Thorolf's body was ice-cold and rigid. He no longer breathed. Isold had vanished. Asla wanted to get up, but her body did not obey her, as if she were tied to her bed. Something stirred in her underbelly, pushed out of her. It paused, twitching, between her legs and then, bulging the furs, crawled up on her. Claws of bone lifted the blanket. A pale skull emerged from the darkness, fixing her with its black holes for eyes, grinning an evil smile at her. Its cold claws reached for her, moving toward her throat—

Asla awoke with a scream. Her heart was beating in her throat, and cold sweat covered her skin. She told herself it was only a nightmare. For a moment, she lay still. Then she felt for Thorolf, who was stirring and muttering something she couldn't understand. His skin felt warmer. His shallow, irregular breathing had given way to deep and even breaths. He had won the battle for his life!

A deep sense of joy warmed her and allowed her to forget the horrible dream. Lovingly, she caressed Thorolf's cheeks and kissed his neck. His recovery must be a sign from the gods! A sign that they did not scorn her and Thorolf and that they approved of their union. Could Hilmar himself have put in a good word with Odin? She thought he might have done just that, for now she saw him smile at her the way he used to. The time was ripe for a fresh start, she realized with relief. She and Thorolf would marry! It would not be a wedding according to the customs of the North, since she had no family to give her to Thorolf. Nor were there many villagers who would attend their celebration with kindness in their hearts. No, theirs would be a very special kind of wedding, to which only the gods would be invited.

The light of the morning streamed through the venthole in a wide beam. Yngvi awoke. He yawned, sat up, rubbed his eyes, and immediately glanced at Thorolf. His brother lay thickly wrapped up between the sleeping women and snored softly. Yngvi was flooded with relief. His brother had made it through the night. Silently Yngvi pulled on his coat and sneaked to the door. Outside the house, he ran into Gudrun, who came to check on her stepson. Her worried face brightened when Yngvi told her that Thorolf seemed better, sleeping peacefully now.

"Then I'd better not disturb him," said Gudrun. "But Ulrik ought to know." She turned on her heel and hurried back to her husband's longhouse.

With a bounce in his step, Yngvi made his way down to the harbor. Perhaps the boats towing the whale were already within sight.

Many villagers had gathered in the harbor to wait for the arrival of the mighty prey. When they spotted Yngvi, they stormed toward him, showering him with questions. He found himself in a tightening circle of people hungry for news, babbling over the top of one another. Högni and the other hunters who had returned the previous day had merely told them that the whale had killed several men and that the hunters had not succeeded in killing the beast. Those villagers who had met Yngvi during the night, however, claimed that they'd heard that Thorolf gave the animal the death blow—but if this were true, then where was the whale?

Soon, Yngvi feared, the crowd would unintentionally squash him to death. He was relieved then when he saw his father with three of his men parting the crowd to make their way to him. Ulrik's followers banged their swords against their shields, forcing the people aside. Once the villagers had calmed, Ulrik bid his men to stop. In his powerful voice, he explained to the people that they would learn details about the whale's fate only once they kept their mouths closed and let his son speak.

Yngvi nodded at the crowd. "First," he declared loudly, "I will answer your most pressing question. It is true: the whale is slain. The beaters have secured it and are towing it hither."

Sighs of relief went through the crowd. Someone shouted, "Why is it taking so long?"

Yngvi replied patiently, "The boats were slowed during last night's foul weather, and the whale's bulk offers great resistance. But they are on their way." He pointed at the fjord and continued in a sharper tone: "If you want to help them get here faster, climb into your boats and row toward them!"

Several freemen took him by his word, calling for their servants and rushing to their boats.

Among the crowd, Yngvi spotted a woman whose face was puffy from crying, holding two children by their hands. Her husband had sat at Högni's steering oar when the whale's tail had smashed the stern and killed him.

Yngvi cleared his throat. "Yesterday's hunt has cost the lives of several of our brave men. Unfortunately, there were further victims that you haven't yet heard of." He named the two freemen, father and son, who had led the beater boat that the whale had rammed and destroyed in front of the neck. A woman cried out. Her two younger sons held her, keeping her on her feet.

Ulrik spoke. "I will send men to the sites of the accidents to search for the bodies of our courageous hunters. If we find them, we will solemnly give them to the fire and ask the gods with a sacrifice to admit them to Valhalla as honorable warriors."

The people nodded. The freemen who had died during the hunt would be treated with the greatest honor. Hardly anyone seemed to spare a thought for the servants at the oars who had also been sent to their wet graves in the fjord.

Yngvi reported what had happened following Högni's failed attempt at killing the whale. In colorful words, he described the whale's flight to the open sea and Thorolf's heroic battle with the giant. He recounted how his brother succeeded in landing the fatal blow in spite of the waves of the sea, and how he dived down into the depths with the wounded colossus, swimming right by the animal's side during its final struggles. He praised Thorolf's courage and his endurance in the ice-cold waters of the Northern Sea.

The crowd—freemen with their wives and older children, as well as some servants and maids—hung on his every word as he brought back to life the events of the previous night. Yngvi felt flattered—he had never before realized that he possessed the talents of a storyteller.

He concluded with the pronouncement that it had not been the giant beast that had pushed his brother to the edge of death, but the cruel cold of the winter seas, sucking nearly all his life from him. "But rest assured. Thorolf lives and will be back to his old strength soon!"

He had scarcely uttered the final words when one of the villagers shouted: "There! There they are!"

Everyone turned to look in the direction of the man's arm. A fresh breeze and the sunshine had dispersed the morning haze that had lingered above the water, and in the distance, they could all see the boats and their black burden, which they towed behind them like an island. Their progress was slow, and it would be some time before they reached their destination.

The whale sped toward him with its mouth gaping. Its bloodied gorge came closer and closer. Any moment now, the monster would swallow him up. The whale shut its mouth around him, its baleen crashing together before shattering into a thousand pieces.

"Look out, you silly goose!" Thorolf heard his stepmother scold as he awoke. "That was a precious glass from the south! You will go hungry for this today."

He groaned, his head aching. What happened? Gradually, the memories from the whale hunt returned. He lifted his heavy eyelids and saw his sister's tousled blonde hair. He felt her warm body against his front, and a second one at his back. Carefully he turned and beheld, to his amazement, the sleeping profile of Asla. Why was she here? He reached up and stroked her hair.

She opened her eyes and smiled at him. "You made it."

"Made what?"

"You were frozen and more dead than alive when Yngvi brought you home. Isold and I took you in our midst and warmed you. I was terribly afraid for you."

Asla propped herself up, drew his head to her, and kissed him softly on his lips. "I am so glad that you are better." He looked into her familiar eyes, which returned his gaze warmly, and felt how the deep bond and affection that used to exist between them were beginning to grow once more.

Thorolf sighed, scarcely able to believe he had won back Asla. "Then you have saved my life." He kissed her forehead, both eyelids, the tip of her nose, and lastly her full lips, where his mouth lingered. "I will thank the other enchanting parts of your body later on," he murmured into her ear, which brought a smile to her face.

Playfully, she whispered back, "It would appear you are quite recovered."

Thorolf toyed with a blonde strand of hair that had slipped into her face. "I believe I am in your debt."

An elbow struck him hard in his kidneys, making him wince with pain.

Isold sat up, her lips pouting. "And I? Did I not help to save your life too? You're also in my debt!" Isold placed a finger on her lips and frowned at the rafters, as if thinking very hard. "A pot of honey! All to myself. That is the least."

Gudrun laughed and gave her sweet-toothed daughter a good-natured nod.

When Gudrun served breakfast, Isold and Asla left their bed and sat at the table. With sparkling eyes, Isold stared at the sweetened porridge in front of her.

Thorolf was hungry, too. He felt as though he might eat half a lamb by himself. But when he tried to stand up in order to dress, the world grew black before his eyes, and he sank back into the furs with a groan.

Asla rushed to his side. "For someone who only just managed to escape the realm of the dead, you ought to take things a little slower, my darling. That is the only request I have of you."

Dusk heralded the beginning of the winter's evening. The freemen and servants in the beater boats towed the whale to a pebble beach some distance away from the harbor, where the land did not drop as steeply into the fjord as on the surrounding shore. The men were utterly exhausted. For nearly two days and one long night, they had rowed in turns, and had, like Yngvi and his servants, sat shivering in the fog and weathered the storm.

When the giant creature ran aground on its stomach, the men undid the ropes and brought their boats ashore with their last remaining strength. Many villagers and residents from the surrounding steadings watched from the shore, gawking at the huge animal. Several women and children rushed down to the wearied whale hunters, who were sitting on the ground. Their wives, sons, and daughters were visibly proud of the deeds of their husbands and fathers, and their faces were filled with joy at being able to clasp the men in their arms, alive and well.

Högni carried his bandaged right arm in a sling. As the original commander of the hunt, he thanked each freeman with his left hand, praising them for their courage and bravery. He overlooked the thralls, but some of the skippers slapped their servants' backs appreciatively.

With his feet planted apart, Högni positioned himself before the spectators. While he was shorter than most men of the North, his thickset, heavily muscled stature commanded respect. His booming voice did the rest. "Don't just stand around idly, men! Light torches and secure our kill! Or else the tide will carry the whale back into the fjord."

"*Our* kill? Are you sure, shipbuilder?" Hafdan stepped forward and positioned himself next to Högni. He fixed his dark eyes on the crowd, wiping his nose with the back of his hand. "As we have all heard, Thorolf killed the whale in the open sea and not in the fjord. Who does the kill belong to, according to our laws, then?" He allowed the question to sink in for a moment. The people watched him uncertainly—few of them knew the answer, which Hafdan now proclaimed with a cynical smile. "To the whale slayer and the hunting party. The rest of us go empty-handed. Or do you think the noble Thorolf Ulrikson gives anything away for nothing?" Hafdan had practically spat the word "noble."

He had the people's undivided attention now, and their expressions darkened.

The members of the hunting party who were resting with their families by their boats were unimpressed by Hafdan's speech. They would receive their fair share either way. But the vast majority of freemen had not participated in the hunt, and now they exchanged disappointed looks. They began to mutter, and one of them shouted defiantly at Högni, "Then let Thorolf and his hunters secure the whale and butcher it. It's nothing to do with us now." The other freemen grumbled their assent.

Hafdan grinned contentedly. He had driven a poisonous thorn into the flesh of the tribe. Now he needed to force it deeper, until there was a festering wound whose pain would push the people's anger at Thorolf and Asla over the edge.

"Do you believe the noble Thorolf Ulrikson, whose whore is responsible for the attack by Halldor's men, cares about the loss of all our households? Is he replacing the cows, sheep, and pigs that burned to death in our stables?"

He was about to continue his malicious speech when Högni harshly cut him off. "Here comes the whale slayer! Let us hear what he has to say."

Thorolf was walking down the track to the beach with Digur and Yngvi. Puzzled, he saw the whale floating unsecured in the water near the shore, while the people gazed at him coldly and with hostility. Why weren't they rejoicing over the big catch?

Hafdan crossed his arms on his chest. "Welcome . . . whale slayer. Go ahead and drag your kill ashore. We won't help you."

Thorolf turned to Högni. "What is going on?"

Thorolf listened to the shipwright's explanation with astonishment. He had not known there was a different law for the slaying of a whale on the open sea than for within the fjord. Ever since he could remember, whales had been killed inside Ulrik's fjord, never at sea.

He did not consider for long. "Men, as you know, Högni transferred the command of the hunt unto me. I killed the whale with Yngvi's help. So who would know better than I where this occurred?" Thorolf paused, gazing into the guarded faces of his audience, men and women whose hope in a share of the rich kill and sufficient food until the end of winter had been disappointed. "I am telling you, I killed the whale inside the fjord!"

The people thought they had misheard, or that Thorolf had made a slip of the tongue.

"Or would anyone like to argue with me about where the waters of the fjord end and the open sea begins? How about you, Hafdan?"

The man remained silent, but his grim stare was enough of an answer for Thorolf. "Well, then, you may stop looking so glum. According to our laws, the meat belongs to us all, and of the remaining spoils of the whale, four-tenths belong to you."

The meaning of Thorolf's words had finally sunk in. First a few individuals expressed their joy, then more joined in, and eventually everyone was cheering and hugging one another. Several men walked up to Thorolf, lifted him upon their shoulders, and carried him hither and thither. Relieved and exuberant, they chanted, "Long live Thorolf, the whale slayer!"

Hafdan, his face filled with bitter disappointment, slunk off.

Högni was forced to shout "Stop it!" three times before the people finally calmed and set Thorolf down on the ground. "By the gods, secure the whale already!"

This, at least, he did not need to say twice. While the women went home with joyous faces, the men and servants set to work, erecting torches so that they could labor into the night, and driving stakes into the stony beach on which to tie the ropes they used to secure the enormous cadaver.

It was still dark when the servants gathered larger stones together and, under the direction of their masters, stacked them in circles to make fire rings. By the time morning broke, copper cauldrons were already hanging above the fires.

When Thorolf visited the beach in the afternoon, the butchering of the whale was in full swing. The first lot of blubber was boiling in one of the cauldrons. The people hardly seemed to notice the foul stench rising from the copper pot as they busily rushed back and forth, sharing the workload. Some men used sharp knives to pull off the whale's skin in wide strips, while others sawed at large chunks of the exposed fat, and others again were removing the flesh below from the ribs. Maidservants picked up the fat and meat with carts. They took the meat to the village, where it was hung beneath roofed constructions in preparation for conservation. The blubber they took to the fires and filled the cauldrons. As soon as one was full, they would light the fire underneath, which would separate out the oil. This process could take up to two days, Thorolf knew. When it was ready, maids would use large wooden spoons to ladle off the precious oil before sieving it and then leaving it to cool in large tubs. Servants would then fill barrels with the oil and take them to the storehouse.

Thorolf studied his once-mighty opponent. Large parts of the beast were still intact, resting in the shallow water. The people would make good use of almost every single part of its body. Skin, blubber, and muscles were the most valuable resources, from which they would produce ropes, oil, and long-lasting dried meat. Clever craftsmen manufactured tools from the bones, and gifted artists whittled combs from them, as well as jewelry, game pieces, or toys for children. Women and maids wove the flexible baleen into baskets. The few bits that were not used served as a meal for the ravens.

Those who passed Thorolf greeted him respectfully, but they never stopped for long. Despite the hard work, folks went about their tasks with cheerful faces. They knew that the whale's treasures would improve their future for a long while and make it more bearable.

Högni approached Thorolf and gave him a friendly slap on his shoulder. "Well done. The people look up to you, and aside from Hafdan, no one claims Halldor had attacked their homes or that you and Asla were to blame."

Thorolf nodded. "I spoke with Digur and Yngvi. We would like to make a special proposal to those who have lost their homes and livestock. In three days, we'll meet with the heads of the families at the tavern. Will you come?"

"Of course. I think I have a hunch what you are going to tell them." Högni winked at him before strutting over to a servant who was standing about idly. The unhappy fellow did not do so for much longer once the stout shipwright was through with him.

The tavernkeeper handed a cup of ale to each of the invited men. They were sitting upon the benches expectantly, staring at the three brothers when they entered the tavern: the tall, dark-skinned, and powerful Digur, athletic Thorolf, and shorter, wiry Yngvi.

In the center of the smoky room, a fire was burning in the hearth, keeping warm a pot of flavorsome stew, which several men were already gobbling from their bowls with wooden spoons. Oil lamps and tallow lights painted the timber walls with speckles of light and shade. It was warm inside the tavern. The brothers took off their coats and ordered ale. While Digur and Yngvi got comfortable on some spare seats among the men, Thorolf strode across the room, positioning himself so that he had a good view of everyone there.

Just when he was about to begin his speech, Högni and Egil arrived. A cold gust sent snowflakes twirling in behind them, leaving small, dark dots on the hard dirt floor. The men quickly slammed the door shut behind themselves, locking out the unwelcome envoys of the wintry night. Once the pair was seated, Thorolf began to speak.

"Men, as you know, Ulrik banished me and my brothers from our home for seven years in order to uphold the allegiance and keep the peace with Halldor. At great length, we pondered the question of where to set ourselves up for the duration of our exile. At first, we intended to sail to our uncle Odur, who has settled on the Faroe Islands, and to set forth on trade voyages from there. But then Egil told us of an island called Catan by its inhabitants. It's an island in the south, where there is no hardship, no cold, but rich fishing grounds and unfarmed, free land for everyone. To that island—an island which, according to Egil, even the gods would delight in—my brothers and I will sail and settle thereupon."

Murmuring broke out, and a few men raised questioning eyebrows.

"We sail in just a few weeks' time. Egil and his trade ships will accompany us as far as the southern land of the Moors, offering us protection. From there, it isn't far to Catan."

Thorolf paused, gazing into the intrigued faces of his listeners. He thought he could see their minds working, their thoughts churning around the questions of why he was telling them of his plans for his banishment and how they themselves might be connected to those plans.

"You have lost your halls, your livestock, and your stores. You are forced to begin again. I know this is bitter. But could this not also be an opportunity for you to attempt a fresh start in a warmer land with fertile fields and luscious meadows?"

Then the men seemed to understand why Thorolf had asked them here.

"Come with us! We invite you to build a new life on Catan with your families and servants."

Thorolf paused again, allowing the audience to digest his offer. Their faces reflected a mix of astonishment, suspicion, and hope.

A haggard farmer who looked as if he had just lived through a winter of famine rose to his feet. "Many of us are left without means. How should we start anew on Catan? We have no animals, no seeds, and not all of us are experienced fishermen."

Thorolf had expected this question. "I own more than two-tenths of the oil we are going to win from the whale's blubber. That means about fifty to sixty barrels. We will take them with us when we sail and use them to buy livestock and seed for all of us at the great markets at Hedeby. We will form a community. When we arrive at Catan, we will herd our sheep, cows, and pigs together. We will clear the land together and sow our fields. As soon as the herds are large enough and there's enough grain for everyone, we'll divide the fruits of our labor fairly among us." Thorolf hesitated for a moment. "I do have one condition, however."

The men's faces turned skeptical. The offer of the jarl's son sounded too good to not have a catch.

"Each freeman who joins me must swear an oath of absolute loyalty to me. In the fall of the following year, I will summon an assembly in our new home. Then I will release you from your oath, and you may choose me or another man as your jarl."

For a few moments, the tavern was silent. The loud crack of a burning log seemed to be the signal for the heads of families to utter remarks, some more witty than others, and to ask questions, talking wildly over one another.

Thorolf raised his hands in a gesture that demanded silence. "We do not expect a decision from you today. You must consider well. I am sure you have many questions about Catan, and Egil is here to answer them. Come see me in the next few days if you wish to sail with us." He nodded at Egil, who rose from his bench.

Högni, who enjoyed the deepest respect from everyone in the tribe, also rose. "Men, I was the first to decide to sail with Thorolf and his brothers to Catan. Harald was the second. I wanted you to know that I am willing to take several of you on my ship."

While Egil answered the men's many questions, the brothers left the tavern. As Thorolf closed the door behind him, he realized that all the farmers and fishermen affected by the attack had accepted his invitation to this gathering. All but one: Hafdan.

Yngvi patted Thorolf's shoulder. "Good speech, brother. I think you've convinced them."

"I hope so. Should the Majo not turn out quite as friendly as described by Egil, we will need as many men capable of bearing arms as possible."

"And we will get them," said Digur into the cold air. "Your proposal is too tempting."

When Thorolf entered his house, Asla greeted him with a warm embrace. She and Ilka had cut whale meat into steaks and fried them in a pan. The smell was delicious. Thorolf's mouth watered, and he sat at the table, which was decked with three cups, three wooden boards, and a jug of ale.

"Who else is joining our meal?" he asked Asla when she sat down opposite him.

"You will find out soon enough, my dear. Allow me to surprise you."

Ilka brought the large pan of fried whale meat. Asla placed three thick steaks upon the board destined for the mysterious visitor. Thorolf frowned but did not ask any further when she placed a finger against her closed lips.

During their meal, Thorolf told her of the meeting.

Asla listened with interest. "Do you think they will come with us?"

Thorolf cut off a piece of the gamey whale meat with his knife and put it in his mouth. While he chewed with relish, he nodded. "They were surprised by our offer. But now they have a choice. Those who do not wish to go viking with my father can sail to Catan with us. Not many of the men are experienced warriors. I believe most of them will join us."

Ilka lifted the pot off the fire and lugged it to the rear of the hall. A short while later, she went outside, refilled the pot with snow, and hung it back above the fire. Thorolf had already watched her do this twice.

"What is Ilka doing with all that water that she's warming?"

"Women's business," replied Asla mischievously. "Men do not need to know everything."

Thorolf grinned. "This appears to be a night full of secrets."

Once they had concluded their meal with cheese, Asla declared: "I am going to show you something."

She picked up a wooden stick that she'd prepared earlier; one side was pointed and the other frayed. She opened her mouth and, with practiced movements, used the stick to clean her immaculate teeth, alternating between the two ends. Then she picked up a cup and rinsed her mouth with its contents before swallowing them.

After she rinsed and swallowed once more, she glowered at Thorolf with mock-severity. "And now it is your turn, my dearest."

"Why should I?"

"Because I do not wish for your teeth to rot and fall out, and then one day you will stink horribly from your mouth like my almost-husband, Hafur."

"I see," said Thorolf. "You are the healer and you know best. Well, then, let me have one of those sticks."

While he cleaned his teeth, she explained to him that the wise Oda had taught her this habit. It cannot be good, the older woman had reckoned, when bits of food rot inside one's mouth. More than a few women could see the truth of this and began cleaning their teeth daily. But many men were reluctant to accept it. "Not Yngvi, by the way. He doesn't have such a radiant, winning smile for nothing. Ask him."

He would, thought Thorolf and picked up the cup with the mysterious brew. It smelled good—of mint and another herb which he could not identify. Once he had rinsed his mouth, he felt pleasantly refreshed, and he conceded that Asla's method of tooth cleaning was by no means unpleasant.

Ilka lifted the kettle of hot water off the fire once more and carried it to the back. Thorolf's eyes followed her curiously. He heard some splashing, and moments later, the area behind the fireplace lit up. Evidently, the maid was lighting oil lamps.

Asla rose. "That will do, Ilka. Go to bed."

She accompanied the maid, who would spend the night at Ulrik's servants' quarters, to the door and barred it behind her. With a mysterious smile on her lips, she took Thorolf by the hand and pulled him to the back of the room. A large wooden tub had been set up there, filled with steaming water.

"Where did that come from?" asked Thorolf, puzzled.

"I borrowed it from your father's sweat-hut. Digur and Yngvi were kind enough to carry it here."

"I see," said Thorolf, at a loss.

Asla started to undress. First she took off her woolen tunic, and then she pulled her long shift over her head. She kept her eyes on Thorolf the whole time, and there was no shame in them. She stood naked before him. He had never seen her like this before. With her long legs, her narrow waist, her stomach slightly rounded from the pregnancy, her well-shaped breasts, her elegant neck, and her long, blonde waves framing her handsome face with her large, sparkling, green-speckled eyes, her delicate nose, her full lips, one of them a little fuller than the other—she seemed to him like an apparition of Frigg, the mother of gods. Thorolf's mouth turned dry, and he felt his erection grow.

Asla stepped up to him and started to undress him. "Have patience, my dearest. We have the whole night to ourselves."

Thorolf would have liked to pull her close, wishing to feel her body right up against his. But a voice inside him told him to rein in his desire. When he stood naked before her, willing his hands to hold still, she glanced with a smile at his arousal and led him to the tub. With a contented sigh, Thorolf lowered himself into the warm water, and Asla climbed in opposite him.

"Here, take this and wash yourself with it."

Thorolf laughed. "What sort of a man do you think I am? Do you believe I do not use soap when I go to the sweat-hut and wash myself?"

Asla shook her head. "No, of course not. But today is a special day. I want us both to wash ourselves with great awareness, as if to cleanse ourselves of our past and prepare ourselves for a new beginning. For tonight, on this evening, I want to celebrate our wedding."

Thorolf swallowed. This was not how he had imagined marrying Asla.

She took his hand. "Don't look so unhappy. It is not possible for us to wed according to the customs of our people. My father has cast me out, and I have no more family who could pass the traditional sword to you. I bring you no dowry. And I am not well-liked among your father's followers. But at least," she added with a grin, "you do not have to pay a bride-price for me this way."

"Oh yes, I did pay a bride-price," he objected with a bitter smile. "I paid with my entire fortune." Thorolf frowned. Disappointed, he went on, "Does that mean we are not going to pledge ourselves to one another in public? We will not exchange rings and sacrifice to the gods to ensure their approval?"

"Yes, we will. All of it! But differently. We will do those things in ways that we can. Look here, I own three rings."

Asla lifted up her right hand. Gold rings gleamed on two of her slender fingers. She leaned over the side of the tub, fished for a leather string with her left hand, and dangled her third ring in front of Thorolf's surprised face. "My ring would not have fit on any of your fingers," she said with a smile. "From now on, you shall wear it around your neck."

She scooted forward, asked him to bow his head, and placed the string around his neck. "One of the two remaining rings on my hand I will sacrifice to the gods tomorrow morning by tossing it into the fjord. The meat and ale for the missing guest were also meant for the gods. I invited them to join our meal. I will give their meat to the flames and hope this small offering and my ring might please them."

Thorolf eyed his wife with fascination. "You are incredible. When did you think up all of this?"

"When I warmed you and woke up in the middle of the night. You were doing better, and I knew then that you would survive. You have no idea how happy that made me." She took his hand and gazed at him with love before continuing. "In that moment, I could think of nothing more wonderful than our wedding. The following morning, I started the preparations."

He hesitated for a moment before replying, deeply moved. "You are wise. And you are very beautiful. But beauty alone would not suffice for me to love you the way I do." He leaned forward and kissed her passionately. His feelings for Asla overpowered him with such force that he ejaculated prematurely into the bathwater. He drew back with a guilty expression. "I am sorry."

Asla gave a cheerful laugh. "I know, my dearest. I don't mind. The night is not over yet."

They used the soap, washing each other, and spoke for a while about Egil's tales of Catan, imagining their future on the warm island. When the water in the tub waxed cold, Thorolf's manhood awoke once more. They climbed out of the tub, dried each other with linen cloths, and lay down on their bed. Thorolf made good on his promise to kiss every part of Asla's body that he had previously never explored with his mouth before. Desiring one another ever more feverishly, he finally glided into her. Asla held onto his broad shoulders, groaning, passionately following his movements—happy and thankful to finally, after all this time, be near him again.

Around noon, a fisherman knocked on Thorolf's door and said he and his family wished to join Thorolf. Other heads of families followed, and three days later, nearly all the freemen Thorolf had asked to the tavern had declared their intention to sail with him to Catan. Even some who had not been affected by Halldor's attack came to him, asking for a place on his ships. When Thorolf began to fear he was losing track, he asked Yngvi, versed in the art of writing, to note down on wax tablets the names of those who wished to come.

At the start of the spring moon, the brothers and Högni

gathered at Thorolf's house. Asla placed a jug of ale and cups on the table and joined them.

Yngvi had brought his wax tablets, upon which he had noted down not only the names of the families who had lost their homes and who wanted to travel to Catan with them, but also those of later-born sons who would inherit nothing. The only hope of such young men to gain wealth was to join viking expeditions or to earn a living as a mercenary. To some of them, the prospect of working their own land and making the acquaintance of Egil's generous island women seemed, by far, the more appealing.

Yngvi had also noted down the names of several young families—men who, with their wives, worked the sparse parcels of barren land they rented from wealthy farmers and which would never yield enough for them to survive.

Behind the names written in Latin symbols, Yngvi had noted the number of family members and servants.

While there were several men in the tribe who knew how to read and write the runes, Yngvi was the only freeman who had mastered the Latin writing and language. Gregor, a monk Ulrik had captured from a monastery ten years prior during one of his raiding voyages, had been his teacher.

On the day he had first addressed the monk, Yngvi had seen thirteen winters and viewed the world with inquisitive eyes, hungry for knowledge. He had observed how Gregor, whenever he was granted a short break from his work, lovingly opened up a leather-bound, box-shaped object. When the monk gazed into this object for long periods of time, his eyes traveling from side to side, his expression, usually filled with a profound sadness, brightened, turning almost cheerful. To Yngvi's question of what sort of a thing this might be into which the monk stared with such pleasure, Gregor replied with a kind smile. What he was holding in his hands was a book, he explained, and he was reading stories written inside it.

How amazed Yngvi had felt that day! How could such an inconspicuous object contain stories? He knew men who chiseled runes into rock and knew how to read them. But those were brief lines in memory of someone dead or to remember the deeds of a hero, not stories like the elders recounted during long winter's nights.

Intrigued, he had asked Gregor to read to him from the book. The monk had laughed and said that the Bible, as he called the book, was written in Latin, a language the people from the North did not understand. That was the moment, Yngvi recalled, when the passionate desire had first sprouted in him to learn this foreign language and to one day explore this mysterious book.

His parents, Ulrik and Gudrun, had been amused by the zeal with which he had pursued the slave, begging him to teach him the strange language. Gregor, however, had shaken his head every time, explaining that he did not have the time.

Ulrik, impressed by Yngvi's perseverance, eventually reached the decision that it could be to his advantage if someone in the family understood the Latin documents and contracts that were the custom in the southern countries. And so Gregor was excused from his other duties in the afternoons to instruct Yngvi in the Latin written and spoken word. As little as three years later, he was able to understand all the stories written inside the Bible.

"There are too many," groaned Thorolf once Yngvi had read out all his notes on his wax tablet. "How are we supposed to travel to Catan with three hundred people? We only have five ships: the four of ours and yours, Högni. We cannot fit more than two hundred if we also want to take livestock and supplies."

The four ships were the *Goldeagle* and three more knarrs

each of the brothers had commissioned from Högni. They had paid the shipbuilder handsomely from the earnings of their trade voyages. Since last fall, the knarrs had waited inside boathouses for their first longer journey in the spring.

Yngvi brushed a strand of hair behind his ear. "The more we are, the better. Egil described Catan's inhabitants as peaceful, but what if they learn that we are no visitors but settlers claiming part of their island?"

"Then we fight," said Digur drily.

Högni stroked his graying beard. "There might be a way. As you perhaps know, my eldest sons, my servants, and I did not work just on your knarrs." He sipped his ale and continued once he felt certain that he held the brothers' undivided attention. "We built three more knarrs in the course of the past year. Two were commissioned by Egil and one by Ragnar, who also wishes to grow his fleet. The ships are not yet paid for, and I would be willing to let you have them, Thorolf, if you pay fifteen barrels of your whale oil per ship to my oldest son, Stefnir, who is going to take over my workshop. Of course, you would have to ask Egil and Ragnar if they're agreeable to receiving their ships later." Högni winked at Thorolf. "Perhaps you can persuade them with a few barrels of oil."

Thorolf thought. "I need the greater part of the oil to purchase livestock, seed, and tools for our new beginning on Catan."

"You will easily get three cattle or fifteen sheep for one barrel of whale oil," replied the shipwright. "But very well—let's say fourteen barrels."

Yngvi, placing a hand on Thorolf's arm, demanded: "Ten!"

Högni laughed. "I'm supposed to give you one of my ships for ten barrels? You know my reputation. No one in the southern Northland builds better knarrs than I do. Your offer is insolent, Yngvi."

Yngvi was surprised at himself. Bartering with his friend Högni went against his nature. But the desire to support his brother motivated him to get involved in the trade. In the end, they agreed on twelve barrels per ship and raised a cup, satisfied with the result.

Egil was prepared to accept the delayed delivery of one of his two knarrs for two barrels of oil. He would simply load his fleet in the spring a little more heavily. Ragnar also accepted the two-barrel offer.

And so there were seven ships for the voyage to Catan of about three hundred people. It would be quite cozy, but it should work.

Spring sent its first messengers. The snow on the fjord's shores melted, the first blossoms lured bees from their hives, and a mild southwest breeze allowed the people to move about without their heavy coats. The whale's cadaver had vanished. Only a few bones that had not yet been washed away by the tide remained, last witnesses of its former mighty existence.

Stacked in the storehouse were more than three hundred barrels of whale oil. The barrel maker and his assistants had toiled day and night to provide sufficient barrels.

The brothers and their servants had hauled their six ships ashore upon round timbers by the harbor. There, they thoroughly checked the planks for leaks, fixing them where necessary with animal hides and tar. Each boat measured around seventy feet long and eighteen feet wide at the middle. Studying the knarrs at the harbor, it struck Thorolf that he was entrusting his life and those of his companions to these ships. He had a good feeling. In contrast to the fast, slender, and agile longships his father used for raiding trips to the shores of Britain and Ireland, the fat-bellied knarrs were able to take more cargo and were better suited to traveling longer distances on the open sea, able to withstand the dangers of storms.

In addition to the gladness of being close to Asla once more, Thorolf's heart leaped with joy at the thought of soon going to sea.

Hafdan sat inside Digur's longhouse, in front of his almost-empty jug of ale, and pondered his bleak future. He was having a bad day. But then again, every day had been bad since he'd lost his farm. He had fought hard every day to get food on the table since he'd taken over his father's run-down property. In the beginning, he could not afford an ox, and so it had been he and his strong wife, Britta, who had painstakingly pulled the plow through the poor soil. A few years ago, he had finally saved up enough silver for a draft animal, and soon he would have been able to afford a servant. But now he had nothing left. All his efforts wasted.

His wife had cautiously asked him to join the emigrants, but he could not bring himself to move past his growing hatred and leave for a new home—not even an admittedly promising one—under the leadership of Thorolf and his whore.

He despised everything in his current life: the unworthy situation of being dependent on Digur, the offspring of a former slave woman; his pale, ugly wife who was irritatingly submissive whenever he was near; his children, forever whining, wearing on him in Digur's crammed accommodation; the loss of his house and his animals; and lastly, the painful loss of his status.

His youngest daughter was crying in the background; she just wouldn't stop. When her initial crowing intensified to a desperate screeching, he roared angrily: "Shut up!"

Britta tried her hardest to soothe her little daughter, cradling her in her arms and muttering softly to her. But none of it helped. With a frightened glance at Hafdan, she nestled her wailing daughter into the small, fur-covered bed and asked Kaja for another jug of ale for her husband.

But Hafdan had had enough. Determined to put an end to the noise, he stood up and staggered toward his daughter's bed. Roughly he picked her up and cursed, shaking her violently.

Britta threw herself on his arm and shouted, "Stop, you are hurting her! She only has a little wind."

Hafdan dropped the infant, now silent, back onto the furs, turning to his wife with hatred. "You dare lecture me?"

Brutally he slammed his fist into her face. Britta screamed and fell to the ground, where he started kicking her. He was about to kick again when arms wrapped themselves around his throat. He bit into one of the arms and freed himself from their clasp. It was Kaja, Digur's maid. Hafdan shoved her aside and ran to the door. He needed silence and fresh air to help him gain clarity over his future.

He jogged down the track to the village. In his thoughts, he was already at the tavern, where, in the company of men and with a fresh jug of ale, his thoughts would be diverted, when he spotted a female figure emerge from the fog. She was looking down and so did not notice him. Blonde hair streamed from beneath her hat. Suddenly he recognized her. It was the whore! The filthy bitch who was to blame for all his misery! The flame of anger still burning inside him grew into a fire that longed for revenge. He drew his knife.

Asla was late. She had hoped to make it home before nightfall, but the birth at which she had assisted Alfhild had been more difficult than anticipated. The mother had lost much blood, but now both she and her child seemed to have made it through the worst. Asla was looking forward to her evening with Thorolf.

The fjord lay shrouded in fog, and dusk was falling when she set off toward home. Asla strode quickly, taking the track up the hill. She held her gaze on the ground so she wouldn't trip in the fading light of day.

Suddenly, a man blocked her path. Startled, Asla looked up and screamed. She was standing opposite Hafdan, his face a grimace of fury.

Not wasting any time, he grabbed her hair and brought his knife to her neck. "Quiet, whore. If you scream again, I will cut your throat."

Asla felt the cold, menacing metal against her skin. She did not resist when the strong man yanked her away from the road and dragged her across the wintry pale grass of the hillside. Her initial surprise had turned into panic-stricken fear. He intended to kill her! Why else would he place a knife at her throat and pull her away from the track, if not to take her life at a secluded spot?

After what felt like an eternity, during which Asla tried to form a clear thought, Hafdan evidently felt there was enough distance between him and the path. He pushed the knife hard against her throat for a moment, then let go and ordered her hoarsely to lie on the ground. It seemed he wanted to rape her before killing her. She slowly did as he asked, desperately trying not to let her fear show, for her fear seemed to arouse Hafdan even more. In the last dim light of dusk, she saw him towering above her, still holding the knife in his right hand, fumbling with his clothing with his left, pulling down his pants. Then he kneeled between her legs, hastily pushing up her clothing, and lay on top of her. His knife moved worrisomely close to her throat again. When she smelled his breath, which reeked of ale and rot, she retched. Asla could not quite prevent her fingers from trembling as she felt for her own knife in its holster on her right upper thigh. Carefully she pulled it out. Thanks to the darkness and his grunting efforts to push inside her, Hafdan did not seem to notice. When she held the knife in her hand, clasping it tightly, her fear dissolved. She had this one chance—her only one.

Now, she thought, grasped his greasy hair with her left hand, and, almost in the same instant, thrust her blade into his throat with her right. She heard him groan, felt warm blood on her skin but saw nothing in the darkness. Then everything happened very fast.

All Asla could do with the weight of the body on top of her was to shift her upper body slightly to the right to bring some distance between her and his knife. She sensed the blade cut her face but felt no pain. Then, wheezing, Hafdan collapsed on top of her. Her breath came in gasps as she lay there, her thoughts muddled. She simply stayed where she was. She lacked the strength and the will to free herself from the burden and stand up.

She did not know how much time had passed when she heard Thorolf call her name. With great effort, she fought herself out of her daze.

"Here," she called out softly. Then, louder, she repeated: "Here!"

Something broke inside her, and tears streamed from her eyes, stinging in the deep gash in her cheek. She cried her pain into the world, but her tears did not take away the darkness and the terror of what she had just endured.

When darkness fell and Asla still had not returned home, Thorolf decided to look for her. He lit a torch and went on his way to

Alfhild. Asla was most likely still there, helping the old healer care for someone sick. But Alfhild shook her head in wonder, informing him that Asla had left for home some time ago.

Deeply worried, Thorolf searched both sides of the path by the light of his torch as he walked back uphill. Again and again, he called her name. In vain. Despair grew inside him as he started to fear some henchman of Halldor's had killed Asla to reap the reward of twenty sheep. But then he heard her answer. She sounded pitiful. His heart thumping heavily, he rushed in the direction of her voice.

His torch illuminated a scene that seemed unreal to him, filling him with horror and making him feel sick to his stomach. Asla was lying on the ground, holding her face with blood-smeared hands and crying uncontrollably. A man whom Thorolf guessed to be Hafdan, by his clothes and stature, was lying still atop her. Protruding from the left side of the farmer's neck was a knife.

Thorolf stared at the scene in shock. Then its meaning dawned on him, and he rammed the shaft of his torch into the ground, dragged the repulsive body off Asla, and kneeled down beside her. Gently he lifted his beloved's hands off her face. A deep cut ran from her left cheekbone to beneath her earlobe. The edges of the wound gaped apart, blood streaming from between them. He folded his arms around her and rocked her, muttering soothing words to her.

When her crying finally eased to soft sobbing, Thorolf placed one hand under her chin, lifted her face, and looked into her reddened eyes. "We must go to Alfhild. She needs to sew the wound."

Thorolf picked up his torch with his right hand, bracing Asla with his left arm. Slowly he walked her back to the path leading to the village.

"Does it look bad?" she asked feebly.

Thorolf nodded. His heart was aching.

Following a two-week return of winter that brought frost and snow, spring came back with force. The sun now spent a long part of the day above the mountains, bestowing upon the fjord its life-giving strength. Thorolf stood in the harbor, shielding his eyes with one hand from the glaring light, and watched the hustle and bustle. The seven ships that would carry the emigrants lay at anchor on the near side of the jetty on which Ulrik's two longships were moored, rocking gently on the fjord's rippled surface.

Thorolf had ordered his servants to load the knarrs with his remaining barrels of whale oil. Contentedly he watched as the thralls rolled the barrels to the shore, lugged them, gasping, through the shallow water, and finally handed them to their comrades on board the ships.

He directed his gaze to the far side of the jetty. There, Egil's seven merchant ships lay at anchor. Servants and maids busily rushed back and forth, filling the boats with cargo from the icy North. One of Egil's men had sailed there at the end of last summer, and he would do so again this year. There Egil's man had traded wine, glassware, jewelry, and high-quality weapons from the south for furs, stockfish, and walrus tusks. The latter especially fetched good prices at the markets of the south. Despite the many wares Egil had stowed in the spacious bellies of his knarrs, there was still much room left in the open cargo holds. Egil planned to fill them with the pretty blonde slave girls and strong slave men he would buy at the great market of Hedeby.

His eyes had sparkled when the cunning trader had told Thorolf that the emir of the Moors loved to surround himself with fair-haired and light-skinned people, and that he paid a fortune for them. The lord of the Moors added the most beautiful women to his harem or gifted them to influential men in his realm. The less beautiful ones were put to work in his household, while the men, following rigorous schooling and their conversion to Islam, found a place among his palace guard.

The day after tomorrow, the ships would leave the fjord and head south. Almost four hundred people had asked to sail to Catan with him, and Thorolf had been grateful for each farmer and every craftsmen who wanted to join him. Others, though, who were merely fueled by a lust for adventure, Thorolf had turned away.

Ulrik had kept a close eye on the lists of those who wished to leave, asking Yngvi to read the names to him. Thorolf was forced to cross out this tradesman or that at his father's behest, if the man in question was too significant for the future of the tribe. On the other hand, Ulrik cared little for the loss of those who owned nothing and such cowards who preferred to peacefully settle new land rather than try their luck on viking raids with him. The gaps those kinds of men left would swiftly be filled by later-born sons of freemen. In the end, just over three hundred people—including families with children, servants, and maids—had received permission to board the seven ships.

Now, during the days leading up to their departure, each person packed their belongings and purchased some last items for their journey: warm weatherproof clothing, tools, cooking utensils, crockery, seeds of healing and kitchen herbs, and other necessities for everyday life.

Asla had followed Thorolf to the harbor. At the water's edge, she spotted a pool of water on whose smooth surface she beheld her reflection. She crouched down to study her face more closely. Hafdan's assault lay three weeks back, and the old healer had done good work despite her failing eyesight. She had removed the thread not long ago, and the wound was healing well. But nonetheless, the bulging, red course of the stitched-up gash disfigured the left side of her face. The fresh scar would become paler in time and no longer be quite so noticeable, but she would have to grow accustomed to people staring at her, not for her beauty but because of her ugly mark.

Unnoticed, Thorolf had stepped up behind her. Softly, as if guessing at her thoughts, he said, "Your injury does not make you ugly, Asla. Your face is no longer without flaw, but your scar does not touch the essence of your beauty, not the magic of your wonderful eyes and not the curve of your lips. When I look at you, your scar fades and all I see is the woman I love."

She rose, turning to him. She could see that he had spoken truthfully. "I thank you for your kind words, Thorolf. I do not wish to discuss with you whether my beauty has withered or not. I have accepted the scar as part of me. It does not lessen my guilt, but it allows me to bear it more easily. My conscience has lightened and my love for you deepened." She quickly rose on her toes and kissed the dimple in his chin. Thorolf appeared surprised. Since laughing still pained her, she smiled a small smile and tugged at his earlobe. "If you don't bend down to me, your chin is my only option, since I cannot reach your mouth."

Thorolf seemed to remember the first cheeky kiss on his chin he had received from her. Gazing at her lovingly, he gladly yielded to the pull on his earlobe. Warm and soft, her lips met his.

That afternoon, Yngvi sat in his father's hall with Gregor over a round of hnefatafl. Following his first trade voyage with Thorolf, his older brother had paid him with a respectable portion in silver from the profits. Yngvi had used part of those earnings to buy the monk off his father. Since Yngvi still lived at his parents' hall, Gregor still had to work upon the estate, but now there was more time for conversations and games of hnefatafl. Yngvi loved conversing with the educated monk in Latin, learning more about the world beyond his horizon and arguing with him over questions of religion or philosophy. By now, Yngvi knew by heart the Latin storybook that Gregor called the Bible.

If asked to describe the appearance of the monk in two words, Yngvi would probably choose "short" and "wide." Even though Yngvi himself wasn't among the tallest of his people, his servant was shorter again by half a head. Gregor's face matched his round stature: sagging cheeks, bags under his eyes, a knobby nose, and a bald head that might lead people to view him as a somewhat unsightly, common man, if it weren't for his lively, intelligent eyes, and for his sharp wits and the keenness of his mind.

Yngvi shifted one of his playing pieces, and Gregor commented with a sigh, "That was not a good move. You will not bring your king to the safety of your fort that way."

Yngvi spotted his mistake. His mind wasn't in the game. Too many thoughts were keeping him busy this close to their departure. One of those thoughts concerned Gregor. Yngvi looked deep into his gray eyes. "Do you want to sail to Catan with me?"

"Why do you ask? I am your thrall, and you command me as you please. It is your decision."

"I ask you because the voyage is dangerous, and you might lose your life. I ask you as my friend and teacher, because I value you and I don't want you to follow me against your will."

Gregor tilted his head to one side, eyeing him with interest. "If I can decide freely, does that make me a freeman?"

Yngvi folded his hands under his chin, then said firmly, "If you wish it, then you are free."

The monk thought. "If I were a freeman, I would have to look after myself. After all, there are no monasteries here that might feed me and clothe me." He paused. "Of course, I could try to return to my home, but most likely, I would starve along the way or be murdered by disappointed robbers who found nothing in my pockets." Gregor rocked his head from side to side. "No, one way or the other: freedom would be synonymous with my demise. So I would rather remain your servant. And yes, I will sail to the island in the south with you. Perhaps the warmth will help dispel the aching from my bones." He smiled roguishly. "The question remains whether in truth you aren't *my* servant, forced to care for me in order to gain more education."

Yngvi laughed and embraced the monk. "We are but friends. Whenever you wish to be free, you shall be."

Gregor was pleased. He loved the bright young man like a son. He would enjoy traveling with him. He did not fear the perils of the voyage—he knew he was in God's hands.

Like many other men in the southern Northland, Digur kept several beehives from which he gained honey and wax. The wax was highly sought after by the blacksmiths. They used it to mold the shape of a weapon or another tool, then embedded the mold in clay. When the clay was baked, the wax would run off, leaving behind a hollow space that could be filled with molten bronze.

Digur and his maid, Kaja, wore hats from whose brims hung nets woven from horsehair. They were standing in front of a roughly two-foot tall, hollowed tree stump that was covered with a round piece of timber. Soft humming from inside told of the colony of bees living within. Kaja was holding a wooden stick in her hand, and attached to the stick was a smoldering pinecone. Digur lifted the round of timber and used a narrow wooden board to fan some of the smoke from the pinecone into the hive.

After they had repeated this process several times, the bees turned calmer and less aggressive. Digur reached for a honeycomb and slowly pulled it out of the trunk. He wasn't perturbed by the few stings he received in the process. He was pleased when he almost immediately found the hive's queen: a bee with a noticeably long abdomen who crawled among her workers seemingly aimlessly. Carefully he pinched her wings between his thumb and forefinger, picked her off the comb, and inserted her into a thick, hollowed-out branch which he immediately sealed with a wax plug. He did the same with some of the worker bees who hadn't stung him. Following a sting, the stinger remained stuck in the skin, and the bee was death-bound and would not be able to feed her queen with the honey Digur would be giving them in their prison.

"What will the bees do now without their queen?" asked Kaja with interest, brushing a strand of her pitch-black hair behind her ear.

Digur shrugged. "A new one is created. I do not know how. But I guess it is as with the people: if one king dies, a new one takes his place. I assume the strongest bee will prevail."

Once they had also robbed the other colonies of their queens, Digur held to his ear the seven hollow branches with their ends sealed with wax, one after the other. Satisfied, he heard the humming of one queen with her small court inside each one. Stowed thus in their narrow compartments, they would travel to Catan with him. In a rare moment of humor, he wondered in a low voice, "How many warriors can claim he's accompanied by seven queens upon his journey?"

That evening, Digur called his servants together. "Otto, you will look after my house and care for my bees. You serve my father for as long as I am in exile. If, upon my return, you have fulfilled your duties well, you will be a freeman. Should I fail to return in seven years, you are also free, and my house is yours." He bestowed Otto with a stern look. "Provided Ulrik is satisfied with your work, of course."

The prospect of being a freeman in just a few years' time lit up Otto's face, and he nodded eagerly at his master. Digur knew he could rely on the man.

"Kaja, Enno, Kilian, the three of you will travel with me. Pack your things. We are leaving tomorrow."

The maid was not surprised. Digur needed her. Whether he loved her, she did not know. But she did see a small chance in her pregnancy, which no one yet knew about. Perhaps he would take her for his wife following their arrival on Catan.

Among the emigrants, there were several freemen who had some experience on the seas with Thorolf, Egil, and the other merchants. Thorolf declared those who, in his view, were the most competent to be the skippers of the three knarrs not under the command of him or his brothers. He also assigned to the men in charge six of his servants who had accompanied him on trade voyages in the last few years and were equally experienced seamen. He promised them their freedom should they reach their destination in good health. He would take his remaining three servants and his maid, Ilka, along on the journey.

For the duration of his absence, he left his house and his

livestock to the care of Britta and her sons. Britta thanked him absently. She had recovered from the beating by her deceased husband, Hafdan, and from his demise, but not from the death of her infant daughter.

Before nightfall, Thorolf checked the ships one last time. Under Högni's instruction, servants had reinforced the floors in the open cargo space between the decks with wooden planks. There, his horses and those of his brothers would begin their journey in the morning, and later on, cattle, pigs, and sheep purchased at Hedeby would be stored there.

On the day of the departure, Digur rode to the charcoal burner's hut before sunrise to fetch Stina. The young woman greeted him with an adventurous sparkle in her eyes. Hilda had done thorough work. With a mixture of ash, coal dust, and tallow, she had dyed Stina's short hair once more and tied her ward's chest flat with a linen cloth. A loose, hooded cloak concealed the young woman's feminine figure. The trousers and leg wraps of the dead charcoal burner completed her disguise as a young lad. She would have to wear this getup until they parted ways with Egil. The merchant knew Stina, and the brothers did not wish to cause trouble for their father should Egil let slip and Halldor learn that Stina, too, had harbored in Ulrik's realm.

Digur looked at Hilda, who was stepping nervously from one foot to the other in her hut, standing between two traveling sacks. At last she came out with what was evidently on her mind. "Please, Digur, take me with you. I cannot bear it here any longer. I would rather die aboard your ships than spend my life in these lonely woods."

Digur shook his head. "We cannot take an experienced charcoal burner away from our father. You have to understand."

A tear ran down Hilda's cheek. But she wasn't about to give up. "Your servant has learned everything there is to know about charcoal making. He can replace me."

Stina planted herself next to Hilda and wrapped an arm around her waist. "Hilda has become a dear friend to me. I won't go without her. She could claim that I'm the son of her late sister."

Digur gave a resigned sigh. He could not oppose Stina's wish. "Very well, then both of you will come. Pack up your things, Hilda. Hurry! I will have to bring you on board together with the first families so that you don't stand out."

Hilda smiled. "I'm all packed."

The servant Digur had lent to Hilda was sleeping inside a small shack he had built following his arrival at Hilda's. He heated his little shack with a coal pan. Digur woke the man and explained that he was now free and responsible for the tribe's charcoal. The newly appointed charcoal burner grinned in happy surprise.

The emigrants streamed toward the harbor, laden heavily with their luggage. Servants loaded the knarrs with enough food provisions and barrels of water for ten days at sea. Yngvi and Gregor used the wax tablets to ensure those climbing aboard the ships were entitled to do so. Hilda's name wasn't upon them, but, exchanging a glance with Digur, Yngvi waved the charcoal burner's wife, Stina, and Loki on his leash through the barrier.

The three skippers appointed by Thorolf proudly welcomed their passengers, who found themselves a free spot on one of the two decks.

While Stina sat quietly in a spot in the stern, Asla and Hilda stood by the *Goldeagle*'s railing and watched the boarding of the last few families. Asla had taken her farewell from Isold and Gudrun earlier that morning. When she had thanked the latter and Ulrik for their hospitality, Gudrun had embraced her and wished her luck and the goodwill of the gods in her marriage with Thorolf. Ulrik had merely given a curt nod and then proceeded to ignore her.

Once all the travelers were on board, servants led the brothers' horses to the knarrs. The animals were accustomed to sea voyages and willingly stepped down planks into the lower open cargo holds between the decks.

Ulrik had come down to the harbor, along with Gudrun, Isold, and Erik, to wish his sons farewell. At the beginning of his brief speech, his voice sounded commanding and firm as always. "In seven years' time, I want to see you back here. Your settlement upon the isle in the south will not prevent you from continuing your trade voyages. I expect that you will return as wealthy merchants." He winked at his sons. "If you don't, I will come to fetch you."

Ulrik was not the sentimental kind, but during his last words, his voice had sounded a little unsteady, as if he doubted he would ever see his sons again.

Gudrun kissed her stepsons, Thorolf and Digur, on their cheeks in farewell. When her slender hands clasped Yngvi's face, her eyes gleamed wet. "Come back healthy, Yngvi." She folded him into her arms and held him tight. Then she let go abruptly, grasped Erik, who looked dejected, by the hand, and walked up the path to the village without turning back. Isold waved to her brothers one last time before trotting after her mother with her head hung.

Ulrik said goodbye to each of his sons, his face and eyes

filled with equal parts love and grief. Then he turned without another word and followed his family.

The brothers exchanged a stricken look. Never before had their father gazed at them thus; never before had he permitted himself the weakness of letting his emotions show.

They were the last to board their knarrs. The helmsmen ordered the anchor stones lifted, and experienced sailors rowed the ships a little distance away from the shallow shore. Each boat possessed four pairs of oars which served to move the ships when there was no wind and to maneuver them in tight spots. One after the other, the crews set the colorful sails. Egil's *Seaserpent* was the first to pick up speed, followed by Thorolf's *Goldeagle*, Digur's *Spearhead*, and Yngvi's *Shieldmaiden*. Soon all fourteen ships of the fleet were moving, heading toward the neck in the fjord. A fresh breeze from the west forced the crews to sail close to the wind.

The passengers gazed back at their old home, waving to the many people who had gathered in the harbor for the occasion. It was not a merry departure, and few people smiled. Most looked pensive. They knew the voyage ahead was a dangerous one. In their faith in a better future, they entrusted their fate to the capricious sea, hoping Thor, the god of the weather and seafarers, would be kindly inclined toward them and safely lead them to their new home.

PART 3
AT SEA

(EARLY SUMMER, AD 860)

CHAPTER 7
CARLA

The sun sent its last rays across the mostly reed-thatched roofs of the large trade center of Hedeby, painting them in warm, golden hues.

Carla hid between empty ale barrels the innkeeper had stacked up outside his tavern. She was so skinny that she had no trouble slipping between the wooden bellies and cowering in their tight midst. Through the narrow gap between the barrels, she had an excellent view of the area in front of the tavern and its entrance. Her filthy dark-brown smock, her short-cropped dark curls, and her soot-stained face concealed her even in broad daylight from passersby who happened to glance in her direction. Once night fell, she would be invisible.

Next to the tavern, quite close to her, there was a loud buzzing. An army of flies occupied a pile of trash and dung which the tavernkeeper added to every morning. A slight breeze wafted the pungent stench of rot up Carla's nose, but it did not bother her much. Inside this city, it always stank. Fumes from the waste heaps mixed with smoke from cooking fires as well as the feces and urine that people left behind in dark corners among the wooden houses and huts.

Sometimes, when a steady breeze blew from the North Sea, Carla sneaked to the western gate, which stood open during the day to let in visitors, merchants, and farmers. Then she would close her eyes and drink in the fresh sea air streaming through the gates, dreaming she would rise up with the wind as a bird does and escape the glum, stinking alleys where she spent her poor existence. Where the wind was supposed to carry her, she did not know. At least there was a dry place for her to sleep in the small shack at the edge of town and occasionally something to eat. The shack belonged to "the mother," as the burly, buxom woman called herself who had plucked Carla and her brother from the gutter nine years ago.

Carla only ever thought of the mother with fear and disgust. She feared the beatings she would receive at night if she came home empty-handed, and she was filled with disgust at the thought of the men, reeking of sweat and ale, who visited the mother during the night.

If she wanted to escape a beating from the hard-hearted woman this evening, and if she didn't want to go to bed hungry, she would have to deliver, had to find a victim that would make for an easy target and wouldn't cost her a hand. Sheer will to live and the fate of her brother had taught her to proceed strategically, to leave nothing to chance, and to avoid unnecessary risks.

This evening, she'd select her victim from the tavern patrons. She would observe each man who entered the pub, studying their habits as best as she might. When and how frequently did he step out to relieve himself? How long did it take him? How quickly was he getting drunk? Would his clothing prove to be an obstacle in her endeavor?

Dimly, Carla remembered happier days, when her parents

were still alive and she and her brother never once went to bed hungry. Carla often longed for the gentle words and hands of her real mother, caressing her, instead of hitting her.

Her parents had been merchants from a town in Frankia whose name she had forgotten. One spring nine years ago, Carla and her family had traveled to Hedeby, the city that would become their downfall. Soon after their arrival, a fever broke out that took the lives of many—including her parents. She and her brother, who was two years older than her, were spared as if by some miracle. The innkeeper's wife had no mercy. Once she'd discarded the parents' corpses, she placed a piece of bread each in Carla's and her brother's hands and showed them the door. The parents' valuable wares, their cart, and their draft horse the woman kept for herself.

For days Carla and her brother had roamed the city hungrily. They found no help anywhere, either because no one understood their language or because nobody gave a damn about two dirty brats. A few times, they received a piece of bread or some small coins from a merchant's wife who took pity on them while striding past in her elegant clothes along the wooden planks that lined the dirty alleys.

And then they were found by "the mother," as she called herself, even though she had no children. She took them into her shack and served them a decent meal. In the beginning, she had treated them kindly, patiently teaching them the art of purse-cutting. She showed Carla's brother how, using a sharp knife, to cut the coin pouch off a wealthy merchant and instructed them how to distract the potential victim. Carla remembered the lesson well. "They all have sad faces, those begging urchins in the gutter. You must be able to cry heart-rendingly if you want to stand out. And if that alone doesn't work, you cling to your victim."

Again and again, the mother had corrected Carla's put-on wailing: "too quiet," "too loud," "too unnatural," "too shrill." It had taken some time until the mother had been satisfied and sent Carla and her brother out thieving. Back then Carla was a pretty, well-nourished little girl who easily drew the attention of a merchant when, with her big dark eyes and her head of brown curls, she suddenly appeared in front of him, sitting on the ground, crying pitifully like the mother had taught her. While the merchant bent down to check on her or tried to pry her off his leg, her brother would deftly cut the purse off the man's belt. Sometimes, those purses would hold many coins and silver; other times, they would not. Following each successful theft, the mother rewarded them with a plentiful meal.

This went well for three years. Until the day they tried to rob the wrong man. Word of their scam had gone around, and the merchants were warned. One day, a merchant leaned down to her, the wailing girl, and in the same instant, he reached at his side and grasped the wrist of her brother who was fiddling with the man's purse. The merchant took him to the city guards. There, they chopped off the thief's hand and poorly sewed up the wound. Ten days later, her brother died from his infected stump. He was only twelve.

Carla shuddered when she thought of the time that followed. For two days, she had cried in her bed, grieving, and the mother had left her in peace. But on the third day, she demanded Carla go back to work. When she refused, the mother thrashed her with a stick until Carla was glad to get out of the miserable shack.

Carla sighed. Since then, she fought the daily battle to survive by herself.

The tavern was well frequented that evening. Carla observed five men who approached the tavern door, busily conversing and laughing: there was a giant with dark skin and black curls; two good-looking fellows—one tall, dark, and strong and the other shorter, blond, and wiry; one well-dressed, evidently wealthy merchant whose weather-beaten face spoke of experience; and lastly, a solidly built man with coarse features and a tousled head of hair. The last man wore no cloak, and the two pouches he carried on his belt bounced with each step. He looked as though he liked his ale. Of the five men, he would be the easiest target, and on his third or fourth visit outside the door, one of his pouches would be ripe for her sharp knife.

Digur was forced to duck under the low doorframe when he entered the pub. For a moment, the loud babel of voices ebbed off. The patrons' curious eyes followed the hulking man, easily recognized as an experienced warrior, on his way to an empty table. The four men behind him aroused less attention; in the wake of the giant, they appeared common. The tavernkeeper scurried over to his latest guests, who had lowered themselves upon the rough-hewn benches made from half logs.

"Two jugs of ale, and a decent portion of your delicious roast for each of us." Egil gestured at the crispy piglet a maid slowly turned on a spit above one of the two fireplaces. Every now and then, fat dripped into the flames with a hiss, infusing the stale, smoky air inside the tavern with the irresistible smell of roast pork.

Yngvi groaned theatrically, holding his rumbling stomach. "After all the dried fish and porridge of the last few days, this piglet strikes me as a gift from the gods."

Laughing, Thorolf gave him a slap on the shoulder. "That's what it is, brother. I, too, can hardly wait to get something decent between my teeth."

Digur, Högni, and Egil nodded their agreement.

Once the man had brought the ale, they filled their cups, and Thorolf raised his. "To Hedeby! May our journey continue as smoothly!" Cheerfully the companions raised their cups to one another.

The day before, after only ten days at sea, thanks to favorable winds, their fleet had reached the mouth of the narrow river that led inland to a harbor west of the large trade metropolis of Hedeby. There they had anchored, paid a mooring fee for two weeks to the guards of the lord steward, and set up camp in a field.

That morning, Thorolf and Egil had hired several oxcarts. The servants of the emigrants loaded Thorolf's carts with all the barrels of whale oil save for two which he intended to take to their new home. Egil's men carried the crates of stockfish and soapstone from his knarrs, lugging them to the carts. Egil left behind the furs, iron ingots, and walrus tusks, which would fetch higher prices in the land of the Moors than in this northern market center. Egil assigned the watch of the fleet to his son, Finnur, and thirty of his warriors.

The drive on the bumpy trade route took only half a day. On their way, they encountered mounted guards of the lord steward, whose task it was to put a stop to thieves and highwaymen and to keep the peace in Hedeby and its surroundings. Egil, Thorolf, and the others did not fear an attack. They were well-armed, and several battle-hardened warriors accompanied them.

Inside the city, Thorolf and Egil rented a countinghouse that would serve them as both accommodation and storage for the next two weeks. Then, with the help of their servants, they unloaded their wares and stored them there. Now, at the end of the day and filled with the feeling they had earned it, they had made for the tavern.

At last the tavernkeeper brought them five wooden boards

with large portions of roast pork and bread. The companions drew their knives and with relish tucked into the meal of juicy, flavorful meat.

By now, every last table in the tavern was filled, and the volume of ale-fueled conversations had risen to deafening levels. Yngvi was forced to shout when he tried to tell a joke. Fragments of speech from a variety of lands reached their ears. Laughing, debating, and arguing at the tables were traveling merchants from the eastern caliphate, dressed in costly garments; rough traders from the North; and elegant merchants from Frankia and Italy.

In the general noise and following his third jug of ale, even the ever-cautious and distrustful Egil failed to notice the three figures clad in hooded cloaks who had sat down at the neighboring table. He did not notice how they furtively studied him and his companions from under their low-hanging hoods, whispering to one another.

Yngvi shoved the last piece of meat into his mouth, chewed briefly, and washed it down with ale. Then he stood up, muttering "Be right back," and strode quickly to the door. Unnoticed, the three hooded men rose from their benches and followed him.

Night had fallen. To help guests find their way to the tavern, the owner had lit oil lamps on two empty barrels to the left and right of the entrance.

Carla was disappointed. Her victim of choice had only stepped outside once so far, pissing against the side of the tavern. He had not swayed and seemed to be in full command of his wits. None of the other guests who had come outside to relieve their urges had seemed ripe for the picking, either. She had to practice patience.

The next person to step outside was the wiry young blond man who had arrived together with the giant. Deciding against the stinking tavern wall, the blond man walked straight toward her. Two figures in hooded cloaks followed him. A third one extinguished the lamps outside the door. With a sigh, the blond one pulled down his trousers and aimed directly into the gap between the two barrels that Carla used as a spyhole. She almost cussed out loud when the steaming spurt brushed her smock. She pressed to the left as far as her constricted hiding place allowed, trying to evade the unwelcome wet.

She could hear footsteps and some muttered words, followed by a dull thud. The stream that had been splattering through the gap broke off abruptly. Carla shifted back to the right and peered through the barrels.

One of the two hooded men was holding the blond one, whose head hung down limply, with both hands under the armpits while the second man pulled a sack over his head. In the dim light, she saw the third hooded man slink back into the tavern, pulling the door shut behind him.

The taller and broader one of the two men wiped his forehead with his sleeve, causing his hood to slide back a little. In the pale light of the moon, Carla caught a glimpse of his profile. She thought she had seen him before. Had he not lain with the mother and afterward refused to pay her? She remembered the hue and cry when the mother, wildly waving a broomstick, chased him out of the shack.

The man crouched down, hoisted the sack with the lifeless body onto his shoulder, and, groaning quietly, straightened up. He trudged off with his heavy load on his back. His shorter companion scuttled after him.

Carla did not hesitate for long. She snaked out of her hiding place and followed them. Her bare feet made no sound as she placed each careful step, and her body became a shadow in the dark. The night was her friend. If she did not want to be seen, she became as one with it. Maybe, she thought, this night would steer her fate into a different direction. Which one, she scarcely cared.

"Where's he got to?" Thorolf looked at the door when it opened. It wasn't Yngvi returning from outside, but instead someone leaving, someone dressed in a hooded cloak.

"I'll go check," grumbled Digur, and rose.

Just then, one of the tavern maids came to their table. Her face was reddened with agitation. "I have a message for you," she stammered.

The hands of the plump older woman trembled. Evidently, she was afraid of misconstruing the message she'd been charged with passing on, and she seemed frightened of the reaction of the giant who was glaring at her with his piercing blue eyes. Eventually she pulled herself together and handed Thorolf, who seemed to strike her as the least intimidating of the men, a large, empty leather pouch. "I am supposed to tell you: if you want your friend to live, then fill this pouch with silver and hand it to a boy who will wait for you tomorrow morning after sunrise outside the tavern. The boy will carry the bronze arm ring of your friend. I must also tell you that the boy is just a messenger. He does not know where your friend is being held. Should you harass him or follow him, your friend will die."

The maid cried out with pain when Digur grasped her hard by her arm. "Are you in league with that riffraff?"

The woman burst out in tears. "No, the man said he would kill me if I didn't pass on the message. What was I supposed to do?" she cried desperately.

Realizing that the maid was but a victim also, Digur dropped her arm.

"What did the man who gave you the message look like?" asked Thorolf.

"He wore a cloak with a hood—like many other men. He kept his face concealed. I think he had a black beard."

Thorolf remembered the figure with the hood who had left the tavern just a few moments ago. He told his companions. "Let us take a look around outside."

Egil paid their tab and followed the others outside. The area in front of the tavern lay in the dark, and the outlines of the neighboring houses and huts barely stood out from the murky sky. Only a handful of stars and the three-quarter moon had enough strength to push a little light through the hazy clouds. Thorolf carried the two oil lamps from the barrels back inside to light them, and then they searched for any traces in the tavern's surroundings but found no hints as to Yngvi's whereabouts.

They were standing together helplessly when, out of nowhere, a gaunt, dirty figure appeared next to Thorolf, tugging at his coat. The small person addressed him with words he did not understand.

"What do you want? Do you speak our language?"

The figure nodded and replied: "Your friend was struck down and carried away. I know where they are keeping him."

Digur grabbed the figure roughly by their shirt with one of his huge hands. "Then spit it out, lad!"

Thorolf held the oil lamp closer to the boy. Big, dark eyes with long eyelashes stared at him anxiously from a soot-stained face with hollow cheeks. Despite Digur's harsh treatment, the bright voice declared firmly, "I will tell you—on one condition."

Digur narrowed his eyes, lifted the boy off the ground a little, and shook him like a rat. "You don't pose any conditions, lad! Either you tell us where he is right now or else I will beat it out of you."

Digur raised his right fist, ready to strike, when Thorolf placed a hand on his arm. "Leave it be. If I am not mistaken, you are about to strike a girl."

Startled, Digur dropped his victim like a piece of hot coal.

Thorolf bent down to her. "My name is Thorolf. The big one is my brother, just like Yngvi, the one who was abducted. What's your name?"

She wrinkled her forehead and hesitated a moment before replying: "Carla."

She probably struggled to believe that the tall, dark-skinned Digur was his and Yngvi's brother. She wasn't the first one to doubt it.

"What do you want, Carla?"

"I want to come with you when you leave town."

Thorolf was surprised. He had expected to be asked for coins, as he was accustomed to from the countless small thieves and beggars roaming the dirty alleys of the city. Never in all the years that he had been visiting Hedeby had one of those lost children approached him with the plea to join him.

He did not at all see why he should feed some filthy girl from Hedeby's gutter on his voyage, and so he replied sharply: "We will give you a few coins if you help us, or a good thrashing if you don't." Thorolf nodded in the direction of grim-looking Digur. "Consider carefully whether you really want to anger me and my brother."

Thorolf thought then the girl would relent and agree to the coins, but instead her skinny body came alive. Egil, however, had preempted her intentions and managed to clasp her by the arm before she managed to run off. Carla squirmed under his tight grip, but finally stopped resisting when Egil grabbed her bony arm harder still. Thorolf held up the lamp to her face once more.

Egil noticed how she glanced nervously at Digur, and he spoke to her in a calm voice. "You speak our Nordic language, and yet it is not your mother tongue. What was the language you grew up with?"

"Frankish," she replied with a shaky voice.

"Do you speak any other languages?"

Carla, who had grown up in the streets of a city where scoundrels, thieves, and cutthroats from many different countries competed for booty, had inevitably learned their languages in order to survive among them. Haltingly, she replied: "Yes. Danish, Anglo-Saxon, and a little Frisian."

"And your parents? Won't they miss you?"

Carla shook her head. "My parents have been dead for many years. Where I live, only the silver I take from careless merchants will be missed."

Egil looked at his companions. "Her knowledge of languages could be of use for us during our business transactions. If I claim that she is my daughter, she can attend negotiations and learn what our partners secretly discuss in their mother tongues."

Carla, evidently glimpsing a glimmer of hope on the horizon, reached into her bag and produced a purse filled with hacksilver, which she held out to Högni. "Languages isn't all I know."

"What are you giving this to me for? Are you trying to bribe me?"

"It's yours."

Högni fingered his belt and found to his astonishment that one of his two pouches was missing. Egil laughed wholeheartedly into the night. Digur and Thorolf also thought the situation was amusing, but their concern for Yngvi stifled their laughter.

Thorolf raised an eyebrow at his companions. Digur eyed

Carla distrustfully and said nothing, but Egil and Högni nodded.

"Very well, Carla," Thorolf said. "You seem to be an unusual girl. We will take you with us, provided you lead us to our brother and we find him alive and well."

Carla gave him a questioning look. "Can I trust you?"

"I give you my word. That will have to be enough for you."

Carla led the men to the edge of town. The houses became increasingly impoverished and run-down, and the lanes, no longer lined with planks, were muddy and covered in puddles. She knew this part of town well. The mother's shack wasn't far from here. While she led the way in her bare feet, light-footed and scarcely making a sound, the men trudged after her with heavy footfall, their boots creating smacking sounds in the mud. Dogs barked and growled from the backyards of the houses.

She stopped by the corner of one house, pointed at a hut diagonally opposite on an intersecting lane, and whispered at Thorolf: "That is where they took your brother."

Thorolf studied the hut. The gable ends of the entire row of houses were connected by timber fences as tall as a man, preventing him from seeing what lay beyond.

"Most of the huts have a back door," Carla told him. "If you want to catch the men who took your brother, you'll have to secure it."

Thorolf nodded. "Then let's do that. Lead Högni to the backyard. Digur, Egil, and I will storm the entrance."

Carla shook her head. "The dogs will bark and warn their owners if you go anywhere near the back. If those men see you, they will put a knife to your brother's throat and use him to force their escape."

The men exchanged puzzled looks.

Carla turned to Digur and held out her hand. "Give me your cloak."

"What do you want with it?"

"To save your brother. Trust me."

Carla led Högni into the lane behind the huts and pointed out the backyard of the one where Yngvi was being held captive. "Wait until you hear the hoot of an owl three times in a row. Then throw stones at the dog. But don't let anyone see you."

Back with the others, she explained her plan to Thorolf, Digur, and Egil. Digur lifted her onto his shoulders. Then she imitated the call of the nocturnal bird before pulling herself onto the roof. Clearly, Högni had heard her signal, because the furious barking of a dog tied up in the backyard drowned out any noise Carla made as she climbed to the ridge of the roof. Some of the wooden rooftiles were rotten and slippery, forcing her to proceed with great caution. The hut's back door was opened and closed again shortly thereafter—one of the occupants appearing to make sure the dog was merely barking at some brazen cat or another noise that represented no danger.

Carla reached the vent in the roof, took Digur's cloak off her shoulder, and used it to cover the hole, thus blocking the smoke's way out. Carefully she crawled along the ridge to the rear gable end of the hut. The dog noticed her and jumped up against the hut wall, barking angrily. Now all she could do was wait.

Soon the men inside began to cough, and one of them tore open the back door. When he followed the dog's bloodthirsty gaze upward and spotted Carla upon the ridge, she jeered at him: "Kind regards from the mother!" Then she withdrew from the edge.

Carla heard the man shout to his companions inside the hut in Frisian: "There's a boy on our roof who has blocked our vent. Go to the front and catch him." Then he made to climb the roof himself while Carla carefully balanced back to the front end of the hut.

Suddenly everything happened very quickly. The front door was unlocked and pushed open. A tall, strongly built man stepped outside.

Digur, hiding with Thorolf and Egil behind the open door, shoved his sword into the rogue's back. This wasn't how he would normally choose to fight, but the life of his brother weighed heavier than the law of decency and honor.

As he pulled his sword from his victim's body, Thorolf and Egil stormed past the dying man into the hut, which was dimly lit by tallow lamps. The back door stood open, and they arrived just in the nick of time. Before the second rogue managed to throw himself with his knife onto Yngvi, who was lying on the ground, Thorolf sank the blade of his sword into his neck. Blood spurted everywhere as the man sank to the ground, gargling.

The hulking dog in the backyard pulled at its chain, blocking the rear exit. Its yapping sounded murderous, and white froth dropped off its jowls. When Egil raised his sword and ended the beast's life, he saw from the corner of his eye a large figure leap off the roof and run away.

Thorolf bent down to Yngvi and pressed an ear to his chest. "He lives!" he declared, relieved. He felt his brother's head and found a substantial bump. "His head has suffered."

"We should take him to Asla," suggested Digur.

Thorolf nodded.

Högni came in the back door, stepping over the dead dog. "One of the scoundrels tried to flee and ran straight into my sword. He must have overlooked it," he observed drily.

Digur picked up a bench and kicked off its legs.

Carla, having climbed down from the roof, held out his sooty cloak. “For his head.”

Digur gave her a thin smile. His gaze was a lot friendlier than earlier. She smiled back, obviously finding the big man a lot less intimidating now.

Gently Thorolf and Digur bedded their unconscious brother on the bench, placing the cloak beneath his neck. Egil and Högni searched the hut and found a chest that contained a few silver coins and some hacksilver.

“This should be enough to buy you some clean clothing, Carla. As my daughter, you can hardly accompany me in your dirty old shift,” Egil said. “Besides—where are you?”

“Here!” replied Carla with a full mouth. She had lifted the pot from its hook and cowered down behind the hearth with it. With a wooden spoon, she scraped the remnants of a stew from the metal vessel.

Digur and Thorolf lifted the bench with Yngvi and carried it out of the hut. Egil and Högni followed, and eventually Carla, too, casting one last hungry glance at the meager remains inside the pot.

Doors that had stood open a crack were quickly closed and barred. The neighbors had not failed to notice the clamor in the villains’ hut, but in this quarter, folk did not look out for one another. Each one was just pleased when trouble kept away from their own doorstep. Ignoring the nosy looks, Thorolf and Digur carried the unconscious Yngvi through the empty lanes to the countinghouse where Egil and Högni would spend the night. By the light of torches, the brothers hitched an ox to a cart, laid Yngvi atop the cart, and set off.

During the bumpy ride, Carla held the head of the unconscious man in her lap to shield it from the jolts. When the first light of day brightened the horizon, she was able to study his face more closely. She liked what she saw. She traced the outlines of his pale countenance with one finger. His face reminded her of her dead brother.

She gave a start when Yngvi suddenly opened his eyes, staring straight into hers. A few moments later, he closed them again, tilted his head to one side, and vomited. *He feels sick,* thought Carla. Probably because of the blow to his head—she had experienced something similar a few years ago. An urchin boy had thumped her on the head with his cudgel to rob her of her few stolen coins. Afterward, she had felt dizzy for days and vomited often. She studied her smelly, soiled smock, hoping the stench of her wouldn't worsen Yngvi's nausea.

She sighed. Finally her ardent wish to escape the filthy city was coming true. But she wasn't filled with happiness, for she did not know what the future held for her. Would the family of the brothers take her in and treat her well? Or would Thorolf put her in chains and sell her as a slave? She did not seriously believe the Northman would break his word, but her experiences at Hedeby had taught her that trust did not get her far in the fight for survival. Still, whatever the future brought, one thing she knew for certain: she would never go back to the mother.

When Asla returned from her morning wash by the river to the tent she shared with Stina and Hilda, erected from wooden poles and skins, Loki came running toward her with a dead young hare in his mouth. He dropped it by her feet and sat on his haunches. Panting, he gazed up at her, asking for praise.

Asla smiled and patted the successful hunter's head. "Well done, Loki. Your kill arrives in perfect time for Hilda's broth."

Barking happily, the dog raced back to his hunting grounds.

Asla was hanging a pot above the fire when she spotted Digur and Thorolf marching toward her. Between them they carried a plank holding the lifeless body of Yngvi. A gaunt figure wearing a filthy and ragged shift slunk along behind them.

Asla clasped a hand to her mouth. "What happened?"

"Much," said Thorolf, nodding at Stina and Hilda, who had emerged from the tent. "I'll explain everything later. First, look after Yngvi. He was struck down and has been unconscious ever since."

"Has he thrown up?" asked Asla, worried.

"Once. On the way here," replied a thin voice.

Asla looked at the emaciated, hollow-cheeked person next to Digur who was studying her with great interest from dark, round eyes. "And who are you?"

"This is Carla," said Thorolf with a smile. "She saved Yngvi's life."

"I see," said Asla, taking a closer look at the skinny girl with short-cropped hair. She seemed to feel ill at ease in this strange environment, nervously glancing this way and that, as if she feared something might happen at any moment that would force her to flee.

The girl scratched her head and then her arm. "I'm hungry."

Asla sighed. Carla appeared to be covered in vermin. "First, we'll wash you and rid you of your fleas as best as we can. Then, you'll get something to eat. Hilda, will you take care of her?" She turned to her sister. "We'd better burn Carla's dress. Please help her out with some clothes of yours. We will buy more at Hedeby."

Stina fetched a piece of soap, a sponge, an undergarment, and a tunic from her luggage. Before handing everything to

Hilda, she sniffed at the soap with longing. The fat mixed with coal dust that Hilda had used to color her hair black exuded an unpleasant, increasingly rancid smell. As soon as they left Hedeby, she decided, she would bathe in the sea at their very next stop on land and abandon her disguise.

While the charcoal burner woman led Carla to the river's edge, Asla examined Yngvi carefully. Speaking to Thorolf and Digur, she said: "There isn't much I can do for him, unfortunately. The blow took his consciousness. We must wait for him to wake up and watch that he does not suffocate when he vomits. When you carry him into the tent, place him on his side. I'll look after him."

Once Hilda had helped Carla to wash in the river, she prepared the first meal of the day. Hilda and Ilka chopped dried whale meat into small pieces, skinned Loki's hare, and gutted it. Then, they tossed everything into the boiling water in the pot. Last, Hilda added salt and herbs that she had collected the day before.

Outside the tent of Högni and his family, Kaja was mixing a dough from rye flour, barley, salt, and ground birch bark. She divided it into several portions. Digur's mouth watered when she fried the flatbreads in a large pan with some fat, the smell of baking wafting to his nose. He liked his maid's bread. He gazed at her from the side.

Kaja had told him that she carried his child, but Digur had not been particularly touched by her revelation. A freeman could have many bastards, and their child would not be the first one fathered by him. He valued Kaja as someone to warm his bed, but he did not love her and nor would he ever consider taking her for his wife. When he told her as much, she had clearly been disappointed but merely nodded in reply.

The sun had not yet reached its highest point when the emigrants sat down outside their tents to eat. With a smile, Hilda filled the wooden bowls with her hearty soup. Diara, too, was in good spirits as she handed out Kaja's freshly made flatbreads. The maids and servants collected their portions and sat down off to the side. It was a warm spring day, causing the birds in the area to sing zealously in their search for a partner and lifting the mood of all those encamped on the field.

The travelers slurped their broth with obvious relish, scooping up the pieces of meat swimming in their bowls. Carla was especially engrossed in her meal. She ate as if nothing existed in the world aside from her bowl and her spoon.

Hilda was appalled by how skinny the girl was. Bones and joints were sticking out sharply on Carla's arms and legs. She urgently needed a little more flesh on her ribs. At least she now wore clean clothing, and her skin was rosy from the sponge Hilda had used to scrub Carla in the cold waters of the river. The charcoal burner woman decided to take the girl under her wing.

With a small sigh, she glanced at the tent inside which Yngvi lay asleep. He would surely have praised her cooking skills with some kind words. Gregor was visiting him at the moment. He was terribly worried about his master's state. Like the monk, Hilda too hoped the kind and cheerful young man would feel better soon. At least he had woken up once thus far, uttering a few muddled words before going back to sleep. Asla said his head needed rest. In a few days' time, he would be back to his old self.

CHAPTER 8
FRIDA

The slave market was situated in Hedeby's port, which was directly connected with the sea in the east through a fjord. When the travelers arrived, the market had been almost completely sold out. Merely a handful of older or ailing slaves had been offered up for sale at brazen prices by their owners. Egil knew this would change with the influx of raiding parties who hadn't made it to Hedeby in time during the fall; instead, they were taking up winter quarters on some benign coast. In the summer and fall, thousands of people would be offered up for sale here.

Only four days following their arrival at the trade center, five ships berthed in the harbor. They belonged to Varangians—Vikings whose longships traveled the rivers of the east. Whenever the Slavs inhabiting the banks of those rivers appeared capable of defending themselves, the Varangians traded with them; if they appeared weak, however, the raiders looted their homes and enslaved them. Such had been the fate of the hundred or so Slavs the Varangians were leading from their boats now. Their ankles bound with iron rings and short chains, the slaves were forced to hobble in small steps.

At this time of the year, only a few traders were interested in slaves at Hedeby, so Egil was able to study the human ware in peace, having brought along four of his men and Carla. He inspected the teeth of the men and women and examined their skin for eczema or other signs of disease. In the end, he decided on eighteen male and female slaves who would satisfy the emir's requirements. Arduous negotiations ensued. The average female slave cost roughly the equivalent of two cows, while a male slave's worth corresponded with three cows. Egil, who had picked the most beautiful women and the strongest men, was forced to pay a great deal more.

Egil had asked Carla to accompany him. The previous day, she had done him a great service when she saved him from being cheated by a Frankish merchant. The Frank, unaware that Carla spoke his language, had murmured to his assistant that Egil's soapstone was of such high quality that he would even pay twice as much for it. Today, though, she had not been able to be of help to Egil since he coped well with the northern tongue of the Varangians.

Carla kept glancing nervously about, keeping a lookout for street children who knew her and who might tell the mother where she was. She was grateful for the hooded coat Asla had lent her, which shielded her relatively well from unwelcome looks. She reassured herself that, should she indeed be discovered, she would be safe in the care of Egil and his followers.

Carla watched the slaves Egil had purchased. She had often visited the slave market in order to reap silver off careless traders amid the hustle and bustle. Therefore, she was used to the sight of the sad-looking people, staring apathetically into space. And yet pity overcame her every time, as it did today. Where would fate take these slaves? If they were fortunate, they would be bought by a master who treated them decently. If they were unlucky, they would end up in households where they'd get beaten, whipped, and, in the worst case, killed like mangy dogs. The life of thralls was worth only as much as their price of purchase. A freeman who killed a slave need not fear punishment.

Carla sighed. While she had never been a slave in the true sense of the word, the mother had treated her as one. Worse: while thralls usually received regular meals and decent clothing, Carla had sometimes lived for days off scraps she found in trash heaps if she'd failed to deliver enough silver. Her real mother had often told Carla about Jesus, and Carla now felt deeply thankful to him for leading her to people who—despite their initial reservations—appeared to be kindly inclined toward her and among whom Carla felt increasingly comfortable.

Once Egil had reached an agreement with his business partners, he ordered his men to take his newly purchased slaves to their camp by the inland harbor. Carla, who was permitted to return to camp with them, looked forward to being reunited with Asla and especially Hilda, whose motherly care she anticipated with great excitement.

While Egil was occupied with the purchase of his slaves, Thorolf and Digur had visited various traders to offer them barrels of whale oil. There was too much oil for a single merchant to afford the lot, but eventually they found sufficient traders willing to buy one or several barrels of the liquid gold for an acceptable amount of silver.

Thorolf came to terms with some farmers from the surrounding area over livestock and grain. He paid deposits for ten cows, two bulls, twenty sheep, ten pigs, thirty chickens, and two sacks each of rye, barley, and oats. The farmers agreed to deliver the grain sewn into waterproof skins. The livestock, its feed, and the grain would be handed over one day before departure, on which occasion the farmers would receive the balance of the purchase price.

On the fifth day after his abduction, Yngvi awoke for the first time with a clear mind. His head ached, and the last thing he remembered was the delicious roast pork he had devoured hungrily. What happened afterward lay concealed behind a gray wall of fog. He looked around. He was lying inside a square tent, and raindrops pattered against the walls sewn together of animal hides. Sitting in a corner of the tent were Asla, Stina, and Hilda, chatting in low voices. Next to them he made out Loki, who was sleeping, and a person he did not know. In the flickering light of the oil lamp, she seemed awfully skinny. He cleared his throat.

Immediately, all eyes turned to him. Trying to focus on his most pressing urges, he uttered, "I am thirsty and hungry," and the women's expressions lit up.

Asla rose with a smile. "At last, you're awake. We were starting to think you enjoyed our care so much that you would never wake again."

Yngvi moved one hand under the blanket and gave a start. He was completely naked.

"Who . . .?" he asked, embarrassed.

"I did," replied Hilda with amusement. "Don't fret—I am quite familiar with the build of a man's body."

Yngvi nodded resignedly. Carefully, he propped himself up and looked at the haggard girl who was gazing at him evenly.

"This is Carla," answered Asla in her stead. "Without her, you would probably be dead."

Stina, in the meantime, had fetched flatbread and dried fish from a storage chest, handing both to him with a smile, along with a cup of water. "Enjoy, Yngvi. I am so pleased that you feel better."

With a grateful nod at Stina, Yngvi drank a long sip of water and sank his teeth into the bread.

"Eat slowly, Yngvi," warned Asla. "Or else the food will come back out as swiftly as you're stuffing it in."

He blinked his assent at Asla, then asked her to tell him what happened. She obliged, and when she was finished, he looked at Carla. Her large, dark eyes, which dominated her drawn face with its hollow cheeks, seemed strangely familiar to him, as if he had known her for longer than just a few moments.

"I thank you, Carla."

"No need," replied the girl in a bright voice. "I did it for myself. Your life was the price for me to come here with you."

An honest reply, thought Yngvi. The kind of reply he liked.

A few days later, ten longships and merchant vessels arrived at the inland port west of Hedeby, where the ships of Egil and the emigrants also moored. That was just what Egil had been waiting for. The Northmen had not made it to the large trade center in time before the winter to sell the wares and slaves they had looted from the shores of Ireland and the Anglo-Saxon kingdoms.

As far as Egil could tell, the Northmen held around two hundred slaves on board their ships. The human cargo emerged one after another from the hulls, their hands tied. Many of them bore blond or red hair. Egil rubbed his hands. Here he would find just what he was looking for. The Northmen loaded their loot onto oxcarts to transport it into the city. The slaves would have to walk. Warriors were herding them together when Egil and some of his followers approached them.

Upon a nearby hill, the lord steward gathered his mounted soldiers. He didn't like the sight of this many Northmen together in one place. Should there be strife or even war between the individual groups, he would intervene. Hedeby was a significant source of income for the Danish king. Preserving the peace in his name was the uppermost duty of the lord steward.

Egil studied the slaves. Among all the weary people, one group of strong, grim-looking men stood out. Despite the humiliations and deprivations they must have suffered, their pride appeared unbroken. Egil supposed they were Irish warriors who'd been taken prisoner after some ill-fated battle. One of them carried his chin particularly proudly. Fresh scars on his face, which was framed by blond hair and a beard of the same color, showed that he had sold himself dearly into slavery. The tall Irishman paid careful attention to his surroundings and the behavior of his guards. He was only waiting for a chance to run, thought Egil, but he would not find it here. The emir would pay good money for him and his companions.

With their owners' permission, Egil picked out the slaves he considered suitable. Once he had made his choice, wild bartering and haggling followed. Eventually, Egil purchased nineteen blond and red-haired Irishmen, whose athletic, muscular bodies told of their belligerent past; roughly the same amount of pretty, mostly fair-haired Irish girls; and almost just as many men and women from the realms of the Anglo-Saxons.

Egil had them taken to the other slaves, who were camped in a hollow patch of the field with no shelter. He provided the men and women, whose feet were chained and who were guarded by his warriors, with warm, weatherproof clothing and sufficient food. He had bought the slaves dearly, after all, and if he wanted to sell them to the emir for multiple times their purchase price, they had to be in excellent condition.

Two days later, more fresh cargo arrived for the slave trader. Danes had plundered the small city of Brema, taking many of its inhabitants prisoner and enslaving them. From Brema, it had taken the raiders only four days to reach the inland harbor of Hedeby. Again Egil was the first trader to inspect the slaves before they were taken to the market at Hedeby. Of the roughly one hundred and thirty prisoners, Egil picked out all young and fair-haired women and men who met his standards.

Yngvi, recovered by now, meandered along the shore of the harbor. The crowd of people by the newly arrived ships captured his interest. From afar he could hear Egil's powerful voice. The trader was in his element, negotiating about slaves he wished to purchase. When Yngvi came closer, he saw that Egil was arguing with a Northman about the price for a woman who endured the haggling over her body with a stony expression. Yngvi studied her attractive profile. Even though she was treated as a slave, she stood out among the bartering men like a queen, standing tall and dignified in her handsomely embroidered (albeit dirty) linen dress. As if she sensed Yngvi's gaze, she turned her face to him. Slightly slanted eyes the color of amber fixed him coldly.

Yngvi's heart skipped a beat, his skin tingling. The sight of her struck a chord inside him which he had not known existed. Instantly he was obsessed with getting to know her.

Once Egil had reached an agreement with the Dane, Yngvi drew his merchant friend aside. "Will you sell me one of your most recent purchases?"

"Which one?" asked Egil, surprised.

"The one with the cat eyes."

Egil knew right away which slave Yngvi spoke of. "Oh, she

is a veritable treasure. The emir will pay me at least six times her purchase price."

"For the sake of our friendship, let double be enough for you. I can hardly afford more."

Egil regarded the young man with amusement. "Don't tell me you lost your heart to the woman. You're willing to pay that much silver for a few cozy hours that any pretty maid could give you?"

"The maids are one thing," said Yngvi with a dismissive gesture. "But this woman has something special."

Egil's expression turned serious. "I warn you, Yngvi. I know women like her. They are unbending and stubborn. They consider themselves to be above the rest, refusing to submit to their fate. If you whip them, their resistance only grows. I do not think the emir would find much happiness with her." Then he laughed. "But that is not of my concern once I've sold her. For our long friendship's sake, I want to be generous with you. I will give her to you for a mere . . ." Egil scratched his head, looked at the sky, then at the ground, then back at Yngvi's face, eventually uttering with dramatic resignation a sum in silver that still amounted to three times her purchase price.

Yngvi beamed as he held out his hand to Egil, who clasped it with the words, "But don't complain to me if she brings you unhappiness."

Yngvi fetched the woman from the camp and ordered for her shackles to be removed. Then he looked straight at her. Pointing at his own chest, he said, "Yngvi."

With an unusually deep voice, she replied evenly, "Frida."

"Frida, I am now your master."

She gazed at him blankly and shook her head. Evidently, she did not speak his tongue.

Asla merely raised an eyebrow when Yngvi arrived outside the tent with his new maid, but Stina and Hilda grinned when, in contrast to his usual eloquent manner, he explained stiffly and awkwardly that he liked Frida and did not wish to leave her to an uncertain fate.

Carla scrutinized the tall, attractive woman and pulled up one corner of her mouth. She had no trouble imagining for what purpose he had bought the slave woman.

Yngvi felt visibly uncomfortable in the company of the women who bestowed him with looks of amusement, as if they weren't taking him seriously. He tried to speak in a matter-of-fact tone. "Carla, Frida comes from Brema. Aren't you from somewhere near there? Perhaps she speaks your language?"

Carla gave a shrug. "I have no idea where Brema lies." Then she uttered a few words at Frida, who nodded and made a curt reply. "Frida speaks my language, even if her accent sounds a little strange," she informed Yngvi.

Yngvi was pleased. "Will you walk with me and Frida over to that hill?" He was pointing to a deserted rise a little way out of camp. Carla nodded and got to her feet.

Yngvi shot Asla, Stina, and Hilda a dark look as he left. What did those women find so amusing?

Once he had moved far enough away from camp, it was Hilda who laughed first, and the sisters joined in mirthfully. "I have never seen Yngvi like this before," she giggled. "As rigid and serious as if he were the servant to a queen."

"I thought he was more like a little boy who was given his first wooden sword," chuckled Stina.

Asla turned serious. "Our Yngvi is stricken. He seems to be under that woman's spell. Let us hope she brings him no ill fortune."

Yngvi lowered himself onto the grass with Carla, signaling for Frida to do the same. His new maid hesitated for a few moments before following his command reluctantly. "Carla, ask her which family she is from and how she was captured."

The skinny girl turned to Frida and translated Yngvi's question.

"Tell him that is none of his concern. Tell him he and all Northmen can go to hell. Tell him to give me a knife so I can first kill him and then myself." Frida's amber eyes seemed to glow while she stared at him, instead of Carla as she spoke.

Yngvi thought he could read hatred in her eyes, and once Carla translated her reply, he knew he had interpreted the expression correctly.

"Ask her why she hates me."

Carla did as she was asked.

Frida ran her fingers through her shoulder-length dark-blonde hair without taking her bitter look of animosity off Yngvi. "Because you are a filthy Northman, a scourge of God, a devil like those who murdered my parents, my husband, and my two small children and who burned down our house. Because you belong to those who then raped me repeatedly, deeply humiliating me. Should you wish to lie with me, it will feel as if you are lying with a thorny stick. And if you want to survive, don't forget to place your knives outside of my reach."

Haltingly, Carla translated the stranger's tirade. Even though she herself had experienced hard times in Hedeby, Frida's fate appeared to touch her.

Yngvi said nothing for a while. It would be difficult, if not impossible, to conquer the heart of this deeply injured woman. Eventually he said, "Tell her that I am no raider and that I will not touch her unless she wants it."

Frida commented on the translation with a cold, mocking smile, then lowered her head in resignation.

Yngvi rose. "Let us go back." In encouragement and more to himself, he murmured, "*Tempus dolores omnes sanat.*"*

Frida looked up with surprise, visibly astonished to hear a Northman speak Latin. As she stood up, she whispered: "*Dolorem meum non sanat.*"†

The following day, Asla, Hilda, Yngvi, and Gregor took an oxcart into the city. Stina had stayed behind with Carla. Too great was the danger that a follower of Halldor's might espy them in Hedeby and recognize the daughter of his king, despite her disguise.

When they arrived at the countinghouse they were renting, Thorolf awaited them in the storeroom. Of the thirty barrels of oil, only three lonely barrels remained in a corner. A merchant had already paid for them, and his servants would fetch them later on. The larger part of the storeroom was filled with wares Thorolf had acquired during the previous days, among them tools, bronze ingots, sacks of coal and salt, and two barrels of tar. If there was still enough silver left after today's purchases, he would also buy some iron ingots off Egil.

Thorolf nodded at Egil's guards when he left the countinghouse with his companions. Their destination was the market at the harbor. After several days of blustery winds and heavy rain that had washed the dirt and trash off the wooden planks on their path, the sun was shining, favoring the people with its warmth.

* Time heals all pain.
† My pain it does not heal.

At the bustling market, people crowded among the shelters and stalls where the city's craftsmen offered their wares up for sale. Everywhere among them, the lord steward's soldiers patrolled, providing protection from pickpockets and other scoundrels.

Asla and Hilda stopped by one of the many clothing stalls. They checked the quality of various linen undergarments and gray tunics made of wool, which the weaver had laid out on her table. The clothing seemed well made, and they negotiated an acceptable price for some new garments for Carla and Frida. The silver for Frida's clothes came from Yngvi, while Egil had paid for Carla's with the hacksilver he'd found inside the hut of Yngvi's abductors.

The weaver placed several weight stones on one side of her scale and upon the other as much of Asla's hacksilver as it took for the pans to hang evenly with each other. Then, she bit the silver and cut into it to see that it was genuine. Finally, she nodded warmly, and the deal was complete.

At two further stalls, they bought shoes and weatherproof cloaks for the two women.

Thorolf, meanwhile, browsed the wares on offer at the stands of smiths. He had already purchased several tools in the days prior, but he was still missing axes and hoes for work in forest and field. Those were the tools they would need most urgently on Catan.

When he strolled past a goldsmith's stall, a finely worked golden choker necklace caught his eye. The ring's two ends consisted of delicately shaped wolf heads. He imagined Asla placing it around her graceful neck and how lovely it would look on her. He bought the choker and decided to gift it to his wife after the birth of their son.

Yngvi and Gregor, meanwhile, were on the hunt for parchment. Yngvi wished to no longer set down important thoughts in perishable wax but note them in ink as to lend everlasting support to his memory.

"Look, here!" called out Gregor. He pointed at a well-used book bound in leather, which lay hidden from superficial glances among candlesticks, crucifixes, silver cups, and all sorts of plunder.

Yngvi picked it up and leafed through the pages of parchment. He had no trouble reading the Latin handwriting. The book was entitled *De re publica* and had been written by someone named Marcus Tullius Cicero. As far as he could tell from his first impressions, the text was about monarchies and other forms of state. He found this thrilling, and he was overcome by excitement almost as intense as when he had first laid eyes on Frida. He wanted to explore this book, dive into it and gain new knowledge. He wanted to own it.

"Your fellow countrymen stole this from a monastery, which surprises me. Normally they only take gemstones and objects of gold and silver. They usually burn the scriptures in the library once the pillagers have finished their destructive work. It is an incredible stroke of luck that we happened upon this rare book here."

Yngvi held the book up to the bored merchant's face. "What do you want for this?"

The merchant gazed into the cloudless sky as if the price were written there. Then he shrugged and named a sum that Yngvi struggled to believe at first. The man wanted only the equivalent of seven chickens for the book.

Gregor elbowed Yngvi's ribs and hissed at him in Latin: "Negotiate! Act angry, as if he had demanded an insolent price. Or else he will start to think his offer was too low, and he'll increase his price. Quickly, boy!"

Yngvi did his best. He was no born trader, and bartering was not his strong point. But still he managed to haggle the price down to the equivalent of six chickens. Then he asked the merchant for parchment. At first, the man did not comprehend. Only when Yngvi pointed at a page in the book and said "Without black" did he understand. He then rummaged in a chest beneath his trestle. After a while, he reemerged, his face bright red from the effort, and held out a bundle of cut sheets of parchment.

"Those must be from the monastery also," said Gregor in Latin.

Yngvi negotiated the price. In total, he paid as much silver as he would have for eleven chickens. His purse did not suffer greatly from this.

As the merchant handed Yngvi his book and parchment, he said, "You are the first madman to take an interest in this trash." Then he laughed. "By the way, they sell kindling much cheaper three stalls over."

Yngvi left the guileless merchant in the belief he had made a good sale, swallowing back the comment that he would have given his horse for the book and the parchment—and that was worth at least three thousand chickens!

At another stall, Yngvi purchased a waterproof satchel made of animal hides for his new acquisitions. The satchel cost him five times what he'd paid for its contents. Last, he bought two combs made of antlers from a craftsman, intending to give one to Carla and the other to Frida. They would put them to good use against their lice.

"Do you hear that?" asked Gregor. "Someone is singing."

Yngvi listened. Through the noise of screeching seagulls and the babble of the crowd among the stalls, he could hear a fine, clear voice. They followed the song toward the water's edge. A little off to the side of a larger group of slaves stood a stocky, burly woman in a threadbare, torn habit who was chanting a wistful melody in a sonorous voice.

"What is she singing?" asked Yngvi, touched by the passionate performance.

"She is a nun—a female monk—and she is singing a church song. I think she is trying to capture the attention of a Christian who might take pity on her and buy her freedom."

"Would you buy her freedom?"

Gregor nodded sadly. "Yes, I would, if I were a freeman and possessed enough silver."

Yngvi, unperturbed by the slave woman's fate, patted Gregor's shoulder. "There are many Christian merchants at this market. I'm sure one of them will come to her aid."

The monk shook his head slowly. "You don't understand." He tore his eyes off the nun and gave his master a forgiving, almost pitying look. "How should you . . ."

When the time for their departure had arrived, the emigrants stowed the wooden poles and the skins of their tents inside the roughly four-foot-high spaces beneath the decks. In the same cargo holds, servants also refilled water barrels and arranged the durable foodstuffs Thorolf and Digur had bought. The farmers had delivered the livestock, its feed, and the grain on time, and soon the ships' bellies resounded with animal voices: cows mooed accusingly, bulls roared angrily, pigs squeaked with agitation, and sheep bleated in fear. The animals weren't accustomed to being penned in aboard a swaying ship. Only the wooden cages of chickens were strangely quiet.

Egil had the more than two hundred slaves distributed among five of his ships. Like the animals, they were kept in the tight spaces of the open cargo holds. Warriors guarded the human freight from the decks above. Egil's two remaining knarrs, commanded by him and his son, were filled with the precious walrus tusks, furs, and iron ingots. So heavy were their loads that these two ships lay low in the water, making them more difficult to maneuver than the other knarrs.

Following Egil's lead, the ships left the inland harbor of Hedeby and soon sailed south along Jutland's west coast. The summerlike weather held, and the sea was calm.

Yngvi, having placed command of the *Shieldmaiden* into the hands of his steersman, was sitting with his back against the ship's side on the front deck, enjoying the sunshine. On his knees, he held an open book. Others sat together in groups, talking or passing the time with a game of dice. To the emigrants, Frida thought, the only blemish on this otherwise perfect day was probably the bleating of the sheep below deck.

In the last few days, she had led several conversations with Gregor. She was glad she could speak with him in Latin, and that he was a fellow Christian. Whenever he mentioned Yngvi, the monk only ever sang his praises. "You can consider yourself lucky that Yngvi bought you. He is the best man you could have encountered in your terrible situation. You may be his servant now, but he will treat you as a person. I promise you he will not touch you against your will."

She decided to give the Northman a chance. She supposed not all of them were necessarily tools of the devil. She crossed the deck, sat down quietly beside Yngvi, hugged her arms around her knees, and eyeballed the book he was engrossed in. In Latin, she remarked, "I have never come across a Northman who can speak and read Latin."

Startled, Yngvi looked up, and a smile formed on his lips. "And I have never met a woman who addressed me in the ancient tongue. Where did you learn it?"

Frida hesitated, wondering whether it was wise to entrust her past to her new master. She decided that it would do no harm. "My father was the wealthiest merchant of Brema and I his only child. Since he had no son, I was supposed to follow in his footsteps at the side of a suitable husband. My apprenticeship started when I was nine years old. He hired an educated monk who taught me mathematics and how to write and read in Latin. When I grew older, my father took me to his countinghouse. There and during his travels, he taught me everything I needed to know as the future wife of a merchant."

"And your father picked a suitable husband for you?"

"Yes, I was made to marry his apprentice."

"Made to? You did not want to?"

"Not at first. But with time, I learned to appreciate him. He was an honorable man, kind with me and, later, with our two children." Frida rested her forehead on her knees. When she looked up, brushing her wavy dark-blonde hair behind her ears, her amber eyes, previously so cold and contemptuous, had softened and darkened. A tear rolled down her cheek. "And then your countrymen came and took everything from me."

"I am very sorry for what my fellow Northmen did to you and your family. But trust me, there are also peace-loving Northmen who would much rather work their fields day in and day out than rob and murder people." Yngvi gave a small smile. "Or, in my case, study books in the old language."

Frida returned his smile, though hers looked strained.

Yngvi placed a hand upon hers, and she allowed it. He gazed straight at her. Though he'd initially been drawn to her by desire and curiosity, in this moment, he mostly felt deep affection for her.

"You do not need to fear me, at least. I hope you know that by now."

Frida nodded, and after a few heartbeats, she said plainly, "I can tell that you have taken a liking to me, and you probably believe that one day I might willingly share your bed. You may as well bury this hope right now." She stood up abruptly, strode to the other side of the deck, and slumped down there, holding her face in her hands.

For three weeks, the ships followed the coastline of Frankia. During foul weather, they went ashore at night, setting up camp, replenishing their water stores, and trying to purchase food that folk at nearby farmsteads and settlements were willing to part with.

Yngvi and Frida now sat together frequently, exchanging stories from their lives and learning about the ways and customs of two different worlds. Yngvi enjoyed the time alone with the beautiful, educated woman. He often longed to stroke her skin and kiss the curve of her lips. Then, he hoped, one thing would lead to the next. But he restrained himself, not once attempting to touch her. One clumsy attempt might be enough to irrevocably destroy the delicate blossom of intimacy that was growing between them.

On this night, they had set up their camp on a beach a short distance before the Breton peninsula. It was raining as if from buckets, and the air had grown colder. The people sat inside their tents, warming one another, and ate bread, onions, and cheese purchased from local farmers. While heavy raindrops pattered down on the protective skins of the small tent, Gregor fished the playing pieces of hnefatafl from a leather pouch and, from his master's travel sack, fetched two painted wooden boards which he connected to make one playing field. Patiently, he explained the game to Frida, who listened attentively. Yngvi watched the many small changes of emotion in her face, from curiosity to surprise, then confusion, followed by realization. He loved this woman with every fiber of his body by now, no longer able to imagine his life without her.

He and Gregor took turns playing with her. Frida learned fast, and it wouldn't be long before she would beat them for the first time. Perhaps the joy would even bring a smile to her face? So far, his humor and jokes had not sufficed to dispel her sadness and cheer her up. Only rarely did the hint of a smile show on her lips, just to vanish moments later, as if she remembered her dead family and forbade herself any kind of pleasure.

While Gregor cleared away the game, she looked at Yngvi with kind eyes. "Would you perhaps let me have one of your knives?"

"Why?" asked Yngvi, remembering the threat she had uttered in the port of Hedeby.

"Perhaps to cut my food like all the others, or to defend myself against a man when you're not around to watch over me? Or perhaps to cut off one of your earlobes in your sleep?" she replied pointedly.

Yngvi sighed but handed her one of his knives. "Careful, it is sharp."

Frida merely rolled her eyes, lay down on her fur, and pulled the blanket over her. Yngvi lay down, too. Gregor lowered himself between them, and was soon snoring softly. Before Yngvi fell asleep, he involuntarily touched his earlobe.

The next day, the weather improved. The rain had stopped, and a stiff breeze from the northeast sped the ships along. The skippers kept their vessels at a distance from each other's to give themselves plenty of space for maneuvering.

Yngvi held the command upon his *Shieldmaiden.* He shouted orders to stay on course, relishing the feeling of riding nine-foot-tall waves. When the knarr was lifted up by a larger wave and then slid into the valley on the other side, her bow dived into the sea, and foaming spray would gush across the decks. The slaves had no trouble scooping the water back out from the bilge. The swell was rough but not dangerous for Högni's stable knarrs. Their flexible timbers did not fight the ever-moving sea but instead bent with it.

Egil decided to make use of the favorable wind and sail through the night. Blowing into his horn, he gave the signal to the other commanders. Before nightfall, the ships passed the western tip of the Breton peninsula, sailing out into the open ocean. The North Star in the almost-cloudless sky reliably guided their way south.

In the morning, the sun rose above a clear horizon. The sea calmed and the wind steadied, moving the fleet along nicely. Yngvi inspected the sail and rigging. They had come through the strong winds fine. From the corner of his eye, he watched Frida, who was sitting in the stern, belaboring something with her knife.

Toward the evening, the wind dropped, and the waves stretching their glittering crests toward the sinking sun were but small. Yngvi passed the command of the knarr to his steersman and walked over to Frida, who stood leaning against the railing, staring listlessly into the sunset.

"What do you say? Shall we sit? I would like to speak with you."

Still gazing across the ocean, she asked, "What about?"

"About you and me," said Yngvi with a smile.

"Not today. I need to be alone tonight, so I can think."

"Very well. Then let us speak tomorrow," he said, conceding to her wish.

She nodded absentmindedly. Yngvi had the feeling that her sadness weighed more heavily upon her on this day than it had on others. So heavily that it cast a deep shadow on his soul, too, casting him into an unusually glum mood.

The moon shone silver from the sky, flooding the decks of the *Shieldmaiden* with its light. The sheep had ceased their bleating, and the only sound came from the burbling of the gentle waves against the boat's hull. Aside from the steersman and two servants who were responsible for operating the rigging, all appeared to be asleep.

Frida pulled out the piece of parchment that she had cut from Yngvi's book and smoothed it against the planks. During the day, she had scraped the page carefully with Yngvi's knife, just enough so that the writing had become pale. Using the knife's point, she pricked one of her fingers, dipped the quill of a feather she'd gathered on a beach into the drop of blood, and began to fill the page with Latin symbols.

When she was done, she softly stepped to the sleeping Yngvi, laid the parchment next to him, and weighed it down with the knife. Then she carefully moved between the bodies of the resting passengers toward the bow, assured herself that she had no witnesses, and jumped.

The rising sun shone into Yngvi's face, waking him. He blinked, rubbed his eyes, and sat up. His glance caught on the knife he had given Frida. Beneath it lay a piece of parchment with words written in reddish ink. Was that blood? Frida's blood?

A terrible sense of foreboding grasped him as he pushed aside the knife and picked up the page with trembling hands.

> *Yngvi, I did not want to leave without saying farewell to you. You are a fine person, and in another life, I might have loved you. In this one, however, there is no future for us. My children and my husband call for me. They were and are my all. I must follow them.*
>
> *Frida*

Even though it was a bright morning, the world before Yngvi's eyes darkened. He was filled by an agony of the soul the likes of which he had never experienced before. He screamed his pain into the world, so loudly and intensely that all those who were awake turned to him with fright, and those who lay still asleep jerked up and glanced about with alarm. Even on the neighboring boats, the people heard his desperate cry.

Gregor awoke as if struck by lightning and turned to look at his master. Yngvi was sitting bolt upright, staring straight ahead.

Gregor shook his arm. "What happened?"

Yngvi gazed at his friend with empty, dull eyes and handed him the parchment.

When Gregor had read the lines, he did not attempt to find words of solace. He knew it was too soon. Instead, he wrapped his fatherly arms around Yngvi, holding the younger man as he suffered through the first powerful waves of grief.

CHAPTER 9
CORONIUM

Only two days later, the fleet reached the coast of Asturias, from where they set their course to the west, keeping the land within sight. At last, they arrived at the sheltered harbor of Coronium. But they were refused entry to the city at first. Armed with swords and pikes, grim-faced men of the city guard stood at the shore with about a hundred archers, ready to prevent the ships from berthing at the docks.

However, when Egil rowed ashore in a small dinghy and the governor of the city gave him a friendly welcome, the tense atmosphere lifted. Egil wasn't visiting this Galician city for the first time. The governor recognized him and knew that he was a peaceful merchant, not one of those raiders who went on viking voyages. Upon his orders, the guard and the archers retreated, and once Egil and Thorolf had paid the berthing fee for three days, they were permitted to dock.

In the late afternoon, Thorolf, Digur, and Egil entered a tavern in the heart of Coronium. There was only one table left with a few empty seats. Sitting at this table was a man in the plain clothing of a farmer, clearly recognizable as a Northman.

His hands and his face bore numerous scars. With a warm smile, he waved at Thorolf and Egil to join him. Digur followed them uninvited.

The farmer introduced himself by the name of Ragnar. Since he was missing his two front teeth, he spoke with a lisp, which sounded rather funny to the ears of the companions. Stifling a grin, Thorolf and Egil also introduced themselves. Digur said nothing.

Ragnar waved his hand, shouting, "Another jug of wine and cups!" The tavernkeeper nodded, and Ragnar turned back to Thorolf and Egil. "I am glad to sit with some fellow countrymen and speak with them in the language of my homeland." With mirth in his eyes, he pointed a finger at Digur. "Does this giant belong to you? Where did you find him?"

"The giant is my brother," explained Thorolf. "And you'd do well not to insult him."

"Oh, that was certainly not my intention. But if that one," he giggled, still pointing at Digur, "is your brother, then I'm a grandson of Odin."

Digur gazed at the farmer, unperturbed, and still said nothing.

Ragnar picked up his cup and raised it in the air. "I myself pressed this wine, you must know. I hope it is to your taste. If it isn't, I would gladly start a brawl with you, if only that fellow wasn't with you." Grinning, he pointed at Digur again.

Digur's hand darted forward, grasped Ragnar's right hand, and squeezed it so hard that the farmer's eyes welled up.

"If you point your filthy finger at me one more time, I will hack it off."

Ragnar nodded at Digur with a painful grimace. Digur let go of the farmer's maltreated hand and crossed his arms on his chest, his expression indifferent, as if nothing had happened.

Thorolf was forced to stifle yet another grin. Digur hated it when people stared at him because of his hulking, impressive stature. He couldn't stand being pointed at as if he were some kind of monster from the Nordic myths. But Ragnar was probably harmless—the kind of man who liked to talk loudly just until things became serious, and then he would quickly put his tail between his legs. To lift the downcast mood, Thorolf picked up the conversation where the farmer had left off.

"You said your wine is served at this tavern? Do you grow it in this area?"

Ragnar kneaded his aching right hand with his left, replying with a rattled glance at Digur. "My house lies but a short walk from the city. There, my wine grows on a south-facing slope. It is the best in all of Galicia. Why else do you think this tavern is so busy? Certainly not for the watery stew the tight-fisted tavern wife keeps warm in her pot and which is at least three days old."

A maid brought the wine. Once their cups were filled, they touched their cups together and drank. Digur, too, raised his cup to the farmer; he was easily angered but did not bear grudges.

Thorolf did not mind the wine, even if he found it a tad sour—it was no match for the wines Egil brought from the deep south. But Thorolf's interest was aroused. In their new, sun-drenched home, he figured, the grapes would certainly develop more sweetness than in rainy Galicia.

"I like your wine. Would you sell me ten barrels and some of your vines?"

Ragnar watched the companions. None of them pulled a face as they set their cups back down. That circumstance in conjunction with Thorolf's words caused him to nod eagerly. "With pleasure. Come with me this evening and spend the night at my house. Tomorrow I will dig out some vines for you. Do you know much about growing wine?"

Thorolf shook his head.

"Not to worry," said Ragnar patronizingly. "I will tell you everything you need to know." Then a funny thought seemed to strike him, for a grin spread on his face. "Don't tell me you plan to grow wine in the Northland?"

Thorolf smiled at the absurd question, explaining to Ragnar that he intended to plant the wine on an island in the south where they planned to establish a settlement and a trading post.

The farmer's face then took on a pensive expression, which vanished when Egil asked him what circumstances had brought him, a Northman, to Coronium.

Cheerfully and gesticulating vividly, he told his tale. "As a young warrior, I went a-viking with my jarl. All I could think about were the masses of gold and silver our leaders promised to us! I felt certain that I would return home a rich man, for never before had the North seen a fleet as large as the one I sailed with. There were almost one hundred ships, and I was one of nearly five thousand fearless warriors hungry for loot. We could scarcely contain our eagerness to rob the south of its treasures. In Aquitaine, we rowed up the rivers, pillaged the surrounding countryside, and gathered anything that gleamed."

Ragnar smiled wistfully, as if counting once more the coins he had pilfered. "Then we sailed on to Asturias. After we had plundered and laid waste to several coastal towns, we were to take Coronium. But our chiefs had not reckoned with the Asturian king, who'd been warned and, together with his warriors, fought us fiercely and fended us off successfully. During the battle outside the city walls, many of my comrades lost their lives or remained heavily wounded on the battlefield. I was one of those unhappy men. When our chiefs deemed their losses were growing too high, they withdrew with their fleet. I heard they attacked towns along the coasts of the Moorish empire and plundered the lands along the rivers they rowed up. But in the end, so I was told, only a few ships of the formerly great fleet made it back to the North, and with very little booty."

Ragnar paused for a moment, sipping his wine. "There I lay, unconscious, among all the dead bodies, gravely injured from an arrow. My savior was a young woman who, with her two brothers, combed the battlefield to search the bodies for valuable or at least useful items. They did not find much, for the king's warriors had done thorough work. My comrades who still breathed were finished off by them. They must have overlooked me—perhaps because I lay pale and peacefully sleeping at the border of life and death. At least, that's what the young woman who found me thought. Later she told me she fell in love with me the moment she beheld me lying on the ground, more dead than alive. I can't blame her. Back then I was a strapping lad with a full mane plaited into braids." Ragnar gave a roguish smile and brushed his hand—almost apologetically—across his thinning hair, which was flecked with gray.

"If my wife wants something, then she gets it. I could sing a song about it." Ragnar chuckled. "Her two brothers stood no chance of talking her out of her intentions to take me to the house of her family. And so they cut the arrow from my wound, bandaged me up as best as they could, and carried me to my new home. The master of the house had no say in the matter, and his wife sided with his daughter. Thanks to her, I got better and was not sold into slavery or worse—" With dramatically wide eyes, raising his eyebrows, the farmer drew his forefinger across his throat and gave a rattling wheeze.

"Thank Odin I was spared such a fate. I soon learned the language of my benefactors, became one of them, and married my savior one year after the battle of Coronium. My father-in-law never regretted having given in to his wife. Instead of wasting my strength in senseless battles, I bettered his farm. When Coronium was attacked once more by a fleet from the North last year, I stood in the first rank among the defenders, helping the governor with my knowledge of my former countrymen to a great victory." With a self-absorbed smile, Ragnar raised a finger and stated in a tone of utter conviction, "If it weren't for me, Coronium would be a pile of rubble today."

Thorolf noticed the tavernkeeper, who was standing nearby, smile to himself. Evidently he understood the Nordic tongue.

Ragnar sipped his wine before continuing. "After they left here with nothing but a bloody nose, I heard, the fleet sailed around the cape at the world's end to the shores of the Moorish lands. They probably found their death there." Clearly tipsy, Ragnar laughed with his mouth wide open, revealing that he also missed three of his bottom front teeth.

"What do you mean?" asked Egil.

"What do I mean about what?"

"Why would they have found their death?"

Ragnar folded his arms on the table and leaned closer to Egil. "Because of the Moorish fleet, of course. After the first attacks from our countrymen, the emir expanded and strengthened it year by year. If the looters were confronted by the dhows of the emir, they would have scarcely stood a chance against the superior Arabic force."

"You forget how fast and agile our longships are," Egil objected. "They will easily outrun the cumbersome Moorish dhows."

Ragnar shrugged. "Perhaps you're right. But what about you? To reach your island in the south you, too, must sail along the Moorish coast. Your wide-bellied knarrs are slower than longships. If you happen across the fleet of the Moors, you will not escape easily."

Shaking his head, Egil smiled confidently. "I am a guest of

the emir's each year, and I hold in my possession a writ that assures me free passage in his realm. The commander of the fleet will accept it."

Ragnar tilted his head from one side to the other, pressing his lips together. "If the rumors are true, then our countrymen murdered the current commander's family during their first attack fifteen years ago. Since then, so I'm told, he is filled with a deep loathing of anything coming from the North." Ragnar reached for his cup. "But I probably see things in too dark a light. The commander cannot simply ignore a deed from the emir. Let us drink to your successful voyage and a happy return home!"

Yngvi sat with Asla and Carla on some crates by the water's edge, supervising the maids who shoveled dung from the cargo holds. Servants had led the horses, cattle, and sheep to the meadows outside the walls of Coronium. The animals grazed peacefully on the lush green while the pigs rooted the ground for worms and other creatures.

Carla studied Yngvi from the side. He was no longer the cheerful, buoyant man who always had a jest at the ready. Since Frida had taken her own life, he seemed withdrawn and taciturn. Whenever someone addressed him, he replied reluctantly and gruffly.

Asla rose. "I should go help Hilda and the maids prepare the evening meal."

Yngvi nodded absently. To him, it was obviously all the same what his sister-in-law did or where she went. Without saying a word, he continued to watch the maids.

After a while, Carla spoke. "Frida was with child. Did you know?"

Yngvi turned his head and gazed at her with surprise. "I never touched her."

"Of course not, you fool. The way you and Gregor watched over her, no one else here could have, either. She was pregnant by one of her assailants."

Yngvi closed his eyes, massaging the top of his nose with his thumb and forefinger. "She told you that?"

"We often spoke, and she confided in me. Her bleeding stopped a few weeks ago, but she didn't think anything of it at first. But once she began feeling sick in the mornings, just like during her first two pregnancies, she knew she was with child. She loathed the child, planted into her body by a brutal Northman. She said it was the spawn of the devil growing inside her."

Yngvi stifled a sob and pressed his right hand over his eyes. Carla reached for his left hand.

"Frida liked you very much—she told me so several times. And maybe time could have healed her wounds eventually, if it weren't for the child in her womb. She could not live with the thought of growing inside her the fruit of a man who murdered her family."

Yngvi tried his hardest to contain himself, but he failed. Tears forced their way out, oozing from beneath his hand. Carla wrapped her arms around his trembling back, holding him tight. They remained in this manner for some time. Several passersby noticed Yngvi's show of weakness but quickly looked the other way when Carla glowered at them.

After a while, Yngvi composed himself. Carla loosened her arms and sat up straight.

"I used to have a brother whom I loved dearly. We shared a difficult time in Hedeby. He died, leaving me behind on my own." Thoughtfully she gazed at Yngvi's profile. "If he lived today, he'd look a lot like you." Carla hesitated for a moment before uttering a wish that had been living in her heart for a while now. "I would like to be your sister."

Wiping his eyes, Yngvi looked at Carla. Hilda's care had done her good. Her cheeks had filled out a little, the dark rings around her big eyes had vanished, and while she was still quite skinny, she was no longer gaunt. He squeezed her hand, which was still holding his in support, and said, "It would please me to be your brother. When you need me, I will be there for you."

Carla beamed at him happily.

CHAPTER 10
ON THE OPEN SEA

After three days, the fleet left the port of Coronium early in the morning. Beneath the low decks, the storage crates were full of foodstuffs and fodder for the livestock, the barrels refilled with water and Iberian wine. The weather smiled upon the people aboard the ships. Now and then, the sun peered out from behind the thick, rushing clouds. A steady and strong northeast wind billowed the sails and carried the boats along swiftly. Not long after noon, they had left the cape at the end of the world behind and sailed to the south. Toward the evening, the clouds thickened further, rendering navigating by the stars impossible. And so Egil led the small fleet to a beach in a sheltered bay and lowered the anchors.

In the morning, the wind had eased, and a light rain forced the people to don their cloaks as the ships glided out of the bay, but around midday, the sun regained its spot in the sky.

As usual, Thorolf's and Egil's knarrs sailed at the front of the convoy within shouting distance of one another, but in the waning wind, their progress had slowed.

Suddenly, the boy Thorolf had sent up the yard that morning yelled out, his voice breaking: "Ships ahead!" He gestured with his left arm excitedly in the direction they were traveling, clinging to the mast with his right.

Thorolf set down his bowl of porridge, rushed to the bow, and peered to the south, but all he saw was an empty horizon whose leaden hue melted almost seamlessly into the gloomy gray of newly gathering clouds. Egil had also heard the boy's shout and had rushed to the bow of the *Seaserpent.*

"How many ships can you see?" shouted Thorolf at the boy.

"Lots and lots!"

Egil, holding his hands to his mouth like a funnel, called to the boy: "What do the sails look like?"

"Three-sided," yelled the boy in reply. "They are white."

Egil blanched. "Those are Moorish dhows. It has to be the emir's war fleet."

After the initial shock, Egil sailed his ship closer to the *Goldeagle.* "Thorolf, I'll sail toward them. The commander must acknowledge the free passage I received from the emir. Until I return, I transfer the command of our fleet to you."

"And if you do not return?"

"Then you will lead my ships until you make land somewhere where you can restock. Then you pass the command of my ships to my son. Give me your word!"

"You have it," said Thorolf, nodding solemnly.

The merchant tossed his horn to the new commander of the fleet. "For your safety, lead our ships west onto the open sea until you've brought enough distance between yourselves and the Moors. Wait for me there."

Egil's son, Finnur, had drawn his ship up beside Egil, and the father informed the son of his intentions and the transfer of command to Thorolf. Finnur, in turn, informed the other men in charge of Egil's ships, while the merchant sailed toward the mighty Moorish war fleet with a white flag raised upon his mast.

Meanwhile, the first dhows came into sight from the bow. Thorolf blew into Egil's horn, blasting several low tones that signaled to the other skippers to change course and sail west.

Asla, whose pregnancy was obvious by now, grasped Thorolf by the arm and asked with concern, "What if the commander of the Moors does not care for Egil's writ?"

Thorolf gently stroked the waning scar on her face. "Then we run. Farther west, probably, onto the open sea. For as long as it takes for the Moors to abandon our pursuit."

Asla grasped his neck with one hand, pulled his head down to her, and kissed his mouth. "Hopefully that won't be necessary. But if it is, I know you will succeed. We, all of us, have faith in you."

He felt the invisible burden on his shoulders grow a little heavier still. And yet he gave her a confident smile. "I will."

Then he turned away, calling for the boy to climb down from his vantage point so Thorolf could scale it himself. From there, he watched events unfold before him.

The *Seaserpent* was about a thousand paces ahead of them now. Her sail barely swelled, and the white flag hung down limply. If the commander of the Moorish fleet accepted Egil's sign of peace, he now ought to give the order to shorten the sails and move forth with his dhow alone to meet the knarr.

Thorolf breathed with relief when he saw the Moors taking in their sails. He started to climb down from the mast, thinking that all would be well after all, when he suddenly froze with shock: the Moors were starting to row. Faster and faster they rowed, and soon three dhows reached Egil's knarr. The sun sent some rays through a gap in the clouds, and in the light, Thorolf saw the glint of steel. Faint screams and battle noises reached his ears. The Arabic warriors boarded the *Seaserpent*. Egil and his men stood no chance against the overwhelming numbers.

Filled with terror, the people on the other decks watched

the end of the great merchant's mission while the crews of the other dhows still rowed at great speed—straight toward them!

Thorolf lifted Egil's horn, which he had hung around his neck. The low, vibrating tones sounded eerie across the still waters, carrying their orders to the other ships: *Take in sails! Row! To the west!* Immediately the crews came alive. The air buzzed with shouted orders, and the planks of the decks shook under the clatter of many feet. Thorolf climbed down, ensuring his orders were carried out on the *Goldeagle.*

The eight freemen and those servants who were accustomed to rowing his ship during periods of slack wind threaded the oars through the oar-ports and dipped them into the sea. One man set the rhythm. Soon the oars bit evenly into the water, speeding the *Goldeagle* onward. Thorolf saw, to his relief, that the other knarrs also gathered speed. Only Finnur's *Bride of the Seas* remained in its place; nothing much seemed to be happening aboard her decks. Evidently, the young man was in shock over his father's fate, incapable of taking any decision. Or perhaps he was considering facing the overwhelming force, so he would meet his father in Valhalla and bring honor to him? Finally, Finnur's stouthearted steersman decided to put an end to the dangerous situation, roaring orders. Moments later, the *Bride of the Seas* started to move as the last ship in the convoy.

Like the knarrs, most of the Moorish ships contained four pairs of oars. But the dhows were not heavily loaded, so they did not lie as low in the water. With each stroke of the oar blades, they came closer. Soon there were only four ships' lengths between the frontmost dhows and Finnur's boat.

Deeply worried, Thorolf glanced at his oarsmen, who groaned as they worked their hardest to shift the *Goldeagle* as swiftly as they could across the calm waters. He decided to swap the exhausted men for rested ones, picking up one of the oars himself. Hilda sat down on a crate on the opposite side of the deck, nodded at him, and clasped the round timber with her strong hands.

At first he had not wanted to allow Hilda to row, but the sturdy woman had braced her hands on her hips, knitted her eyebrows, and told him sternly, "Do you think a charcoal burner woman does nothing but cook soup and sit on her ass all day? I can work as hard as anyone. You don't mean to doubt me, do you?"

On the other ships, too, oarsmen were rotated. Since Egil's crews consisted of only eight to ten warriors and seamen, they fetched the strongest slaves from the holds and put them to work on the rowers' benches. He who was reluctant, not pulling the oar as hard as he might or disturbing the rhythm, received a taste of the whip.

Hilda fulfilled her task with dedication but did not quite last until the end of the second shift. Drenched with sweat and red in the face, she passed her oar to a burly farmer's wife. Thorolf nodded at the charcoal burner, his eyes filled with respect for her effort. Soon he ordered the first team back to the oars. Then he made his way to the stern, watching the unfolding drama with a heavy heart.

Despite the strenuous efforts of the rowers, the *Bride of the Seas* made slow progress. The fastest dhow had come closer still, now running less than two ships' lengths behind her. Some of the Moorish warriors reached for their bows and loosened arrows upon the fleeing knarr. Those of Finnur's men who weren't rowing cowered behind their shields, but the oarsmen were exposed to the missiles.

Finnur took over the oar of a mercenary who sank to the floor, struck by an arrow. Moments later, an arrow pierced

Finnur's shoulder. Gritting his teeth, he ignored the pain and continued to pull on his oar. Then the slave in front of him took an arrow to his neck. Immediately, one of the warriors dragged his body out of the way and took his place.

When another slave was struck in the chest and died, Finnur accepted that they would not escape their pursuers. The Moors would shoot one oarsman after the other.

He sprang to his feet with determination, picked up his shield and shouted, "Cease rowing! Form shield wall!" He would give the Moors a fight even the skalds in Valhalla would sing about.

The ship's crew and his followers answered his call, rushing to his side on the rear deck with their shields, pikes, and swords. Standing shoulder to shoulder, one shield touching the next, they were protected from arrows.

Finnur roared, "Valhalla! Valhalla!" and the men joined in his hoarse battle cry. They would sell their lives as dearly as possible.

The *Bride of the Seas* quickly lost momentum, and soon the first dhow reached her. The Moors threw ropes over the gunwale, and grappling hooks bit into the timber with a crunching sound. Some of the thirty or so Arabic soldiers certainly shuddered at the Northmen's fierce, ominous cries, but nonetheless they pulled their ship alongside the *Bride of the Seas* relentlessly.

When the Moors made to climb aboard the knarr, the warriors around Finnur suddenly stepped apart and hurled their spears at them. Almost every one struck home. The emir's soldiers retreated, and Finnur and his men successfully stormed the enemy vessel. They slashed their swords viciously, blocking attacks and hacking through the flesh and bones of their opponents. They hardly appeared to notice the blows they themselves received, up to the moment when they were struck down by a fatal cut.

All of a sudden, the fight was over.

Surrounded by six of his warriors, most of whom could

scarcely stand on account of their grievous wounds, Finnur stood among dead and severely injured bodies. Raising his sword into the air, he shouted once more, "Valhalla!"

His men joined in with his cry, drunk from their victory but knowing they would not be able to withstand the soldiers on the approaching dhows.

The ugly sound of iron hooks digging into the timbers of the conquered dhow announced the beginning of the final verse of the hero's poem the skalds might someday perform about the last battle of Finnur and his companions.

Thorolf placed an arm around Asla as he watched with a bitter face the end of Egil's eldest son and his last followers. The young man had undoubtedly been brave and dauntless, but perhaps Finnur could have saved the lives of his men and his ship if he had decided to throw his precious wares overboard and flee sooner. Now the emir could rejoice at having won a second ship filled with the treasures of the North without having to pay for them. Maybe that had been his plan from the onset.

The ships of Digur and Yngvi glided through the water at a little less than one ship's length to the left and right of the *Goldeagle*. Together they formed the rear guard of their small fleet. For them there was no question that they would stick together and, along with the freemen still capable of fighting, put up as great a fight as possible should the Moors succeed in catching up to them.

Right then, it did not look like that would happen. The Moors kept their dhows close together now, the fastest ones holding back to stay with the slower ones. They would not repeat the mistake of sending one single dhow against a ship full of Northmen who were staring death in the eye.

When evening approached, the Moors had gained several feet on them. Thorolf estimated the distance between the last ships of his convoy and the dhows to still be ten ships' lengths.

A bluish-gray front of clouds pushed closer from the south-eastern horizon, devouring the white-gray clouds that had intermittently allowed the sun to peek out throughout the day. It started to rain, and with the rain came the wind.

Relieved, Thorolf blew into his horn, whereupon the commanders hoisted the sails which immediately filled with the steady breeze from the east, increasing the ships' speed. The rowers drew in their oars. Utterly exhausted, most of them lay down on their furs and fell asleep within moments. Thorolf raised his horn to his lips again, telling his ships to set a down-wind course. He could no longer make out the Moorish dhows in the falling darkness and heavy rain.

He sighed. Now it was out of his control. All he could do was hope the gods were not playing games with them.

Thorolf's steersman, Hakon, was more rested, so he transferred the command over the *Goldeagle* unto him, ordering him to blow the horn from time to time so that the other ships had a point of orientation and would not sail too far from their convoy. The fact that the Moors would hear the horn too was the lesser evil.

Now he needed to sleep.

When Thorolf awoke in the low-ceilinged cabin in the *Goldeagle*'s bow, a space that was his right to occupy as the ship's owner and commander, pale light streamed through the gap between the two animal hides that shielded the tiny room from rain and prying eyes. He peeled himself out of the waterproof sleeping sack, which Asla and Gudrun had sewn together from furs and which was large enough for both him and his wife. But still he could not avoid waking Asla.

She asked anxiously, "Are they still following us?"

Thorolf shook his head. "Probably not. Hakon would have woken me if they were within sight."

"Thank the gods," she muttered, reassured, and soon went back to sleep.

Thorolf carefully sat up and peered through the gap. The sun had risen, but it was muffled by a thick blanket of cloud, unable to give out more than a dull twilight. He pulled on his boots, reached for his raincoat, and crawled outside.

Yawning, he stretched his arms into the air, his muscles aching unpleasantly from yesterday's hard rowing. He turned his face into the mild rain, wiping the refreshing drops across his eyes and cheeks, and looked around. Most families still lay asleep underneath the skins they had stretched between the mast, the ship's sides and heavy crates providing shelter from the rain. During the day, they would catch the water pouring from the skins with buckets and use it to refill the water barrels. A boy, perched atop the yard, peered into the distance.

On his way toward the ship's stern, Thorolf walked past the lower-lying open cargo hold. Loki, who was tied up in there, greeted him with his typical bright yap, and the horses snickered. The cows mooed discontentedly, waiting to be fed and milked. A maid would soon see to them. Next to the cows, two servants used buckets to remove bilge water from the ship's lowest area. Stina peered out from the low storage space beneath the deck, sleepily raising one hand. There, in the narrow corridor left between the crates and barrels that were fastened in place in ropes, Thorolf had assigned dry sleeping places to her, Hilda, and Carla.

All seemed well, and Hakon, his steersman, had everything under control. Thorolf knew he could rely upon the experienced old sailor. Hakon had been going to sea since before Thorolf was born.

The bald steersman shuffled toward him. His left leg had remained stiff after a battle injury, but it did not hinder him much. With a calm face and eyes that had seen much suffering, Hakon reported that none of the convoy's ships had gone missing and that the boy up the mast had not seen any Moorish ships this morning, but that didn't signify much since the rain impaired their vision.

Thorolf shared the old man's opinion and decided to stick to the downwind course for now. Should the Moorish commander persist in his pursuit of them, the Northmen would gain a safe lead, thanks to their large, square sails.

"What direction do you think we're traveling?" he asked Hakon.

The lanky steersman scratched his wrinkled neck. "Not sure," he replied slowly. "The sky was overcast the whole night through, and the wind turned slightly several times. My guess is that we are still more or less headed west."

Thorolf nodded, told Hakon to get some sleep, and relieved his second steersman at the steering oar; the man thanked him with a tired, sleep-deprived look. Thorolf loved steering the *Goldeagle* himself in the early morning, while watching the men and women on board wake up and begin their day.

In the course of the morning, the wind picked up further, driving before it ever-growing waves. Thorolf knew the harbingers of foul weather: a storm was coming. He ordered the sail to be halved and grabbed his horn to warn the other ships of the impending threat. Like an echo sounded the dull, low tones from the horns of the neighboring commanders, passing on the message to the farther-away ships to prepare for the storm.

Thorolf instructed the people on board to pack up their

tent skins and attach themselves to the ship's side with ropes. The crew would need room for their maneuvers. His second steersman took an armful of ropes and three servants down to the cargo holds, where they tied the legs of the horses and cows, forcing them to lie on their sides. Thorolf hoped this measure to spare the ship's walls would only need to be in place until the evening, or else the horses would fall ill and die. He thought of the two bulls who would be similarly bound on Digur's *Spearhead*. Before their departure from Hedeby, he'd had their mighty horns cut off. He hated to imagine what those powerful animals would otherwise do to the ship's floor, even while lying on their sides.

Around noontime, the wind had become a gale. The mast groaned and creaked. Thorolf, fearing a powerful gust might rip it from its footing, shouted to one of his crew over the noise of the rolling breakers to shorten the sail again to a quarter. He was pleased to see the other commanders follow his example.

The knarrs pitched through the tossing sea in front of the waves coming at them from astern. Reducing speed had been a sound decision, Thorolf found. This way, the ships were less likely to push their bows into the back of the wave in front of them and become flooded by its waters. Already, servants and maids were frantically bailing water from the ship's belly, and even some freemen helped with the arduous task, knowing their lives and those of their families depended on the seaworthiness of the vessels, which were but tiny, fragile nutshells to this huge, angry ocean.

Thorolf, who roared his orders into the storm from the steering oar, guessed the waves were around eighteen feet by now. When they broke, they left behind white, whirling foam, sending dull rumblings across the sea. The sun had been concealed behind leaden clouds chasing across the sky all day, and

Thorolf had no idea in which direction the storm blew them. His heart thumping heavily, he hoped the weather would not worsen, and that Thor would take mercy on them, preserving the ships from sinking.

The steering of the *Goldeagle* in front of the gale-force winds and upon the turbulent waters demanded Thorolf's full attention. Most critical were those moments when, after reaching the crest of a wave, the *Goldeagle* dived down into the trough. Then the bow pointed downward and the rudder in the stern lost contact with the water for a moment. To prevent the ship from veering sideways, Thorolf had to react instantly once the rudder dipped back into the water, or else the ship might broach to and a wave might strike her from the side. So far, Thorolf and the other commanders had successfully avoided getting broadsided—until Digur failed to.

Thorolf watched in fear as his brother's knarr was grasped side-on by a wave. The *Spearhead* tilted precipitously and almost listed, but Digur was lucky: the wave did not break, and so the knarr was not buried under masses of foaming water. The passengers aboard the *Spearhead* had survived the danger. When the steersman managed to turn the knarr back downwind, Thorolf thanked Thor, promising him a sacrifice should he deliver them safely to Catan.

By the afternoon, Thorolf was so exhausted that he could no longer steer the *Goldeagle* with the concentration the task demanded. He handed the steering oar to Hakon, knowing his first steersman was more than capable, just like the other experienced helmsmen on the ships. Slowly, hand over hand, he made his way along the gunwale toward his cabin. The knarr's pitching as the waves lifted her up and down, and her rolling from side to side, rendered every step difficult. Carefully he clambered across the legs and bodies of men and women who, together with their children, had tied themselves to the bulwarks. Several of them had vomited, staring vacantly ahead, while others gazed anxiously at their captain, hoping for a sign of encouragement. Thorolf tried for a confident expression, nodding at them reassuringly.

Inside the small cabin, Asla received him with a warm embrace. She said nothing, but he saw admiration in her eyes. Whenever she looked at him thus, he felt certain that he would love her until the end of his days. Gratefully, he accepted the dry bread and the skin of water she offered him.

Wearily, he murmured, "I need to sleep for a while. I'll return to the steering oar at nightfall. Wake me when it's time."

Asla fastened a rope around his body and rested his head in her lap. In spite of the *Goldeagle*'s endless pitching and tossing, Thorolf soon sank into a deep, dreamless sleep.

When he left his cabin that evening, the storm had eased, even if the *Goldeagle* still pitched heavily. Hope sparked in Thorolf that he would bring his ships safely through the night. When he took over the steering oar and his horn, he bade the old steersman to untie the horses and care for the animals.

The following day, the weather remained largely unchanged; only the rain eased. The crests of the waves were down to about fifteen feet, but the knarrs still swayed significantly. As the day before, men and women with gray faces leaned across the gunwale, passing every last drop of bile to the ocean, or else they hung apathetically in their ropes against the ship's sides. Those who fared better helped to bail water.

Thorolf took turns with Hakon at the steering oar, continuing to set the course downwind. As long as he could not steer by the sun or the stars, he saw no point in changing their direction, especially since the heavy swell of the ebbing storm could still prove dangerous to the ships if they did not sail with the waves.

After Hakon had relieved him in the middle of the night and Thorolf had staggered back to his cabin, he had struggled to find sleep at first. He was plagued by nightmarish images, seeing in his mind's eye his ships smashing against a rocky shore, crashing onto reefs, or plunging to their death down an enormous waterfall at the world's end. Now and then, he nodded off, but he started back up every time the horn sounded to keep the ships together.

Asla, sensing his restlessness, grasped his hand. "My dearest, Gundahar, who knows how to read the runes, has foretold you that our firstborn is going to achieve great things. And so he will be born. And he can only be born if we survive this voyage."

The undeniable logic behind Asla's words calmed Thorolf. Thankful, he squeezed her hand, and, soothed, closed his eyes.

On the third day of their stormy passage into the unknown, the sun began to peek through gaps in the clouds. *Finally*, Thorolf thought with relief. By the sun's high position, he gathered it was around noontime. As the clouds gradually disappeared from the sky, the wind likewise began to ease and the waves to shrink into dwarves. In the afternoon, the swell had decreased enough that Digur and Yngvi could successfully bring their ships alongside the *Goldeagle*, tying their three vessels together.

Thorolf greeted his brothers, embracing them both warmly. At last they would be able to exchange their thoughts in peace rather than shouting a few hasty words from the sides of their ships.

Their faces filled with hope for the first time in days, they sat down upon storage chests hastily carried over by servants. Asla sat beside Thorolf and leaned against his shoulder. Several freemen and women formed a circle around them, eager to hear the brothers' thoughts on their situation.

Thorolf broached the subject on everyone's mind. "We do not know which direction the storm blew us in. Hakon and I suspect that we are somewhere west or northwest of the land of the Moors."

Yngvi nodded. "I agree. We ought to sail southeast to get closer to the Hot Land."

Digur said drily, "And how do you propose to sail with no wind?"

Thorolf and Yngvi glanced at the limp sailcloth, no more than a gentle breeze tugging at its edges here and there. Almost simultaneously they replied, "It will come."

"I doubt it," objected Hakon, stepping into the circle. His glum expression made his weather-beaten face look even more wrinkled. "I have seen periods of no wind that lasted several days. One time, even two weeks." Squinting, he peered into the sky. "Most started off like this. A storm would pass, and then there'd be a change to fair, windless weather within a day. The quick easing of the swell suggests there is a large area of fair weather ahead. I'm afraid we've sailed right into it and will have to expect long days without wind."

The brothers said nothing for a while, contemplating the experienced sailor's words.

"We'll row," suggested Digur.

Hakon shook his head decisively. "That is the last thing we want to do. The water barrels may be full, but they'll not last for more than four or five days. I'm not in charge of overseeing our provisions, but I'd guess we've used at least half. If we make our men row in the heat that is about to descend upon us, we won't make it far, and our stores will be depleted even sooner."

The men looked expectantly at Thorolf, who clearly wrestled with a decision. Finally, he said, "We will not drift aimlessly like sheep, not knowing for how long we might be without wind. We'll row at night when it is cooler, trying to reach an area with winds."

"Won't do much," said Hakon. "We won't get far with four pairs of oars."

"Better than nothing," decided Thorolf in a tone that allowed no further contradiction.

He rose and blew his horn, signaling to the other ships to shorten sail and tie all boats together. That way, during the day, his men and the crews from Egil's remaining ships would be able to easily move from ship to ship.

"Yngvi, you get an overview of our stocks of food and water." Thorolf turned to Hakon. "Carry my decision to all the other skippers. Tell them to divide everyone aboard into groups who'll take turns rowing during the night."

When Digur made to return to his ship, Stina approached him with a smile. "Come with me, big man, and join us for our evening meal."

Shortly after their departure from Hedeby, she had abandoned her charade, taking care to avoid Egil and his men. The free folk aboard the *Goldeagle* had watched her transformation with suspicion at first, but once she told them her story, they soon stopped worrying themselves about her. The lords of their old home and their quarrels no longer concerned them; their minds were on the future, and their thoughts were preoccupied with the fear of falling victim to the ocean and never setting foot upon their new home.

When Digur appeared undecided, Stina grasped him by the

hand, leaving him no choice but to follow her to the rear deck, where Hilda and Carla had prepared cheese and dried fish on a large wooden platter. Digur was struck by Carla's transformation. He hadn't properly seen her since Hedeby. The haggard, hollow-cheeked girl had turned into a young woman with healthy features in her heart-shaped face still dominated by large, dark eyes. Her dark-brown curls shone in the sunlight and reached almost to her shoulders.

Hilda noticed Digur's look of astonishment and asked mischievously, "Haven't I done well with her?"

Without waiting for a reply from the taciturn giant, she laughed heartily, wrapped her arms around Carla, and squeezed her tight, which Carla didn't seem to mind.

Digur smiled as he sat down beside Stina and helped himself to dried fish. Hilda, he thought, was a good mother, even if she had no children of her own.

Together with Thorolf, Yngvi climbed aboard one of Egil's knarrs. The pungent, revolting stench of urine and human excrement wafted from the cargo holds where the slaves were being kept, forcing him to breathe through his mouth. The sheep aboard the *Shieldmaiden* also soiled the planks, but Yngvi had the dung collected regularly and thrown overboard.

His gaze traveled across the young women and men, shackled by their feet and forced to sit in their own muck, staring vacantly straight ahead. One slave woman caught his eye; she looked vaguely like Frida. Had she suffered a similar fate? Maybe her children, too, had been murdered before her eyes, and their killer had raped and impregnated her afterward?

At the thought of Frida, he felt fiercely repulsed by the

crimes his fellow countrymen committed against others. More clearly than ever he recognized how wrong it was to rob people of their freedom and treat them like animals.

He was reminded of his many conversations with Gregor about Christian teachings. His friend's words about love, compassion, and forgiveness had always sounded strange and weak to his ears; he'd been brought up from infancy with Nordic values like loyalty, bravery, and honor. But following Frida's fate, which had pushed her to her death, he had increasingly mulled over the Christian values. And the more he had done so, the more familiar and truthful they had appeared to him. What he now saw and experienced on board the ships of Egil's men was the absolute opposite of those values: reigning here were indifference, greed, and contempt for human dignity.

Yngvi watched Thorolf as he spoke with the skippers of Egil's ships. His brother had grown into the role as the emigrants' chief and commander of his fleet. He spoke clearly and decisively with his innate sense of authority.

"Tomorrow morning, I will call a meeting with the leaders of each family." Thorolf gestured at the cargo holds at his feet. "Until then I expect you to clean up these pigsties aboard your ships. Further, you will lead the slaves onto the decks in groups during the day and allow them to move. At night, you may use the strongest ones among them to row. You cannot sell a dead slave, and if disease breaks out among them, it could spell the end for us all. Also, I expect your report in the morning with regard to your stocks of foodstuffs and drinking water."

Thorolf was about to turn away when one of the ships' leaders, a strong, black-bearded man, spoke up. "You can't order me around. I am Kilian, a nephew of Egil's and his last living relative here. It is my right to command the ships of my uncle. And so I am telling you: our slaves and our stocks are none of your concern. As soon as the wind picks up, we are going our separate ways."

Thorolf looked straight into the man's cold, challenging eyes, waving his horn. "Egil entrusted this to me—and with it the responsibility and command over his knarrs. I will exercise this right, according to his will, for as long as it takes for us to reach land where we can replenish our water barrels and provisions. Only then will we part ways. If you do not accept this, I will have you bound and replaced by one of my men."

Angry veins throbbing in his temples, Egil's nephew roared angrily, "You will do no such thing!" Then he unsheathed his sword.

With a hissing sound, Thorolf, too, drew his blade. Yngvi and the other commanders took a few steps back to make room for the opponents. No one was permitted to intervene in an honorable one-on-one combat.

Thorolf studied his opponent. The man was arrogant, convinced of his own capabilities. Those were attributes that were not of advantage in a fight. Thorolf would let Kilian come at him, watch his movements closely, and find a response in a suitable moment.

After Kilian's first few attacks, which he fended off with ease, Thorolf knew all he needed to know about his opponent's skills. Egil's nephew considered himself to be a far better swordsman than he actually was. His angry, erratic attacks were predictable, and his defense was miserable. Thorolf made short work of him. Driving Kilian backward with two slashes, which the man still managed to block, Thorolf feinted and then sank the tip of his sword into the left side of Kilian's chest.

The fatally wounded sailor staggered backward and fell into

the cargo hold, landing in the piles of stinking feces. The last thing Kilian saw in his life was the face of a bearded blond slave who leaned over him and spat in his face.

Thorolf sheathed his sword, glowering at the four remaining skippers. "Is there anyone else among you who would like to question my position as your commander?"

The men shook their heads.

"Very well. Choose someone from your ranks to lead Kilian's ship from now on and follow my orders."

By the following morning, all ships had reported their stocks. Yngvi noted on a wax tablet the amounts of dried fish, dried whale meat, onions, oat and barley flour, and cheese. Adding them together, he gauged how much was needed.

Finally, he looked up, regarding Thorolf with a serious expression. "If we continue to eat and drink as before, our supplies will not last longer than two or three days. Nor will the feed for the livestock."

Thorolf, having feared as much, called together all men in charge of ships and heads of families aboard his *Goldeagle*.

To get a better view of all those gathered before him, he climbed atop a crate. The men gazed up at him with worried faces, and the decks of the two neighboring knarrs were filling up with women, older children, crew, maids, and servants. Anxiously they awaited his words. The sun stood at its highest point, burning down on the skin of men and beast. Not even the smallest breath of wind came to bring them some relief. While the humans waved their hands to fan some air unto them, the dogs, cattle, and sheep in the cargo holds panted to dissipate heat from their bodies.

Wiping the sweat off his forehead, Thorolf explained the

situation to the people who had entrusted their lives to him. "Even though we are rowing at night," he said, "we have to expect to remain adrift without wind for several days yet. Therefore, we must ration our stores of water and food. From now on, every freeman and woman will receive only one meal a day. Children younger than ten winters, servants, maids, and slaves receive half a portion."

Unperturbed by grumbling and moaning here and there, he carried on. "The daily feed for the livestock will also be halved. The water will be rationed so that it should last us for seven days. Pregnant women will receive milk for as long as the cows give any. Protect yourselves and the animals from the sun by stretching any skins you have above your decks and storage rooms."

He shot a stern glare at the leaders of the slave boats who stood together in a group. "You will follow my orders exactly as I gave them! He who fails to do so will regret it."

The men nodded—they had seen what Thorolf was capable of.

One of the freemen, a burly farmer, spoke up. "Why are we still feeding Egil's slaves? They're of no use."

Thorolf had expected this question. "I gave Egil my word that I would protect his ships and his goods until we safely reach land."

Another man wanted to know why they weren't slaughtering the animals.

"We need the animals so their offspring can feed and clothe us someday. We will only slaughter them when there is no other way to save us from death."

Thorolf gazed at the group of heads of families and skippers, bestowing each man with a brief, intense look. As he did so, he reached for the golden arm ring that adorned his right upper arm, pulling it off slowly before raising it into the air.

"We know the gods are capricious. Let us brighten their mood!" Even the last man stopped whispering when Thorolf declared in a booming voice, "I sacrifice this arm ring, which was a gift from my grandfather when I still lay in my cradle, to Odin, father of gods, and Thor, the ruler of the winds."

With a powerful thrust, he tossed the ring over the *Goldeagle*'s stern. It flew in a wide arc before piercing the sea's perfectly smooth surface, tumbling down to its depths. Digur followed suit, sacrificing two of his four silver arm rings. Men and women followed the brothers' example, parting with their rings, pendants, arm rings, and necklaces, hoping to win the gods' favor amid their desperate situation. Those free women who did not possess any jewelry used their knives to saw off strands of hair, sending them flying across the railing.

Carla was unfazed by the goings-on around her—the Nordic gods were foreign to her. In the stories the men told at night, Odin, Thor, or Freya often acted violently, erratically, and all too human. She preferred to believe in the kind, forgiving, and loving Jesus her mother liked to speak of. If there was a god who might send them winds, then it was Jesus, the son of the god of her dead parents. She felt sure of it.

On the first day of lying adrift with no wind, several men climbed into the dinghies, studding the hooks of their rods with small pieces of dried whale meat. Others tried their luck with a net, which they dragged between two boats as they rowed them along. Now and then, a fish would bite or a small fish would get caught in the net, but rarely any that were large enough to feed a grown man.

On the third day, they were lucky. A large creature that looked like a lizard carrying a shield on its back surfaced beside the dinghy where Yngvi and two of his men were fishing. Yngvi had never seen such an animal before. The shield was approximately five feet from head to tail, and the creature's weight looked to be around that of a burly man.

"There is bound to be a lot of meat in there," one of the men remarked.

"The thing is far too large and heavy. We'll never get it into the boat," replied the other man.

Yngvi agreed. While the imposing sea creature paddled past them with its wide front fins, sluggishly and seemingly unafraid, Yngvi tied the end of a rope to a loop and then pulled the rope's other end through the loop, forming a snare. With a few gentle strokes of the oar, they caught up with the armored animal, and Yngvi let it swim right into the trap. With a jerk, he pulled the snare tight around the leathery neck. The strange creature appeared to comprehend that its life was in danger. Flapping its front fins up and down, not unlike the wings of a bird, the animal tried to dive but did not get far. Yngvi and his companions held on tight to the rope, tying it to a bench. With their prey in tow, they rowed to the nearest knarr, and together with the men waiting for them up on deck, they heaved their heavy quarry on board.

When Hakon saw the animal, he nodded appreciatively at the decent catch. "I have come across such a creature before, years ago during one of my voyages in the south. Back then we called it 'shield lizard.'"

Yngvi thought it was a fitting name.

The next day, Högni succeeded in capturing another shield lizard.

The creatures they wrested from the sea and consumed raw stretched their provisions, but they were far from satisfying the daily needs of five hundred people, and on the fifth day with no wind, it was clear that the food would last only until the following day. The water in the barrels would probably last another two days.

Lethargic, the people sat or lay in the shade of the skins, trying to forget their hunger and thirst. The livestock also suffered. Some people held shut their ears to block out the accusing mooing, baaing, and squeaking for a while.

Yngvi sat with Gregor and Carla in the stern of his ship. The animal hide above their heads protected them from the searing sun, making sitting on the deck bearable. Yngvi was talking with Gregor about the book he had purchased at Hedeby, *De re publica*, which he had been perusing that morning. For the sake of Carla, who listened with interest to their conversation, they were speaking in the Nordic tongue. Several Latin terms in the book were new to Yngvi, and if there was no equivalent for a certain word in the Nordic language, then Gregor found words in Yngvi's mother tongue to describe it with.

But as much as Gregor tried to answer his questions, Yngvi was forced to concede that he had not yet grasped much of the book's content. He decided to study the text for a second time. Maybe then he would better understand what it was Cicero had tried to convey to his readers. But right now, he was not in the mood to discuss the difficult work any further. Like everyone else on the ships, he was tormented by thirst, and he longed for the noontime ration of water his steersman would distribute among the passengers on the *Shieldmaiden*.

Leaning against the ship's side, Yngvi folded his hands behind his head and asked Gregor, "Who was this Cicero? A monk like you?"

Gregor laughed and shook his head at Yngvi's ignorance. Then he told him about the Romans who, in centuries past, had conquered many lands and ruled a great empire. "Cicero was a Roman politician and philosopher."

Yngvi gave him a questioning look. "Philosopher?"

"A philosopher is a man," explained Gregor, "who poses questions about the world and humankind. Cicero asked himself which form of government was the best. *De re publica* is his answer."

Glancing at Carla, Gregor occasionally noticed the glimmer of understanding in her eyes. He wondered at the young woman. Was she simply wishing to be near Yngvi, whom she treated as a brother? Or was she longing to learn more about the world and broaden the narrow horizon that life in Hedeby had forced upon her? Probably some of both, he thought.

Yngvi sat up straight again, resting his chin in his hand. "Are all monks as well-read and educated as you?"

"No, certainly not. Most do not even know how to read or write, learning only the most important Latin words for their prayers." He hesitated for a moment. "Besides, I am not really a monk—nor am I a Saxon."

"Then what are you?"

"A Roman cardinal, a high-ranking church official. When your people took me prisoner at the monastery, I was traveling Britain in the name of his holiness the pope, the uppermost lord of Christendom. He instructed me to inspect the local monasteries and compile a report on the godliness of his lambs upon the isle. Well, as you know, I never got that far."

Ryan trudged across the deck in small steps. If he wasn't careful, the short chain between the shackles clasping his ankles would trip him up, which would please the armed guards. They would laugh at him and mock him—him, the firstborn son of an Irish king.

Together with his men, he had fought those sons of whores from the North who were trying to claim his father's land. They had fought valiantly for their king, but in the end, too many Northmen had streamed from the dragon ships, and the Irishmen lost the battle. When Ryan recovered from a blow to the head and opened his eyes, he found himself a prisoner of his enemies. A few weeks ago, at the slave market of Hedeby, the heathens had sold him and several of his men who, like him, were not fortunate enough to die on the battlefield.

Now they were penned up like cattle inside a stinking cargo hold, sleeping and eating upon the hard, soiled planks, suffering hunger and thirst. His boundless hatred of the Northmen alone gave him the strength to carry on breathing and to cling to this dismal life. One day, he would take his revenge. Of this, he felt certain.

A few days ago, the ships' commander had improved their situation somewhat. He had argued with the man named Kilian, killing the slave driver after a brief fight. Ryan had been filled with satisfaction when the bastard had landed in the muck right in front of him. With relish, the Irishman spat into the loathsome face that had stared up at him with disbelief.

Since that day, two slaves were released from their chains once a day to collect the worst of the filth with shovels and toss it overboard. They had been given buckets for their needs, and at night, Ryan and the strongest of his comrades were put to the oars. He who did not pull the oars hard enough was given a taste of the whip. Once a day, they were led up on deck in small groups to exercise by walking in circles.

Ryan enjoyed the movement, but most of all, he treasured the change for his eyes. Instead of perpetually staring at the drawn faces of the other slaves inside the crammed cargo hold, he watched the goings-on aboard the ships that were tied together side by side in a long row. The decks had become quiet in the last few days. The thirst and heat were hard on everyone.

Unless people had urgent tasks to fulfill, they dozed underneath the outstretched skins.

Ryan's eyes scanned the timbers of the deck and the ship's sides. He hoped to find a loose nail or something similar, and he prayed to God and Jesus Christ to show him one such small tool that might help him become the master of his chains.

At last, on this day, he was lucky. Just four paces away, he spied a nail whose rust-red color scarcely differed from the wood. The nail had been driven in crookedly, and the movement of the planks in the waves must have loosened it. Now, the nail's head cast a shadow from the slanting rays of the sun, without which Ryan never would have spotted it. When he neared the spot after another round, he pretended to trip over his chain and fell against the ship's side. As expected, the guards jeered at his misfortune. But he didn't mind. While he braced himself with his left hand, he grasped the head of the nail with the thumb and forefinger of his right hand and levered it out of the timber. When he straightened up, he was smiling. The hook-shaped piece of iron burned inside his fist like a propitious gem. For the first time in a long while, Ryan felt hope sprout in his heart. If he was lucky and God was with him, he would be able to pick open the locks of his shackles and those of his companions with the nail. Then he would only need to wait for an opportune moment . . .

In the early hours of the evening, when the sun stood about two handsbreadths above the horizon, Thorolf stood with Asla by the gunwale and gazed across the calm sea. He sighed. "I haven't the faintest inkling where we are. If Yngvi is right, the sea's current carried us to the southwest in the last few days."

"What makes him think that?" asked Asla, frowning.

"He believes the shield lizards are lazy, preferring to swim with the current. The two creatures we caught were both paddling to the southwest."

She understood. "So, the shield lizards are drifting along the same current as us?"

Thorolf nodded. "At night, we row to the southeast, and during the day, the current carries us to the southwest. But even if it is true, this knowledge does not help us. If there is still no wind tomorrow, and no sign from the gods, we will have to slaughter the horses." Glum, he stared at the almost unmoving surface of the ocean, which reflected the sky's blue. "I wish my ship would live up to its name."

"How do you mean?" she asked.

"Just imagine if the *Goldeagle* grew wings. Then she could lift off like an eagle and find land."

Asla glanced at him sidelong. Had their situation not been so serious, she would have smiled at his fantasies. But as it were, she merely nodded, automatically running her dry tongue across her cracked lips. She could hardly wait for the final cup of water for today, to feel the refreshing moisture in her mouth.

A bright voice behind her called her name. Asla turned and saw Carla, a piece of dried fish in her hand.

"Take it," said the dark-haired young woman. "I'm not hungry."

"I don't believe you. I thank you for your offering, but I cannot accept it."

"Yes, you can. You must eat for two, after all." Carla pointed at Asla's rounded belly. "So think of your child. If you won't eat my fish, it will gladly return to the ocean."

Carla lifted the hand holding the piece of fish above her head and pretended to throw it overboard. Asla noticed the mischievous glint in the young woman's eyes and knew that Carla would make true to her word if she had to, and so Asla eventually relented, accepting the gift.

Before her benefactress could slink off, Asla drew her into her arms. "I thank you, my dear. You are a good friend." She planted a dry kiss on the shorter woman's forehead.

Carla smiled when she returned to Hilda. The embrace and the kiss from Asla had been worth giving up her daily ration. She was accustomed to hunger from her time at the mother's in Hedeby, whereas affection and love were new to her.

Thorolf's eyes followed her. "I like the girl. She is a gain for our community."

Asla took his hand. "Community? I would prefer 'family,' since Yngvi regards her as his sister. And I have grown quite fond of her, too."

For a while, they stood together in silence. Then Asla pointed at a bird that dived headfirst into the sea not far from the *Goldeagle*'s bow, only to emerge moments later with a twitching fish in its yellow beak. The bird straightened up, stretched its long wings, and, following a number of awkward steps on the water's surface, elegantly rose into the air. Thorolf watched the bird's flight. The yellow-beak, as Thorolf called it in his mind, did not alter its course, flying to the southwest in a straight line.

"What a curious bird," said Asla with a smile. "I'm sure it's taking the fish to its young."

Realization struck Thorolf and Asla in the same instant: birds did not nest on water! There must be land nearby to which the yellow-beak was returning! Land to the southwest. They exchanged a look, and their eyes were filled with hope. Thor had sent them a sign.

Thorolf gazed longingly into the cloudless sky. "Now all we need is wind."

She squeezed his hand. "We shall have it. Trust me. The gods have accepted our sacrifice, and they will help us."

Thorolf folded his wife in his arms, whispering lovingly into her ear, "Why are you always so damned confident?"

"As you know, I believe in the prophecies of the wise Oda and your man Gundahar, who knows the runes."

Deep down, however, Asla wasn't as certain as she claimed. She knew that even those who read the runes could be mistaken. But she couldn't let her doubts show. She believed in Thorolf and his ability to save her, her unborn child, and everyone else on the ships. But to do so, he needed hope. And, she knew, only she could give him the belief that the gods would bestow their favor unto them.

Thorolf shared his and Asla's observation with his brothers and the other ships' commanders, informing them of their conclusion: there must be land to the southwest.

The men's joy was muted; they might have a destination now, but they could not reach it without wind. Thorolf briefly considered letting the ships row but abandoned the thought almost immediately. Their meager water supplies would only last the following day, and as a result of the severely rationed meals, the men were not in the best of health.

But Asla was proven right: shortly after sunset, the first few clouds appeared in the sky, and they were soon followed by wind. Thorolf blew his horn, ordering the ships to be untied from one another and the sails to be set. The people rose to their feet on the decks, cheering. At last the days of no wind, of fearful fretting, of hoping and of despair seemed to be over. The wind freshened and filled the sails. They struck Thorolf to be as hungry beasts finally able to sate themselves, joyfully pushing the boats across the sea. The sky was star-spangled, and they could clearly make out the North Star. The few clouds trying to conceal it moved past swiftly.

The following morning, the clouds thickened, and the wind picked up some more. The sun peered through gaps often enough for Thorolf to use his sun compass to correct their course to the southwest. Around noon, they saw more birds: once they spotted a bird of prey whose outline was similar to a goshawk and who seemed to watch them inquisitively as it drew its circles high above them, and another time, they saw a yellow-beak deftly sailing past them.

In the late afternoon, the boy perched upon the yard shouted excitedly, "Land! Land ho!"

Immediately, the people aboard the ships dropped whatever they were doing and rushed to the front decks of the knarrs, staring hard at the gray seas on the horizon. They could not yet make out anything, but it wasn't long before a woman pointed ahead, shouting eagerly, "There! I can see it!"

So far, it was nothing but a long, narrow ribbon on the horizon, its blue-gray barely differing from the gray of the sea and the lighter gray of the clouds above, but it was definitely land.

Men and women laughed and embraced. Some grasped each other by the hand and danced with sheer joy. Several servants and maids started with surprise when they found themselves in the arms of their master or mistress. The children, infected by the grown-ups' elation, danced and cheered among them.

As though the land wished to send them a special welcome, it started to rain. The people raised their hands and their joyous faces heavenward. Grateful, they received the drops of rain as if they were a gift from the gods. But they soon recollected themselves, for the gods would not fill their barrels. Quickly they placed buckets in those places where the water trickled off the skins. The rain grew heavier, swallowing the ships' surroundings in a monotonous gray. The masses of water pouring off the skins filled the buckets faster than the passengers managed to empty them into the barrels.

Thorolf, who had taken the *Goldeagle*'s steering oar, grinned at Harald, who, instead of carrying his bucket to a barrel, lifted the heavy wooden pail to his lips and drank greedily. Once his thirst was quenched, he set the bucket down so that Abena and his children were able to drink, ladling the water with their hands.

Thorolf ordered his fleet to shorten their sails by half. Visibility was less than a hundred paces, and he did not want to risk the ships hitting any offshore rocks.

Carla made her way toward him through the thick rain. Her dark curls hung wet and heavy. She carried a large cup in her hands. She nimbly balanced out the ship's rolling and succeeded in delivering the clay vessel almost full. "Asla sends me. With the pitching and tossing, she doesn't want to walk longer distances anymore with her belly."

Thorolf gave a laugh. "Asla would have arrived here with an empty cup, if any cup at all."

With a satisfied grunt, he tipped back the water, then wiped his mouth and held out the cup to Carla with a friendly expression. "I am still thirsty. Can you fill it once more?"

Carla nodded eagerly, evidently pleased to be of use.

When the rain stopped as abruptly as it had arrived, the sun peered out from between the clouds, and the wind dropped.

They had come a good deal closer to the coast of the unknown land. A shallow beach stretched along the water's edge, dappled with rocky gray and grassy green. A luscious green forest lay beyond the beach, rising steadily until the tops of the trees disappeared in the haze of low-hanging clouds. Offshore from the beach, rocks protruded from the surf, and there might well have been reefs lurking beneath the water's surface, waiting to slit open their ships and sink them. Thorolf blew the signal to take in the sails and row. He called to the boy on the yard to keep his eyes peeled for any rocks below the surface, and he sent a seaman to the bow to do the same.

The people on board the ships reverently gazed at the approaching land, which was to be their new home. The air was summery and warm, and the shore with the gently sloping woods did not differ too greatly from Egil's description of the coast of the island. Most were convinced that they had arrived at Catan.

While Thorolf ordered his men at the oars to row more slowly, and Digur, Yngvi, and the other skippers behind him followed his example, two slave ships sailed past the *Goldeagle* with their sails reefed to half. Either their commanders had not heard his orders, or they simply ignored them. Thorolf's eyes tensely followed the knarrs, and he exhaled with relief when the men in charge of the ships finally, about a hundred paces in front of them, followed his order to take in the sails.

For one of the two slave ships, however, the maneuver came too late. The man in the bow shouted a cry of warning when he spied a rock just beneath the water's surface, but the knarr was too fast for the steersman to dodge the reef. With an ugly crunching noise, the sharp rock ripped open the hull, creating a wide gap for the water to pour in hungrily. Thorolf watched with horror as the knarr filled within moments and listed.

The sailors and slaves screamed in mortal fear as they tumbled across the bulwarks into the sea. Those who could swim managed to stay afloat, while those who could not paddled awkwardly with their arms or slapped them desperately against the water's surface. Crying for help, they disappeared beneath a wave, swallowing water, and emerged coughing and gasping for air, just to go back under moments later. The slaves, managing but small movements with their shackles, were dragged down mercilessly by their chains.

The men of the second speeding slave ship threw ropes at their comrades. Urgently the seamen grabbed the lifesaving ropes and were pulled aboard by the others. Soon the *Goldeagle* and the *Shieldmaiden* arrived at the site of the accident, helping with the rescue efforts.

Yngvi leaped into a dinghy together with two other men to search for survivors. He had already saved two utterly exhausted slave girls when he noticed another who was sinking toward the bottom of the sea, unmoving. He jumped into the water, dived, grasped the drowning woman by her shirt, and pulled her to his boat, where his companions lifted her aboard. Yngvi was pleased to see her cough and spit out water. Fifteen paces away from him, another slave girl surfaced, trying to gulp some air when the next wave buried her. Yngvi swam toward her.

Carla, watching him trying to save as many drowning slaves as possible like a man possessed, guessed at his motivation. With every slave girl he saved, he atoned, begging Frida for forgiveness for what members of his people had done to her. In the end, he had wrested six slave women and one man from the sea. Two of them did not wake up.

Thorolf seethed with rage at the two commanders who had ignored his orders. Now that they had reached land, he had no authority over them and would not be able to punish them, but he would not return the twelve slaves his men had saved. Instead he would divide them among the families as maids and servants. The new settlers needed every hand they could get.

The water was now shallow enough, and Thorolf ordered the anchors dropped. There were about a thousand paces left between the ships and the beach, with breakers taller than a man crashing in the surf. The risk seemed too great to beach the knarrs in these rough conditions. They would have to wait for the sea to calm, even if their provisions were used up. Only the livestock had received one final feed. At least they had enough water following the rain.

During the first half of the night, the wind and the waves eased, and the ships lay more calmly in the water. A heavy downpour rained almost vertically onto the decks, filling the last remaining empty barrels. The freemen took turns with the servants and maids at scooping the large amounts of water from the ships' bellies, while the slaves were forced to complete this task on board Egil's ships. If, weakened from hunger, they paused for a moment, the overseers whipped them cruelly.

Several freemen and women used the mild rain and the darkness to wash themselves. Despite the gnawing hunger, they enjoyed the feeling of rubbing the sweat, dust, and salt from their skin. Thorolf and Asla, too, rubbed each other down with a wet cloth and scrubbed their clothing on the deck's rough planks.

When they snuggled up together in the warm sleeping sack inside their cabin afterward, Asla whispered to him, "Our son will come soon."

"I know. I will control myself."

He kissed her gently and started to caress her entire body . . .

In the early morning, Thorolf pulled on his damp clothes, squeezed his way out of the low cabin, and straightened up. A surprised smile spread on his face at the sight of the landscape before him. The light of the morning sun painted the beach in golden hues, and the sky's blue reflected on the gentle waves meandering toward the shore. The previous day, when gloomy clouds had dominated the sky, the jagged rocks enshrouded by the spray of the crashing waves had seemed menacing. Now they looked harmless and peaceful as they cast their long shadows across the beach and the water. The air was clear, allowing Thorolf to see far. In the distance, above the sloping, wonderfully green forest, oddly shaped white-gray mountaintops rose into the deep-blue sky. Their narrow peaks were separated from one another by deep gashes, as if Ymir, the forefather of the giants, had slashed angry cuts into the rock with his axe.

Awestruck, Asla, who had stepped up beside him, pointed at a particularly conspicuous formation. "Look, there! Don't you think those rocks look as though a giant was reaching into the sky with four fingers?"

Thorolf gave her a gentle nudge. "What a shame he has lost his thumb."

Giggling, Asla leaned against him. "Do you think we have reached the island Egil told us about?"

Thorolf tilted his head, considering. "Egil described Catan differently. He spoke of rolling hills. He never mentioned tall mountains. And besides, I believe this land is farther west of the Hot Land and much larger than the island described by Egil."

"Never mind," replied Asla. "Our new home must have a name. Why don't we stick with Catan? I think 'land of the sun' is a beautiful meaning. The name is a good omen. Don't you think?"

Bending down his head to her, he whispered softly: "If it is the wish of a king's daughter, then who am I to deny it?"

Thorolf smiled contentedly as he watched the emigrants wake up by and by, gaping with amazement at the impressive scenery of beach, woods, and mountains. He was filled with a deep sense of pride at having led these people to their new home without significant losses. He did not blame himself for the demise of Finnur's knarr and the sinking of the second slave vessel—those came down because of the stupidity of the ships' commanders, who had disregarded his orders. As soon as they were on land, they would hunt anything that ran, flew, or swam, and trade food with the island's inhabitants, so that hunger would remain but a brief episode under his leadership. He wanted to be a good chieftain to the settlers and rule over them for their well-being. The people of his new tribe would adore and revere him for his deeds. He liked the thought. And he liked the power to rule over their destinies. It felt good.

Meanwhile, Yngvi and Gregor stood in the *Shieldmaiden's* bow, relishing the wonderful views of the coastline. A feeble breeze blew into their faces from the land.

"Can you smell that?" Yngvi asked his friend.

"What do you mean?" Gregor held his knobby nose into the wind and sniffed for a few moments before wrinkling it in disappointment. "I can't smell anything in particular at all. Your nose appears to be more sensitive than mine."

"It is a woody scent, the likes of which I have never smelled before. It reminds me of damp soil and moss, mixed with a tinge of rot. I like it. It fills me with the feeling that something new awaits us."

"Something new?" asked Gregor. "I see a sandy beach, rocks, forest, and mountains. You can find those anywhere. How is that supposed to be new?"

Yngvi rocked his head from side to side. "I don't mean it like that. If this land is uninhabited, we might have the opportunity to reinvent the way we live together. A life without oppression, wars, and murder of women and children."

Gregor laughed kindly. "I think the scent of this land has

bewitched not only your nose but also your senses. Even if many people are peace-loving, there are always some who long for power and who will stop at nothing to attain it."

Yngvi made no reply, thinking of Frida. For her sake, he would cling to his dream and fight for it. He glanced at Gregor with a small, dreamy smile which the churchman did not know how to read.

Digur looked over to the *Goldeagle* and saw his brother lifting the horn to his lips to give the signal to row the ships to the beach. Digur had already had the skins packed away and ordered men to the oars. Everything was ready. Once the anchor was lifted, they began to row slowly. A woman stood in the bow, calling instructions to the man at the rudder for what to do if the clearly visible rocks under the calm surface demanded a change of course.

Digur studied the shore with mixed feelings. Would the inhabitants of the foreign land be peaceful, and would they meekly accept the new arrivals challenging them for part of their territory? Or would they be belligerent, waiting to offer a bloody welcome? If so, he would instill terror into them.

Splitting skulls with his axe and hacking off limbs with his sword did not perturb him. But nor did it satisfy him. After each of the many battles during which he had thinned out the enemies' ranks, he had been filled neither with pride at the praise from his comrades nor with a sense of victory. He had killed with his hands, but created nothing. There was an emptiness inside him that remained the same before and after the killing.

But sometimes, in his dreams, he saw himself plowing fields and harvesting the fruits of his labor. When he awoke, he would begin the day in a happy mood.

PART 4
THE ARRIVAL

(SUMMER, AD 860)

CHAPTER 11
HUNGER

The *Goldeagle*'s bow came to a crunching halt on the sandy beach. To her left and right landed the other six knarrs. With expectant expressions, the people jumped into the knee-high water. Fathers turned to their wives, who handed down their children across the railing, and then the men helped the women off the ships. Many of the settlers swayed as they walked onto the land. After weeks on board a moving ship, they were unaccustomed to firm ground beneath their feet, and to walking without constantly having to keep their balance.

Thorolf climbed atop a flat rock with his brothers and Högni, waiting for everyone to gather around them. The slave ships landed over a thousand paces farther down the beach. Evidently Egil's men wished to remain among themselves and forge their own fortunes. This suited Thorolf. He had fulfilled his pledge to Egil as best as he was able.

"What will they do with the slaves?" asked Yngvi pensively.

Högni pulled a cynical face. "Those slaves are worth a fortune. I bet since Egil, his son, and his nephew have passed on, they'll sell them off on their own accounts."

"But until then, they will have to feed them," remarked Digur drily.

Thorolf crossed his arms on his chest. "Yes, they're facing the same problem as us: no food. It could take weeks before they accumulate enough smoked meat and fish for their return voyage."

"A return voyage into the unknown." Högni paused. "Or do you have any idea where we have come to? I, for one, haven't the faintest inkling in which direction I would have to sail to get home."

"Well, first to the east, I would say," replied Thorolf unconvincingly. "And it would certainly be a long and dangerous voyage."

By now, everyone had assembled before the rock, waiting with eager anticipation for their chieftain's words.

Thorolf briefly thought about what to say before declaring: "The gods have accepted our sacrifice and saved us! We are arrived."

Clearing his throat, he waited for enthusiastic applause. The applause came, but it turned out rather muted.

Somewhat disappointed, but with no less fervor, he went on. "Yesterday, the lords of Valhalla sent us a bird with a beak as yellow as the sun. It led us to this shore. At first, I believed we'd arrived at the island Egil told us about—Catan. But in truth, we have landed on the shores of a different, much more distant land."

Thorolf read no surprise on the faces of his audience. Many of them had probably reached the same conclusion at the sight of the tall mountains farther inland. "I will call our new home Catan nevertheless, for in the tongue of the Majo, Catan signifies 'land of the sun.' Such a name promises warmth, life, and fertility. I am telling you: the gods not only sent us the yellow-beak, but also gave us the name Catan as an omen for a bright future!"

Some of the men showed their support with brief shouts of encouragement, and Thorolf nodded at them. "We do not yet know what awaits us here. Is there prey in the woods for us to hunt? Are there people living somewhere in the forest? Have they already spotted us? If so, they may not be as peaceful as the Majos on Egil's isle. But we will find out!" He raised his voice, thumping his right fist into the air in the rhythm of his words. "But should there be resistance, we will break it and make this land ours!"

He was trying to rekindle the excitement that had taken hold of his people upon first laying eyes on the coast of this unknown land—but it wasn't working. The people's faces, no matter whether man or woman, young or old, free or unfree, were filled with one need only: to satisfy their hunger.

"I know your stomachs are grumbling. We all need food urgently. But we mustn't forget our safety. Maybe enemies are lurking in the woods right now, planning their attack. Therefore, we will split into groups. I'll go hunting with the three best bowmen among you. Fishermen, go with Yngvi and Högni. They will take you to the deeper waters off the coast aboard the *Shieldmaiden*. There you shall receive ample opportunity to bring honor to your profession." He gestured at Digur. "All men who know how to handle a sword and shield, report to my brother. He is going to select twenty of the most experienced warriors among you, whose task it will be to secure and guard our camp. Asla, together with the other women, will oversee the erection of the tents and firepits."

He winked at Hilda, who was standing in the front row with Carla and Stina. "Hilda, take a few maids to gather wood with you and ensure that every available pot is hung above a fire. By evenfall, I want water for a rich stew to simmer in each pot. We men will provide the ingredients."

Hilda nodded at him, her cheeks flushed. Having spent many years as the charcoal burner's wife at the side of a tight-lipped man living remotely in the woods, she wasn't used to standing at the center of so many people and being endowed with an important task.

Thorolf's eyes found Harald, who was standing in the third row with his maid, Abena, and his children. "Harald, take a few servants and make them fasten the ships to the beach. Then get them to unload the horses and the livestock. There are grasses here and there for the grazing animals, and as for the pigs and chickens, lead them to the edge of the woods. I am sure they will find fodder there." That was all there was to say for now. "Let's get to work."

The settlers scattered, and soon each person had found a group that best suited their abilities.

Thorolf was taking preparations to go hunting when two sailors from the slave ships arrived at his camp. One of them was Runar, a dubious sort of a fellow that Egil used to employ as the skipper of one of his ships. Thorolf raised his hand in greeting at the man and his companion. "What do you want?"

Runar spoke with a flat voice, and Thorolf felt unease at the cold and calculating stare of the pale-blue eyes. "I now carry the command over Egil's ships. We need a fishing net."

Thorolf crossed his arms on his chest. "I am no longer responsible for you—you made this very clear. Why should I give you a net?"

"Because we need food in order to fulfill our task."

"What task?"

"We want to return home and sell the slaves there."

Thorolf asked Yngvi, who was nearby, how many fishing nets were in their possession. When Yngvi held up two full hands, he turned back to the men.

"I am prepared to give you one net, Runar. However, I do have one condition: Swear by the gods that Egil's family will receive half of the winnings."

Runar swore in a monotonous tone and with a traitorous

sparkle in his eyes, which Thorolf did not fail to notice. He decided to give them the net regardless. This would be his final service to his friend Egil, even if the likelihood of Runar keeping his word was rather slim. If he ever would be in a position to keep his word at all, thought Thorolf. The journey was long and the sea treacherous.

Near the spot where their camp would be, Digur selected three rock formations upon which two armed men each would keep watch. Then he sent several of his men to the edge of the forest to collect wood for the fires, which would be built one hundred paces in front of each sentry post at night, illuminating their surroundings.

Asla rested on a crate, holding her aching back. The child in her belly moved, seeming impatient to be born. Asla sensed that it would not be long now, and she thanked the gods that her son would be born on land.

"Look who it is!" called out Stina.

It was Loki, zigzagging between the half-built tents and firepits toward them. His snout was bloodied, and he was holding something furry between his teeth. Evidently he had already devoured one of his victims. Asla received his offering and hugged the loyal dog who, whimpering happily, licked his mistress's neck. When she released him, he gave a curt bark and ran off toward the woods once more.

Asla studied Loki's catch. The animal looked like a young hare, but with a stouter build and shorter ears. "I've never seen an animal like this before," she said, more to herself than to anyone in particular.

Gregor, having overheard her, explained. "This is a rabbit. They only exist in the southern lands."

Asla looked at the monk with friendly eyes. "Is its meat good?"

Gregor closed his eyes, his face taking on a dreamy expression. "Oh yes, it is. Properly roasted and seasoned, it is delicious—even more so than hare."

Asla asked her sister, who had listened to Gregor's words, to take the rabbit to Hilda for the stew.

"I will do no such thing," replied Stina firmly. "This is your rabbit. Loki gave it to you as a gift. You need strength for you and your son. Give me a little while—I'll roast it for you."

Asla did not object. Her mouth watered at the thought of roast meat. She needed to distract herself until it was cooked.

"Come with me?" she asked Carla, who was sitting on the crate beside her, patiently disentangling some rope. "Thorolf is about to head to the forest with his hunters. I'll ask him if we may come along."

"What do you want to go to the forest for? To hunt? In your state?" asked the younger woman incredulously.

Asla giggled. "No, even though I am good with a bow. I want to study the plants that grow here. Perhaps there are some I know."

Carla thought that sounded exciting. She was intrigued by Asla's ability to heal illnesses and by her knowledge of plants. "Of course I'll come," she replied eagerly.

Thorolf was not at all thrilled at the request of his heavily pregnant wife to join him on his exploration of the forest. But once she explained that she intended to search for plants with edible bulbs and roots for Hilda's stew, he gave in.

The forest was like a foreign, mystical world. Many of the trees did not possess one main trunk like those in the woods of the North. Instead, just above their roots, they branched into multiple thicker and thinner trunks, some of which sought the sun in a straight line while others writhed crookedly in all directions, as if they had been eager in their youth to explore their surroundings. Some trees started off straight before bending back toward the ground, and then, as if they had recognized their mistake, they curved back again toward the sun like a snake. In some places, the trunks and branches of neighboring trees grew wildly around and within one another, and seemed to suffocate rather than embrace each other in their desperate search for gaps of light in the dense canopy. Damp moss grew on the bark, forming fat cushions on rotting tree trunks. The air smelled of sodden soil and moss.

The hunters made their way through the difficult undergrowth, followed by Asla and Carla. Many times they were forced to clamber across fallen logs or navigate around large ferns with huge fronds. Carla held her pregnant friend's hand to keep her from falling.

Asla thought the woods were eerie. Every now and then, they heard birds cawing or singing, and they passed small islands of flowers with yellow blossoms that took away some of the threatening nature of this green wilderness. But still she feared that, at any moment, a horde of evil trolls with cudgels might emerge from behind trees and bushes, putting an end to all their lives.

Suddenly Thorolf raised one hand, turned to his companions, and placed a forefinger against his lips. Slowly and almost soundlessly, he drew an arrow from his quiver, lifting his bow at the ready. His three fellow hunters copied him. Thus they stood, still, for quite some time, until Asla and Carla finally noticed the reason for their pause: about fifteen paces ahead of them, a rabbit emerged from some low scrub atop a small mound. Thorolf must have spotted the furry creature when, startled by their noisy approach, it fled into its hideout. Now it sniffed the air, took a few hops, and eyeballed the six motionless humans who appeared strange but seemingly not threatening. Evidently encouraged by the example of their friend, more rabbits soon emerged.

Slowly and silently the hunters drew their bows, aimed, and loosed their arrows in quick succession. Two animals were lying on the ground with twitching hindquarters, while a third one had been struck by two arrows at once, killing it instantly. The other rabbits scattered, disappearing into the undergrowth with fright. The men collected their prey and returned the precious arrows to their quivers.

Thorolf placed his hand on Asla's shoulder. "I will continue to search for game with the men, but this is too exhausting for you. Please go back with Carla. Tell the others we will be back before dusk. Be careful!"

Thorolf did not need to ask twice. The walk through the dense underbrush had been more strenuous than she cared to admit. She stroked his bearded cheek. "I will, my darling. Do not worry. You, too, take care. This forest frightens me."

While the hunters went deeper into the woods, Asla and Carla carefully stepped over tangled roots, smaller rocks, and broken branches. They could not get lost, knowing they only needed to descend the gentle slope to reach their camp.

At the edge of the woods, Asla bent down with her knife and dug out a plant. The whitish root was thicker at the top, and its narrower tip had broken off. The light-green leaves were delicately feathered. Asla rubbed one leaf, holding out her green-dyed fingers to Carla.

"Do you recognize the smell?"

"No, never smelled it before. But it's nice."

Asla smiled sympathetically. "And how should you have encountered it in filthy Hedeby, you poor thing. This smell is typical for the carrot."

"I see. And what is the carrot good for?"

"It's nutritious and adds flavor to a stew. Look at it closely. When we get back to camp, take a few maids and dig out as many carrot plants as you can. Take only the young plants that haven't flowered yet. The root grows too hard once they flower. Hilda will be pleased about the carrots for her meal."

Carla nodded eagerly and ran ahead to the camp, while Asla trudged after her slowly, excited about the roasted rabbit she would naturally share with her sister and her friend.

Meanwhile, Yngvi and Högni had boarded the *Shieldmaiden* with fifteen men. In a slow rhythm, they rowed the knarr, which carried six dinghies tied to her stern, out of the rocky danger zone and into deeper waters, where they dropped the anchor. In pairs, the fishermen climbed into the smaller boats, and while one man operated the two short oars, the other unfurled a thirty-foot seine net with a fisherman in one of the other boats, pulling it tight between the two vessels. Wooden sticks along the top edge kept the net on the surface, while lead weights dragged its bottom edge down.

Yngvi and Högni leaned against the *Shieldmaiden*'s side, watching the fishermen's maneuvers. Propelled by the oars, two boats glided across the calm sea with the net taut between them. After a while, they would turn and row back toward the *Shieldmaiden*. Shortly before reaching her, the two smaller boats approached one another and the fishermen brought in the net, passing it to their companions at the railing.

"Now we will learn how abundant the fish are on these shores," said Högni with eager anticipation as the men beside them lifted the first folded-up net. The shipbuilder's face fell in view of the meager contents. There were but three larger and several smaller fish captured in the net's middle.

Toward the evening, however, the fishermen were not entirely dissatisfied with their catch. The smaller fish would be cooked in a soup, and the larger fish would be fried to ease the worst of the people's hunger.

Yngvi, who was helping to gut the caught fish, was about to give the order to return to the shore when he noticed yellow-beaks landing in the water all around them, a few at first, then more and more. Soon there were hundreds of birds, greeting the cliffs and rocks of the shore with their squawking cries of *doo doo doo huh*. Yngvi suspected they'd built their nests within the cavities and on the rifts of those rocks. Curious rather than nervous, they eyed the humans in their boats, swimming alongside them without shyness just a few feet away.

Yngvi thoughtfully stroked his blond beard, which had grown thick by then. "I believe these birds have not yet had any bad experiences with people—if they've ever encountered any at all."

Högni brought his calloused hand down on Yngvi's shoulder, grinning at him from his broad face. "That we will change tomorrow, when we bring our bows. I can hardly wait to see those birds roasting on spits."

Pleased at the prospect of a new source of food, Yngvi nodded at the shipbuilder who—like all the settlers—was visibly suffering from hunger.

When the dinghies were secured at the *Shieldmaiden*'s stern, the men sat down at the oars and began to row the knarr back to the beach. Deep in thought, Yngvi watched the gray-brown birds that innocently paddled on the water by the last light of the setting sun, spreading and retracting their wings, grooming their feathers, diving under and singing their funny song. Not only had the yellow-beaks led them to Catan, but they would also help them conquer their hunger.

Thorolf and his hunters had killed nearly forty rabbits, which he shared evenly, just like the larger fish, among the families. The smaller fish, the edible innards of the rabbits, and the carrots were tossed into the pots of boiling water. That evening, the people's good mood returned. The fish and skinned rabbits roasting above the fires exuded an irresistible savory aroma that promised full stomachs.

With an unusually serious expression, Hilda stood between two kettles from which maids scooped the soup with wooden ladles, distributing it among the bowls of the settlers. The meal had not turned out particularly well, but she'd had little control over the broth's flavor. She had added anything nutritious and usable at hand, having run out of the herbs she would have normally added to improve her meals. The only flavorings available to her were the seawater, which made up half of the broth's base, and the carrot roots. But to her amazement, everyone looked satisfied as they slurped up their soup. Most likely, Hilda suspected wryly, they would have gobbled up soup made with flies in their hunger.

With a sigh, she slumped down between Carla and Stina, who were sitting around a fire with Asla and the brothers. She was surprised to see Yngvi's servant, Gregor, sitting beside his master and among the freemen. She liked the monk. He was by no means an attractive man, though he had lost a little weight and the sun had tanned his skin, but his kind manner and the intelligent, sensitive look in his eyes when he gazed at her appealed to her.

Asla passed her a piece of the fish Thorolf had taken off

the spit above the fire and cut up. When she handed a piece to Gregor also, Thorolf looked at Yngvi with his brow wrinkled. "Since when is it the custom for a servant to sit with us and share our food?"

Annoyed, Yngvi replied a little more sharply than he'd probably intended, "I don't see any servants here. Should you refer to Gregor, then let me tell you that, as of this morning, he is a freeman. If you don't like it, I will gladly sit elsewhere with my friend."

Gregor stared at his former master with surprise. Evidently, he had not been told of his recent release. Asla and Hilda smiled at the monk's befuddled expression.

Thorolf, too, could not help but smile. "Settle down, little brother. How was I supposed to know that you've released Gregor when he does not even know it himself?"

Now they all laughed, save for Yngvi, who looked a little abashed.

Thorolf raised his cup and turned to the monk. "Welcome to our ranks, Gregor! What a pity we have only water and not wine to drink to you. You have been a good teacher and friend to my brother for many years, and I am sure you have earned your freedom." Glancing at Yngvi, who seemed surprised at his brother's good-humored reaction, he added: "And so you have in my eyes, too."

Gregor picked up his cup and thanked Thorolf for the kind welcome into the class of freemen. Amicably, he boxed his former master in the side, remarking mockingly: "You I already thanked this morning, as I'm sure you will remember."

Now Yngvi laughed too, wrapping an arm around his friend's shoulder. The tense moment had passed. As Hilda gazed into the monk's cheerful face, listening to his warm voice, he suddenly appeared a lot less unsightly to her.

Gregor noticed the charcoal burner's furtive glances. Ever

since he had known her, she had seemed to him as an angel amid the coarse world of the Northern people. The warm gleam in her brown eyes that intensified when she smiled enchanted him and drew him in a way he could not explain. When he peeked at her ample bosom and wide hips, he had more than once caught himself in reveries wherein she lay in his arms.

Gregor sighed. The pope would not approve of such sinful thoughts. Those who served the church ought to have no wife to distract them from their tasks. Gregor had never particularly struggled to keep the celibacy which the church might not have demanded but expected nonetheless, for his manifold responsibilities in the church and his studies had hardly left any time for a private life. But even though he had lived in abstinence for such a long time, the tiny flame inside him that longed for the closeness of a woman had never completely died. Now that Hilda had entered his life, the flame had been nourished, warming his heart. *And why not*, he thought. The pope and Rome were far away, and he would probably never return there.

Digur tore meat off a rabbit's leg with his teeth. It seemed he couldn't eat fast enough, and there was still room for plenty more before his stomach would feel sated for the first time in many days.

With a full mouth, he asked Thorolf, "How was the forest?"

"The forest we saw is completely different from the forests in our old home. Many trees here grow wildly intertwined with crooked trunks, unsuitable for building houses. But thankfully, there is the occasional straight branch or trunk." Thorolf's expression turned thoughtful. "The rabbits were the only game we came across. No roe, no red deer, no boars. And no sign of them. We found no tree whose bark was gnawed, and no patches of churned ground. Nor did we come across any game paths. It seems strange. I wonder why these little furry creatures exist in a land that seems to hold no animals other than birds and lizards," Thorolf sighed. "Be that as it may. In this part of Catan, at least, we will have to content ourselves with the hunt of rabbits and fishing."

"Don't forget the yellow-beaks," said Yngvi, telling the others about the trusting birds that gathered near the coast in large numbers in the evening. "We will catch some of those tomorrow."

As the first day on Catan came to an end, many settlers bathed on the beach before turning in for the night. The air was mild, and most preferred to sleep under the clear, starry sky, instead of in their tents.

On the third day following their arrival, Thorolf ordered his skippers Olaf and Tjörvi and their crews to explore the coast. He gave them two days. Their task was to keep a lookout for a suitable place to settle, and for a river or a creek to fill their empty water barrels. The sun shone and a steady breeze blew when the men rowed the two knarrs out of the surf. By now they knew which way to take to reach the open sea safely past the hazardous rocks. Once at sea, one of the knarrs made course for the southeast and the other sailed northwest, both remaining within sight of the shore.

When darkness fell, the settlers cheerfully welcomed Thorolf and his hunters back to camp. The thin trunks they carried in pairs were bending under the weight of all the rabbits they had killed. By then the men had learned that the furry creatures were most likely to be found outside their burrows in the morning and toward the end of the day and had adjusted their hunting times accordingly.

Women, maids, and servants eagerly fetched the dead

animals to skin and gut them. The water in Hilda's pots was already boiling when Yngvi and Högni, too, returned laden with prey. Many smaller and significantly more larger fish than in the last couple of days had swum into their nets, and more than four dozen yellow-beaks waited to be plucked, gutted, and roasted.

Satisfied, Thorolf watched the people in their busy doings. The meat of the animals they had hunted would not only feed them this evening; for the first time, there was sufficient food to last for a second meal the following day.

The ship that had sailed to the northwest returned the following afternoon already, its water barrels filled. The heads of families assailed Olaf, the man in charge of the first ship, with questions, but he refused to give answers until Thorolf returned from hunting in the woods.

Thorolf, Yngvi, and Högni arrived back at camp almost at the same time. As the day before, they were bringing home rich spoils from the forest and the sea. The leaders and everyone who was not helping with the preparation of this evening's meal gathered around Thorolf and his brothers, who greeted Olaf and asked him to tell them of his exploratory trip.

They did not need to ask twice. The tall, strongly built seaman, who wore his brown hair in plaits, was ready. "To begin with, the coast hardly altered. Sandy beaches, some with more rocks, some with fewer, alternated with rocky cliffs. Beyond the beaches were the woods, just like here. But in the late afternoon, the forest retreated and gave way to a delta with luscious green meadows. We rowed up a wide river in the delta and decided to make camp at a spot were the river branched out. Thankfully we chose an elevated place for our camp or else our backsides would have got wet." Olaf laughed. "For when we woke up in the morning, the sea had flooded the delta, and the grass only stuck out from the water by half its length. Farther upriver, the meadows were replaced by woods that came right down to the banks. At the same time, the river became narrower and its current stronger, and the surrounding land rose to above fifteen feet. At the end of our journey, we reached a large lake." He drew an oval shape in the air with both hands to illustrate the lake's outline. "From the south, a roughly seven-foot waterfall drains into the lake. We beached the ship, and I hiked up the wooded hill, found myself a nice tall tree, and climbed up. From there I could see far across the land. What do you think I saw?"

Olaf paused expectantly, enjoying the group's eager expressions. He loved being the center of attention.

When it seemed that he would not speak on, Harald's patience ran out. "Spit it out already! Giants, troll, dragons?"

Olaf laughed. "No. I saw woods, woods, and more woods. Like a sea of green, growing up the mountains in the distance, only giving way to rocky gray at great heights." Olaf looked his chieftain in the eye. "If you ask me, Thorolf, I would select the shore of this lake for our settlement. There, we have all that we need: a sheltered harbor, fresh water, and wood—plenty of wood. And there is grazing for the animals in the nearby delta."

Thorolf grasped his skipper's right forearm, and he in turn grasped Thorolf's. "Well done, Olaf. Sounds as if that place could be right for us." He looked at his brothers, who nodded their approval, and then glanced into the round of leading men. "Once Tjörvi returns, we will break up this camp as quickly as possible. Unless he tells us of an even better place to build our home, Olaf will lead us to this lake. There we shall settle."

Thorolf saw relief and joy in the people's faces. He knew what they were thinking: at last something was happening; at last they would arrive at a place where they could hopefully build a home.

Tjörvi returned shortly before dusk and reported about his trip to the southeast. The shore, he said, did not differ much from where they were now. Twice they passed bays with wide sandy beaches. The first one wasn't far from here, and it contained the mouth of a creek, but neither of the bays held grazing ground for the livestock.

And so Thorolf's decision stood. The next day they would leave for the place described by Olaf to settle.

CHAPTER 12
THE CHAIN WIELDERS

Ryan pinched dead a louse—one of many torturing him and the other slaves, and one of many tortures they were forced to endure. For him, the worst was the hunger. Not because of the gnawing sensation in his innards, but because of the feeling of powerlessness in the face of his dwindling strength.

Soon after their arrival on the foreign shore, the Northmen had herded them off the ships and divided them into two groups of about eighty slaves each. Each group they forced to dig out a shallow pit, heaping up banks around it, and within the pits, the slaves were permitted to move freely—as much as their short ankle chains allowed. The slave drivers had made it unmistakably clear that anyone who crossed the banks would be killed. Six Northmen armed with spears and bows stayed behind to watch them, while the rest hunted in the woods or fished in the sea. There was no lack of drinking water; evidently, the Northmen had discovered a source of fresh water nearby.

In the evenings, the guards threaded ropes through the rings on the slaves' chains, tying the ends to posts outside the pit. Thus tied together, the men and women were scarcely able to move.

The tough ropes were knotted from walrus hide and would be difficult to cut even with a sharp knife. Some of the slave girls, however, the Northmen released from their chains and led down the beach, forcing them to take off their rags and wash. In the dark of night, the grunting and moaning of the men mixed with the cries of pain from the women.

On the second day, the slaves were finally offered food. Four armed guards with drawn swords placed a basket of small fish in their midst, and no sooner had they left the pit than fighting over the slippery sea creatures broke out. The men had a clear advantage, securing the larger part.

From the corner of his eye, Ryan noticed Runar standing at the edge of the pit. The new master of the slave ships bore a wide grin on his face. Clearly, he was amused by the undignified spectacle performed by Ryan and his companions.

The constant anger simmering inside the Irish prince boiled over. He clenched his fists, longing to smash the grin off the Northman's face. But he needed to be patient—the time to take revenge on his tormentors would come. Ryan bit off the head of one of the four fish he had secured, furiously grinding it between his teeth. The taste did not bother him. All that mattered was the strength the animal gave him.

When darkness fell, Ryan reached for his nail. Arduously, he had sharpened and shaped it between two smooth stones during moments when he was unobserved, practicing until he had mastered the mechanism inside the locks and was able to open and close the iron shackles at will.

Tonight their fate would be decided. Either he would gain freedom together with his fellow prisoners, or they would die.

For four nights Ryan had studied the habits of the Northmen. As soon as the slaves' shackles were bound together with the ropes, they reduced the number of guards. Only two men, armed with swords and spears, would then sit together on crates between the two pits, keeping an eye on the slaves. Between the sentries, a fire would be lit, emitting just enough light to outline the bodies inside the pits. At some point around the middle of the night, the guards would be relieved by others.

On the first two nights, the guards took their task very seriously, casting their eyes regularly across the pits. When occasionally one of them nodded off, he would be awakened immediately by his companion. On the third and especially the fourth night, they had become increasingly lax. At times, both sentries dozed at once, clearly evident from their sagging shoulders and hung heads.

On this night, Ryan hoped their jailers would be even more careless. The other slaves in the pit were informed. The night before, Ryan had shared his plan with the men chained to either side of him, and they, in turn, had passed on the message to their neighbors. In the course of the day, the Irishmen had tried their best to convey their leader's plan with furtive gestures and signals to the Anglo-Saxon, Frankish, and Slavic men and women.

When it was dark enough, Ryan unlocked his shackles and passed the nail to his neighbor. Since they had not practiced picking their locks, it took a long while before everyone in the pit had freed themselves from their chains. Ryan was relieved at the discipline of his fellow prisoners; everyone adhered to his order to not alter their behavior. They continued to moan, complaining of hunger and rattling their chains as if they still carried their iron shackles around their ankles. Now and then, the guards would cast bored glances into the pit while they chatted. But at some point, they fell silent. The fire between them had burned right down, with only some embers giving off a faint red glow. The air was mild, and hazy clouds dampened the light from the stars in a moonless sky.

Ryan knew the fresh guards would arrive soon. He signaled to Brennan, his friend and most capable companion in battle, and they took off their torn tunics. Now they were naked. In the darkness, their pale skin and fair hair barely stood out from the light-colored sand upon which they silently crawled out of the pit. Relying more on feeling than eyesight, they found themselves rocks that were large enough and fit well in the palms of their hands. Then each man carefully approached one of the two Northmen from behind.

Ryan paused on all fours behind the broad back of the softly snoring warrior whose death he would bring about, when the guard's bald-headed companion opposite him yawned heartily, glancing left and right into the pits but evidently not noticing anything out of the ordinary. He spat into the embers, his saliva turning to steam with a hiss, and, with a contented smacking of his mouth, folded his arms more tightly across his chest. Soon his head began to slump forward in small jerks.

Ryan crouched, then rose silently and lifted the rock above his head with his right hand. Vaguely, he made out Brennan's outline behind the bald man—his friend, too, was ready. With all his might, nourished by anger and deep resentment, Ryan struck. The Northman slipped off the crate and collapsed on the sand, his skull smashed in. His bald-headed companion opened his eyes wide, but before he could do anything, Brennan's stone struck him on the temple and made him tilt to the side.

The two Irishmen took the knives of their victims and passed them to their fellow countrymen Owen and Liam, who, as agreed, came climbing out of the pit. The guards had also carried daggers, which Ryan and Brennan kept for themselves. When the bald man unexpectedly began to groan, Brennan cut his throat.

Quickly, they undressed the two corpses, and Owen and

Liam dragged them away, hiding them behind a rock. Ryan and Brennan pulled the Northmen's tunics over their heads and donned their sword belts and cloaks. Then they sat down on the crates and pretended to be asleep. Brennan, sitting in the place of the bald man, pulled his hood over his thick head of hair.

They were ready for the relieving guards to arrive.

Owen sneaked back down the pit and handed the knife to one of the men who then sawed through the walrus rope in several places, thus freeing the chains from the ropes. This way, each person would be able to hold a weapon: a chain with heavy shackles at the ends, which they could swing at their enemies' unprotected heads.

Meanwhile, Liam showed the slaves in the second pit how to pick open their shackles with the nail. Excited, one after the other began fiddling with their locks. Many of them did so with trembling hands, tense and nervous, if their efforts did not succeed at first. While Liam cut the rope in several places, he used simple gestures to explain to the mostly Anglo-Saxon, Slavic, and Frankish women and men how to use their chains in combat. When it was time, he signaled to them he would lead them.

All was quiet in the Northmen's camp, about sixty paces away. None of the sailors and warriors sleeping on their furs seemed to have noticed the attack on the sentries. Ryan gave a strained smile. So far, so good. The first part of his plan was fulfilled. If the men and women inside the two pits played their part, the Northmen's fate was sealed.

Time dragged on. When Ryan began to fear the fresh guards were not coming, he heard crunching footsteps in the sand. Moments later, a hoarse voice said in his back: "We overslept. But as I can see, you aren't working too hard, either."

Two pairs of feet appeared in his limited field of vision. Wood was dropped beside the red glimmering embers of the fireplace. One of the men nudged his shoulder harshly, snarling, "Hey, man. Change of guards!"

Ryan lifted his head, muttering something incomprehensible. Slowly he rose to his feet, and at the same moment that the Northman identified him as a foreigner, freezing with shock, Ryan plunged the dagger into his chest. The second Northman gaped with surprise and made to draw his sword, but before he could scream, Brennan, who was behind him, slit his throat.

Tense, Ryan glanced in the direction of the Northmen's camp. Someone was fidgeting with the fire, which flared up brightly moments later. Luckily, it was sufficiently far away; the light of the flames did not reach the events at the slave pits. They did not have much time. Soon the guards from the first shift would be missed, or one of the Northmen would notice that the watchmen's fire had gone out.

Ryan and his Irish comrades now possessed four swords, four daggers, three knives, and four spears, which had been stuck in the sand with their shafts next to the fire. Fifteen weapons for nineteen men. Not enough to withstand the more than thirty remaining battle-seasoned seamen and well-armed warriors from the North in an open conflict. But Ryan had two allies: surprise and sheer numbers, there being more than one hundred and fifty desperate slaves.

Ryan, Brennan, and Owen were armed solely with heavy rocks as they crawled on their bellies toward the Northmen's camp. They had left their swords, daggers, and spears to their fellow Irishmen, who were crawling behind them. Behind the cover of a rock, Ryan gave the signal to stop. The Northmen were sleeping on their furs about thirty feet away. There was only one guard posted. Thankfully the man was sitting with his back to them in front of his fire. Aside from snoring, all was quiet. Ryan got to his feet and ran, doubled over, to the edge of the camp. Brennan, Owen, and the other warriors followed him as quietly as they could.

The first three Northmen died in their sleep when the Irishmen brought down the heavy rocks on their heads. Swiftly Ryan grabbed the sword belt that was lying next to his victim and drew the blade from its scabbard. Brennan and Owen did the same.

And not a moment too soon: the first few Northmen were awakened by the noise, leaping to their feet and drawing their swords also. Ryan roared a battle cry and ran with his warriors at the astonished enemies.

That was the signal for Liam to lead more than one hundred men and women to the Northmen's rear. Few among them had any experience in battle, and all of them were weakened from hunger, but hatred of their tormentors gave them unexpected strength, turning their chains into deadly weapons.

When Ryan, fighting side by side with Brennan and Owen, parried the attack of an opponent, the face of a woman suddenly appeared behind the Northman's shoulder, wildly determined and twisted with hatred. With both hands, the slave woman threw her chain over the man's head, dropped to the ground, and pulled with all her weight on her former shackles. The Northman's head jerked back. Ryan did not hesitate, thrusting his blade into his chest. He withdrew his sword from the dying man's body just in time to parry the attack of a foe from the right. His blood rushed through his veins, dispelling the weakness he had felt at the beginning of the fight. His reactions were as fast as they usually were, and he swung his sword with deadly precision.

With a groan, Owen fell to his knees to Ryan's left. The tip of a blade had pierced his chest. When the opponent withdrew his weapon, blood gushed from the wound. Brennan roared angrily and avenged his friend's death by sinking his sword into the Northman's neck. Another Northman was struck on the head by some shackles, staggering toward Ryan half-unconscious. In one fluid motion, the Irishman slit open his belly and blocked the attack of the next opponent.

Many of the Irish warriors had died by the Northmen's blades, and the battle's outcome hung in the balance. Without Liam's chain-wielding troop, Ryan knew he and his warriors would never have stood a chance against the superior force of the battle-hardened Northmen.

But the tables had indeed turned. The ranks of the Northmen thinned out under the valiant efforts of the remaining warriors and the men and women swinging their chains like berserks. In the end, only Runar and three of his followers were left, fighting bitterly. But the Northmen could not attack, block, and protect their heads from the chains of their former slaves all at once. Runar was the last of the enemy warriors to fall into the sand, pierced by Liam's sword.

Utterly exhausted, Ryan sank to his knees. The strength that had carried him through the battle left him abruptly. But there was no time for rest. Dawn would not be long. Once daylight arrived, Thorolf's settlers would soon notice that something was amiss.

With great effort, he straightened up and called together the survivors. Of his Irish warriors, only Liam and Brennan, as well as five other men—some of them gravely wounded—had survived, and of the chain wielders, as he had come to call the colorfully mixed troop of former slaves in his mind, only about half were standing.

Ryan nodded at them with a strained smile, speaking in a husky voice. "You fought bravely for our freedom. Thanks to your courage and God's help, we have vanquished those devils!"

Conscious of the former slaves' varied backgrounds, Ryan accompanied his words with facial expressions and vivid gestures. "You probably wonder how we are to carry on from here.

Where should we go? We cannot return home. Or do any of you know how to maneuver a Nordic ship through tall breakers?"

Ryan paused. None of the men and women wearily staring at him raised their hand. He had not expected anything else.

"We have no choice but to find a place in this land for the time being. It's not going to be easy. But we will make it and we will survive." Defiantly, he raised his clenched fist, adding in a tone of determination, "This I swear by God!"

Ryan gazed into the people's tired faces, faintly illuminated by the fire, and was satisfied to glimpse a hint of hope in at least some of them.

"We don't have much time. The settlers will bash in our heads when they find out that we killed their fellow countrymen. Therefore, do exactly as I tell you now: take off the Northmen's clothes and shoes. Whoever knows something about healing, care for our wounded. Collect the weapons and search the camp for useful items and food. Those dogs probably had something prepared for their breakfast. Carry everything to this ship." Ryan pointed in the direction of a knarr and clapped his hands. "Go on, get moving! Our new enemy is time."

The former slaves did not question Ryan's role as their leader. They were relieved to be told what to do. Weary, they shuffled and limped to work. The other Irishmen continued to explain with gestures to those who had not understood Ryan. Many of them probably thought their lives could not get any worse.

At the edge of camp, they found five bound and injured women who'd been used by the Northmen the previous night, including two Irishwomen. Ryan nodded at Brennan. "Untie them. We'll take them with us."

Ryan inspected the scene of the battle. The women were starting to undress the fallen Northmen. Those who had not succumbed to their injuries yet, lying groaning in the sand, they killed without batting an eyelid. Filled with hatred, they pulled the shoes off the corpses and tore the clothes from their bodies.

A red-haired Irishwoman addressed Ryan, her voice hoarse. "Seven of our people will survive their injuries, provided their wounds don't fester. We will carry them to the ship as soon as we've cared for them. But there are six we cannot help. What would you have us do with them?"

Ryan only fleetingly knew the woman, who had not been among the slaves on his ship. He studied her in silence as he contemplated her question. Her oval, even face was smeared with dirt and blood from a wound on her forehead. By the light of the campfire, her deep-blue eyes stood in contrast with the dark red of her matted hair. Ryan could only guess at the beauty she must have been before her monthslong period of suffering as a slave, a beauty now shrouded behind a veil of misery with sunken cheeks and dark rings around her eyes.

"What is your name?"

"Enya."

"Take me to them."

Enya first led him to a dying Irishwoman. She had received a stomach wound during the fight, her innards spilling to the outside. She was trembling, gazing at Ryan from glassy eyes.

He knelt down beside her and clasped her hands in his, praying in a gentle voice. "The Lord is my shepherd, I shall not want. He maketh me to lie down in green pastures, he leadeth me beside the still waters. He restoreth my soul . . ." Ryan had forgotten the rest of the psalm.

The Irishwoman closed her eyes and breathed more calmly. While he continued to hold the woman's delicate hands with his left, his right hand drew the dagger from his belt. Pressing his lips together tightly, Ryan plunged the dagger into the woman's heart. Her eyes opened wide, and her body jerked twice. Then she lay still. Ryan gently closed her lids and rose to his feet, a look of agony in his eyes.

He proceeded in the same manner with the other mortally wounded men and women. Even though the two Anglo-Saxons and the Slavic woman did not understand the meaning of his words, they were soothed by his deep, pleasant voice as he spoke to them, holding their hands.

Enya stood next to him in silence while he comforted the dying before relieving them of their suffering. "Where do you know this prayer from?" she asked eventually.

Ryan smoothed back his tangled hair. "There was a man of God at my father's court. My mother was a very pious woman. She asked him to teach her some Bible passages in our tongue. When I was little, she used to say those prayers with me."

Enya gazed at him with renewed interest. Not only was he a brave and merciless warrior, but he was also gentle and kind. She could see those contrasting characteristics reflected in his gray eyes. When, shortly after the battle's end, she had first looked into his face covered with its wild reddish-blond beard, she had been met by a cold, hard stare. But now, following his service to their moribund companions, the eyes she saw were warm and filled with empathy. Even though his words were not directed at her, she, too, felt soothed by him. He gave her the feeling that they still had something left to fight for. From one moment to the next, he became the focus of her existence.

Ryan walked over to Liam, who had called him to the former watchfire of the Northmen. The fire's embers had been fed with fresh wood, and the flickering flames illuminated more than twenty frightened women cowering together in one of the pits.

Liam shot a contemptuous look at the women. "They refused to aid us in our fight, even though we had freed them from their chains."

Ryan felt fury well up in him, and he unleashed a volley of curses at the slave women. In the end, he said, "Since you cowardly hags did not join our fight, you can rot here. You don't deserve to sail back home with us." He turned to Liam. "Tie them with ropes. We will take the chains, for we'll need the iron."

Ryan had recognized a fair-haired woman in the pit. She was Irish, and possibly the only one who understood him. He felt certain she would be able to convey to the settlers and their leader—with gestures, if need be—that the runaway slaves intended to sail back to their home. The Northmen had no way of knowing that there was not a single experienced sailor among his people—no one who would be able to handle a ship on the open sea.

As Ryan had guessed, their former masters had already prepared something for their morning meal. The chain wielders found cooked fish and roasted rabbits wrapped in skins. One pot was half-filled with a fish soup.

They lifted any useful possessions of the slave traders from the cargo holds of three of the knarrs, storing them inside the fourth ship, which Ryan named *Freedom*. There were numerous useful items that would help them survive in the wilderness of this unknown country—axes, weapons, a barrel of salt, copper pots, cups, bowls, firestones, animal hides, and a fishing net. The biggest surprise was hidden in some chests they found concealed at the very back of one of the cargo holds. Three chests were filled to the brim with dried fish, and another by about half. Obviously, the men in charge of the ships had kept these provisions secret from the settlers. No wonder their tormentors had not appeared plagued by hunger.

Dawn spread her first diffuse light across the horizon; it was high time. On Ryan's order, twenty-four women and twenty-five men climbed on board the *Freedom*. Together with the wounded who had already been carried aboard, the chain wielders numbered a little more than fifty heads.

Slowly, the strongest among them rowed the ship past the treacherous rocks. With mixed emotions, they gazed back at the beach where their luck had turned for the better, but where many of their companions had met their death. They had carried the bodies onto the three remaining knarrs and set fire in the ships' bellies. The first flames now licked up the bulwarks. Soon there would be nothing left of the three ships and the bodies but glowing logs and charred bones.

Out on the open water, the former slaves tried to raise the sail. They had observed the procedure many times but never done it with their own hands, and even though the sea was calm and the wind gentle, it took them several failed attempts before they managed to set the sail to the wind and bring the *Freedom* to move at least somewhat in the desired direction along the coast.

At last the *Freedom* glided to the southeast. Anyone who wasn't battling the stubborn sail or the steering oar filled their belly with the pilfered provisions. When Ryan gazed into the faces of the people this time, he could see that many of them had faith in him, radiating a guarded sense of hope for the future that lay ahead of them.

Hakon yawned. Around midnight, he had taken the second shift with Bran, a former servant whom Thorolf had freed upon their arrival, as promised. The night was quiet. Only the gentle rushing of the small waves and the occasional cracking of a burning branch on the fire in front of their watch post broke the silence. They had been keeping watch for a while when Hakon thought he heard the sounds of fighting in the distance. Bran could hear the muffled sounds, too. They squinted in the direction of Egil's former men, but all they saw was a small column of light from the fire their fellow countrymen kept going through the night.

"They're probably arguing," muttered Bran into his beard. "Probably over the silver they will make from the sale of the slaves."

Hakon shrugged indifferently. "What's it to us? Let them bash in each other's skulls. We have naught more to do with them."

It wasn't until after sunrise that they realized something was seriously wrong in the camp of their fellow Northmen. Smoke was pouring from three of the knarrs, and the camp appeared deserted. While Bran remained at his post, Hakon ran to Thorolf's tent. Thorolf was immediately wide awake. He dressed and sent a servant to wake his brothers and some heads of families.

The sun stood above the ocean by a handsbreadth when Thorolf, Yngvi, Digur, and twenty other armed men arrived at the camp of the slave traders. With horror they beheld the many naked corpses strewn wildly around the fire, which had since gone out. They were, without exception, Egil's former seamen and warriors. Instinctively, some of the men reached for their swords, fastening their gaze on the edge of the woods distrustfully. Had warlike inhabitants of Catan arrived from there during the night, slaying Runar and his men in their sleep? This question and many others sprang to Thorolf's mind when he studied the bodies more closely. Why were all naked? Why did many of the dead bear head wounds that looked to have been caused by some sort of projectile?

Yngvi searched the surrounding area and discovered about twenty bound women sitting in a shallow pit. When they spotted him at the edge of the pit, they started to wail and babble wildly over the top of one another. Yngvi couldn't understand a word. He shouted for his brothers.

The sight of the women was a new puzzle for Thorolf. Why were these slaves here while the others had vanished? Had the mysterious warriors taken but some of the unfreemen and women, intending to come back later for the rest?

"I'll fetch Carla," Yngvi decided. "I think there are Anglo-Saxons among these women. Carla speaks their language."

Soon Yngvi returned with Carla. The settlers had untied the women's fetters but commanded them to remain where they were. Carla stood at the edge of the pit and asked the slave women whether any of them were from the land of the Anglo-Saxons. Many of them raised their hands. Carla asked several questions, and the women replied readily. Thorolf, not understanding any of it, tapped his foot impatiently.

At last Carla turned to him. "The slaves broke free in the night and attacked their masters. They mentioned the name Ryan several times. It seems he was their leader. The women claim they had been too afraid to join in the fight, especially since their only weapons were their chains, which they were supposed to wield during the battle. As punishment for their refusal, Ryan had them tied up and would not take them along on the ship the slaves escaped on."

In Thorolf's thoughts, the questions that had tormented him became pieced together like the shards of a broken jug to form a whole. Even if the death of Egil's former men pained him, he couldn't help but feel relief that it had not been hitherto undiscovered natives of Catan who butchered the Northmen.

"Ask them what the slaves did with their dead and how many of them survived."

Digur added, "How did they free themselves from their chains?"

Carla spoke with the women again. "They say Ryan freed them using a nail. He worked the nail until he could open shackles with it. They burned their dead with the ships. Most of the women are unsure how many slaves survived the fight and left with Ryan, but one showed both her hands five times."

"And where have the slaves gone to?" asked Yngvi.

Once Carla had translated his question, the Anglo-Saxon women exchanged puzzled looks. Then one of them pointed at a woman in their midst. Yngvi looked at the fair-haired, evidently pregnant woman, spoke the name "Ryan" and, a questioning expression on his face, held out his arm in various directions.

The Irishwoman stepped forward, placed her hand on her chest and said, "Caitlin." She crouched down and drew a cross in the sand, and then pointed in turns at herself and the cross. Yngvi copied her and nodded, signaling to her that he understood the meaning of the cross as their current position. Then she drew a long line into the sand about two feet away from the cross, stuck one finger into the cross, and slowly dragged it through the sand. As her finger traveled away from the cross, she repeated the name "Ryan," bloating her cheeks and blowing out air through her pouting lips until her finger reached the line in the sand.

Yngvi looked at his brother. "It would seem they decided to sail back home."

"Without provisions?" asked Thorolf. "I doubt that."

Yngvi raised one eyebrow, tilting his head. "What if Egil's men weren't entirely honest with us and kept some of their provisions hidden in the holds?"

"I wouldn't put it past them," grumbled Digur. "They did not strike me as men suffering from hunger."

"In the end, it is one and the same whether the slaves sailed back for their homeland or have gone to search for a place on Catan," said Thorolf, ending the discussion. "We do not currently have the means to comb the land for escapee slaves with a troop of armed men. We need every hand to secure our food supplies and build our domiciles."

His brothers agreed.

One of the Anglo-Saxon women said something. "The women would like to know what's going to happen to them," Carla translated.

Thorolf did not think for long. "Tell them they will join our community as maids. After all, they did not participate in the attack on our fellow countrymen."

He turned to Yngvi. "With Carla's help, try to make them understand that it's not going to be easy. They will have to earn their daily bread, same as all thralls, with hard work. If they disobey, they will be punished. Distribute them among the families as you see fit. But tell the head of each family that it is I who decides over the women's future. They are but a loan for now."

Before Yngvi did as his brother asked him, he placed an arm around Carla. "You helped us greatly, little sister. I'm glad we have you."

He gave her a warm, winning smile—the kind of smile she'd last seen on him when he still lived in the hope of sharing a future with Frida.

Delighted, Carla brushed a dark curl behind her ear and rose on the tips of her toes, planting a kiss on his cheek. "Thank you, big brother."

Yngvi scanned the slave women. They were filthy, and their drawn faces were marked by hunger and deprivation. Thin, bony limbs stuck out from their threadbare shifts. But even their pitiful state could not conceal the inherent beauty of these women. Yngvi feared the new maids' looks would bring strife to their community. Not every head of a family would keep his fingers off the unfree woman Yngvi assigned to them, and not every wife would stand by idly. And it would be the new maids who would suffer from it all.

Yngvi decided to take under his own wing the fair-haired Irish woman who had introduced herself as Caitlin and who had explained Ryan's intentions to them. The reason, however, was not her pleasing appearance but the rounded belly showing under her shift. If Frida were still alive, he thought, her pregnancy would be similarly advanced now.

CHAPTER 13
WOODHAVEN

The tide was low when the seven knarrs rode into the wide main branch of the delta. Men, women, and children stood on the decks in cloaks, gazing with interest at the landscape passing slowly by. The banks were overgrown with grasses and a variety of weeds. The scent of the plants mingled with that of the sea, infusing the humid air with a foreign, pleasant aroma. The low evening sun occasionally hid behind swiftly moving clouds, and every now and then, a brief shower would sweep across the ships.

In the early evening, they reached the place where the river branched. This was where the lush meadows lay. Thorolf estimated the distance to the edge of the forest, which surrounded the fields in the east, south, and west in a half-circle, to be at least three thousand paces. It looked as though the trees were keeping a respectful distance from the salty seawater which, during high tide, probably flooded large parts of the meadows. This place, Thorolf thought, was ideal for their livestock. The horses, sheep, and cows would flourish from the rich grasses and soon procreate.

Before darkness fully fell, servants led the grazing livestock off the boats. With relish the animals began to pluck at the blades right away. The cages of chickens, too, were unloaded and opened. The poultry would find plenty to peck here. The settlers spent the night on board their ships.

In the early morning, they led the pigs on land. Thorolf ordered one of his servants to herd the animals to the edge of the woods, where they could scour not only the meadow but also the forest floor for insects and nutritious roots and bulbs. Thorolf advised him to herd the pigs until someone came to relieve him. Then he entrusted the supervision of the grazing animals to the capable daughter of a freeman, assigning her a servant from her family and one of the two sheepdogs Thorolf had bought in Hedeby as helpers.

Once the animals were looked after, Thorolf ordered the men to row the boats farther up the Saltmarsh River, as they had named the lazy stream. They made good progress; they could feel the current, though it was weak. The river's edges became increasingly overgrown by dense reeds, and beyond them, the realm of the forest began.

As the day before, the weather was changeable. Sunny periods alternated abruptly with clouds, and the next rain shower was never far away. In the late morning, they reached the lake Olaf had scouted out. To the east, the woods reached right up to the lake's reed-lined shores, also covering a peninsula that curved out into the water for about a thousand feet, forming a natural harbor. The lake's distant shores to the west and south lay enshrouded by haze.

Thorolf led the ships into the bay, ordering the anchors dropped and the ships bound together. Then he called his brothers and all heads of families to the *Goldeagle*.

"Men, we have arrived at the destination of our voyage. We will settle on the shores of this bay." With his hand, Thorolf drew a half-circle from the left shore to the tip of the peninsula. "Here, we will found our first settlement, which I am naming Woodhaven. But first we must overcome mighty adversaries."

When some of the men cast worried glances at the shore, searching for armed figures among the trees, Thorolf laughed.

"It will cost us much sweat to vanquish them with our axes—one after the other. Tree by tree, we will claim the land from the woods. Land for our fields, our livestock, and our halls! Are you strong enough to take up this fight?"

The men roared "Yes!" and they cheered and shook the *Goldeagle*'s timbers under their stamping feet. Thorolf, pleased to see confidence on the faces of his people, shared their enthusiasm. At last they would begin their future in their new home, shaping it according to their will.

Thorolf went on. "We have not discovered any sign of humans. We are likely to be the first people to set foot on this land. I believe one post of sentries will suffice for our safety, down by the fork in the Saltmarsh. If, unexpectedly, foreign ships were to come up the river, the watch would warn us in time." He pointed at his steersman. "Hakon, you carry the command over the sentries and those who herd the animals in the delta." The old seaman nodded eagerly, visibly pleased to avoid the task of swinging an axe in the woods. Thorolf wet his lips. "Our most pressing tasks are the provision of food and the clearing of the peninsula. As on our arrival, I will hunt for rabbits in the woods with a handful of men. Yngvi and Högni will continue to take their crew fishing at sea, securing our supply of fish and yellow-beaks. Digur will oversee the clearing of the peninsula."

Thorolf noticed the blacksmith frowning. "Do you have a better suggestion, Harald?"

"Why don't we just burn down the trees on the peninsula?"

"If you had come hunting with us, you would know that

the forest is simply too damp. The trunks and branches of the trees are thickly covered with moss which never seems to dry out. And even if we succeeded in setting fire to a few trees, a downpour would arrive and ruin our efforts."

As if the dark clouds in the sky wanted to prove Thorolf right, they opened their floodgates, speckling the settlers' cloaks with heavy drops.

As they did every day, Yngvi, Högni, and the fishermen had climbed aboard the *Shieldmaiden* at dawn, maneuvering her down the Saltmarsh. Long before the sun reached its zenith in the sky, they arrived on the open sea, where on this day they were witness to an impressive spectacle.

Paying no heed to the ship, more than a hundred yellow-beaks ran on the water's surface, flapping their wings, then dived and reemerged with fish in their beaks. Dolphins swam in circles around the birds' hunting ground, occasionally diving deep and blowing out air underwater, sending large bubbles to the surface here and there.

"Look down, Högni!" called Yngvi to his friend, who stood at the ship's side with him, watching the spectacle.

The shipwright did, gasping when he beheld hundreds of fish packed tightly in the clear water. "There's a huge school of mackerel underneath us. Apparently the dolphins herd them together and the yellow-beaks reap the rewards."

"And so will we in a moment," said Yngvi cheerfully, ordering the seamen to row the *Shieldmaiden* out of the dolphins' hunting ground before lowering the dinghies into the water and plundering the school with their nets.

When Yngvi and Högni anchored the *Shieldmaiden* in the

bay that evening, the settlers watched in amazement while the men rowed their huge catch ashore in several trips.

Hilda called together a few maids, and the women worked by the light of torches into the night until all fish were gutted and rubbed with salt. They urgently needed huts to smoke the mackerel.

Digur lifted his axe and sank it into the trunk. He worked the same way he fought: focused and efficiently. No other man had felled as many trees as he, and no other man lasted as long. When the tree finally toppled, Digur suddenly felt ravenous and thought it a good time to take a break. He ran a thumb across the axe's cutting edge and found that it was blunt. He decided to take it to Harald, who had stored his tools beneath a makeshift shelter of trunks and reeds.

The smith was sharpening an axe when Digur came by, leaning his own axe against a post. Harald's old servant sat on a log in front of a crate full of rusty tools, working to free some pliers from the rough, red marks which the salty sea breeze had eaten into its iron. Next to him sat Abena, heavily pregnant by now, smearing tallow on the cleaned tools. Harald gave a whistle. A strong young servant rushed over and took the freshly sharpened axe from him. He would carry it to his master, with whom the servant took turns at felling trees.

Wiping sweat off his forehead, Harald picked up Digur's axe. "This one needs honing. It'll take time. Come back later."

The hulk nodded and trudged off. Abena couldn't help but smile. When those two taciturn men met, it was a miracle if any words came out at all.

Digur was pleased with their progress. In the last five days, the settlers had cleared nearly half of the peninsula, which had to be two or three hundred feet wide. Any tree trunks that were straight and therefore potential future building material were stacked in one area. Crooked timber was cut into firewood. Because the lumber would need to dry out, Digur had the men build a shelter to protect it from the weather until it was ready to use. Wherever there was room, the families had hung up their pots, lighting fires with great difficulty and using less-damp heartwood from the trunks.

Stina was pleased to see Digur approach. He looked sullen, as usual when he was very hungry. Quickly she opened the lid of a wicker basket and produced a roasted rabbit, holding it out to him. "I put this aside for you. With regards from Loki, who brought it to Asla last night."

Digur's face brightened at the sight of the meat, and he accepted it with a small smile for his benefactress.

Stina studied the large, athletic man as he ate with obvious relish, sucking the cold but still tender and juicy meat off the bones. She did not know how Digur felt about her. Sometimes, when she felt his gaze on her and turned her face unexpectedly, she thought she detected a hint of longing in his eyes. She wasn't sure if that emotion related to her, for he never made any attempts to get close to her. When she gave him a kiss on the cheek, it seemed to please him, but he never returned the tender gesture.

Nor was Stina entirely certain of her own feelings for Digur. She felt at ease near him, sensed the strength that resided within him, and the kindness and fairness in his heart. She herself had experienced how caring he could be. She liked it when the big man was nearby, but she would have to wait and see what the future held for them.

Digur tossed a clean rabbit bone into the fire. "Where are the other women?"

"Asla isn't feeling well this morning and stayed in her cabin. Hilda is tending to her. Carla, Kaja, Ilka, and Caitlin are helping the women cut reeds."

"Who is Caitlin?"

"One of the slave women who were given to the families as maids. Yngvi kept the Irishwoman as his own maid."

Digur pulled his lips into something that was probably supposed to be a smirk, Stina guessed. "Then she must be very pretty."

"She is," said Stina. "But I don't think Yngvi wanted her for that reason. He is still grieving for his lost love. I suspect he wishes to protect Caitlin because she reminds him of Frida."

Digur understood. Sucking the last remains of the roast off his fingers, he rose to his feet. "I'd better carry on."

On this day, Thorolf stayed on the peninsula, sending his hunters into the woods by themselves. Asla felt certain their son would be born soon, so he wanted to stay near his wife. Besides, it was time for him to check on things at Woodhaven and listen to the concerns and needs of his people. When he spoke with men near where the trees were being felled, Thorolf was forced to raise his voice to be heard. Axe blows resounded in various rhythms and, along with shouted orders from the woodsmen, formed a wall of background noise that made conversation at a normal volume impossible.

From his right, Thorolf could hear the blows of a hammer. He was pleased about the progress on the smoking huts. He had bestowed this task on some settlers who were gifted with carpentry skills. While two men split logs with their axes, producing even planks, two other men nailed the planks to the frames of the emerging smokehouses. As soon as the following day, the women would be able to hang the first lots of salted mackerel and smoke them.

Near the peninsula's tip, Thorolf spotted the wide back of Digur, who seemed to be working on something while crouching down.

"What are you doing, brother?"

Digur stood, brushing his hand over his unfamiliarly short, curly hair. Kaja had cropped it that morning with a sharp knife.

"I am making a new home for my three queen bees."

"Didn't you have seven?"

"Yes," replied Digur bitterly, "but four of them did not survive the journey."

Thorolf looked at the three hollowed-out tree trunks, each about a foot wide and two feet high, which Digur had stood up on wooden boards. At the bottom, each log had a small opening. He watched with interest as his brother dipped his finger into a pot of honey and smeared it on the twigs of four skinny, leafless branches.

Digur was pleased at Thorolf's evident interest. "With the honey," he explained, "the worker bees feed their queen. And when there is none left, they will have to venture outside to find food in blossoms."

"There are plenty of blossoms here," Thorolf observed. "And what are you doing with those branches?"

Digur inserted them into the hollow space. "The bees build their combs between the twigs. Once they are done, I lift two of the branches and drain off the honey."

"Why don't you lift all of them?"

"That would rob the bees of too much honey, weakening them," replied Digur patiently. "Now all we need are the bees."

Digur removed the wax plug from one end of the oblong wooden cylinder, in whose hollow interior the queen and her workers had spent the last few weeks. Carefully he lowered the transport vessel through the twigs, placing it on the hive's floor. The first worker bee soon crawled from her prison. Digur quickly covered the log's open top with a wooden board, weighing it down with a stone.

Thorolf experienced one of those rare moments in which his older brother smiled. For Digur, it was almost a big smile, and he rarely was this talkative. Clearly spending time with these small, hardworking creatures brought him enormous joy.

"When can we expect our first mead?"

Digur's face reverted to its usual serious expression. "Yuletide at the earliest. And not much, either."

"Better than nothing!" Thorolf patted his brother's broad shoulders. As he walked away, he remembered his vines. He had kept them damp during their voyage, and now it was time for them to go in the ground. In the early evening, he planted them near Digur's beehives. There they would be able to remain until he found a better spot for them.

Before he returned to the *Goldeagle* for the night, he continued to work for a while on the cradle for his son, which he was building in Harald's shelter with boards cut from the first trees felled upon Catan. His heir's first bed was almost completed—it needed only a few finishing touches here and there.

The first labor pains came in the early morning. Thorolf helped Asla out of the low, cramped cabin and led her to the tent his servants had erected on the front deck. In the tent's center stood a stool upon which Asla lowered herself with a sigh. She would give birth to her child sitting on the stool, as was the custom in the North.

Thorolf kneeled before her, taking her left hand in his. "What can I do?"

Asla brushed her free right hand across his cheek, reddened with excitement, and smiled at him lovingly. "Fetch Hilda and give this to Stina." She placed a leather satchel in his hand. "Tell her to bring a pot of water to boil and toss the herbs and some linen cloths inside. Once the brew has cooled off, ask her to bring it here with the help of a servant." Leaning forward, she kissed him softly. "Do not fret—our son is well. It is going to be an ordinary birth. I know it."

Suddenly, her head jerked up, and she drew breath sharply through clenched teeth. Her hand cramped around his, and she breathed deeply in and out with her eyes closed. After a few moments, her breathing calmed, and she relaxed.

"The pains are more frequent now. Please leave. What comes next is women's business."

Thorolf clasped the satchel, squeezed Asla's hand one more time in farewell, and almost collided with Hilda as he left the tent with the unpleasant feeling of being helpless in the face of what was to come. He would have liked to position himself in front of his wife with his sword drawn to protect her and his son from any evil that might threaten them in the coming hours. But he knew that would be in vain. It was in the hands of the gods now.

Hilda touched his arm. "Is it time?"

"Yes. She asked for you."

Hilda scuttled past him and into the tent. Behind her, Stina had stood waiting, and she now looked at him with wide eyes. Thorolf beckoned for her to follow him.

"Asla has a task for you. Let us return to the peninsula."

At noontime, his son still wasn't born.

Thorolf was sitting on a crate in the stern of his ship, staring at the tent in the bow. Asla's muted cries, ringing out in increasingly quick succession, tortured him. He would have loved to bear the pain in her stead, or at least to share it with her. Erratically, he whittled at a thick branch, not knowing what it was he was making.

Then, suddenly, silence. Thorolf shot to his feet, dropping his piece of wood. Was it time?

A few long, agonizing moments later, he heard the wailing of a newborn child. Nothing could stop him now: he ran along the ship's side and ducked through the tent's entrance.

Asla sat on her stool, pale-faced, with dark shadows under her eyes. Stina stood behind her, gently brushing back her sister's sweaty, sticky hair. Hilda handed the young mother a bundle of linen with a tiny head and a few dark hairs. Pressing her child to her chest, Asla looked up at her husband with a disheartened smile. Thorolf was overcome by an ominous feeling. Something was wrong.

"Is he healthy? Is everything all right with him?"

Slowly, she shook her head. "Our child is well. But it isn't a son. You have a beautiful daughter."

Thorolf's jaw dropped. The disappointment in his face was obvious. Thus, he stood for a while, unable to utter a word.

Finally, Asla pressed her lips together, frowning angrily. "If you do not rejoice over the birth of a healthy daughter, then please leave!"

Thorolf was forced to admit that he did not rejoice—quite the opposite. He was deeply disappointed. Never once had he doubted Gundahar's prophecy that his firstborn would change the fate of his tribe for the better. He thought he could hear the gods laughing at him, the simpleminded fool who had fallen for one of their tricks.

"Asla, I—"

"Leave!"

A curse on his lips, he walked out of the tent. Hilda and Stina's eyes followed him, abashed.

Tears rolled down Asla's cheeks, dripping onto the linen swaddling the newborn. Stina kneeled beside her, placing a soothing hand on that of her sister. She liked Thorolf, but the behavior he had just displayed disgruntled her too. After all the hardships of the voyage, Asla had made it through an exhausting, strength-sapping birth, bearing him a healthy daughter. He could have shown at least a little joy—if not over the birth of a daughter, then at least at the fact that his wife was doing well, considering the circumstances.

As though Asla had read her mind, she said, "He did not even bother to ask how I was doing. He did not seem to care at all."

Hilda, always eager to keep everyone at peace, said, "That is just what men are like. They pay little consideration to the needs of us women."

Asla wiped the tears from her eyes, her face hardening. In a firm voice laced with anger, she retorted, "I did not want a man who is like *men*. I thought Thorolf was different, or else I would never have gone with him. If he does not apologize to me and learn to respect and love his daughter, then I will divorce him. I cannot and will not live with a man who is becoming just like my father."

With his jaw clenched, Thorolf rowed back to the shore. Rarely had the settlers seen their chieftain in so foul a mood. When asked whether Asla had given birth yet, he growled curtly: "A daughter."

At least the clearing of the land progressed to his satisfaction. The woodsmen had removed all the trees from the peninsula, except for a meager few toward the land. Tomorrow morning, he would send for the two bulls from the grazing grounds in the delta. With the help of the strong beasts, they would pull the stumps from the ground.

Hilda missed Gregor during their shared meals. When she asked Yngvi where he had got to, he told her that the monk was spending time near the outpost in the delta.

"What is he doing there?"

Yngvi smiled mysteriously. "Go find out."

Since Asla and her little girl were doing well and Ilka was looking after them, Hilda decided to travel to the delta with Thorolf's steersman, Hakon, the following day.

When Hilda climbed aboard Digur's *Spearhead*, the morning was warm and sunny. Hakon was already on board, with the women and men who would relieve the sentries and herders at the outpost. As she had on prior days, Hilda had put together provisions for the workers in the delta. For Gregor, she had packed two tasty mackerels from the first batch smoked in the new smoke huts.

Since they were traveling downriver, it wasn't long before the knarr arrived at the delta. Standing upon a flat-topped rise, the monk watched as the men fastened the *Spearhead* to the shore. Hilda waved at him, and he waved back, clearly pleased at the sight of her.

Gregor welcomed Hilda warmly. His camp consisted of a

low tent Yngvi had given him and a fire with a small pot hanging above it. A few steps to the side, the grass was trodden down, and protruding from the hardened ground was a pole with a sharpened tip, about as tall as a man. The pole stood in the center of a circle marked with small stones and sticks, some longer, some shorter. Hilda thought the whole arrangement looked like the mysterious work of a wizard.

"What is that?" she asked. "Do you use it to speak with your god?"

Gregor laughed, his eyes sparkling with mirth. "No, certainly not." He pointed at the pole. "Do you see the shadow it casts? The higher the sun is in the sky, the shorter the shadow becomes. When the sun rises or sets, I use sticks to mark the spot where the shadow touches the circle."

Hilda did not follow. "And what good is that for?"

"With this, I can determine when day and night are of the same length in the spring and fall, and which day in summer is the longest and which one in winter is the shortest. I will be able to tell you when the time has come for your Yule fest, or that we are now very close to the longest day of the year. If my observations are correct, your sun month begins tomorrow or the day after."

"I see," said Hilda, who, while practical-minded, had no knowledge of the positions of the sun. After all, anyone could see how high the sun was in the sky, and it was the chief of the tribe who determined the time of the Yule fest.

A little embarrassed, she handed Gregor the two mackerels in a cloth. "I wanted to bring you something to eat."

Gregor, unaccustomed to such kindness from a female being, placed one hand on her shoulder. "I thank you for your generosity, Hilda. May God bless you."

Hilda liked the touch of his hand. It felt warm on her

shoulder, and she thought she could feel something of the strength that lay within him.

Hilda and Gregor jumped at the guttural roar of a bull. The animal, pulled by four servants with a rope and pushed from behind to get him aboard Digur's *Spearhead*, raged and stamped its hooves powerfully on the wooden planks leading to the ship. Furiously, it swung its head, sending one of the servants flying into the shallow water. The servant most likely thanked the gods that the bull's horns had been removed, and stood up unharmed.

"It seems the bull does not feel like leaving behind his green pastures and his cows," said Hilda, recovered from the fright.

"Who can blame him? After the long journey, this delta must seem like paradise to him." Gregor gave a cheeky smile. "If I were in his skin, all the servants would be in the water by now."

Hilda giggled. "That's how strong a bull you would be?"

"Even if I appear to you as a gentle servant of my God—emotions like annoyance, wrath . . . and even passion are not unknown to me."

Hilda detected a look in his eyes that was new but not unpleasant to her. She tore her eyes off him and glanced at the *Spearhead*. The two bulls were loaded, and a servant carried a barrel of milk across the planks. "The ship is about to leave. I must go."

Gregor took her hand. "Stay. Let us spend the day together. I would like to find out more about you."

Hilda considered. She wasn't urgently needed on the peninsula. There was a capable farmer's wife who would surely be able to oversee the handing out of food. In a spontaneous decision, she called to Hakon that she would stay in the delta until the evening ship. The steersman nodded and gave the order to set off.

It would turn out to be one of the most wonderful days Hilda had ever experienced. She told Gregor of her childhood, of married life with Oddur, and of her work as a charcoal burner. Gregor was an attentive listener. He asked questions in the right places and would often make her laugh with his witty comments. During a moment of silence, which Hilda found anything but awkward, she compared Gregor to her late husband. It was like comparing a dry winter twig with a summery branch of elderflower, heavy with blossoms.

After they shared one of the mackerels around noontime, Gregor took Yngvi's fishing rod from his tent, and together they sat at the bank of the Saltmarsh River. Now it was Gregor's turn to speak of his life. Hilda learned that he'd been born the son of wealthy parents in Rome and grew up there. Her eyes grew wide when he described the tall stone houses and churches of the Eternal City, and she was scarcely able to believe him when he told her of pipes and bridges that brought clean water from the mountains to the city and even inside people's houses. With delight she listened as he spoke of the many amenities visitors could find at the numerous thermal baths. Even though he spoke modestly about his role in the church, Hilda understood that, in his former life, Gregor had been more than a simple monk. He used to belong to the inner circle of one of the most powerful men in the world. Considering this, his fate as a slave seemed like a cruel jest of the gods.

In the afternoon, Gregor caught a two-foot eel. They roasted it above the fire, contentedly chatting and joking about funny and awkward situations among the settlers.

When the *Spearhead* returned in the evening, Hilda did not climb aboard. She spent the night with Gregor.

Late the following morning, Hilda returned on board the *Spearhead.* Immediately she asked a servant to row her to the

Goldeagle to check on Asla. With relief she spotted the young mother sitting outside her tent, nursing the newborn. Stina kept her sister company, stitching a torn undergarment with needle and thread.

Asla rose, scrutinizing Hilda's tousled hair. She smiled. "I gather you must have experienced a very special night, happy and wild-haired as you look."

Hilda nodded, embarrassed.

Her curiosity aroused, Stina set down her needlework. "Who is it?"

Before Hilda had a chance to reply, Asla raised her hand. "Wait—don't tell us. Let us guess."

The sisters eagerly listed names of freemen who lived alone and were roughly the same age as Hilda, or a little older. Amused, the charcoal burner shook her head at each one.

Stina eventually ran out of patience. "Go on, tell us. Who is it?" She giggled. "Who sweetened your night?"

Softly, unable to contain her smile, Hilda whispered, "Gregor."

She did not fail to notice the look of surprise Asla and Stina exchanged. It was not only astonishment that Hilda read in their eyes, but also a sense of concern, disapproval, even. A flame of anger flared up inside Hilda.

"What issue could you possibly take with Gregor? Do you despise him because he is not a strapping lad like Thorolf, and because he's bald? Or perhaps because he was a slave until recently? You don't even know him! Gregor is the most decent, humorous man I have met in my entire life!" She had talked herself into a state, unable to stop herself from casting a stinging remark at Asla. "Gregor would be just as pleased about a daughter as he would be about a son, and he wouldn't leave his wife alone so long after the birth, as Thorolf is obviously doing.

Gregor is a fine person. He's the first man to take a genuine interest in me and my thoughts—he does not just see the cook and the servant in me." Hilda paused for a moment before carrying on defiantly. "Even if you can't understand it, I feel good when I'm with him. And yes, I love him, and I will spend the coming night with him, too."

Stina listened to Hilda's outburst with her mouth open. She was surprised and astonished to see the older woman, who normally met her with nothing but kindness and equanimity, so annoyed—angry, even. Meanwhile, Hilda's comment about Thorolf's behavior struck Asla right in the heart, stirring the wound her husband had inflicted upon her, and causing a moment of inattention in which her arm slumped down a little. The newborn child cried fiercely in protest.

While Asla helped her little daughter back to the nipple she had lost, murmuring soothing words, Stina raised both hands. "I'm sorry if we gave you the feeling that we spurned Gregor. We believe you if you say that he is a good man. Yngvi speaks highly of him, and Carla, too, values him."

Hilda stood there with flushed cheeks, as if she had startled herself with the intensity of her words.

Stina set aside her sewing things and embraced the older woman. "Hilda, we are happy for you and wish you and Gregor well."

She turned to Asla, who nodded but couldn't manage more than a thin smile. Hilda's remark about Thorolf had cut her to the quick.

Hilda returned Stina's embrace, holding her tightly. "Forgive my harsh words. It's just that it is important to me that you like Gregor. You will see me at his side more often from now on, and you will have ample opportunity to get to know him better."

Across Stina's shoulder, she saw Thorolf being rowed toward

the *Goldeagle* by a servant. "Oh, the father of the child is on his way. I might as well catch his boat back to land." She winked at Stina. "Are you coming?"

Stina understood. It was important to give Thorolf and Asla time to talk now.

Thorolf stepped toward his wife. She kept her head down, hiding her face and the infant behind her thick curtain of hair. He wished to apologize for his demeanor but struggled to find the right words.

"Asla, look at me."

She did not react.

Thorolf cleared his throat. "I am sorry."

She lifted her face, brushing her hair behind her ears with her free hand. "What are you sorry for?" Her eyes narrowing, an angry furrow carved itself into her brow. "Are you sorry for looking at me like I gave birth to a repulsive toad two days ago? Or are you sorry for making me feel I had to protect my daughter from you? Protect her from you abandoning her in the woods like a cripple? No, my guess is that you're sorry that I am holding in my arms a healthy little girl who failed to die during her birth." A tear rolled down her cheek. "Get out of my sight!"

The last words had sounded shrill, frightening the newborn, who ceased to suckle, whining pitifully instead.

Thorolf knew his wife by now. Most of the time, she was even-tempered, treating him and everyone else kindly. If, however, she became annoyed at someone's behavior, then her annoyance was like a worm burrowing through her insides, burning and fueling a seething fury which took some time to ebb off after its eruption. He had no choice but to give her that time.

"You know that isn't true. I will leave now. Maybe you'll have calmed down when I return. Then we can speak properly."

Asla ignored him, trying to soothe her daughter with gentle humming.

Once again Thorolf returned to the peninsula with a grim face. This time, no one dared to address him.

There was no tree left on the peninsula now. The men worked hard to remove the last few stumps from the ground. Once a stump was pulled out halfway, they chopped off the deeper-reaching roots.

The bulls were unaccustomed to the yoke, which chafed off the hair on their withers. They had to be whipped with a stick and pulled with a rope before they would step forward, lowing angrily. Once the cows had calved, Thorolf decided, he would castrate the male calves to raise docile oxen for field work.

Toward the afternoon, the settlers were finally ready to hitch the plow to the bulls and horses that had been brought up from the delta that morning. In a crisscross pattern, they pulled the plows across the forest floor, burying rotten leaves, low ferns, and shrubs under the soil, which broke open dark-brown and moist, exuding a smell of fertility.

In spite of his foul mood, Thorolf couldn't help but smile when he saw Digur ram the iron blade of his plow deep into the ground as if he were striking a mighty opponent, and then laboriously driving it through the earth with the help of his horse. Though plowing was hard work, his brother looked happy.

The maids and servants who had dug out larger ferns and bushes the day before were now breaking apart the big clods of earth left behind by the plows. In two days' time, Thorolf guessed, the fields on the peninsula would be ready to take the seed they had purchased in Hedeby.

Thorolf finished the cradle before sunset. He may not have

received a son to gift it to, but it would serve as a bed for his daughter just as well. Maybe, he hoped, it would someday become the cradle of his firstborn son, who, as his worthy successor, would change the future of the settlers of Catan for the better, just as Gundahar had foretold him.

Like many of the families, Thorolf spent the night on the peninsula. The air was mild, and one fur and a woolen blanket sufficed for his bed. Before he fell asleep, he thought about him and Asla. Would he have agreed to a fight for life or death with his friend Hilmar if the wise woman had foretold that Asla would bear a daughter, instead of a son? Would he then have renounced his love, respecting Asla's wish to go with her brother?

Maybe.

Thorolf knew such thoughts were futile. What was done was done. He loved Asla, and he did not want to fall out with her over a false prophecy. He would learn to accept that he had a daughter. Their next child would surely be a boy. With this comforting thought, he fell asleep.

Thorolf was awakened the next morning by scattered, heavy drops. By the time he arrived at Asla's tent, it was pouring. He slipped through the tent's entrance with the cradle in his arms. Asla was kneeling on a fur, wrapping the babe in fresh cloths.

He set down the wet bed and peeled off his cloak. "This is for our daughter."

Asla looked up, brushing Thorolf's gift with a brief glance. "Our daughter? Yours, too?"

Thorolf held out his arms. "Give her to me."

Asla picked up the tightly wrapped bundle from the furs and placed her into the arms of her husband. Thorolf gazed into his daughter's deep-blue eyes, which seemed to regard him with interest. Never before had he looked twice at an infant, but his daughter's pretty face touched him in a strange way and led him to gaze at it for longer.

In a low voice so as not to startle the child, he turned to Asla. "Of course I acknowledge my daughter. That is not a question. I was merely led to believe we would have a son."

"Then give your daughter a name," Asla replied curtly.

Thorolf thought for a moment. "Jora."

"Jora? Where did you hear that one?"

"No idea. At a tavern in Hedeby, perhaps? I liked it when I heard it; that's why I remembered it."

"I hope it wasn't a whore whose name was so unforgettable to you," she jeered. Thorolf gathered from her hard, sarcastic tone that she had not yet forgiven him.

Asla transferred the soft fur her daughter had been sleeping on into the cradle. "Very well. Hand Jora to me, then. It is time for her to sleep."

Once she had set down her daughter in the new cradle, she stood awkwardly for a while, as if unsure how things were supposed to proceed between them now. Thorolf fiddled with the large pouch he carried on his belt and asked her to close her eyes.

"Why?"

"Please, do it."

Asla gave in. Thorolf picked up her right hand, and she felt something metallic placed inside it.

"I bought this golden necklace for you in Hedeby. I was going to give it to you for the birth of our son. Now you have borne me a daughter, but you still deserve this ring, for you are not to blame for the whims of the gods."

Thorolf felt certain that Asla would beam with joy when she beheld the golden masterpiece in her hand, and that she would wrap her arms around him in gratitude. But, evidently, he did not know his wife as well as he thought he did.

Asla opened her eyes, studied the piece of jewelry in her hand, and tossed it at his feet. "Take it and place it around the neck of the first cow to give birth to a male calf in this land." Her eyes blazed with anger. "Our daughter is a whim of the gods? You reward me because I carry no fault in this misfortune? How generous of you!"

Thorolf stood as if struck by thunder.

Asla sighed and carried on in a calmer tone for the sake of her daughter. "Don't you understand? My father loved only Hilmar, his sole legitimate son. Stina and I were but *girls* to him. Our only worth consisted in marrying us off so that his power would grow. And now you are well on your way to treating our daughter in the same contemptuous manner. In doing so, you hurt me, too, and give me the feeling that the main reason for my existence is to bear you as many sons as possible."

Thorolf sat down opposite her. Heavy raindrops pattered onto the roof, and streams of water ran down on both the outside and the inside of the tent walls. "I think I understand what you mean. I am going to try to be a better father to Jora than Halldor was to you. And I see so much more in you than just the mother of my future sons. You ought to know that already."

Asla folded her hands in her lap. She gazed at him in silence for a few moments. Her lips, pressed into a tight line until then, relaxed a little, and her eyes grew a little warmer.

"It isn't your fault. The constant battle for survival in our old land forced men to become that way. But now we are here, in an uninhabited, wonderful land. Here, there are no rival jarls, no neighbors threatening our existence with warfare and death. We are making a fresh start. We have the opportunity to change things."

"And what would you like to change?"

"There is so much we could do better. Nearest to my heart would be the issue of forcing girls of age into marriage. They ought to be allowed to decide freely who to bind themselves to. Would you as chieftain support such a law?"

Thorolf raised his eyebrows. "The heads of the families won't like that. They are accustomed to the old tradition of choosing their children's spouse in order to grow their wealth and influence."

"With the only difference that sons may decline a union, whereas daughters cannot," she replied pointedly.

"Women can divorce their husbands."

Asla smiled derisively. "Only the bravest ones dare to do so, those who do not fear their husband's revenge and who can trust in the support of their family. You know that as well as I do."

Crossing his arms on his chest, Thorolf asked ironically, "And next thing you will want women to take part in the assembly of the heads of families?"

Asla squared her shoulders and gazed at him defiantly. "Why not? If a woman is the head of a family because her husband passed away? In my father's territory, there were more than a few women whose men never returned from a viking voyage or a battle. They all mastered their fate, successfully carrying on their farms in the same way their dead husbands would have—just like those women always did when their men were away for long parts of the year. Why shouldn't such women be allowed to speak for themselves, their children, and their servants, if it is about the future of the tribe and therefore their own future, too?"

Thorolf was astounded. Asla's arguments were not illogical, but she suggested that a woman should have the right to speak at an assembly, as if equal to men? Traditionally, women had to be represented by a man during an assembly, and none of the male settlers would put up with such a radical change. But he did not tell Asla that. Not now. He wanted peace with her.

"I will think it over. It is still more than a year before I offer myself up for election."

Asla nodded. Evidently, she hadn't expected anything more.

When Thorolf walked out, he left the golden choker on the ground.

He returned to Asla in the evening. He watched as she nursed Jora and swaddled her in fresh cloths. Once the little one was satisfied, Thorolf took the baby in his arms. When Jora started to cry, he tried to hand her back to her mother, but Asla said that his daughter only needed to burp. She showed him what to do, and Thorolf placed the bundle against his shoulder, gently patting his daughter's back. She burped softly and stopped crying. When he carefully lifted her off his shoulder and gazed into her face, it seemed to him that she smiled. He smiled back.

That was the moment when Thorolf began to love his daughter, and the moment when Asla forgave him. For now.

Ryan and the former slaves sailed for two days along the shore, which rose gently, sometimes rocky, sometimes sandy. The gentle wind and calm sea were forgiving of the mistakes the men and women still made when setting the sail and steering the ship. At night, they anchored in sheltered bays.

At the start of the third day, the appearance of the coast changed. In the distance, they saw a cone-shaped mountain from whose flat top rose a thin column of smoke. Stretching into the sea from the mountain's foot was a wide ridge of debris with gray rocks of all shapes and sizes, covered here and there with small patches of mossy green. The sharp-edged gravel and boulders had created a peninsula that reached far into the sea. To the people aboard the *Freedom,* it seemed as if giants had climbed out of this mountain, furiously hurling the rocks down the slope from the mountain's interior. It took them quite some time to circumnavigate the desolate headland. On the other side, they sailed along a shore of gentle sand dunes. Beyond the dunes, the forest started, rising steadily until it became swallowed up by hazy clouds. Soon thereafter, sheer cliffs rose straight out of the water, barring their sight of the landscape beyond.

Toward evening, they sailed into a wide fjord with tall rock faces on either side. After a while, the inlet narrowed, giving way to a slow-moving river. Soon they were forced to take down the sail and row instead. Then the rock walls retreated, and the people could see that the ridges on either side of them were, in fact, foothills of a mighty mountain range in the distance. Wide belts of reeds lined the banks. Then, a few trees at first, then more and more overpowered the reeds, forming a dense forest. The increasingly strong current and the once more narrowing banks would have made it difficult to continue up the river. Ryan ordered the rowers to cease rowing and drop anchor.

Ryan took counsel with Brennan and Liam. They agreed to set up camp at the end of the reed belt. If they took down the mast, the dense growth would conceal the knarr, as well as the four dinghies tied to the stern, from the eyes of any Northmen who might pass by.

Enya wrapped her arms around Ryan. They had become close in the last few nights. Whatever fate held in store for them, she felt confident that he would master and make the best of any situation.

PART 5
THE OUTLAWS

(FALL, AD 860)

CHAPTER 14
HARVEST FEAST

Thorolf stood outside the modest house that he had built, with the help of his brothers and his servants, upon a rise about fifty paces from the lakeshore. Two weeks ago, he and Asla and their relatives had moved in. In a festive ceremony, he had sacrificed a sheep to the gods to secure their favor on their new home. The highlight of the modest celebration had been taking the eagle Thorolf had carved for Asla almost a year ago and mounting it above the door, from whence it greeted visitors as well as those at home here.

From the rise, Thorolf had a good view over the settlement. The air was uncommonly dry on this warm, sunny morning, and he could see across the entire lake to its distant, reed-lined shores.

On the peninsula's landward third, rye grew golden in the warm light of the new day. The barley field behind it had already been harvested, the sheaves drying in the sun. The oats at the peninsula's far end would be ready for harvest in a week.

Four knarrs lay at anchor in the bay. The fifth ship, the *Spearhead*, was moored to a jetty about twenty feet long, which had been built under Högni's supervision. Hakon would shortly set off with the knarr on his daily trip to the outpost in the delta.

Thorolf was proud of what each and every person in the community had accomplished under his leadership in the four moons since their arrival on Catan. Beyond the village, they had wrested more land from the forest and started to plow new fields, which they would sow sometime after midwinter. The exact point in time depended on the weather. Many suspected that the winter on Catan would be significantly milder than in their old home, but they would only know for certain around Yule time, when the days were shortest.

To his right and left stood rows of modest houses. Modeled on the houses in their former homeland, the roof constructions rested on frames of squared timbers, and the wall spaces between the studs were filled with woven branches plastered with clay. Several still lacked the reeds on their roofs. The settlers had left generous gaps between the buildings, allowing space for the larger longhouses they'd build at a later stage. Then the existing simpler houses would serve different purposes. Some of the women had already set up gardens where they grew beans, peas, and onions, or kitchen herbs from the seeds they'd brought from their old home.

The settlers were planning to improve the two roads, which crossed outside Thorolf's hall, with planks or pounded dirt in the next few weeks, similar to the alleys in Hedeby. It did not rain as much on Catan as it did in the large trade center, but when it did rain, it was as if the gods were wringing out the clouds like huge linen cloths above the island to vex the settlers with muddy and barely usable tracks.

Asla crawled with Jora out of the tent next to their new home. Even though the days were shortening now, the nights were still pleasantly mild. When it wasn't raining, she and Thorolf preferred to sleep outside. Their modest hall was too crowded for them, and too noisy when Thorolf's brothers, Stina, Carla, Hilda, Gregor, and, in a separate chamber, their servants and maids all snored in unison and gave off plenty of other irritating sounds.

Thorolf sighed softly. Soon this crowded situation would come to an end. Only the thatch was missing on the neighboring houses of Digur, Yngvi, and Hilda.

Little Jora's entire face beamed when she spotted her father and held out her little arms to him. Thorolf smiled as he took his daughter on his arm, and the girl responded with a joyful gurgling sound. Gently he stroked her thin dark hair.

Asla leaned against his side. "I don't think they're coming back."

Thorolf placed his free arm around his wife's shoulder and gave her a downcast look. At his order, Olaf and Gunnar had set out to sea with two knarrs three weeks earlier during the best of weather. He had told the men to sail east for seven days. If they did not reach the Hot Land or the emir's empire within seven days, they were to turn around. By now, their return was overdue by a week, and Thorolf felt gravely concerned over the whereabouts of his two ships and their crews.

Thorolf sighed. "I fervently hoped the Hot Land or some other shores known to us were reachable within just a few days' sailing."

"Why?" asked Asla, uncomprehending. "You are banished from the Northland for seven years. Why do you want to sail there?"

"As soon as our settlement is established, I had hoped to take back up my trading voyages between Hedeby and the southern lands. Trade and seafaring are in my blood, and when I step before my father in seven years' time, I want to do so as a successful merchant."

Asla wrinkled her nose. "You are vain and ungrateful, Thorolf Ulrikson. This way you will never win the gods' favor.

You should be contented that we landed on this wonderful island, that we have enough food, and that no other tribe threatens us with war, death, and suffering. And besides, you would leave me and Jora for a long time." Flippantly, she added, "So long, perhaps, that we two girls would have to find ourselves a new husband and father."

Thorolf took his wife's speech with good humor, planting a kiss on her forehead. More than once, her frank words had brought him back down to earth when plans ripened inside him that were too ambitious.

He replied jokingly, "Well, if that is the case, I will challenge any man you might consider to single combat before my departure." Pulling up one eyebrow, he whispered into her ear, "You know that isn't the only thing I am good at."

Asla laughed, ramming her elbow in his side. "You monster. Before you dispatch innocent men to Valhalla, I would sooner accompany you on your travels."

Stina and Carla emerged from the house, chatting, followed by Caitlin, heavily pregnant now, and Kaja. Kaja had given birth to her daughter just a few weeks after Jora was born, carrying her in a cloth tied around her shoulder. Following the birth, Digur had merely glanced at the infant before going to visit his beehives, in which he took far greater interest than in his progeny. As a slave woman, Kaja had no choice but to accept this.

The women gave Thorolf and Asla a cheerful greeting as they walked past, taking the short path down to the peninsula. Today they would help bring in the rye. As with the barley, the harvest would be much richer than anyone could have predicted. In the rough climate of their old home, they had reaped two or (in a good year) three grains for every seed they put into the ground. Responsible for the poor harvests were the depleted ground, wet summers, hail, and crows that destroyed great parts of the seeds and young stalks. These adversaries were absent on Catan, and if the farmers weren't mistaken, they would reap at least seven times the rye they sowed.

Three men came walking up the track toward Thorolf and Asla. It was the archers, who normally scoured the woods for rabbits. But today, instead of their bows, they carried hand nets.

The rabbit numbers had steadily declined over the last few weeks. The hunters had been forced ever deeper into the woods to find new colonies. Even though rabbits seemed to be fast breeders, the settlers had evidently decimated their population significantly. Today they would visit a more lucrative source of food.

Thorolf handed little Jora back to his wife. "Let us take care of our feast this evening."

Asla nodded. "Hilda, Ilka, Diara, and a few maids will help me with the preparations."

Thorolf and the other hunters walked along the lake on the path that led to the waterfall. Halfway there, Yngvi joined them. Soon they reached the upper Saltmarsh, whose waters wound their way through the woods from the south, rushing past rocks, gurgling down smaller falls, and finally pouring in a thundering, seven-foot waterfall into the lake they'd begun to call Lake Woodhaven.

About a week ago, they had spotted the first big salmon attempting to overcome the waterfall with powerful leaps. At first, there had been a few, but now, dozens of salmon that had traveled up the Saltmarsh River from the sea were gathered in front of the barrier, which prevented them from swimming upriver to the stream's source to spawn there. Again and again, they darted out of the water, thrashing about. Most of the time, they fell back down, unsuccessful. Every now and then, a fortunate salmon would clear the obstacle during its first few attempts. However, those who did manage to leap to the top of the fall found a new danger awaiting them: Thorolf, Yngvi, and the three hunters were standing in the rushing waters at the fall's edge, their hand nets stretched between them, poised to catch the leaping fish. Their patience was rewarded. Again and again, one of the salmon would finish its leap inside Thorolf and Yngvi's net. Their companions, too, proved deft at catching the fish.

"Got another one," cheered one of the hunters when a three-foot salmon landed in his net following a powerful leap. But the skinny man lost control over the handle with the heavy catch in his net, and the net's wooden frame wasn't strong enough. Thrashing about wildly, the fish demolished its prison and swam upriver, sweeping its strong tail from side to side. The luckless hunter's face fell as he stared at his ruined dip net. Thorolf grinned. The man reminded him of a child gaping at a broken toy in dismay.

Around midday, they gutted their catch, hung the fish on wooden poles, and carried them on their shoulders back to the village.

Hilda clasped her hands above her head at the sight of the many fish. "That's enough! We have plenty of salmon for tonight, and the smoke huts are full!"

On the field, several women were busy harvesting rye. Since they did not possess enough sickles, they took turns at work. Spurred on by the singing of those resting by the field's edge, they cut the ears halfway down the stalk, bundled them into sheaves, and propped them up for drying.

When Yngvi walked along the peninsula, he heard a merry song from his Nordic homeland. Carla was among the singers—he recognized her bright, clear voice among all others. Her singing touched him. It seemed to him as though the sounds that came from her throat arose from some kind of pure, untouched core deep inside of her, which not even the darkest experiences during her time in Hedeby managed to taint.

Carla had told him of her life in the city—how hunger had forced her to steal, to betray, and to lie. Several of the terrible events she had witnessed and the abysses of the human soul she had seen brought tears to her eyes. But when she spoke of the memories of her earlier happy childhood and of her real mother, she smiled, and it was as if she opened a small treasure chest which she guarded carefully and which had helped her emerge from the swamp and misery of Hedeby unbroken.

Two servants trudged past Yngvi, carrying the last few of the dried barley sheaves up to the barn. Yngvi followed them. From afar he could hear the rhythmical thuds of the flails the men and women used to thresh the barley. Outside the barn, they used shallow baskets and the wind to separate the chaff from the grain. Then they carried the clean barley seeds inside and poured them into a large wooden storage tub.

Yngvi gazed at the impressive storehouse. It was, by far, the largest building of the emerging settlement and the first to be completed. Here they stored the harvest and the precious tools they all shared. When they weren't threshing grain on the solid, pounded-dirt floor of the barn, the settlers used the building as a meeting place during foul weather.

In the large area outside the barn, the freemen would celebrate the harvest feast with their wives and older children this evening. The servants had already set up tables and carried over anything that might serve as a seat.

Yngvi worried that the collection of benches, crates, barrels, and blocks of wood might lead to arguments. Which proud leading family member would want to spend the entire evening upon a low crate while his neighbor towered over him on a tall log, able to spit on his head in the case of an argument?

To his left, Hilda, Asla, Diara, and some maids prepared fires, where the meal for the feast would be cooked. Fat salmon waited on a table to be roasted crisp on spits, along with the gutted and plucked yellow-beaks hanging from poles with their feet tied.

To Yngvi's right, Thorolf's plot of land bordered the village square. His brother was seated at a table outside the house, talking to one of the settlers. Six other men were waiting to be heard. Curious, Yngvi walked up to Thorolf and sat down beside him. His older brother did not mind his presence. When Thorolf, as their chieftain, received the freemen of Woodhaven to listen to their important matters or complaints, he was sometimes even grateful for Yngvi's wise counsel.

Next in line was a young man. His face was flushed, and his hands nervously kneaded a hat. It was Bran—one of the servants who used to sail with Thorolf on his trade voyages. Before their departure, Thorolf had assigned him to the *Shieldmaiden* and, as promised, gave him his freedom upon their arrival on Catan. Yngvi liked the handsome young red-haired man who had been taken from the land of the Anglo-Saxons as a youth. He had served Yngvi as a second steersman on their crossing, and Yngvi had come to view him as a reliable, upright, and pleasant-natured man.

"Master, I am speaking for myself and my friends." Bran gestured at the five young men standing behind him. "We have something to ask of you."

Thorolf folded his hands and rested his chin on them. "Don't call me *master*, Bran. You have been a freeman for four moons. What do you want?"

"You may have given us our freedom, and yet we are not treated as freemen. The heads of families turn us away when we ask for the hands of their daughters. They curse us and claim we are not true freemen."

Yngvi knew what Bran was speaking of. Often, back in their homeland, only the grandson of a released servant was considered a truly freeman.

Thorolf shrugged, crossing his arms on his chest. "I can't force the heads of families to give you their daughters for wives."

Bran nodded. "I know. That is why we started looking among the maids. Particularly among those left behind by the slaves."

Yngvi could not stifle a remark. "No wonder—they are of rare beauty. But many of them possess one blemish: they are with child."

Bran nodded again, and there was a carefree smile on his lips. "I know. That does not bother us. I ask for your permission, chieftain, to wed the maids that we have chosen."

Yngvi whispered something to his brother, whereupon Thorolf signaled to Bran to take a few steps aside. Then he turned to Yngvi. "You do not need to persuade me to yield to Bran's demand. I like his idea. Men need women, and our community must grow. If Bran and his companions wish to marry the former slaves, that is fine by me. They are mine to command."

Yngvi grinned. "That was not what I was going to say. I knew that was how you would decide."

Thorolf raised his eyebrows in astonishment. "Is that right? And how did my clever little brother know that?"

"You did not keep the guardianship over Egil's slave women for no reason. You knew your former servants stood no chance of marrying a free woman. And no freeman would give away one of his maids."

Thorolf laughed, slapping Yngvi's shoulder. "You got me. But then what was it you wanted to say to me in private?"

"Allow the maids to decide freely whether they want to wed the man who chose them. It is the only way to avoid bitterness, misery, and hatred in the homes of the new families."

Yngvi, thought Thorolf, sounded almost like Asla, who increasingly pestered him about giving more speaking rights to women—and now even to unfree women? He shuddered at the thought of his brother and his wife joining forces against him some day. His good mood suddenly evaporated.

"Very well," he said nonetheless. "Let us ask them. No, better yet, you ask them. I make you responsible for the whole affair." Thorolf stood abruptly and marched off.

Yngvi had a hunch as to what it was that bugged his brother. He waved Bran and his friends over, explaining the situation, and the former servants reacted with relief. Yngvi promised to speak with the chosen maids soon and report back to the men thereafter.

They were lucky with the weather. Once the sun went down, a bright full moon lit the clear night sky. All freemen had followed Thorolf's invitation: the young, unmarried men who had claimed two tables for themselves, as well as the heads of families, who had brought their wives and older sons and daughters; the younger children they had left in the care of their housemaids. Around two hundred people sat at the tables upon which maids had placed jugs of water. Torches soaked with pitch and the cooking fires bathed the square in a warm light.

Asla, Stina, and Carla were still missing. Thorolf guessed they still needed time to ready themselves. Impatiently he kept glancing at his house until he finally saw them step into the glow of the fires. Like most women on this evening, they had taken special care with their appearance, accentuating their eyes with coal and combing their hair until it shone like silk. All three women drew the gaze of men, but Thorolf only had eyes for Asla, who stepped toward him between Stina and Carla with her chin raised. Her narrowly cut tunic showed off her figure, the low-cut neckline revealing the tops of her breasts. The whiteish scar on her face did little to disturb the harmony of her features. Around her neck, she wore the golden ring with the wolf heads, which she had thrown at his feet in the heat of their argument. Now it made her appearance even more queenly.

Thorolf rose, welcoming his wife with a heartfelt embrace. Yngvi rapped his fist on the table, and many of the settlers fell in with him.

Once they were seated, Thorolf leaned over to Asla, whispering in her ear, "It pleases me to see that you have accepted my gift."

Asla smiled, whispering back, "And I am pleased that you have learned to love our daughter."

All was said.

Thorolf reached for a wooden cup and hammered with it on the table until all conversations had ceased and he was holding the people's undivided attention.

"Today we harvested our rye. As with the barley, the harvest was rich—richer than we ever dared dream. Catan smiles upon us. The gods are well-disposed toward us, and the Norns seem to spin their threads in good humor. Let us give thanks to the gods!"

While the settlers waited with bated breath to find out how their chieftain would thank the gods for their favor, Thorolf signaled to two servants, prompting the men to carry over a barrel marked with a rune. They set it down upright, opened the plug, and poured a clear yellowish liquid into a large wooden pail.

Thorolf picked up the heavy bucket, lifting it into the air effortlessly. "This is no water. There is wine in this pail! The best of wine, which I bought off a farmer in Coronium. Five barrels of this will sweeten our night tonight."

The men cheered excitedly, drumming their fists and cups on the tables. They had not expected this, and all the greater was their joy at not having to celebrate the harvest feast with boring, flavorless water.

When the cheering ebbed off, Thorolf tilted the bucket, tipping the wine on the ground in a wide stream. "This is our thanks to the gods. May they be our guests and continue to bestow their favor upon us." Then, turning to the servants and maids, he shouted: "Wine for everyone! Fill the cups!"

Again the settlers cheered, chanting passionately and several times in a row: "Long live Thorolf!"

The chieftain enjoyed the love and appreciation shown to him. When he sat back down next to Asla, high in spirits, she took his hand and squeezed it. "Thank you."

Thorolf clasped her face with his hands and planted a good-humored and somewhat boisterous kiss on her mouth. Originally, he had intended to feast with the heads of households alone, as it was the custom in the Northland. Asla had not been keen on this idea at all, however, and, following endless discussions, she had persuaded him to break with old tradition. To celebrate once a year together into the night, she maintained, would strengthen their sense of community. And a strong sense of community was important for the future of the settlers. Additionally, the presence of the women and older children would deter the men from overindulging in wine and thus lessen the likelihood of fighting. When Thorolf had replied that, to the men, fighting was the eagerly anticipated highlight of any feast, she had merely gazed at him pityingly and shaken her head. He insisted that at least one evening of the coming Yule feast would be celebrated solely among men.

Now the servants busily followed Thorolf's orders, filling jugs with wine and carrying them to the tables, while Hilda conducted the maids, who swiftly took the crisply roasted yellow-beaks and salmon off their spits, cutting them into pieces on wooden boards and refilling the spits with fresh meat.

Yngvi sipped from his cup. He liked wine but took care not to drink too much of it, for it only caused him suffering the following morning. Evidently, others did not appear to share this affliction. Ansgar, a farmer, drank particularly eagerly. Yngvi watched how the corpulent man knocked back his first cup of wine as if he were dying of thirst. Then he drained the cups of both his wife and his daughter, who had merely sipped on theirs.

When the food was served, the freemen and women picked up their knives and ate with great appetite. Particularly popular were the flatbreads fried in pans, and not just because of their crisp texture and well-seasoned flavor—the bread came with a sense of pride, for most of it was baked from the ground barley they had sown in their new home and which, under the care of the settlers, had ripened in the Catan sunshine.

Hakon's exploratory voyage was the foremost topic at the feast. The old sailor moved from table to table, patiently recounting his trip to satisfy the people's curiosity. Three weeks prior, Thorolf had sent his experienced steersman out with the *Goldeagle* to explore the shores of Catan to the northwest, and three days ago, Hakon had returned from the southeast. Catan was an island! And a large one at that, the sailor told them. In his younger days, he'd served on a ship that had circumnavigated the isle of the Irish. That journey had taken a similar amount of time as sailing around Catan. The lanky steersman told them of endless woods stretching inland from the coast and of tall mountains visible in the distance on fine days. He described varying coastlines and mentioned a smoking mountain and a wide, meandering river in Catan's south, which, surrounded by meadows, lazily flowed into the sea. But wherever he and his men anchored at night, whether off rocky shores or inside sheltered bays, nowhere had they seen humans or signs of humans.

Yngvi barely listened when Hakon came to their table—he had heard the story plenty of times. Carla, sitting opposite him, had not. Yngvi watched her as she listened to the words of the old seaman as if spellbound. Her small mouth with its full lips stood slightly open, her dark eyes framed by long lashes sparkling and reflecting the lights of the fires. When she reached up to brush a strand of her dark-brown curls behind her ear, her eyes met his. She shot him a quick smile before turning back to Hakon, who was just answering a question from Stina about the smoking mountain.

Yngvi felt he was seeing Carla for the first time as a woman, not as the lonely girl with a sad past who'd sought and found a brother and a family in him.

Once everyone had filled their bellies and the maids had cleared the tables, a man sat down with a drum at the edge of the round space between the tables, and two more joined him with flutes, and the men struck up a merry tune. Asla stood up and grasped Thorolf's hand, pulling him off his crate. Other women followed her example, leading their men to the dancefloor. The settlers clasped hands, formed a circle, and started to dance. Taking quick steps toward the center, they tightened the circle until the dancers briefly stood elbow to elbow before moving outward again, turning their upper bodies first to the right and then to the left. After a few more steps, each dancer took the spot of his or her left neighbor.

The joy in the people's faces mirrored not only their love for moving to the rhythm of the music but also their happiness and gratitude at having arrived at Catan—an island that promised a golden future, free from hunger and warfare.

Yngvi couldn't help but smile about one of the younger girls who did not yet know her steps too well, stumbling over her own feet clumsily more than she was dancing. He was about to ask Carla if she felt like learning the dance when Einar, the eldest son of well-respected fisherman Fenrir, turned up next to her and grasped her hand as if it were the most natural thing in the world, pulling her up from her seat. Carla appeared too surprised to protest against the good-looking young man. Yngvi suspected that she was feeling quite anxious right now, for she'd confessed to him before the feast that she had never danced before. But Carla was brave. At first, her efforts to keep pace were harder to watch than those of the clumsy girl's. But Carla was naturally graceful and a quick leaner. By the time the musicians started their next tune, she knew the steps. One of the flute players accompanied the song with his voice, and, by and by, many of the settlers joined him in singing. Carla's face, strained with concentration at first, softened and lit up with merriment, which made her look especially beautiful. Carla obviously relished the feeling of being part of a circle which, on this evening, was a symbol for the community of all free settlers.

Even though Yngvi liked to sing and dance, he did not feel the urge to join the circle, preferring to watch the festivities from his seat. He saw Hilda whisper something into Gregor's ear. It must have been some extraordinary news, because Gregor's eyes widened with surprise and his jaw dropped. Then his mouth spread into a wide grin. He clasped Hilda's head with both hands and pressed a kiss on her lips. When he let go of her, a blissful expression on his face, she wrapped both her arms around him and repaid him with a kiss that lasted twice as long. After a sip of wine, Gregor dragged his wife to the dancing circle, wildly determined. Like Carla, he had obviously never danced before, but after tripping over his own and other people's feet a few times—earning him some glowering stares from the neighbors whose rhythm he had disturbed—he began to learn the sequence of steps better and better. The blissful, almost simple grin on his face was to remain there for the entire rest of the night.

Only Stina and Digur were left at Yngvi's table. Stina was talking insistently, trying to persuade him to dance, but Digur sat upon his wooden block as if he were one with it. Yngvi knew that his brother never had moved to music, and he was ready to bet his right hand that he never would. Eventually Stina gave up and joined the dancers by herself.

Yngvi sat with his brother. "I think Stina likes you."

Digur replied sullenly, "Perhaps. But she is still a child."

"You can't fool me—you like her, too. You'd have to be blind not to see it. With her nearly seventeen winters, she is of marriageable age, and she has several admirers. What will you do if one of her suitors asks her to marry him?"

"Stina is Thorolf's ward. Our brother will ask me." Digur gulped a sip of wine, crossed his powerful arms on his chest, and looked away—an unmistakable hint to end the conversation.

Yngvi's eyes traveled to Ansgar, who was staring at a jug of wine, too drunk to join the dancers. His gaunt, thin-faced wife sat next to him, a bitter expression around her mouth. If Yngvi remembered correctly, her name was Hedda. Even though her pinned-up hair was completely gray, Yngvi guessed her age at fewer than forty winters. It was obvious that Hedda was not enjoying the evening. He saw how she stood up, grasped her husband by the arm, and whispered something into his ear. Ansgar lifted his heavy head and slapped her hand away. Then he stood angrily and rammed his fist into her chest. Hedda fell. Yngvi couldn't hear what it was that Ansgar shouted at her over the noise of the revelers. Hedda struggled to her feet and, with her head hung, fetched her daughter from the dance circle, quickly disappearing into the darkness with her. Ansgar sat back down and refilled his cup with wine.

After five dances, Carla left the circle. Einar followed her, catching her by the arm. Carla spun around, and before she could do anything, he planted a cheeky kiss on her mouth.

Yngvi held his breath and felt his heart skip a beat. To his relief, Carla did not return the kiss; instead, she pulled away from the young man. Yngvi was surprised at himself. Was he jealous?

Carla sat down, poured water into a cup, and drained it in one gulp. In the light of the torches, her face glowed with exertion and beamed with exhilaration.

"I believe you have an admirer, little sister."

She tilted her head to one side playfully. "Do you think he means it sincerely, big brother?"

"No idea," lied Yngvi, knowing full well that Einar was one of the community's biggest woman-chasers. He was all too familiar with this kind of good-looking young lad, pursuing one skirt after the other, for he used to be one of those lads before he met Frida. He patted her hand in a brotherly gesture. "You can rely on me. I will sound him out for you."

Gregor and Hilda also returned to the table. Yngvi's fatherly friend wiped a hand across his sweaty, blotchy forehead, beaming at Yngvi. Noticing the unspoken question in Yngvi's eyes, Gregor burst out with the happy news: "Hilda is with child! I am going to be a father, with my forty-two years! Can you imagine?"

Yngvi's eyebrows shot up in genuine surprise, and he congratulated Gregor with a joyful smile. "I hope your god is well-disposed toward you. May Hilda give birth to a healthy child."

Carla, who had overheard them, stared at Hilda's face, which wasn't just flushed from the dancing; Carla was first astonished and then glad. She sprang to her feet and rushed over, embracing the woman she had so much to thank for.

Yngvi, at last, felt like dancing. "Will you come?" he asked Carla. When she nodded eagerly, he took her hand. Warm and delicate, it rested inside his. It felt good.

Some time after midnight, most of the guests had gone home. Only a handful of men were left, babbling nonsense and drinking the last of the wine. Eventually, Thorolf, who seemed surprisingly sober to Yngvi, broke up this last small group.

Ansgar had fallen asleep with his head on the table. Thorolf shook him hard by the shoulder. When this did not help, he emptied a jug of water over the farmer's head. The drunkard awoke with a grumpy growl, opening his bloodshot eyes. Confused, he stared at his chieftain, who glowered at him with knitted brows.

Thorolf tugged at his sleeve. "Get up and go home."

The farmer rose with a groan. For a few moments, he just stood there, swaying, as if he didn't know what to do next. Then he dropped back down onto the crate he had been sitting on. Thorolf called for his servant, Dag, ordering him to take the farmer home. Dag did as he was asked, helping the drunk man to his feet. Ansgar pitched like a ship in a stormy sea when he started to walk, and the servant had a difficult time of keeping the heavyset man from falling. Yngvi hoped for the sake of Hedda and her children that the drunkard would fall asleep the moment Dag dropped him on his bed.

CHAPTER 15
THE MURDER

Hedda still lay awake when she heard her husband's grousing. She shuddered. Ansgar was a despicable person even when he was sober. He never uttered a kind word to her or the children and always lashed out when he was in a foul mood. But when he was drunk, he turned into a monster. Then he rampaged, raped her, and beat her with his fists or his belt. Even his daughter he had violated in a drunken stupor, which had turned the girl quiet and withdrawn.

Since their departure for Catan, those cruel nights had stopped. In the cramped conditions among the other families aboard Digur's knarr, Ansgar had pulled himself together—and he had also simply lacked opportunity to get drunk. But tonight he had indulged in the wine. Hedda knew the nightmare would return tonight. And it was here to stay, for Thorolf's vines were thriving in Catan's soil.

The door was yanked open. Hedda, pretending to be asleep, watched from under lowered eyelids how Ansgar stumbled across the threshold. Dag helped him back to his feet. She had left a few tallow lamps burning, so her husband would find his way to his bed. But that was not where he was headed.

"I want the redhead," said Ansgar, his speech slurred, and he staggered across the room toward and into the servants' chamber. In the weak light of the tallow lamps, Hedda could see the object of Ansgar's desire: Edvina.

The handsome maid, who'd been one of Egil's slaves, sat up in her bed and stared at her master with fright. He fidgeted clumsily with the clasp of his belt, then dropped his pants, exposing his half-erect penis. With a rough grunt, he threw himself on top of the young woman, who screamed out in panic, squirming under Ansgar's heavy body and pummeling him with her fists. Ansgar punched her brutally in the face.

Bert and Luke, the servants who shared the small chamber with Edvina, had scrambled to their feet with shock. Bert, who was ponderous and portly, pressed himself against the wall in fear. He had been made to feel his master's whip and belt many times and did not dare to help Edvina.

Before Dag had a chance to intervene, Luke, who was simpleminded, grabbed Ansgar by his tunic with both hands, shouting imploringly, "Master, don't!" and finally pulling him off the whimpering maid with a strong jerk.

The master of the house landed on his back and, for a moment, waved his arms and legs in the air like a fat maybug. He glared at Luke furiously. "You dare lay hands on your master? You will pay for this, you filthy mongrel."

Breathing heavily, Ansgar got to his feet, bent down, and picked up his belt. Grunting with effort, he whipped Luke with the buckle. In the small space of the chamber, the servant was unable to dodge the blows, and the metal clasp struck him painfully on his shoulder and arms as he tried to shield his head. Bert, standing trembling by the wall, fell victim to a stray lash of the belt, which ripped open his cheek.

Dag could no longer watch Ansgar lay into the harmless

servant with a mixture of rage and sadistic pleasure. He grabbed Ansgar by the arm, screaming, "Stop it!"

Dag hoped against hope that Ansgar would see reason. But the farmer stared at him from crazed, bloodshot eyes, yanked free his arm, and swung his belt at Dag. It seemed as if sexual arousal and anger had somewhat sobered Ansgar. He swung the belt hard again and again, cutting bloody slashes into Dag's arms, which he was holding up to protect his face.

All of a sudden, Ansgar froze. He opened his eyes wide in disbelief, and the belt slipped out of his hand. Like a sack that had suddenly been drained, the fat man collapsed in a heap on the ground.

Lowering his arms, Dag saw Edvina standing above Ansgar's lifeless body with a jug in her hands. She was shaking violently and seemed incapable of moving.

Hedda, who was standing in the doorframe and had seen everything, kneeled down beside her husband and touched her hand to his throat. While she felt that Ansgar's heart beat strongly, a daring plan sprouted in her mind. In an even voice, she declared, "He is dead." She stood up. "You have raised your hand against a freeman and killed him. They will execute you for this."

She looked into the thralls' horrified faces. They were scarcely able to grasp what had just happened, and it took a while for them to understand that their lives had fundamentally changed within just a few moments.

Hedda grasped Bert by the arm. "You've got to flee!"

Dag was the first to recover from the shock. The farmer's wife was right. Thralls who raised a hand against their master were sentenced to death. It did not even matter whether the victim survived the attacks, or who had placed the fatal blow—they all bore the wounds of a fight and had laden guilt upon them. Dag wondered why Hedda wasn't running outside, crying for help, but was instead trying to help them. He kneeled down and picked up the sheathed dagger that had slipped off Ansgar's belt. The wounds on Dag's forearms bled.

Edvina finally moved, too. She dropped the jug, picked up a satchel, and filled it erratically with her meager belongings. Last she folded up the blanket on which she had slept. The two servants followed her example.

"Wait," said Hedda. She rummaged through a chest and started to fill a large sack with blankets, firestones, a pouch of tinder, a knife, two bowls, two wooden spoons, and a small pot. "You are going to need this in the wilderness." She handed the sack to Luke. "Do any of you know how to handle a bow?"

The servants exchanged a look, both shaking their heads.

"I do," said Edvina quietly.

Hedda raised her eyebrows with surprise, then left the room. When she returned, she handed the maid a hunting bow and a quiver filled with arrows and spare bowstrings. With a glance at her husband's lifeless body, she said: "He won't need it anymore."

Her daughter appeared behind her, staring blankly at her father on the ground.

"Why are you helping us?" asked Bert.

Hedda did not think for long. "You freed me from a monster. You shouldn't have to die for this." She braced her hands on her hips. "Now go! I will wait for a while before I shout for help. Follow the river up into the mountains. I will tell them you were going to escape by sea. That will gain you some time."

Dag, Edvina, and the two servants left the house, quietly disappearing into the dark of night. Hedda closed the door behind them and quickly checked on her two small boys. Like always, when their father rampaged in the night, they were hiding under their blankets. Then she returned to the chamber. Ansgar groaned softly. It was high time.

With both hands, Hedda grasped the heavy jug, casting a questioning look at her daughter standing in the doorway. The girl nodded. Hedda lifted the jug, then brought it down hard on her husband's skull. Once, twice, and a third time. Each time, there was a crunching sound. Just to be absolutely sure, she thought, feeling deeply relieved.

For a while, Hedda and her daughter remained beside the loathed corpse. They sat in silence, holding hands. There was nothing to say. At last Hedda stood. "It is time to play our roles."

Her daughter nodded.

Yngvi and Thorolf were awakened by Hedda's hysterical cries for help. They swiftly dressed, and on their way to her house, Ansgar's wife told the brothers in a teary voice how her servants and Dag had attacked Ansgar with a jug when he tried to rape Edvina in his drunkenness.

The story sounded plausible enough, and yet something seemed off to Yngvi. The role of Dag, his brother's calm, level-headed servant, did not seem to fit the picture. Yngvi did not think him capable of murdering a freeman, not even to help a maid in distress.

He and Thorolf looked around the chamber in which Ansgar had died. The murder weapon, a heavy clay jug with a blood-smeared bottom, lay beside the victim's head. On the back of Ansgar's head, Yngvi found a lump, but a blow that could have caused that would not have killed him. What had killed him were three fatal blows that had smashed in the farmer's skull. Yngvi inspected the belt that was lying next to the dead man. There was blood on the buckle. Blood was also splattered on the ground a few feet away from the corpse—blood that could not have come from Ansgar, who must have already been on the ground when he received his fatal injuries. Yngvi pieced together what must have happened in this room. Looking at Hedda, the traitorous gleam in her eyes confirmed his suspicions. A servant might have struck Ansgar down, but it was Hedda who killed him.

However, Yngvi kept his observation to himself. For the blow to the back of Ansgar's head, at least, one of the thralls was responsible. If they were captured, they stood no chance of avoiding execution. And he did not wish to expose Hedda, who was holding her daughter and two small sons in her arms, to the suspicion of having murdered her husband. She had suffered enough.

Before Hedda had raised the alarm, Dag had quietly opened the back door to Thorolf's hall. Dag shared a small chamber with two other servants; Ilka was permitted to sleep in the main hall. In the feeble light of a tallow lamp one of the servants had left burning, Dag had lifted his carry sack off the wall and, taking care to not make any sounds, filled it with his personal belongings.

Now they ran, looking over their shoulders again and again, up the path to the waterfall. From there they followed the Saltmarsh upstream. Whenever the river was shallow and calm near the bank, they waded in the water, hoping to confuse any dogs their pursuers might use. Dag was grateful for the full moon that lit the river in a silver light, making their progress easier. In places with rapids and waterfalls, they moved along the river bank, struggling through the dense underbrush with great difficulty. In a spot where the Saltmarsh flowed along wide and lazy, they crossed the river.

When morning dawned, Edvina slumped down exhaustedly on a rock by the river, rubbing her calves. "I need a break."

Bert seemed glad he wasn't the first to utter those words. He wasn't used to walking for long stretches. His bright-red face and the beads of sweat gleaming on his forehead and saturating his smock testified to the enormous effort it had cost him to keep pace with his companions. Panting, he sat down on a fallen log, whose bare branches rotted in the river's waters, and wiped the sweat off his brow. Luke followed suit. A tall, muscular servant whom Northmen had captured in Britain, he often copied Bert's actions. Not to poke fun at his friend, but because his wits had suffered following a serious head injury, and it gave him a sense of security to orient himself by whatever Bert was doing.

Dag looked at the motley troop: one burly, middle-aged man gasping for air; one strong giant staring dumbly into space; one pretty young woman who was almost still a girl; and himself, Dag, forever unlucky.

His ill fortune had begun with the death of his mother at his birth. Just a few years later, his father had died from a festering wound. The uncle running his father's farm bullied him. When Dag grew up, he went to sea—first with Egil and later with Thorolf. He sold the farm to his uncle, borrowed silver from Thorolf, and commissioned his own knarr. During her maiden voyage, she capsized in a storm. The expensive wares in the cargo hold were lost, and Dag survived in the dinghy by the skin of his teeth. When, a year later, he was unable to pay back the money he had borrowed, he was forced to enter Thorolf's service as a thrall for four years. And now he had reached the lowest level of his existence as an outlaw. Outlawed for a murder he did not commit.

"We must keep going!" Dag looked at Edvina. "We have killed a freeman. Our pursuers won't give up that easily."

"I'm hungry," moaned Bert. Luke repeated the phrase monotonously.

Dag wasn't in the mood to argue. "Fine, then you just wait here until our pursuers bring you something to eat. I, for one, am leaving."

Faced with such a choice, his companions followed him.

Their path grew steeper and the river narrower, foaming downhill among rocks, damming up here and there behind rocky ledges or fallen trees before rushing into the depths on the other side. Only rarely now could they find safe spots to change sides or walk in the water for any longer periods of time. Toward noon, they took a break near a creek that flowed into the Saltmarsh.

Edvina sat down in the shade of a large, foreign-looking tree, cooling her aching calves in the clear water.

Dag sat down beside her. "How come you know how to use a bow?"

The young woman looked at him with her large ice-blue eyes, which both fascinated and alienated Dag at once, for it seemed that rarely did an emotion surface from their hazy depths. Dag never quite knew how to read the red-haired woman.

Edvina twisted her beautifully shaped lips into a mocking smile. "Forgive me if I still struggle with your Nordic tongue at times, but if I understand you correctly, you are asking why a simple, silly maid knows how to shoot a bow?" Edvina lowered her face, studying her blurry reflection on the water's rippled surface. "My father was a thane, a high-ranking follower of a Saxon king. I was his only daughter and grew up with three brothers. My two older brothers taught me the use of a bow, and I was permitted to accompany them in the hunt. We shot partridges, ducks, and hares."

She paused for a moment, as if recalling fond memories. Then she turned her face back to Dag, once more bestowing him with the attention of her fascinating eyes. She continued proudly, "My brothers took me along not only because they loved me, their only sister, but also because of my skill with the bow. None of them brought home more game than I did."

"Then how did you end up here?"

"It happened a little over a year ago, on the very day that I was married to the son of an allied thane. I counted nineteen summers—I was practically an old maid. My father took his time in the selection of my husband, asking my opinion on each and every suitor. I was so grateful to him. When the right one came along, I was happy. At least until the evening of the wedding feast, when Northmen came from the sea. No one expected an attack, and since we lived at peace with our neighbors, there was no reason to garrison the palisades. That proved a fatal mistake, for those devils set my father's hall on fire and wreaked havoc with their swords among our guests. My father's men stood no chance. Most of them were too drunk, and those who managed to stand up and draw a weapon were soon cut down. Save for me, a young maid, and my younger brother, Godric, they killed everyone, even my parents and the priest who blessed our union in the name of God. We were taken to ships and, in the spring, sold at Hedeby. You know the rest of the story."

Dag thought he could see a wet gleam in her eyes. "Then you must hate all Northmen," he observed.

"Yes, I do. Especially Ansgar, that pig. I loathe him deeply, and I am glad he is dead."

"Do you hate me also?" asked Dag.

Edvina looked at him with surprise. "Why should I hate you?"

"I am a Northman too."

"But you're indentured to them as a servant? Although . . . looking at you, I could almost believe you're one of them."

Dag sighed. "Even a free Northman can become a servant if he cannot pay back silver he has borrowed. That's what happened to me. In three years' time, I would have worked off my debts to Thorolf and become a freeman once more."

Edvina paused for a moment before she spoke. "Then you are probably the first Northman I cannot despise. You and Luke saved me from getting raped by that monster. That was a brave thing to do."

Dag nodded, wondering where his bravery had taken him. He knew, however, that if he were in that situation again, he would act the same way.

When they set off, heavy gray clouds swallowed the sunlight, and soon afterward it started to rain. The escapees fetched their cloaks from their carry sacks and climbed uphill, their strength dwindling. The rain grew heavier and more persistent, drumming on leaves and the waters of the river in a monotonous song that was broken only by Bert's whining.

Thorolf called together a handful of armed men and fetched Loki. He took the dog to Edvina's bed on the ground. Loki picked up her scent and led the men up the path to the waterfall.

Thorolf turned to Yngvi, who was walking behind him, and said, "I struggle to believe that Dag should be capable of such a brutal deed. He is a decent man who always completes his work well. He would have been free in two years' time; I was going to gift him one year. And Ansgar's servants are harmless fellows. I can't believe they would have dealt so cruelly with their master, either. It puzzles me."

Not me, thought Yngvi. But he merely said, "We will only solve the puzzle when we have caught the servants and the maid." Secretly he hoped that would not happen.

The search party's progress was slow. Loki kept losing their trail whenever it seemed to lead into the water. When the rain became heavy, Thorolf broke off the search. Loki would no longer be able to follow their scent reliably, and he wished to be back in the village before sunset. Without food and tools, the runaway servants would not survive in the wild for long.

When they returned to Woodhaven, Yngvi visited Hedda, the widow, and told her of their unsuccessful search. Hedda, who was preparing a meal amid her happily playing boys, took the news stoically.

"Whether you find them or not, Ansgar will not rise from the dead." *And I thank the gods for it*, she added in her thoughts.

Wouldn't hurt for a widow to act a little more aggrieved, thought Yngvi, but he said nothing, taking his leave.

The rain stopped as abruptly as it had arrived. The sun gradually began peering out from behind the clouds until it reigned alone in the blue sky once more. Bert refused to take another step, breathing heavily as he collapsed onto the wet forest floor. Dag saw that no ruse and no reason would move the heavyset man now.

"Very well, then we make camp here. I saw salmon leaping along the way. Shall we catch some, Edvina?"

The young woman set down her bundle, her quiver, and her bow. "Without a spear? Just with your hands? Have you tried that before?"

Dag said he had not. "Let's give it a try. I'll bring my cloak. If we catch ahold of one, we'll toss it in." He looked at Luke, who had lowered himself next to Bert. "Will you come help us?"

Luke nodded eagerly. He liked it when he was needed.

Bert did not wish to sit about idly while his companions took care of their evening meal. "I will get a fire going." The big man rummaged through the sack for the firestones and the pouch of tinder. "I just need to rest for a little while longer."

Dag, Edvina, and Luke walked the short distance to the Saltmarsh and searched for a suitable spot for their endeavor behind some rapids. They found a calm, knee-deep area near the bank where they could see clearly to the gravelly riverbed.

Dag planted his feet apart and held out his hands, ready to strike at the right moment. The first few salmon that swam past his feet against the current were either too large or too quick. But then a middle-sized one paused right beneath his hands. Dag grabbed at it swiftly and caught hold of it, but when he lifted his prey out of the water, the fish struggled hard, bending and stretching its slippery body until it glided out of Dag's hands. He rushed forward to capture the fleeing salmon a second time, but his foot caught on a rock, and he fell flat into the water.

Edvina laughed merrily.

When Dag straightened up, he saw that even Luke was grinning. He sighed. He always had been and still was the unlucky one. He fared no better with the next two salmon he caught—the only difference being that he chose not to chase after the fleeing fish. He did not wish to entertain Edvina and Luke at his own expense again.

Eventually he gave up. "There's no point. We need a spear. Edvina, do you want to try with your bow?"

"What if I miss and the current carries the arrow away, or if the fish swims away with it? We only have seven arrows. We need to use them sparingly."

"Luke take care of it," said their tall companion unexpectedly.

Dag scrutinized the Anglo-Saxon, who probably wasn't much shorter than Digur, the tallest man among the settlers. Luke's hands and feet, however, were bound to be the largest of anyone's. As Luke stood in the water, slightly bent, dangling his muscular arms above the surface, Dag gazed at the man's hands and couldn't help but think of shovels.

The Anglo-Saxon proved nimble. The first salmon he grabbed with his big hands almost landed in the cloak Dag and Edvina held out between them, but the fish managed to slip away at the last second. Luke, unfazed, returned to his position. When he caught hold of a second salmon, he dug his fingers into the gills and held it in a viselike grip. Then, in a mighty throw, he hurled it across the cloak and onto the nearby bank. Before the large, nearly three-foot salmon was able to squirm and flounce its way back to the water, Dag tossed the cloak on top of it, dragged it away from the bank, and thrust his dagger between its gills.

"Well done," said Edvina to the big man. "Now you are Luke the Salmon Catcher."

The Anglo-Saxon beamed, though his left eyelid and one corner of his mouth did not entirely participate in the joyful expression.

"Luke Salmon Catcher," he repeated blissfully, positioning himself in the water once more.

Edvina gently tugged at his sleeve. "Come. The fish is big enough for us all. Let's go eat it. Tomorrow you can catch us another one."

The big man straightened up. "Eating is good. Luke Salmon Catcher is hungry." Amenably, he walked after Edvina and Dag.

"Olaf is back!" shouted a boy excitedly. Soon other children picked up the cry.

Everyone who was in the village streamed down to the harbor, waving at the men rowing toward them with a shortened sail. Olaf, unmistakable with his brown plaits and large nose, was standing in the bow, waving back.

As the knarr came closer, it became obvious that something was wrong with the mast: it was significantly shorter than normal. The ship must have suffered a broken mast during its voyage. It looked like the men had used ropes to tie the broken piece to the remaining mast and then reinforced it with oars. The sailors ceased rowing and dropped the anchor. Olaf climbed into the dinghy with three men, and one of them rowed them ashore.

Thorolf made his way through the crowd. Everyone eagerly anticipated the returnee's story. Thorolf, greatly relieved to see his skipper alive and well, grasped Olaf by both arms. "Where is Gunnar's ship?"

Olaf's face darkened. "He capsized. Gunnar and five of his men drowned."

Thorolf's heart sank. The loss of the men pained him. They had been good men who had gone to sea at his command—and now they lay dead at the bottom of the ocean. "What happened?"

"We sailed east for seven days. For the first four days, a brisk wind from the west brought us good progress. Then the wind turned south and weakened, but still filled our sails. There was no land in sight on the seventh day, and so, as you ordered, we decided to turn back. That was when misfortune struck." Olaf widened his eyes dramatically, as if he were going to tell them that Aegir, the lord of the sea himself, had appeared and dragged Gunnar's ship down to his watery realm. His audience waited with bated breath. "We were sailing before a weak breeze under a full sail. I was sitting at the steering oar, enjoying the sunny day, when my attention was caught by a cloud that grew incredibly fast. At the same time, I noticed that whitecaps were beginning to form all of a sudden. I could tell something was wrong. I remembered a tale from an old sailor I heard at a tavern many years ago. He described the signs I was witnessing as the harbingers of Thor's white hammer. At last, I understood, and I yelled as loud as I could to shorten sail—but too late. Like a mighty fist from the heavens, a gust more powerful than I've ever experienced struck us. Our mast broke like a twig, crashing onto the deck right beside me and smashing a gap into the side. I lay buried beneath the sail." Swallowing hard, Olaf went on with a glum voice. "When I struggled from underneath the cloth, I could only see half my men on the decks. The others had been swept into the sea. I could hear them crying for help, and that's when I noticed that Gunnar's knarr leaned to the side. His mast had been ripped from its footing and cut a huge breach in the area of the steering oar, destroying parts of the ship's side. Two of his men were able to save themselves in the dinghy just before the knarr went down. I took them on board, and we fished any survivors from the water. Unfortunately, Gunnar was not among them." Olaf wiped his nose. "It was eerie. In a matter of moments, we had lost one knarr and five men, and the sun merrily shone from the sky. Just as if the gust never existed. It took us two days to fix the mast and the sail. There wasn't much wind, which made our work easier but prevented us from returning home in a timely manner."

One of the villagers shouted, "It was a sign from the gods!"

Another man added, "They punish us if we leave the island they led us to."

Others called out their agreement.

Thorolf grieved for the loss of his men and ship, but at least he had gained certainty: Catan lay alone in the ocean, far away from the lands he knew and whose coasts could lead him back to the shores of home. The long crossing was a dangerous gamble. Thorolf buried his dream of resuming his trade voyages and one day returning to his father.

Yngvi inspected the progress on his house. The roof construction was covered with a first layer of reeds, and the servants had begun the second layer. He could not find any fault.

Thorolf stepped to his side. "Day after tomorrow, your roof will be completed. Then it's Digur's turn. Come with me—there's something I need to discuss with you."

They sat down on the bench outside Thorolf's house. For a while, they didn't speak, enjoying the view of the golden-yellow sun as it sank into a glowing red veil of haze and eventually disappeared behind the horizon.

Yngvi was the first to break the silence. "I spoke with the maids Bran and his friends chose as their brides. All but one are agreeable to the matches."

Thorolf gave a knowing smile. "The one refusing is called Caitlin."

"How did you know?" asked Yngvi, astonished.

"A good chieftain knows everything," replied Thorolf with a grin. "It appears Olaf has taken a liking to her. He has asked for my permission to marry her. And it would seem his love is reciprocated. It is my decision to grant Olaf's wish—but Caitlin is under your care, and I did not want to decide without you. Do you agree?"

Yngvi nodded. "Of course. Olaf is a decent man. He will treat her well, and her child, too, when it arrives."

Thorolf cleared his throat. "There is something else. Sievert, the third son of farmer Sören, has proposed marriage to Carla. Since she lives in my household, he has asked for my permission."

Yngvi felt his stomach turn. "How did she respond?"

"She said she wanted to think it over. I believe she will say yes. Sievert is a good fellow, and she will hardly find better." Thorolf looked into his brother's face. "You have grown so pale! Are you feeling ill?"

Lowering his head, Yngvi tried to bring his thoughts in order. When he looked up again, he murmured, "I love Carla."

Now it was out. Finally he had said out loud the truth he'd been carrying around for a while, but which he had refused to accept until now. Suddenly Yngvi felt free from bonds he'd kept tied around himself since Frida's death.

At first Thorolf probably thought he had misheard, but then he laughed out loud. "I never would have guessed, brother. We all thought Carla was but a little sister to you. You have concealed your true feelings for her exceedingly well."

"I even concealed them from myself," Yngvi admitted.

Thorolf slapped his brother's shoulder. "I congratulate you on your choice. Carla is a warmhearted and clever young woman. When are you going to tell her?"

"Tomorrow. Please don't speak of it to anyone—not even Asla."

Thorolf promised.

It was bath day, the day when all settlers set down their tasks for a while, dedicating themselves (more or less thoroughly) to washing themselves and their clothing. Like many others, Yngvi bathed in the cool waters of the lake, washing his hair and cleaning his body with the help of a pathetic scrap of soap. It was high time he purchased a new chunk from Hilda. The charcoal burner was skilled at producing soap from the fat of yellow-beaks and wood ash.

He had already cleaned his teeth that morning, as well as shaved his short stubble with a sharp knife. At the lakeshore, he had prepared clothes—freshly washed by Ilka—and when he slipped them on, he felt clean and pleasantly refreshed. As on every bath day, he was meeting Carla at noon. The young woman was intent on learning to read and write, and Yngvi had come up with a method of easing her access to the Latin alphabet. He had whittled forty small wooden tiles and etched a letter into each one—some only once, and others, which were used more frequently, twice or thrice. Then he had blackened the carved lines with soot ink.

Yngvi was sitting on the jetty in the harbor, his feet dangling above the water. Carla wasn't late. He spotted her from afar as she meandered along the path from the bay on the far side of the peninsula, where she had gone to bathe with the other women.

She wore a plain, undyed linen dress, and her full curls were still wet, sitting heavily on the scarf around her shoulders. Around her neck was a leather string with a wooden cross.

"Hello, big brother," she greeted him cheerfully, brushing one hand across his head as she sat down beside him. Her own scent mixed with that of soap surrounded her like a cloud.

"Hello, little sister." Yngvi took a cloth pouch off his belt and tipped the letter tiles onto the wooden planks, turning them all letter-side up.

"Let's see if you can find the right letters for the word 'tree' and line them up in the right order."

Yngvi watched his student as she became engrossed in her task, shaping the sounds of the word's consonants and vowels with her mouth. She picked the letters from the pile and placed them in the correct order in front of her.

She looked at him proudly and pointed at the letters one by one, pronouncing them slowly, "T-r-ee."

"Well done, Carla." Yngvi winked at her, smiling. "We'll make a scholar of you yet."

Pleased at the praise, she gave him a smile that went straight to his heart.

Placing the letters back on the pile, Yngvi asked casually, "I heard Sievert asked for your hand in marriage?"

Carla sighed. "Yes, it's true."

"That doesn't sound like you're overly pleased."

"Sievert would treat me well, I'm sure. But I do not love him." She gazed at the peninsula, where pigs grunted as they scoured the harvested fields for edible morsels. "Maybe I can learn to love him."

"So, you will give your consent?"

"I think so. I will hardly find a better man. I am old enough to marry, and I don't wish to be a burden on Thorolf and Asla forever. And I like the thought of running my own household."

Yngvi nodded, changing the subject. "For your next task, you must read and understand an entire sentence. The sentence describes a thought of mine."

Yngvi picked out a number of tiles and used them to form three words in front of Carla.

Carla read them haltingly, "I . . . I lo . . . love you." She repeated the sentence, "I love you." For a moment, it seemed as if she waited for praise for her reading skills, but then the meaning of the words sank in. Her small mouth opened with surprise, and she stared at him from wide eyes, unable to put her astonishment into words.

Yngvi held her gaze. "Yes, that's how I feel about you, Carla. Now you have two suitors for your hand. Sievert and me. You must take your pick."

Carla sat as if frozen. Yngvi feared she might jump up and run off at any moment. But she did not. Her eyes gleamed with tears. Then, with a deep sigh, she threw her arms around him, kissing his forehead, his eyes, his cheeks, and finally his lips.

Yngvi returned her kiss passionately, feeling how the emptiness he had carried inside him since Frida's death became filled with Carla's closeness.

Lovingly she pressed her face against his neck. "You have been more than a brother to me for a while now. But you loved Frida so deeply, even long after her death."

"That is true. But your company was good for me. Aside from Gregor, you were the only one able to bring me comfort." Yngvi gently clasped her face between his hands. "Frida still holds a special place in my heart. But her death lies almost half a year back now, and I have learned to live with it. The more I came to terms with what happened, the more my feelings for you grew. But I wasn't ready to admit my feelings to myself—until yesterday, when I heard of Sievert's proposal."

Carla embraced him, and Yngvi folded his arms around her, holding her tight. For a while they sat thus in silence, each trying to sort their thoughts.

Yngvi softly brushed aside her curls and whispered, "Will you be my wife?"

Loosening herself from his embrace, she looked deeply into his eyes. "Yes, I will, with my whole heart." She paused for a moment. "But I do have one request."

"Whatever it is, you shall have it."

"I am a Christian, like my deceased parents. When I was a little girl, my mother used to tell me stories about Jesus and his love for humanity. Those stories helped me through the difficult time in Hedeby. And more recently, Gregor has answered many of my questions about Christianity, strengthening my faith in God."

Yngvi picked up her hands. "Carla, I know all that. What is it that you want?"

"I want God's blessing for our union. I would like Gregor to marry us." Carla lowered her head. "I would like for you to become a Christian."

Yngvi gently lifted her chin with one hand and sought her eyes, in which he read fear that he might disapprove of her request. He didn't care whether he was Christian or not. With a cheerful smile and his typical dry humor, he said, "If that is all, then I'll become a Christian tomorrow, and we marry the day after."

Carla laughed and covered his face with little kisses.

The next morning, Yngvi met Gregor outside his almost-finished house. The former cardinal was focused on working a longish board with his axe. He had learned this technique from Högni.

"I have already made a table," he declared proudly. "Once the bench here is finished, I am planning to make a chest."

"You seem to enjoy this work."

Gregor smiled. "Immensely. Creating something durable with one's hands is deeply satisfying. And besides, our savior was a carpenter too, as I'm sure you know. I like the thought of treading in his footsteps."

Yngvi looked around. "Where is Hilda?"

"My dear wife is in the woods with Stina, checking on the charcoal. She has to visit those two servants every day to ensure the pits are running properly. Harald is impatient. He urgently needs coal to extract iron from the rare lumps of ore."

Yngvi nodded. "The settlers are pressing Harald to manufacture new tools, for the old ones are becoming more worn by the day and will soon be unusable."

"One puts pressure on the next," mused Gregor. "And he who refuses to be pressed or is unable to keep up, finds himself discarded. Such is the price of progress."

Yngvi grinned a little at his friend's philosophical outburst. "How come you never tried to persuade me to become Christian?"

"I am a priest, not a missionary. It has always been against my nature to impose my religion upon others. I'm always glad to teach anyone about the message of Christ, though, if they want to learn more about my faith. But there is nothing I can tell you about it—you know my Bible by heart."

"Then it won't be a problem for you to baptize me."

Gregor raised his eyebrows in surprise and set down his axe. "You wish to become a Christian and denounce your gods? Are you not afraid of Odin's, Thor's, or Freya's wrath?"

"No. I stopped believing in them a long time ago."

"Do you believe in the Creator?"

For once, Yngvi decided to make no excuses and give an honest reply. He did not wish to fool his friend. "I doubt his existence, but I like the Christian teachings. You know that. I prefer it to our own high-handed gods, who are often all too human and bloodthirsty. Who knows? Perhaps, one day, I will find my way to your God."

"Then why do you wish to be baptized?"

Yngvi gave a shrug. "I asked Carla to be my wife. She has

consented, but she wants you to bless our union in the name of God."

Gregor's wide smile showed how pleased he was at the news. "I am happy for you and Carla. She is a fine girl."

"I know."

Gregor's smile vanished, and instead a wrinkle appeared on his forehead. "But you expect me to baptize you, even though you don't believe in the almighty?"

"I do not *expect* it of you. I am asking you."

Gregor muttered a few words Yngvi did not catch. Then he made up his mind. "You are a better person than many Christians I have encountered. There are many who only turn Christian in order to do business with other Christians, feigning their belief in God. At least you are honest with me, and therefore, you are honest with God. I will baptize you under one condition: you must never admit to anyone else that you do not believe in our Creator or doubt his existence."

Yngvi grinned and bowed low. "Rest assured, venerable Father. That I promise. May Odin, father of gods, be my witness."

Gregor admonished him gently. "Leave your jests be. We don't joke about matters of God."

Yngvi nodded with pretend contrition. But then his face turned serious once more, and he folded Gregor into his arms. "I promise you in the name of our friendship, which means very much to me."

It did not bother Yngvi that his new life as a Christian began with an agreement to keep up a lie.

A cool breeze from the mountains was driving light showers across the land when Gregor and Yngvi, wearing only their pants, waded out into the river above the waterfall. The water had cooled noticeably. They stopped when the river reached up to Gregor's hips.

Hilda stood on the bank with Carla, both wrapped in their gray cloaks against the damp.

Once Yngvi had uttered the words to profess his faith, Gregor placed a hand on his head and pushed him under the water for a few moments, speaking the Latin words of baptism, "*Ego te baptizo in nomine Patris, et Filii, et Spiritus Sancti.*"*

When Yngvi reemerged, Gregor concluded the ceremony with the words, "Now you belong to the community of Christians. Live according to the commandments of our Lord." He lifted a leather string with a wooden cross over his head and slipped it over Yngvi's. "May this cross protect you and help you to resist the temptations of evil."

Yngvi felt strangely touched. He still did not believe in the God of the Christians, but in some inexplicable manner he had come a little closer to this God.

Ten days later, the wedding took place in Yngvi's almost-finished house. Wearing his best clothing, the groom kneeled beside his bride while Gregor spoke the solemn words.

Yngvi couldn't take his eyes off Carla. She wore the simple, tight-fitting tunic he loved so on her. Her shoulders were adorned by a shrug of rabbit furs which she had sewn together herself with instructions from Stina. Asla had braided Carla's curly hair into many small plaits and pinned them up. Two large

* I baptize you in the name of the Father, and of the Son, and of the Holy Spirit.

blue blossoms, one on the right and one on the left, completed Asla's work of art. Yngvi thought it all went well with Carla's kind and natural manner, intertwining her inner beauty with her external one. Before he could stop himself, he planted a kiss on her cheek. Carla tried to stifle a giggle, but Gregor still heard it.

Muddling his words, Gregor shot the couple an irritated glance. "I did not think I had finished."

The guests behind the couple laughed, and Högni laughed loudest of all, holding his stomach and wiping tears from his eyes.

Yngvi lowered his head, trying hard to repress his grin. "Forgive me, honorable Father. The presence of our Lord caused my love to overflow."

Now Gregor was laughing, too, and finished his blessing. "Well, Yngvi, now you may give free rein to your love and kiss your wife."

And kiss they did, long and passionately. Swept up in the enthusiasm, the guests accompanied the kiss with cheers, clapping, and stamping. Then they handed the newlywed couple their gifts.

Högni, who made furniture for himself and other settlers, surprised them with a wooden bed frame. His wife, Diara, contributed a mattress stuffed with straw and a pillow that she and her maid had sewn from linen and filled with the feathers of yellow-beaks.

Asla and Stina gave Carla a jug, cups, and bowls from clay which they had shaped with their own hands and baked in the village's pottery kiln.

Digur gave Carla a pot that was closed with an animal skin and a string. She removed the skin and exclaimed with delight, "Honey!"

Her evident joy brought a smile to the big man's lips. "It's the first honey I have harvested on Catan," he declared proudly.

Hilda gave three bundles of dried kitchen herbs and a pouch of seeds for Carla's future herb garden.

Dragging a bench seat toward Yngvi, Gregor said, "This is the bench I was working on when you told me you wished to become a Christian. When you rest upon it, remember the promise you gave me."

Harald offered an iron pan. The taciturn blacksmith nodded at the cooking tool. "Some of the iron in this pan comes from Catan."

Carla gave her husband a look of gladness. "Now I can cook flatbread for us every day."

"Maybe not every day," said Yngvi with a smile. "I do like other foods, too."

Lastly, Thorolf presented his gifts. He signaled to a servant who had been waiting by the door, and the man disappeared outside and returned moments later with two jugs. A dainty woman followed him into Yngvi's humble hall.

"This wine I give you for your feast," Thorolf said. Then he pointed at the young woman behind his servants. "This is Edna. She is one of Egil's former slaves. Edna is a good worker and will serve you well as a maid."

Yngvi studied the young woman. She was one of the few former slaves who was not blessed with extraordinary beauty. Her warm, brown eyes and her wheat-blonde hair were pretty enough, but her hooked nose seemed a little too large for her thin face, and the corners of her mouth pointed sullenly downward. Yngvi suspected Egil had had her in mind as a kitchen maid for the emir's household. Was his brother afraid a prettier maid would have made Carla jealous?

Carla was visibly moved, thanking each of her guests with a warm embrace. Yngvi asked his guests to sit down at the two tables Asla had loaned them. Since the firepit in Yngvi's house was not yet completed, Ilka had prepared the meal in Thorolf's house. She and Edna fetched the food while Thorolf's servant filled the cups with wine.

Thorolf had no quarrel with the Christians, but he did not comprehend his brother's reasons for denouncing the gods of the North. After two cups of wine, he stated that the god of the Christians couldn't be very powerful if he allowed his son to bleed to death at the cross rather than handing him a flaming sword to destroy his enemies. No son of Odin's would let himself be nailed to a cross. He would sooner cut down hundreds of his enemies and then, following his honorable death, he would happily be taken to Valhalla by the Valkyries. *If* he lost the battle in the first place.

Högni and Harald laughed and agreed with Thorolf, while Digur sat in thoughtful silence. Yngvi glanced at Gregor, and the priest gave a small shake of the head. On this evening, they would not try to change the minds of Thorolf, Högni, or Harald.

Dag and Edvina reached the edge of the woods. Cautiously they pushed aside the branches of a wide bush and saw the cleared land and busy goings-on of the settlement beyond. On the plowed fields, pigs rooted for plants, worms, larvae, and other creatures. Three sows had given birth to piglets, some of which were running after their mothers, trying to catch a nipple. Not far from Dag and Edvina's hiding place, the girl who minded the pigs stood leaning against the enclosure she would herd the animals into come evening. A freeman trudged after a horse and plow, while some servants and maids cut up the overturned lumps of soil.

"I know the swineherd," whispered Edvina. "Her name is Nele. We were on one of the slave ships together."

Dag rubbed his beard. "I've met her a few times, too. Do you think we can trust her?"

"I don't know her well enough to be certain. But what choice do we have? We have to risk it if we want to survive."

Dag rustled the branches of the bush they were cowering behind. Nele looked up and peered in their direction. Dag shook the branches a few more times until curiosity made her walk over.

Once Nele was close enough, Edvina called softly, "Nele, it's us, Dag and Edvina." She parted the branches so the girl could see their faces.

The strong, round-faced maid gaped at her former fellow slave and her companion with bafflement. "What on earth are you doing here? If they catch you, you're done for."

"To avoid that from happening, act like you need to pee. It looks suspicious if you stand by the edge of the woods, talking to the trees."

Nele did as Edvina asked and soon sat behind the bush with her and Dag. "Thank God the settlers didn't find you. You are heroes to most of the thralls, because you dared to stand up to the violence of a freeman. Ansgar deserved to die. That pig did not only use his whip on his own servants. He would torture anyone's maid, especially when he happened upon them by themselves."

The two outlaws listened to Nele's words with relief. She was obviously on their side.

Dag spoke, "We found a place, one and a half days' walk from here—a place that offers us protection from the weather and from unwelcome visitors. Maybe we'll make it through the winter there, maybe we won't."

"We are lacking so many things," said Edvina with a sigh and grasped Nele's hand, squeezing it tightly. "Please help us."

"What do you need?"

Edvina counted on her fingers. "Salt, flax, a spindle, scissors, wool, grain, a pan—"

Dag added, "Two axes, a hammer, a hoe, whetstones, nails, and"—Dag's eyes turned to one of the sows who had lain down on her side to feed her young—"and two piglets."

Nele frowned, asking drily, "And how about two cows and ten sheep?" She shook her head with irritation. "How am I supposed to get all that without anyone noticing the theft? It's impossible on my own."

"Ask Ortwin," said Dag. "He is my friend and I trust him. I'm sure he will help us."

"We can rely on Luba, too," suggested Edvina. "We supported and comforted one another during our time on the slave ship."

Nele gave a resigned shrug. "All right. I will help you. But don't build your hopes too high. Come back in ten days' time. I'll leave anything that I manage to steal without arousing suspicion behind this bush and cover it with leaves. The two piglets you can have today. No one counts them. They are seven weeks old now and will be fine without their mother's milk. Wait until it gets dark and the farmers leave."

In the evening, Nele handed Dag a little sow and Edvina a little boar. The piglets squealed in fear when the two outlaws stuffed them into sacks.

Ortwin had served Högni for as long as he could remember. Northmen had abducted him and his mother twenty years ago from Frankia. He had been but a small boy then. He still remembered the day Högni purchased them at the slave market. Two years later, his mother died, and Ortwin had grieved for the only person who showed him love and care.

Högni and Diara took him under their wings, raising him alongside their sons. They were stern, but they did not differentiate much between him and their own children. Diara, who was warmhearted and spirited, did not exclude him when she cuddled the other boys, and in time, it seemed almost as if Ortwin were a part of the family. Even though he wasn't free, he liked his place in the world. Högni did not use him too hard as a common servant, and as Ortwin grew older, he was often permitted to watch his master perform his craft, and later he even helped. Högni praised his cleverness, entrusting him with ever more difficult tasks.

When Nele approached him outside the barn, telling him of her meeting with the outlaws, Ortwin immediately agreed to help his friend Dag. But he would not steal from Högni and Diara. That was out of the question for him.

Luba was one of the slaves Egil had bought at the market at Hedeby. Normally, the slave trader only purchased blonde or red-haired young women for the emir, but in the case of the black-haired Slav from the steppes of the East, Egil had made an exception, for he who beheld Luba's face once would never forget it. Well-shaped, bushy eyebrows, long lashes, and almond-shaped eyes that seemed to gleam black captivated anyone who gazed into them. With her high cheekbones, delicate nose, luscious full lips, and soft, tanned skin, she struck many as the embodiment of a goddess of love.

Nele watched Luba as she strode to the well and lowered a pail, admiring the young woman's lithe, elegant movements. Even though Nele did not think of herself as ugly, next to the Slavic woman, she felt very plain.

On board the ship, Nele remembered, Luba's beauty had not been as noticeable. Whenever the slaves were offered the opportunity to wash, Luba had declined it. On the contrary, she had smeared her face with dirt, hiding it behind her matted hair whenever an overseer walked past her. After a while, she reeked so awfully that even her fellow slaves, who did not smell of roses themselves, kept as much distance from her as possible. Edvina alone had been unperturbed by the stench.

It was not until Thorolf, the chieftain of the freemen, had loaned Luba to a man who only had eyes for his wife and paid no heed to pretty maids that she turned herself back into the immaculate beauty she was.

Nele walked over and helped Luba retrieve the pail as she told her of her encounter with Edvina and Dag. Luba immediately agreed to help. The thought of stealing from her master gave her no pangs of conscience. The chance to help those who killed the man who, a few weeks earlier, had lain in wait for her, tortured her, and almost raped her caused her heart to leap with joy.

As agreed, Dag and Edvina returned ten days later. They found several of the items they had asked of Nele in the hiding place. Dag was especially pleased about the axe and whetstone, while Edvina happily picked up a spindle, sewing needles, scissors, a sack of flax fibers that were ready to weave, and a smaller sack of salt.

Ortwin was standing by the pig enclosure with Nele. Since the farmers and their servants were working some distance away, Dag dared to whistle to capture the pair's attention. Ortwin strode leisurely toward the hiding spot.

The friends grasped each other by the arms and exchanged a sad smile. Edvina liked the calm, levelheaded manner of Ortwin, who lived in Högni's household almost as a freeman. As expected from servants, he wore his dark-brown hair short, and his trimmed beard was groomed. Next to Dag with his blond hair and even features, Ortwin was not a good-looking man. While the tip of his broad nose pointed to the right, his mouth dominated the left side of his face and made it seem crooked. But that was precisely what Edvina found appealing.

Dag thanked his friend for the assistance he and Nele had given them.

Waving dismissively, Ortwin replied that Luba, too, had contributed. "Is there anything else you need?" he asked eventually.

Dag and Edvina exchanged a look, answering almost simultaneously, "Grain."

Dag explained. "We want to sow a field with rye and barley, and a second axe would be good so that Luke and I can both fell trees."

"We are also missing ropes. And a hoe would be useful," Edvina said.

Ortwin tilted his head back and forth. "We can probably get you some grain and ropes. Folks will hardly notice if some of those are missing. But it is too soon to steal more tools. They're missing the axe I took from the barn a few days ago. If another one goes missing, they will grow suspicious and investigate."

Dag nodded. "I understand. That's a risk you don't want to take."

Before they parted ways, Ortwin handed a pouch to the outlaws. "Beans, peas, and some onions. I hope you find a spot to grow them. Come back here in ten days. Then we'll have the grain and ropes ready for you."

Before leaving the bush, Ortwin asked Dag to describe to

them the way to their hiding place, just in case they would need to find them one day.

Dag looked at Edvina, an unspoken question in his eyes. She nodded in agreement.

One week later, Ortwin, Nele, and Luba met outside the barn at night. The air was mild, even though it was late in the year. Ortwin carried a torch, but he wouldn't light it on his tallow lamp until they were inside. Nele and Luba had brought empty sacks. They agreed that Luba would keep watch at the door while Nele and Ortwin would search the barn for useful items for the outlaws.

A few houses farther on, Harald was struggling to fall asleep. He wished Abena were still here, lying next to him, so that he could listen to her soft breathing. He missed the maid more than he ever thought he would. Three moons ago, just a few weeks after Asla had given birth to her daughter, Abena, too, had gone into labor. It was a difficult birth, and the tiny infant did not survive. Ten days later, his mother followed him to the grave. In spite of all her efforts, Asla did not manage to vanquish Abena's childbed fever.

Following Abena's death, Thorolf had offered Harald one of the maids he commanded, but the blacksmith had turned down the offer. For now, at least. He was not ready for a new woman in his house to disturb his peace and to grow accustomed to. With their eleven and nine winters, his sons Runar and Knut were capable of looking after themselves and little Caven. Asla loaned him her maid, Ilka, for half the day to feed him and his children.

With a sigh, Harald rose from his bed. It would do him good to stretch his legs. When he stepped outside, he noticed a small light outside the barn, which lay about seventy paces away. Harald wondered who had any business there at this time of night. Returning to his house, he fetched a torch and lit it on the hearth's embers. Caven muttered in his sleep. The boy, still suffering from his mother's death, was probably having a nightmare.

When he stepped back out, the small light had disappeared, but Harald still hurried to the barn with determination. A few days ago, one of the axes stored there vanished. Harald had not seriously considered that one of the settlers had stolen it—what for? They felled the trees as a community, and no one particularly enjoyed this task. But what if someone had stolen it after all?

When Luba saw the approaching light of Harald's torch, she knocked on the barn door and dashed around the corner of the building.

Ortwin and Nele started when they heard the warning knocks. Swiftly, Ortwin stamped out the torch. "Hide!" he urged Nele before hastily grabbing his half-filled sack and diving behind a stack of timber. Not a moment too soon, Nele also found a hiding place.

When the door opened with a soft creak, Ortwin cursed inwardly. He had forgotten his small tallow lamp. It was standing next to the doorway, and now, in the draft of the open door, it flickered brightly, instantly catching Harald's eye. "Come out, you wretched thief! I know you're here."

Thinking on the spot, Nele undid her shift and bared a breast, stepping out from her hiding place. "Forgive me, master, Ortwin and I met here in secret, hoping to be undisturbed."

Ortwin emerged from behind the stack of timber, seconding Nele's claim with a guilty nod.

Harald gaped at the maid's large breast. Then he noticed

the sack Nele had failed to conceal in her panic. "And what's this?" The smith bent down and picked up the sack. Grains of rye scattered and bounced across the hard dirt floor.

Harald's face turned red with anger. "You are thieves! I'll bet you also stole the other things that have gone missing in the last two weeks. You might as well prepare yourselves now, for we will cut off your ears or shorten your nose. Maybe both. Everyone is going to see you for the miserable thieves that you are!"

"Are you going to cut off my nose, too?" asked a low woman's voice from behind him.

Harald spun around with surprise and found Luba standing naked in the glow of his torch. Transfixed, his eyes traveled from the dark triangle between her legs to the erect nipples of her firm breasts, eventually coming to rest on her immaculate face. Opening her mouth seductively, she ran her tongue along her upper lip. But Harald saw through the maid's maneuver. She was trying to buy his silence with her charms.

His eyes narrowed. "You miserable wench, we are going to cut out your tongue—"

Silenced by a blow to the back of his head, Harald collapsed on the ground. Ortwin dropped the log he'd used to strike the smith and picked up the torch Harald had dropped.

Cussing quietly, Luba pulled her shift and her plain dress back on. "By all the gods, Ortwin, I thought you would never hit him. What were you waiting for?"

Ortwin and Nele stood rooted to the spot, shocked by the recent events. Luba bent down and picked up the squared log, raising it in the air with both hands. Before she could take a swing at Harald's head, Ortwin held her back. "No. We are thieves, not murderers. Harald isn't the worst of the freemen."

Luba's dark eyes blazed angrily in the flickering light of the torch. "Do you want to lose your nose or your ears? Or your life, even? You've attacked a freeman, and maybe even killed him. Is he still alive?"

Ortwin kneeled down and held his ear against Harald's chest. "His heart is beating." Rising to his feet, he made a decision. "Harald is a friend of my stepfather's, and I will not allow you to murder him, Luba. Our only option is to run. We will bind and gag Harald, take as much as we can carry, and make our way to Edvina and Dag. Harald won't be found until the morning. That should give us enough of a head start."

Nele tried to seek the good in the situation. She touched Luba by the arm. "What is keeping us here?" she said, thinking out loud. "We are going to toil as maids until the day we die. If we're lucky, our master allows us to marry a servant. If not, they get us with child. Then we raise children who will share the same fate as we do." The thought of being the mistress of her own life seemed to appeal to her.

Luba was torn. She had consented to marrying one of the former servants freed by Thorolf. If she ran away, she was abandoning the chance of becoming a free woman herself—but on the other hand, she would escape the duty of sleeping with a man who had the right to pull his prick out of his pants whenever he felt like it and stick it inside her. The thought alone made her feel nauseated every time. In the end, she concluded that escaping might bring her both—freedom and independence from men. She would simply have to take care of her own clothing and food from now on.

Luba dropped the log. "Fine. We will let him live." She pointed at a wall where some coils of rope hung. "Let's tie and gag the fellow."

They did not return to their homes to fetch their sparse belongings. Too great was the danger of being caught by a freeman.

Instead, they packed as many supplies and tools into the sacks as they could shoulder, then quietly left the barn.

There was no moon, but the stars provided enough light for the small group to follow the Saltmarsh River upstream. In his right hand, Ortwin carried an axe—a tool suitable not only for felling trees, but also for defending oneself if need be.

The next morning, when Yngvi came to the barn with one of Thorolf's servants in order to prepare the families' weekly grain rations, he discovered the smith in a corner, tied up and gagged. Yngvi freed him from his bonds and ordered the servant to fetch Thorolf.

Harald spat out the gag and cursed vociferously. "Those bastards! We have to go after them!"

"Go after who?" asked Yngvi.

Massaging his wrists, Harald told him of last night's events. When he finished, Thorolf and several other heads of households arrived at the barn, and Harald told his story once more.

The damage was considerable. Three axes were gone, a length of rope, and various other tools that all the settlers used together. Several wooden handles were lying on the ground, evidently having been removed from the tools' metal heads. There also seemed to be less grain.

Everyone was in agreement: the servants' crime mustn't go unpunished. This time they would not break off the search after half a day. Not even if rain washed away the tracks. Thorolf put together a large search party of armed settlers. Two men brought their dogs, and Thorolf took Loki.

The men led the dogs to Högni's house and let them sniff

Ortwin's clothing. The animals barked excitedly, eager to follow the trail of scent.

Diara, watching the men, sighed deeply. Högni had planned to give his stepson his freedom at this year's Yule feast and employ him in his workshop as a freeman. Now these plans were crushed. Instead, Ortwin was facing a death sentence.

As in the first pursuit, the dogs led them up the path to the waterfall and along the river. When the dogs lost the scent, sniffing searchingly all over the ground, Thorolf gave the order to keep following the river. They had no time to waste. As fast as they could, they forced their way through the dense underbrush, climbing across fallen logs, bypassing huge ferns, and using their swords to cut swaths through tall, tangled bushes. In the afternoon, they rested at a spot where a creek flowed into the Saltmarsh. Then they followed Loki, who, barking impatiently, had taken up the runaways' scent again.

Ortwin, Nele, and Luba waded through a slow-moving part of the river. Low, moss-covered rocks rose from the wide, rocky riverbed and continued to jut out from the ground here and there in the forest that bordered the river. As the sun neared the horizon, the rocks became more numerous and larger, some as tall as a man.

"Look, there!" Ortwin called to Nele. "That must be the 'Guardian of the Portal' Dag told us about."

Nele, who had been focusing on her step in the stony riverbed, looked up and beheld the strange rock formation. It was about fifteen feet tall and divided into three towers by jagged cracks running from top to bottom. Together, the three columns, which were narrower at the bottom and wider toward the top, with the middle column rising above its neighbors, created the illusion of a fearful mountain troll towering possessively above the river with his two mighty arms and his massive head resting on his broad shoulders. Nele shuddered at the thought of this giant coming to life.

Behind the awe-inspiring rock formation, the land rose starkly, and at the slope's upper ridge, the river came gushing out through a portal of rock, and then, foaming and spluttering, it rushed down the steep hillside, whirling and twisting around rocky obstacles before finally calming by the feet of the stone troll, where it flowed peaceably toward Nele and her companions. It truly seemed as though a mighty mountain troll was watching over the river portal at his back.

In the last light of the evening sun, the runaways scaled the twenty-foot slope with their sacks on their backs, then dragged themselves through the woods with their last remaining strength. They had been on the move almost nonstop, and the arduous hike through rough terrain took its toll: their feet and calves ached, and they were hungry. But even greater was their need for sleep. Groaning, they slumped down on the soft mossy ground, lying huddled together to spite the cold of the night, and, after exchanging a few words, sank into a deep sleep.

Was he dreaming? No, there it was again—the barking of a dog, distant but unmistakable. Ortwin sat up with a jerk and woke his companions. "They have caught up with us!"

Swiftly they relieved themselves in the pale light of dawn, then shouldered their sacks and ran off. The Saltmarsh flowed evenly and calmy in its gravelly bed here, allowing them to walk upriver in ankle-deep water once more. After they followed the river around a few bends, the bed became narrower and the current swifter. Even right at the edge, the water reached up to their knees now, and with the heavy packs on their shoulders, they did not always manage to keep their balance. More than once, Nele and Luba fell into the water, but so far, with Ortwin's help, they had successfully scrambled back to their feet every time. The current was not quite strong enough yet to carry them away in an instant.

The land on both sides of the river began to rise ever more steeply, soon forming a gorge with rocky sides. A few skinny trees and bushes had sprouted here and there in the cracks of the weathered rock, breaking up the gray walls with their green leaves and beautifying the otherwise dark, steep valley. They were now in the foothills of the tall mountain range whose peaks were visible from Woodhaven on sunny days—although today, as so often, those peaks were shrouded in cloud.

There was less and less room for the escapees to walk on either side of the river, and the ground was rough. The slopes waxed steeper until they finally reached vertically into the sky for a hundred feet. In the distance, they heard the rushing of a waterfall.

The sun stood high in the sky by the time they reached the end of the gorge, arriving at the lake enclosed by tall rock walls that Dag had described to them. At the lake's far side, about five hundred paces away, the waters of the Saltmarsh came gushing across the top of the rock wall, pouring down in several misty strands for at least a hundred and fifty feet, bursting and splattering on protruding rocks along the way and finally roaring into the lake in white clouds of spray. The view made the three companions pause for a moment with amazement.

Luba, who had not been present when Dag explained to them the way to their hideout, tore the others from their thoughts.

Dropping her sack on a rock, she breathed deeply. "And now? Is this where our escape ends? Or will we have to climb up the rock face? Can anyone tell me how we're supposed to accomplish that?"

"No. There's a concealed cave on the right-hand shore that leads to our friends' camp," explained Ortwin.

He led the women along the lake's right shore, wading around a rock that protruded into the lake. On the other side, the lake stretched to the west by a fair way, and here, too, its shores were lined by steep slopes.

The water became deeper and deeper. When it reached up to Nele's hips, she cried out fearfully, "I can't swim!"

"I can't either," said Luba reassuringly. "But we still have ground under our feet for now."

Ortwin set down his sack and the axe on a dry ledge and told the women to do the same. "Here we are out of sight when our pursuers come up the river."

A dog barked in the distance. Nele shot Ortwin a nervous look. "They're getting closer."

He nodded. "We must hurry."

He crouched down to take off his shoes and stuffed them into a sack from which he produced a long coil of rope. He tied the tops of the three sacks to the rope, then clamped one end of the rope between his teeth. He swam with powerful strokes to a rocky island that lay about twenty paces away, rising out of the lake about twelve feet high. He found stable footing before pulling the sacks from the shore across to him. Then he vanished with them behind the island.

The barking of dogs grew louder.

"Where has Ortwin got to?" asked Nele nervously. "I hope nothing's happened to him."

"If we knew how to swim, we'd be safe by now," said Luba. "Shall we try?"

"You can't be serious!" exclaimed Nele, aghast.

"I am. I would rather drown than be caught by those Northmen."

Before Luba had a chance to put her plan into action, Ortwin came swimming back around the rocky island. When he was about halfway between the island and the shore, he tossed the end of the rope to the women. "Hold on tight. Luba, bring the axe."

The young woman nodded. One hand would have to do to hang on to the rope. Ortwin swam back to the rocky island, and from there he pulled the women toward him as swiftly as he could. They heard the voices of men—their pursuers must have reached the lake. "Quickly," Ortwin urged in a low voice. "We hide behind the rock."

Her teeth chattering, Nele uttered a prayer. Only God could help them now.

The dogs had lost the trail. After one day and one night, they did not seem to remember Ortwin's scent.

Thorolf counseled with the men, and they decided to split. He would follow the river up the gorge with his men, while the other two groups were to scour the rising banks on either side of the Saltmarsh.

Together with his men, Thorolf left the narrow bank and began to trudge through the shallow water. As it grew deeper, Loki barked reproachfully. The dog increasingly struggled with the current, and eventually Thorolf was forced to carry him. But nor did Loki feel at ease in Thorolf's arms, glancing downward and kicking his legs as he continued to bark.

"Quiet, now," Thorolf commanded, staring into the dog's eyes. That, finally, worked.

At the gorge's end, they reached a lake with a mighty waterfall at its end. Sheer cliffs rose straight from the water, and Thorolf saw no way to climb them. There was no way out of here, he realized. He passed Loki to one of his men, whereupon the dog started to bark unhappily once more.

Intrigued, Thorolf waded around a rocky outcrop to his right and saw that the remainder of the lake lay hidden behind it. A longish rock island jutted out from the water, but once again, he saw no evidence of the runaways, nor any way they could have scaled these steep slopes.

Disappointed, he called to his men, "They are not here. Let us go back and take a closer look at the spot where the thieves rested. Perhaps we overlooked something."

"They might have climbed up the bank somewhere along the gorge," suggested one of the men. "They weren't as steep there as these rock walls here."

Thorolf nodded. "Maybe. In that case, one of the other two search parties should find their tracks."

Ortwin exhaled with relief when he heard Thorolf break off the search along the lake. Luba's and Nele's teeth chattered pitifully.

"Where are the sacks?" whispered Luba falteringly.

He grinned. "In the same place where you are going to be in a moment."

When the voices of the men trailed off in the distance, Ortwin placed one end of the rope into Nele's hand, bit onto the other end, and pushed himself off the rocky island. Once he reached the far shore, he found footholds on some rock ledges below the water, which reached up to his chest.

Next to him, Luba noticed a dark crack in the rock above the water's surface, about a foot and a half long. Pointing at the crack, she asked: "Is that the entrance to the cave Ortwin spoke of?"

Nele nodded. "Yes, it mostly lies underwater. We must pass through there."

Luba wondered at Nele's even tone, as if she didn't mind squeezing through a narrow, dark hole—and like Luba, she couldn't swim. Luba, in contrast, shuddered at the mere thought of having to swim through there. Even as a child, she had feared darkness and tight spaces.

Ortwin signaled to Nele, pulled her across with the rope, and then supported her with one arm.

Luba heard a splash nearby and looked in the direction of the sound. Ripples on the water grew outward in rings, and underneath, she saw a shadow dart off. Evidently there were salmon here too. Her stomach rumbled at the thought.

When her eyes returned to the cave, she saw that Nele had vanished. The back of Ortwin's head was just disappearing in the darkness of the gap.

She felt terribly cold, but shivered not only on account of her wet clothes but also in fear of the dark hole. Angry thoughts crept into her mind. Why was Ortwin making her wait for so long? When he finally reemerged, she was clawing out his eyes in her imagination.

Luba's trembling hands were stiff, and she failed to catch the end of the rope he threw at her. She finally caught it on the third attempt. Ortwin pulled and Luba glided, freezing, into the water.

He helped her find some footing. The water reached up to her chin. She felt so afraid that she clung to him desperately.

Ortwin took the axe from her hand and spoke to her in a soothing voice. "Trust me. I'm going to help you into the cave now. You will continue to feel ground under your feet. Use your hands to hold on to the sides and feel your way forward. I'm right behind you. It won't be long before you can walk normally."

Luba whimpered softly as Ortwin guided her through the entrance to the cave. His right hand held on tight to the scruff of her tunic, which gave her a vague sense of security. Her feet touched the ground, and she managed to keep her head above the water. She grasped the uneven surface of the rock walls to pull herself along. At last, the narrow corridor began to rise, and she found, to her relief, that she was able to push herself off the ground with her feet. Soon the water was down to her hips.

The sparse light streaming through the cave's entrance reflected off gray rock gleaming with dampness. In the spot where Luba fully emerged from the water, a small stream flowed into the lake, bubbling merrily across small obstacles on the cave floor. Luba's eyes had adjusted well enough to the dim light by now for her to make out a paddle and logs that had been tied together. The makeshift raft was narrow enough to fit through the cave entrance. If a person were lying down upon it, they could probably leave the cave halfway dry. To her right, Luba spotted the sacks and, sitting behind them, Nele, shivering as she held her arms clasped firmly around her knees. Luba sat down beside her. The women hugged, trying to stop their chilled bodies from losing any more heat.

Holding the coiled-up rope in one hand and the axe in the other, Ortwin came over to them. "It won't get better if you sit here. We must keep moving."

"Without light?" asked Nele, her voice shaking.

"Do you have a better suggestion?" retorted Ortwin with irritation. "Do you suggest we return to the woods and make a fire? As you know, they're still searching for us there."

Luba stood up. "Aren't you cold?"

"I am," replied Ortwin. "But I've been moving." He pointed

at the sacks. "We will leave those here and fetch them later. Let us tie ourselves together with the rope. I'll go first."

"I can lead you."

Startled, they all looked in the direction of the voice. It was Edvina, climbing down the cave toward them. She carried a torch in her right hand, bathing the rocky walls in a warm glow.

"Were you expecting us?" asked Ortwin.

"No. I had no idea it was you. I was hunting for rabbits early this morning. Standing at the edge of the gorge, I could make out three figures coming up the river. I couldn't tell who it was, but I feared you were settlers who had not given up hope of capturing us. I quickly climbed down the bank, ran back to the lake, and paddled across to the cave on the raft. I've been keeping watch here ever since, praying to God the settlers would not find the entrance to our hideout."

"We must have given you an awful fright when we entered the cave," said Ortwin.

"You sure did. I was about to go warn the others when I recognized your voice."

Edvina was wearing a woolen tunic and, around her shoulders, a cloak made of rabbit furs. She undid the brooch holding it together and passed the cloak to Nele. "Once you feel a little warmer, pass it to Luba. You can tell me your story later, when we're with the others."

Edvina led them up the cave. "Mind your feet and heads," she told the others.

Despite the warning, Ortwin cursed a short while later when a sharp rock growing from the low ceiling ripped open the skin on his head. His first instinct was to hurl his axe at the rock, but then he stopped himself. Not long after, Nele slipped and fell on a slimy rock, landing hard on her elbow. Her cry of pain echoed eerily off the cave walls. Luba was spared such accidents.

She wasn't particularly tall and didn't need to fear the low ceiling. Graceful by nature, she moved nimbly across the uneven, slippery ground.

The corridor widened and the ceiling rose higher, and eventually the passage ended in a grotto. "This is our bath," declared Edvina proudly. In the light of her torch, the companions saw a small pond that was fed by the waters of the stream. "Did you notice that it has become warmer?"

Ortwin nodded. Now that Edvina pointed it out, he noticed.

"The water is warmer than the sea in the summer," she raved.

Luba and Nele eyed the steaming pool longingly. They would have loved to take a bath right then, but Edvina walked on.

The grotto turned lower and narrower, and soon they were back inside a corridor that continued to lead uphill. Luba feared this underground hike would never end. Then, finally, after following the cave around a bend, they could make out light in the distance.

Nearer to its exit, the cave grew larger once more. This was where Edvina and her companions had set up camp. Their simple sleeping places to the right and left of the stream consisted of blankets and sewn-together furs, which they had padded with fallen leaves and moss. Skinned and gutted rabbits hung from a wooden structure.

Edvina gathered the blankets off the beds and brought them to the new arrivals. "Take off your wet things. We don't need sick people here."

Wrapped up in the blankets, Ortwin, Luba, and Nele stepped out of the cave. They found themselves on a small, sunny clearing which Dag and Luke must have wrested from the woods. Tree stumps in the ground and trunks fallen among the surrounding trees testified to their efforts. In the clearing's center, the small stream flowed into the cave. Beside the stream, four logs sat arranged around a fireplace enclosed by stones. A little way off to the side, Bert and Luke sat with their backs to them, scraping the insides of rabbit skins. The two stolen piglets rooted the ground for food.

Dag gaped in surprise when he spotted the new arrivals. Quickly he set down the axe he had been using to carve a groove into a trunk. Disquieted, he hurried toward Ortwin and grasped him by the arm. "What happened? Why are you here?"

Luke and Bert, too, spun around with astonishment and set down their work.

Ortwin, soaking up the warm sunshine just like Nele and Luba were, looked from person to person. "It's a long story. We'll tell you later. First we should fetch the sacks. The grain has become wet, and we need to dry it as soon as possible."

Nele's eye was caught by a fried salmon resting upon leaves by the fire. Her stomach grumbled loudly.

"I can hear that you are hungry," said Edvina with a smile. "Why don't you sit and eat the fish. Once I've put your wet clothes in the sun to dry, Dag and Luke and I will fetch the sacks and my rabbits from the cave."

The new arrivals did not need to be asked twice as they sat down in the warm sunshine and helped themselves to the fish. Bert also snatched a few pieces. He wasn't starving like Ortwin, Nele, and Luba, but he was always hungry.

The sacks' contents were a revelation for Edvina, Dag, and Bert. Luke watched with dull eyes as they spread the treasures before them. The outlaws gave cries of delight at the sight of axes, sickles, hoes, and hammers, which Ortwin had freed from their handles for ease of transport. Their faces lit up further when they saw seeds of flax, barley, and rye, as well as nails and arrowheads. Edvina spread a blanket to dry the damp grains. Meanwhile, Bert skinned and gutted the rabbits Edvina had killed that morning.

He tossed the edible innards into their pot, filled it with water, and hung it on a makeshift construction above the fire.

Toward the evening, the group of now seven outlaws gathered around the fire. Bert turned an impaled rabbit above the small flames while Ortwin, Luba, and Nele took turns telling the tale of their escape.

When they were finished, Dag shook his head slowly. "It's our fault that you have become outlaws like us. If we had not asked for your help, you would not have been forced to flee."

"Then we would still be maids and servants, at the mercy of the freemen," Luba replied. Then she smiled, glancing at Edvina. "I like it here. I do not regret running."

Nele nodded. "Here, we are free, and whatever work we do is for our own benefit, not for the settlers."

Edvina dampened the women's expectations. "Our life here is not all milk and honey. Every day we fight to find sufficient food. Hunting rabbits is dangerous because of the hunters from the village. No one can tell when and where they might appear. Big salmon are becoming scarce, and we only planted your beans, peas, and onions the day before yesterday." She pointed at a patch of freshly dug soil. Beside it lay a roughly carved spade and a makeshift hoe consisting of a branch with a pointed rock attached to its end.

"It is going to take time before we have cleared enough forest to sow the grain. And winter is almost upon us. No one knows how cold and wet it's going to be," said Dag, adding to Edvina's gloomy observations.

Ortwin nodded. "I will make myself a bow. Then I can help you shoot rabbits, Edvina."

Bert glanced longingly at the two piglets and sighed. "It's going to take a long while yet before those two can produce offspring. Too long, if you ask me. We ought to slaughter them once they have put on a little more weight."

Bert received dark looks from Dag and Edvina for his comment and hung his head guiltily.

Luba looked around. "Where exactly are we?"

"We are at the start of a narrow, wooded valley," replied Edvina. "It's surrounded by tall rocks all the way around. If you follow the stream, you come to its spring—the end of our small world. The walk to the spring and back takes about half a morning."

"Do you think we're safe from the settlers here?" asked Nele.

Dag shrugged. "I hope so. The entrance to the cave lies mostly underwater and is well hidden. We discovered it by chance when I swam to the rocky island out of curiosity."

"Is there no other access?"

"No direct one. Coming from the direction of Woodhaven, you wouldn't suspect this valley here behind the tall foothills. No one will bother scaling those steep cliffs. The settlers can't search every single nook and cranny of this island for us. At some point, they will believe we died in the wilderness. So we must proceed with extreme caution during our future raids if we want them to remain in this belief."

"Raids?" asked Ortwin. "What do you mean?"

Edvina grinned mischievously. "Dag and I are planning to visit their flock of sheep one night and steal a few lambs."

Nele frowned. "Isn't that too dangerous? If the sheepdog barks, the sentries will be alerted."

Edvina shook her head. "I herded the sheep for a few weeks. The dog knows me. Once he's sniffed me, he'll be fine."

"It's worth the risk for a crispy roast lamb," said Bert. "A little variety in the diet never hurt anyone."

"The lambs aren't meant for your fat belly," Edvina groused. "Once they're fully grown, we'll shear them and weave new clothing from the wool. Just look at your threadbare tunic. If your gut doesn't rip it to shreds first, it will simply fall apart sooner or later."

"We still have flax," replied Bert sheepishly.

"Yes, we do. But it's only just enough to spin the thread we need to sew together the rabbit furs. And besides, we still don't have a loom. If you want to make yourself useful, build us one."

Bert said nothing. He invariably came off second best when locking horns with sharp-tongued Edvina. In his thoughts, he made peace with the subject: there would be neither pork nor lamb roast for him. Thank God she had no quarrel with roast rabbits.

Bert's mouth watered when he pulled the crispy meat off the spit. He placed the next rabbit on the stick before dividing the roast into six roughly even-sized pieces for his companions, while retaining the two hind legs for himself. That was only fair, he figured, since he had been turning the spit.

Edvina furrowed her brow and snatched one of the rabbit legs from him, handing it to Luke, who gave her a smile, and she thought she could glimpse in the depths of his eyes something that defined the man he used to be before his injury: kindness, gentleness, and generosity.

The morning turned out foggy, and the outlaws were in agreement that they ought not to go hunting or fishing that day. Too great was the risk of running into settlers. Thorolf and his men were bound to still be in the area, searching for the runaways.

They sat together to discuss the day's work, but in the end, it was Dag and Edvina who decided who would do which task, and no one questioned their decisions.

Dag summarized, "Since we now possess two axes, Luke and I will both fell trees. Ortwin, you make handles for the third axe and one of the hoes and help us later. Bert, you prepare our meals and take care of the piglets. I hope you know what I mean by 'take care of.'"

Bert nodded.

Edvina spoke. "Luba and I will spin yarn. Nele, you search for carrots in the woods. Do you know what the plant looks like?"

"Of course." Nele pulled a face. "I also know what they taste like."

When they all gathered by the fire around noon, the sun and wind had won their battle against the fog. The women and Bert were in good spirits as they sat down, while Dag and Ortwin slumped heavily on their wooden seats, sweating and visibly exhausted. Luke, on the other hand, did not look at all as if the tree-felling work had been strenuous to him. In silence they fished out lumps of meat from the broth Bert had cooked from the rabbits' innards the previous day.

After a while, Nele wrinkled her nose. "It's not what you'd call tasty. A little salt would have gone a long way."

Edvina slurped the rest of her broth from the wooden bowl. "Then you should have brought more salt. The little we have we intend to save for special occasions. But if you don't like it, give it to the fat one. I'm sure he'd love it."

Bert shot Edvina an indignant look before shaking his head decidedly.

In the afternoon, the men set to pull one of the stumps out of the ground. With the aid of the wooden spade and a hoe which Ortwin cleverly fixed to a handle, they cleared the upper layer of the stump's roots until they were able to secure two ropes in suitable places.

Edvina and Luba sat outside the cave, spinning flax while watching the men's efforts. Their faces reddened with exertion, Dag and Luke pulled on the ropes with all their might while Ortwin chopped through the roots that held the stump in the ground.

Edvina had shown Luba how to use the spindle, and Luba proved to be a good student. Deftly, she used one hand to feed the yarn attached to the spindle with fibers from the bundle of flax, while her other hand rotated the spindle, thus entwining the loose fibers and growing the yarn bit by bit.

Edvina, who had helped her mother spin as a young girl, marveled at Luba's handiness. Her yarn was growing almost as fast as her own, and soon Luba would surpass her. That irritated Edvina, and it wasn't the only reason she nursed wrathful thoughts about the other woman. *You minx—not only will you spin better than me in no time at all, but you also draw the men like a dunghill draws blowflies. Well, except for Bert. He only thinks of filling his belly. And Luke lives in another world. But Dag and Ortwin eyeball you. They seem to think Nele and I don't notice their secret looks. You can have Dag for all I care. But I will fight you for Ortwin.*

A dull thud, followed by a muted cry of pain and hearty cussing, interrupted Edvina's ill-humored thoughts. She looked up. Evidently, the last root holding the stump in the ground had just been severed, releasing the ropes from their tension and sending Luke and Dag flying forward. Luke was rubbing his forehead where he had hit a tree. Then he shook his head and picked up the rope again.

Edvina resumed her work, but Luba's hands lay still as she gazed sidelong at her friend. After a few moments, Luba placed a hand on Edvina's cheek and leaned over to her, whispering, "I like you. I like you very much." Gently, Luba turned Edvina's face toward her and kissed her on the lips.

Edvina was stunned—this was the last thing she had expected. When Luba's kiss became more urgent, she pulled herself free, staring at her friend with bewilderment. Then Edvina broke out in ringing laughter. Once she started laughing, she couldn't stop; tears ran down her cheeks and she gasped for air.

Luba pinched her arm hard. "What is it? Why are you laughing?"

Edvina finally calmed down. "Because . . . because I was jealous and angry with you. I saw Ortwin's eyes following you with admiration. I had no idea you liked women."

"Are you only interested in men?"

"Yes," she replied, turning serious once more. "Ortwin and I are going to become a couple. Only, he doesn't know it yet."

Luba's face filled with regret. "What a shame. We talked so much on the ship, spent so much time together. You brought me comfort. I thought something more had grown between us."

Edvina picked up Luba's hand. "And so it has. Friendship. But, from my side, nothing more than that. I would like us to remain good friends."

Luba nodded with disappointment.

CHAPTER 16
RYAN

For four days, they sailed the *Freedom* along the coast without spotting any sign of the settlers. On the morning of the fifth day, Ryan had his men steer the knarr up the main arm of a delta. After a while, they spied, in the distance, a wooden watchtower that appeared to be unoccupied. At last! They had found the settlers.

Ryan ordered the *Freedom* to stop. He and Enya climbed into the dinghy, then had Liam pass down a pouch and a larger, heavy sack. Ryan held his friend's steady gaze and grasped his hand in farewell. "If we haven't returned in ten days, my mission failed. You know what to do then."

Liam nodded. For a while, he watched as Ryan pulled himself and Enya into an uncertain fate with powerful strokes of the oars. Before ordering the men to set course back to their village, he raised his hand in farewell one last time.

While Ryan pulled the oars through the water in a steady rhythm, he watched his companion, who was studying their surroundings with alert eyes.

At first he had refused Enya's demand to accompany him

on this mission. "It's too dangerous, and you are pregnant," he had repeated to her a dozen times.

She had replied invariably with, "I am your wife and belong at your side." Eventually she had drawn the last arrow from her quiver of arguments by declaring that, in any case, she would kill herself if he did not return to her alive. And so he had yielded. He had become tired of the endless arguing and knew that Enya meant it. She was a straightforward person who never lied and always followed up her words with deeds.

A gentle breeze played with her thick red hair, the rays of the sun causing it to gleam copper. Her beauty scarcely stood out among the chain wielder women, and Ryan often wondered what Egil's plans had been for the comely slaves.

When Enya noticed his eyes upon her, she turned her face to him. Her heart-shaped lips formed a smile whose warmth was reflected in her deep-blue eyes. Sweetly, she asked: "Why are you looking at me thus?"

Ryan returned her smile. "I usually look in this direction while I'm rowing. And today—and not entirely by chance—there happens to sit a lady I don't at all mind looking at."

Thorolf was in a foul mood when he left the smithy. Harald, who had spent several days searching the mountain foothills for ore with his apprentice, Bran, had returned with the news that the rocks contained as much ore as the yellow-beaks bore scales.

There was a serious shortfall of tools. The tools they had were becoming noticeably worn—frequent sharpening and honing meant the axes' cutting edges were becoming thinner and the hoes' blades shorter. And the runaway servants had stolen some. Thorolf cursed the thieves. For five days, they had searched for the scoundrels, combing the dense woods far and wide on either side of the Saltmarsh River. For nothing. It was as if the earth had swallowed up the outlaws. As a measure of precaution, he had bestowed Harald with the task of manufacturing locks for the barn and the smithy. In the meantime, Thorolf posted guards outside the two buildings at night.

The lack of tools hampered Woodhaven's development. The clearing of trees to create more fields had slowed, and the settlers were growing discontented by the shortfall of numerous everyday items: daggers, which were customarily gifted to a male youth upon becoming a man, chisels, hammers, new shears for shearing the sheep, nails for building houses.

Thorolf had already asked the leading family members to hand in their swords so that Harald could use the metal to forge urgently needed tools. They would not need their weapons, he had told them. There were no enemies on Catan, and later, once they had found a vein of ore in the mountains, Harald would be able to forge them new swords. The men had stared at him with shock and disbelief, as if he had just asked them to strip naked. One farmer had said out loud what they all thought, "You can't have *my Wolf Slayer*! I would sooner give you my left hand. I received the sword from my father, and he received it from his father. It is the sword of our family, and when the time is ripe, I will place it into the hands of my firstborn son."

Thorolf, too, had been forced to concede that he would be loath to see his own sword, *Bearkiller*, reforged. The superior Frankish weapon had cost him a fortune. The blade with the inscription *Ulfberht* was particularly flexible yet hard.

On the way back to his hall, he saw his younger brother step out of the barn.

Yngvi, looking good-humored as ever, walked toward him.

"Thorolf, what is it? You look as though you swallowed a slimy toad."

"Something of the kind," replied Thorolf. "I have just spoken with Harald. He found no ore in the mountains."

Yngvi's smile vanished. "That is bad news indeed. Then we must content ourselves with the little iron that is in the forest floor. Or else we send Harald around Catan on a ship. There's bound to be ore somewhere on this island."

"We can't do without him for that long. Bran only started his apprenticeship two moons ago, and the servant I lent Harald merely fetches and carries."

Yngvi was about to reply when his eyes were caught by an approaching ship. Pointing it out to Thorolf, he asked the question they were both thinking: "Why is the *Spearhead* returning at noontime from the delta?"

A short while later, Thorolf and Yngvi saw Hakon disembark from the ship followed by a man and a woman. The brothers exchanged a puzzled look. They did not know the pair. Where had they come from? Were they not alone on Catan after all?

With bated breath, they waited for Hakon as he limped up the track with his crooked leg. The old sailor briefly bowed his head to his chieftain.

"Thorolf, two strangers arrived at the delta in a dinghy. I did not understand their business, for they do not speak our tongue. I believe they are Irish. They kept saying your name, and so I gathered they wish to speak with you, and I thought it important to bring them to you right away."

"You made the right decision," said Thorolf. "Tell the strangers to wait for me by the jetty."

Hakon nodded and limped back down the hill.

Thorolf turned to Yngvi. "I must get changed. Fetch Caitlin, Digur, Harald, Högni, and as many other leaders as you can find."

Soon after, Thorolf descended to the jetty with Asla at his side and several men behind him. He wore his best tunic and the bearskin from his old homeland. On his belt, he carried his precious sword.

The stranger raised his left hand in greeting, while his right hand rested on the hilt of his sword. The man was tall and had an athletic build. His blond hair reached down to his chin and was well-kempt, as was his trimmed beard. Beneath the elegant fur-trimmed cloak, he wore a tunic that had seen better days. The red-haired woman at his side was handsome, but her clothing did not fit her, being too wide and too long for her delicate figure. The plain cloak she wore over the top was also too large. It almost seemed as if she wore a man's clothing.

Thorolf addressed the stranger. "Greetings. My name is Thorolf Ulrikson. I am the chieftain of our settlement of Woodhaven. I hope you come in peace."

The new arrivals looked at him blankly, and Thorolf asked Caitlin to translate his words.

Caitlin's face had darkened when she recognized the stranger. He was the leader of the slaves who had left her and the others tied in the pit. But she readily translated Thorolf's greeting into Irish nonetheless.

The stranger nodded and spoke some words which Caitlin translated to Thorolf. "Greetings to you also, Thorolf Ulrikson, chief of the Northmen. I am called Ryan, the eldest son of the Irish king Máel Sechnaill mac Máele Ruanaid. Rest assured that my wife, Enya, and I come in peace."

And all of a sudden, Thorolf knew who was standing in front of him: the same Ryan whose name the slave women had uttered over and over—the same man who was responsible for the death of Egil's men. Thorolf felt hatred and fury rise up in him. He pressed his lips into a thin line, flared his nostrils, and narrowed his eyes. Then he drew his sword.

Ryan followed suit, positioning himself in front of his wife. Asla cried out and clasped her hands to her mouth.

Before the two men had a chance to begin their fight, Yngvi grasped hold of Thorolf's sword arm and clung to it while Ryan remained in his pose, ready to defend himself.

"Thorolf," he entreated his brother, "wait and hear what he has to say. He came without any warriors, alone with his wife. We can still pronounce judgment over him later."

Digur placed one of his big hands on Thorolf's shoulder. "This Ryan is a brave man. Let him speak."

Thorolf ground his teeth. Eventually he succeeded in taming his anger. He agreed with his brothers. He could always kill the Irishman later to avenge his countrymen. Sheathing his sword, he uttered a curse and snarled at Ryan, "You're the leader of the slaves who attacked their masters and killed them. The punishment for that is a painful death."

Ryan, too, sheathed his sword. Once Caitlin had translated, he answered in a calm, deep voice. "I never had a master and never was a *slave*." He spoke the last word with contempt. "My compatriots and I lost a battle against pillaging Northmen while defending the land of my father. It is true that they took us prisoner. But we never considered ourselves slaves. Rather, we were captive warriors. As such, we freed ourselves and defeated your countrymen honorably in battle." Ryan paused while Caitlin translated. "You can kill me. But if I do not return to my people within ten days, you will never find peace in this land again. Those of our men who did not know how to use sword and shield before do so now, astounding even us trained warriors with their skill. We have taught our women to shoot with bow and arrow, and by now, they can strike a rabbit at thirty paces. If you kill me, my people will not only avenge me on your cattle—they will bring you a bloody feud."

Against his will, Thorolf admired the Irishman's courage and determination. He recognized that he was looking at a strong, charismatic leader whose people would do as he threatened they would. With consternation Thorolf realized that he was standing at a crossroads. Whichever way he chose, the settlers' life was facing drastic changes. They were no longer alone on Catan.

Before he had made up his mind, Yngvi spoke. "Why are you here?"

Ryan was relieved that he and Enya had survived their arrival and that the settlers were speaking with him. The first part of his plan had succeeded. He took a heavy pouch from his belt and stepped forward, emptying the contents before Thorolf's feet. Metallic lumps of various sizes gleamed yellowish in the light of the afternoon sun. "This is for you," declared Ryan, adding ironically: "It is my gift for my host."

The settlers gaped in astonishment at the gold the Irishman had tossed at their feet. In their old home, it would have been a fortune.

"Is there a smith among you?" Caitlin translated the question, and Harald lifted his hand.

"Step forward."

His curiosity aroused, Harald approached the Irishman.

"This is for you." Ryan picked up the heavy sack he had set down beside himself and lifted it into Harald's arms.

Harald opened the sack, peered inside, and finally emptied its contents onto the jetty. Reddish marbled chunks of stone thudded onto the timber planks. Harald crouched down and studied the rocks more closely. Then he picked up a lump as large as his fist and held it up to Thorolf. "There is more iron in this than in ten crates full of this accursed forest soil."

Ryan placed his left arm around Enya, who leaned against him. He silently uttered a prayer of thanks to God. Judging by the smith's reaction, there was no or very little iron in the ground near the village. The second and highly uncertain part of his plan was fulfilled: he possessed the monopoly of a resource that was vital to the settlers' survival.

"You can have more of this if you are willing to trade it for goods that we are in urgent need of. In the name of my people, I offer you peace between our communities. If we trade with one another, everyone benefits."

Once Caitlin finished translating, Yngvi whispered something to Thorolf. The latter nodded, turned around, and, without uttering another word, marched up the path to his house. The men who followed their leader cast longing glances at the sparkling lumps of gold, but no one had so far dared to touch it. It was Gregor who collected the gold and returned it to its pouch.

Yngvi gestured for Ryan and Enya to follow them up to the village. On the way, he explained to them, with Caitlin's help, that Gregor would welcome them as guests in his house until Thorolf decided what to do with them.

When Yngvi entered Thorolf's small hall a short while later, the men were hotly discussing the matter. Fenrir, a lanky fisherman, grumbled, "The slave must die. He murdered our brothers. What are we coming to if thralls may raise their hand against their masters and go unpunished?"

Harald agreed with him. "There are more of us than of them. Why trade if we can take the ore for nothing?"

Högni ran his hand through his shaggy hair. "Taking their ore won't be as easy as that. I believe the Irishman when he says that they will meet us with drawn swords. After all, they took all of Egil's men's swords, shields, and bows."

Fenrir, who in his younger days went on viking raids, replied sharply: "Are we little girls? We know the slaves count barely more than fifty heads. If half of those are men, we can face them with three times as many warriors. What are we waiting for? Let us cut off the heads of Ryan and his woman. Then we buckle our swords, board our ships, and take the ore of those lousy slaves!" Thirst for action and adventure sparkled in the fisherman's eyes.

Most of the gathered men expressed their agreement with loud cheering; only a handful of them seemed pensive. One of those was Digur.

Yngvi raised his voice. "Have you who shout so loudly to take up arms forgotten how you lost your home and livestock in our old homeland? Wasn't it because of the eternal discord among the tribes?"

He glanced at Asla, who encouraged him to speak on with a nod and a slow blink of her eyes.

"Do we not wish for a better future for us and our sons and daughters upon this warm, fruitful island? Do we not wish to graze our animals and till our fields in peace?" Yngvi allowed the question to sink in for a moment before continuing. "And now you want to once again risk your houses, your provisions, and your lives? Are you truly ready to bring war to this island—war that will demand a high blood toll from us, even if we win? I ask you: Are you too lazy or too cowardly to break with old traditions and instead bravely carve new paths in a new world?"

Several leading men grumbled and strafed him with boos. The loudest among them was Fenrir, also called The Red—not only for his fiery red hair but also for his choleric outbursts, which would turn the skin of his long skull with its deep-set, suspicious eyes a striking shade of red.

Thorolf's tense expression showed that he was wrestling for the right decision.

Digur stepped beside Yngvi and placed a demonstrative hand on his shoulder. "The Irishman is a great warrior. He has beaten our countrymen fairly in an open fight."

Digur spoke slowly. He rarely became involved in discussions, and most settlers were unaccustomed to hearing him string several sentences together. And it was this circumstance that made them all listen closely to the words of the famous hero of many battles.

"This island is big," he continued. "There is enough room for everyone. Even for the Irishman and his people. Trading with them will be of advantage to us all." The tall warrior gazed into the eyes of one man after another. "If you are foolish enough to start a war, then go ahead. But do not expect me to join you. I will stay here and plow our fields."

There was silence. Yngvi gave Digur an appreciative nod. His big brother had impressed the men more with a few simple words than he had been able to do. Stina, too, gazed proudly at Digur, but he did not notice. Asla, who was sitting beside her sister, rose and came next to Thorolf. Not wishing to embarrass her husband in front of the men, she said nothing. Instead, she took his hand and squeezed it tight.

Thorolf understood her silent message: *I am behind you, no matter what you decide. But you know my opinion on this.* He looked into her trusting eyes and knew what she would say to him.

Thorolf cleared his throat. He had reached a decision. "I agree with my brothers. We ought to cut new paths. I will acknowledge Ryan as a warrior and an equal—a chieftain who won his freedom in honorable battle. By trading with him and his people, we will hopefully get enough iron to produce sufficient tools and all those other commodities we urgently require. We do not need his gold. It does not fill our bellies. But we shall welcome some pretty jewelry for our wives and a few arm rings for us men."

Asla squeezed his hand a second time, and this time for longer. Most heads of households present seemed to accept his decision; only Fenrir and two others continued to display dismissive, gloomy faces.

Hilda was sitting with Carla outside her house when she saw Gregor approach the house with Caitlin and two strangers. The autumnal afternoon sun warmed their backs. While Carla spun, Hilda had been weaving some cloth for a new dress for herself. She was proud of Gregor, who had built Hilda her very own loom, using Asla's as a model. It worked wonderfully.

She set aside her loom and stood up. Gregor introduced the strangers to them, explaining briefly what had happened.

Hilda wasn't entirely sure what to make of all this, but the imposing stranger and his pretty wife were her guests now, and she knew her duties as a hostess.

While she and Carla vanished into the house, her husband asked the Irish guests and Caitlin to take a seat on the bench. Gregor felt pleased every time his eyes beheld the solid table between the two benches. Högni had called his work a small masterpiece, and Gregor had immediately prayed for God's forgiveness for the sense of pride that the shipwright's praise had filled him with.

Gregor preferred to dwell out of doors rather than inside the dim twilight of his house. He could scarcely believe how mild—warm, even—the air was on Catan at the start of the Yulemoon.*

* December

The days were still significantly longer than in the North at this time of year, and longer even than in his native Rome. Gregor felt certain by now that Catan did not have proper winters with snow and ice—or at least not in the low-lying regions near the coast.

Hilda set cups on the table, and Carla filled them with mint tea. Even though Caitlin had to translate everything, a lively conversation ensued.

Ryan pointed at the wooden crosses that Hilda, Gregor, and Carla wore on leather strings around their necks. "You are Christian?"

"Yes," replied Gregor. "Same as you. As far as I know, the Irish have been Christian for several centuries."

Ryan nodded. "The Christian faith is a big part of life back home. Unfortunately, here on the island, we do not have a priest among our ranks who can ask for God's blessing for our unions, like my marriage to Enya."

"Gregor can do that," said Hilda eagerly. "He even used to be a good friend of the pope," she added proudly.

As much as he loved Hilda, right then Gregor wished for a tiny, tiny moment she would be swallowed up by the earth.

Ryan studied the burly, stocky man with new interest while Gregor struggled to find an appropriate response. "It is true. I used to be a cardi—er, a priest in the pope's service. As such, I am authorized to bless marriages in the name of God."

Once Caitlin had finished translating, Enya's eyes lit up. Leaning across the table, she grasped Gregor's hand. "Would you bless our union? Now?"

Gregor felt put on the spot. "Do you not wish for a more solemn setting for the blessing of your union before the eyes of God?"

Enya shook her head gravely. "We do not yet know which judgment your chief will pass on us. Should he condemn us to death, I want to step before our Lord as Ryan's Christian wife."

Gregor clasped Enya's hand. "Do not fret. Yngvi, our chieftain's brother, is a great advocate of yours."

Ryan raised his eyebrows. "Why? He does not know us."

Carla replied in Gregor's stead. "But we know Yngvi. He is my husband and Christian like us. But that isn't the reason he will help you and therewith us all—it is because he deeply, and for good reason, despises the enslavement of people. And yet he will not argue that it is wrong or sinful to rob a person of their freedom." Quietly, more to herself, she added, "The settlers aren't quite there yet . . ."

The fact that Carla considered taking away people's freedom a sin made Gregor think. Could it be that, of the ten commandments God gave to Moses, one was missing? One that said, "Thou shalt not subject another person and take their will and freedom"? Was it in truth *eleven* commandments the Lord proclaimed to the Israelites? Why was this one missing? Had Moses perhaps misheard or forgotten this last commandment? It seemed unlikely to Gregor. After all, God's chosen people suffered for a long time under Egyptian rule and were bound to despise slavery profoundly. Gregor decided to pick this thought up again during a quieter moment.

Ryan gazed pensively at Carla. Then he turned to Gregor. "If you're right and we will be permitted to return to our people, would you accompany us? There are other couples besides Enya and me who long for God's blessing for their union." He cast a glance at Hilda. "Of course, your wife is also welcome."

Gregor did not need to think for long. As the only ordained priest upon the island, he viewed it as his sacred duty to tend to those children of God who found themselves on Catan, be they Northmen, Irishmen, Anglo-Saxons, Slavs, or Franks.

"I will accompany you. Hilda must speak for herself. She is

an experienced charcoal burner, and I don't know if the settlers can make do without her for long periods of time."

Ryan listened up when Caitlin translated. "You are a charcoal burner?"

Hilda nodded.

"Then it is my special wish to invite you to our settlement. Our smith hails from Frankia, and while he is skilled at extracting iron from ore and manufacturing tools, he does not know how to produce coal in large quantities. You could teach our people how it is done properly. We would pay you in gold."

Hilda looked at the Irishman warmly. "I have no need for your gold. But I will gladly go with my husband, if my friend Stina agrees to supervise the charcoal servants in my place."

Enya asked Hilda to fill her cup once more with the mint tea, saying, "This is so refreshing. There are no such delicious brews at our settlement."

Hilda liked Enya. Not only did the Irishwoman speak with a gentle voice, she also seemed to have a sensitive and warm-hearted nature. While the men continued their conversation with Caitlin's help, Hilda took Enya by the hand and led her around the side of the house to her herb garden. From the seeds she had brought with her, she had raised strong plants, including summer savory, mint, chervil, chives, parsley, and sage. Hilda picked a leaf of mint and rubbed it between her thumb and forefinger, holding it up to Enya's nose. "That's what I make the tea from."

The young Irishwoman inhaled the scent of the mint and gave Hilda a smile. Returning the smile, Hilda made a decision: should she accompany Gregor on his journey, she would dig out some of her plants and help Enya set up her own herb garden.

Shortly before sunset, Thorolf, Yngvi, and Digur arrived at Gregor's house. Ryan stood up when he saw the brothers approach.

Thorolf stopped a few steps away from the leader of the chain wielders and locked eyes with him. "I accept your offer of peace, Irishman. And we are prepared to do trade with you. My brother Yngvi stewards our stores. He will lead negotiations with you and return you and your wife to your people the day after tomorrow. Until your departure, you will remain the guests of Gregor and Hilda."

Thorolf briefly looked to the ground before continuing. "Unfortunately, there are those among us who still demand your death. To prevent our agreement from failing and to avoid a bloodbath, Högni, our shipbuilder, and Digur, my brother, will take turns guarding this house for the next two nights. Both of them are well-respected men in our community, and no one will dare attack them. Now swear by your God that you will keep the peace and that you will threaten neither us nor our livestock."

Ryan rejoiced inwardly. The third part of his plan was a success. He thought Thorolf and his younger brother Yngvi seemed trustworthy, though he still wasn't sure how to gauge the third brother, the hulking Digur, who was staring at him blankly from piercing blue eyes. One thing, however, he knew for certain: if he were to survive a fight against the huge warrior at all, it would be only with God's help.

He raised his hand to make his oath. "I, Ryan, son of the glorious King Máel Sechnaill mac Máele Ruanaid, swear by the almighty Lord to keep the peace between our two communities."

Thorolf took a step toward the Irishman. "I, Thorolf Ulrikson, son of the glorious Jarl Ulrik Ragnarson, swear by the gods of my people to keep the peace with you and your people."

He offered his hand to Ryan, who clasped it without hesitation.

The next morning, a cool wind from the north chased thick clouds across the land, and intermittent rain showers poured upon the settlers. When the forebodings of foul weather had become evident the previous night, Gregor had carried the table and benches inside. Now Yngvi and Ryan sat at the table to negotiate the trade of goods. Caitlin joined them to translate, while Carla and Enya sat on logs by the fireplace. By the sparse light streaming in through the vent in the roof, Carla taught Enya the use of a spindle. Gregor and Hilda had gone outside; he to work on a chest under the shelter of a roof, and she to check on the charcoal pits in the woods.

Yngvi was astounded at the amount of goods the chain wielders seemed to be lacking. Most pressing were the needs for flax and wool to produce new clothing, but nor did they have grain to sow in the field that, according to Ryan's description, they had wrested from the forest.

When Yngvi asked the Irishman why they'd cut a field without owning any seeds to sow in it, Ryan shrugged and replied drily, "If you had killed me, my people would have come and taken the grain by force."

Yngvi explained to the Irishman that he would not be able to give him much grain. The farmers had brought in only one harvest so far, and of that, they would need at least a third to sow their new, larger fields. They did not have much wool or flax either, and Yngvi was unable to spare any of it. Instead he offered Ryan some young pigs.

Ryan shook his head decisively. "We will never reach an

agreement this way. If you want our iron ore, your people will have to cut back."

After some back and forth, they eventually came to terms. Yngvi would load the *Goldeagle* with one sack each of oats, barley, and rye, as well as three sacks each of flax fibers and wool. Additionally, he would provide the chain wielders with two young sows and one boar. In exchange, he would return to Woodhaven with seven crates of iron ore. He agreed with Ryan to fill the crates with as much ore as two grown men of average height were able to lift and carry for at least ten steps.

Yngvi liked the Irishman, even if Ryan had put much pressure on him during the negotiations. Ryan appeared unaffected by the airs and graces of most chieftains. He seemed upright, like a man who had taken responsibility for people and now tried to do the best he could to live up to it.

"We call it the Shannon," Ryan told Gregor and Yngvi when, four days later, they sailed up a fjord. "I named it after the largest river of my old homeland."

The three men were standing in the bow of the *Goldeagle* as the sheer cliffs on either side of the river passed them by. The steep walls reminded Yngvi of the fjord back home, which he would probably never see again. But the sight did not evoke homesickness in him—on the contrary. His relatives aside, he did not miss his old home.

It was one of those rare days at the coast when the air was dry enough to permit visibility far into the distance. When the servants rowed the *Goldeagle* around a bend, the rocks retreated from the banks, revealing a view of reeds and trees. In the distance, the white of snowcapped mountain peaks contrasted sharply with the clear blue sky.

"Winter isn't far away," predicted Ryan.

"Cold and snow will only take hold in the mountains," said Gregor. "By the coast and on the low-lying areas, they will lose the battle against the mild sea breezes and the sun."

"I hope you're right."

A horn sounded. The low tones, two short ones and a longer one at the end, sounded eerie.

"What was that?" asked Yngvi, frowning.

"Do not worry, friend. The guards have seen us and informed the village of my return." Ryan pointed at the light-gray cloth tied to the top of the mast. "That is how they knew I'm on board."

Only after they cruised past a squat tree with a thick trunk did Yngvi spot the well-disguised watch post. It was a platform built into the fork of three branches. A young blonde woman stood on the timber planks, waving excitedly. Ryan raised a hand and returned the greeting with a smile.

A short while later, Ryan's village came into view to their portside. The chain wielders had erected palisades as tall as a man from logs with sharpened points. Outside the palisades, they had cleared some land and plowed it. Beyond the fence huddled a collection of reed-thatched wooden huts. The double gates stood open. The villagers lined the riverbank, cheering. Several women carried newborns wrapped in furs, bawling at the unaccustomed racket.

Hilda and Carla stood leaning on the gunwale, studying the scruffy figures. The people's trousers and tunics were little more than rags sewn together. Some of them wore vests of rabbit skins.

Carla realized that most of the shouts of greeting from the chain wielders were in Anglo-Saxon. She tried addressing Enya, who had come up next to her husband, in this language. "Your people greet you in the tongue of the Anglo-Saxons. Why not in Irish?"

Enya's eyes widened. "You speak Anglo-Saxon?" Then she remembered Carla's question. "We Irish folk are the minority. Most of our men and women fell when we fought the Northmen. Aside from us, there are a handful of Franks and some women from the East, but more than half of our people are Anglo-Saxon." Enya shrugged. "And so their language is most commonly spoken."

The servants fastened the *Goldeagle* to the *Freedom*. Ryan jumped over the ship's side into the knee-high water, then helped Enya climb off board. Even before the two of them had made it ashore, the people crowded them. They joyfully embraced their leader and his wife, patting their backs and ruffling their hair.

"They love Ryan and Enya," said Gregor thoughtfully.

Yngvi nodded. "They seem to have every reason. Even if they still look like slaves in their rags, thanks to the Irishman, they are free people. And well-fed to boot."

Gregor agreed. "If Thorolf had killed Ryan, we would regret it bitterly. These people would have avenged their leader's death unto their last drop of blood." Gregor gave Yngvi a friendly nudge with his elbow. "I hear that it was you who persuaded Thorolf to choose the road of peace."

Yngvi shook his head. "In the end, it was Digur who swayed him."

When the visitors from Woodhaven disembarked from the *Goldeagle*, they were at first met with dark and suspicious glances. Then, an Anglo-Saxon woman spied the wooden crosses around their necks and cried, "They are Christian!" Then the chain wielders' faces brightened. But they regarded the new arrivals with true warmth and friendship only once Ryan presented

Gregor to them on the small square amid their houses. "This man is named Gregor. He is an ordained priest and willing to give God's blessing to those men and women among us who have found one another. Furthermore, he is going to hold a service and will hear anyone who wishes to confess."

The ship servants had carried the Woodhaven wares from the *Goldeagle* to the square. Now Ryan untied the ropes they were bound with and reached into every sack, one after the other, showing its contents to his people. The chain wielders cheered each time he raised a filled hand. "Barley for our ale! Wool for new clothes! Rye for our bread!"

"They won't be able to make much new clothing from the flax and the wool in those sacks," said Hilda glumly.

"The next time we shear our sheep and harvest flax, they will get new supplies in exchange for their ore. At some point, they will have enough clothes for everyone," replied Carla.

Once it started to rain, Ryan and Enya invited their guests into their plain log cabin. Around the time of the evening meal, they were joined by Ryan's friends and former comrades-at-arms Liam and Brennan, as well as their women. Enya served up smoked fish, cold roast rabbit, and fried pigeons.

While Liam and Brennan listened more than they spoke, their gregarious Anglo-Saxon wives took eager part in the conversation. They wanted to know everything: What did it look like in Woodhaven, was there any game other than rabbits, had they found any edible fruit or bulbs? Carla had her hands full keeping up translating the two women's gushing words from Anglo-Saxon into the Northern tongue. Caitlin was needed only every now and then, when one of the Irish reverted to their mother tongue. That suited the young Irishwoman just fine, since it gave her time to nurse her three-month-old baby boy.

Ryan was interested in learning more about the land at

whose shores they had ended up. Yngvi told them of Olaf and Hakon's exploratory voyages, reporting that they were upon an island that lay remotely in the middle of the ocean, and that it appeared to be of similar size to the homeland of the Irish chain wielders. His brother Thorolf, he said, had named the island Catan, which in the tongue of a foreign people meant 'land of the sun.'

The name and its meaning seemed to appeal to Ryan. He raised his cup—filled, to the dismay of all, with water only—and cried to Liam and Brennan, "To Catan, the land of the sun. To the friendship between our communities!"

His friends, too, raised their cups and repeated their chieftain's words. Everyone present gladly joined in.

The rain clouds withdrew, leaving in their wake a cheerful blue sky. Hilda shook her head when she inspected the pathetic pits inside which the wood burned rather than smoldered.

"No wonder your smith is short on coal," she observed, looking into the helpless faces of the two Irishmen standing in front of her. "Let's get to it! Pick up your spades and dig out a decent pit."

Caitlin translated while her little son kicked restlessly inside the cloth tied to her chest. She couldn't help but smile at the energetic way in which the charcoal burner, her hands on her hips, ordered about the pair of strong young men who were each a head taller than her.

Hilda watched as the boys dug swiftly with their spades. At least they were good workers. But she would hardly be able to teach them more than a few basic skills in the span of a day. It would be better if one of them were to learn the trade from the ground up in Woodhaven for a few moons. Hilda decided to broach the subject with Ryan and Yngvi.

While his wife oversaw the excavation of a pit, Gregor positioned himself in the center of the village square. He was clad in a threadbare and torn brown habit. Waiting for his priestly blessing in a half-circle in front of him were Ryan and Enya, as well as twelve more couples, among them Liam and Brennan with their women. Babbling noisily behind him were almost all remaining villagers, who did not want to miss the ceremony. Most chain wielders were not dressed any differently from the previous day; they owned no clothing other than their old rags and the clothes they'd pulled off the bodies of their dead enemies and whatever they had found on board the ship. With eager anticipation, the assembled villagers watched the priest and awaited his words. Gregor spoke in the tongue of the North, and Carla repeated his words in Anglo-Saxon.

"As you can see, I am dressed no better than you are. This is the habit I wore when I first became a slave."

Some of his audience gasped with astonishment.

"Yes, you heard right. I, too, was once a slave, a thrall at the mercy of my worldly masters. Before Yngvi's father bought me at a slave market and made me a servant in his household, I was humiliated and beaten. This habit became my second skin, inside which I learned to become humble, shed my arrogance and become a different person. I often prayed to God—not like earlier in my life, superficially and dutiful, but from the bottom of my heart. I grew modest and did not allow myself to ask our Lord to give me my freedom. Why should he work a miracle for me while others—better people than myself, and innocent children—died every day from illness and war? But I did beg for his closeness and asked him for the strength to accept my fate and bear my load. When at last I felt his presence, I was filled with joy."

Sinking to his knees, Gregor lowered his head, folded his hands, and said nothing. After a few moments he looked up again, rose to his feet, and went on. "In this old habit which I'm wearing before you, I made the transformation from a God-fearing man to a God-loving one. That is why I never could bring myself to throw it out. And on this day, it is my honor to wear it for you."

While Carla translated, Gregor's eyes scanned the couples waiting for his blessing. Everyone listened in utter silence.

"Today, you seek the closeness of God. Like myself, you have not lost your faith in him during your time as slaves, but have emerged from your dreary fate stronger and perhaps even reformed. I gladly bless you in the name of God, his Son, and the Holy Ghost."

Gregor solemnly raised his arms. "Kneel."

With measured strides, he walked from couple to couple, placed a hand each on the head of man and woman and uttered the Latin formulas of blessing and the *ego vos coniungo.** He knew that many Christians believed that, in the Latin tongue, God spoke directly to them through the mouth of the priest. Gregor did not share their belief, but he had no desire to disillusion anyone.

At the end of the ritual, several women crowded around Gregor and tried to kiss the hem of his habit. Feeling embarrassed and uncomfortable, he fended them off by saying, "I am but a simple priest, not a saint!"

* I join you.

In the afternoon, Gregor instructed three Slavic women in the Christian faith. During his next visit, he promised, he would fill the gaps in their knowledge and baptize them. The young women's motivation for becoming Christian wasn't so much a longing for God but rather the desire to share the same faith with the other men and women in the chain wielder community.

During the evening, which the guests from Woodhaven again spent in Ryan's and Enya's home, Yngvi inquired after the sources of the gold and the iron ore.

Ryan gave a diplomatic reply. "They lie in that part of the land which we claim as ours."

"Then I only hope," replied Yngvi lightly, "that I do not need to return to my brother with the news that you and your chain wielders claimed the whole of Catan as your land."

Ryan laughed. "No, certainly not. Every place that we can reach on foot or with our ship within one day at midsummer we consider to be the boundaries of our area."

"Then we will hardly be in each other's way," observed Yngvi, and the subject was closed.

After their meal, there was a knock at the door. Ryan bid the late guest welcome, placing an arm around the shoulders of the young red-haired man. "This is Godric. Godric has a particular request, and I support him in it."

Yngvi guessed Godric had seen around seventeen or eighteen winters. He was of slender build and, aside from a few pimples flourishing on his nose and chin, was of winsome appearance. Yngvi particularly noticed the boy's ice-blue eyes, which reminded him of someone he couldn't place.

Ryan sat back down while Godric remained standing, fixing

his eyes on Gregor. Rubbing his hands nervously, he did not bother making a complicated introduction, getting straight to the point with a shaky voice, "Lord, I wish to become a priest, and I ask you to walk this road with me and instruct me."

He spoke in Anglo-Saxon, and Carla translated.

Gregor was too surprised to answer at first. Godric, mistaking the priest's silence as rejection, added desperately, "Lord, ever since I can remember, I've been wanting to serve God. I am the third-born son of a thane. Since I cannot be his heir, my father decreed a godly life for me. He had bought a place for me in a monastery. This suited me fine. But shortly before I was able to take up my place there as a novice, Northmen assailed my father's court, taking me and my sister prisoner."

The words "sister" and "thane" jogged Yngvi's memory. Godric had the same striking red hair and ice-blue eyes as Edvina, who with three other servants was accused of the murder of Ansgar. Carla had told him the maid was the daughter of an Anglo-Saxon nobleman.

Gregor had listened attentively to the young man's speech and discovered no falsehood in his manner and words. Godric appeared genuinely filled with the desire to become a priest. And why not? The chain wielders needed a priest. Gregor himself would fill this position to begin with, taking the trip to Ryan's village two or three times a year, perhaps. Then, in a few years' time, once Godric had internalized the Christian teachings and received his holy orders, the young man would be able to take over this role.

"Godric, take a seat." Gregor pointed his finger at an empty log.

"Yes, lord."

"First of all, don't call me lord, but Father Gregor."

"Yes, lord Father Gregor."

Laughter rang out following Carla's translation. "Just Father Gregor."

Godric nodded. His face had flushed red.

Gregor continued. "If you wish to become a priest, you will have to learn Latin and to read and write the ancient language. Then you must study my Bible, copy the most important passages, and learn them by heart. Do you think you can do all that?"

The young man's expression grew more confident. "Yes, Father Gregor. I already possess some command of reading and writing Latin texts. My father deemed the knowledge of Latin indispensable for my ascent in the church. He paid a clergyman to teach me the ancient tongue."

Gregor was surprised. Few noblemen had their sons instructed in reading and writing, let alone in Latin. "That is excellent! You would receive daily tutoring from me. But the larger part of your days would be spent working hard to pay for the roof over your head and your apprenticeship. Do you agree?"

Godric agreed without hesitation.

Gregor turned to look at Hilda, an unspoken question in his eyes. She smiled and gave a curt nod. And so it was decided. "Very well. Then we shall try it together," he told Godric in Latin.

His face filled with joy, the boy kneeled before the priest and replied, also in Latin, "You will not regret it, Father Gregor."

The servants lifted the anchor and began to row the *Goldeagle* down the Shannon. The crates of iron ore were safely stored in the cargo hold. Ryan, Enya, and the other couples whose unions Gregor had blessed in the name of God stood on the bank, waving.

Yngvi knew the chain wielders' heartfelt farewell was mostly for Gregor. As a priest, Gregor stood above the communities. Should there be strife between the settlers of Woodhaven and Ryan's people someday, Gregor might be the only person able to mediate.

The sea was calm when they reached it, and Yngvi assigned an experienced servant to the steering oar. He and Carla sat down in a sunny spot by the ship's side, enjoying the warmth. Sitting diagonally across from them sat Caitlin and Conor, an Irishman come to learn the charcoal-making trade from Hilda in Woodhaven. The two of them led an animated conversation in their mother tongue. Yngvi didn't understand a word, but he disliked the interested looks the Irishwoman and her fellow countryman exchanged. Apparently, Conor wasn't perturbed by Caitlin's standing as a married woman nor by her infant son.

Carla confirmed his concerns when she suddenly stated, "I believe those two have taken a liking to one another."

"Looks that way," said Yngvi. "There will be trouble if they can't keep their hands off each other. Olaf is a hothead. He'll lose his temper if Caitlin makes a cuckold of him."

Godric stepped up to them and addressed Yngvi in Latin, "May I ask you something?"

"Sure. Sit," replied Yngvi.

"I have a sister who was sold into slavery with me. Her name is Edvina. We arrived here on different ships. I was injured and knocked unconscious during the fight against the Northmen. When I awoke, I found myself on board the *Freedom*. In vain I searched for Edvina among the survivors. Ryan said she either died during the fight or she was one of the slave women he left behind. Do you know anything of her whereabouts? I have already asked Gregor. He sent me to speak with you."

Yngvi had expected the question. He briefly explained to Godric what happened to Edvina. However, he did not share with the boy his suspicion that Ansgar had not died by the hand of the servants. "We lost the trail of your sister and her accomplices along the upper Saltmarsh."

Grief wrestled with hope in Godric's face. "So she might still be alive?"

"It is possible," said Yngvi. "But I would not raise my hopes too high if I were you. Even if she survived in the wilderness, she is still an outlaw. Should she be discovered, she will be executed."

Godric stood up and leaned on the gunwale, gazing gloomily across the waves.

PART 6
CHANGES

(SUMMER, AD 861)

CHAPTER 17
INFIDELITY

A buzzard cruised in circles above summery Woodhaven. The bird of prey did not understand the nature of the many yellow and green areas amid the green-speckled brown beneath it. The figures moving among them were too big to serve as prey to the bird, and its instincts warned it from getting too close to them.

If what the bird perceived were seen by a person, they would have recognized a thriving settlement on the eastern shores of a lake. Houses and huts of varying sizes with gardens in between lined up along three parallel paths, which, in their middle, were crossed by a wider road. The paths led out of the settlement toward the east, cutting through a half-circle of harvested yellow-brown fields. Pigs rooted there for small creatures, searched for any grains that had fallen to the ground, and devoured with relish the fresh shoots of green among the leftover stubble, all the while fertilizing the soil with their droppings. At the edge of the woods, which lay quite some distance from the village now, people were felling more trees, robbing more land of the dense, dark greenery.

There had, indeed, not been a winter in Woodhaven—or at

least, none of the kind the settlers were accustomed to from the North: winters with long, dark nights, heavy frosts, and snow that tumbled down on the land in huge quantities, burying it under a thick, cold coat. To the settlers, the winter on Catan had seemed like a capricious spring: bright, mild sunny days that alternated with chilly rainy ones, and occasionally storms that whipped the sea against the shores. Then the wind would churn the surf into tall breakers, preventing even the bravest fishermen from practicing their trade.

Never had it turned properly cold, at least not by the coast and in the lower-lying regions. Winter had possessed some power only over the higher altitudes of the towering mountain range beyond the rising woodland. One clear morning several weeks before midwinter, the settlers beheld, with amazement, the sight of the mountains dusted in sparkling white halfway down their slopes.

Six weeks after the Yule feast, during which Thorolf had emptied two barrels of Coronium wine together with a handpicked group of leading men, according to old tradition, the settlers sowed for the second time. Their new fields, too, proved enormously fertile. The grain and flax flourished, and now, not long after midsummer, the farmers had brought in a harvest that exceeded their expectations and left contented smiles on their faces.

Olaf was a sailor, and no use for field work. He much preferred to go to sea with the fishermen, enjoying the breeze in his face and the tangy scent of the ocean. When he sat in the small boat Thorolf had gifted to him as thanks for the dangerous exploratory voyage and sailed it homeward, laden with fish, he often thought of Caitlin. He loved the pretty blonde Irishwoman he had married last fall. She was deferential, taking care of his household and rarely turning him down when lust for her body overcame him. He sensed that she liked him, but he never seemed to get truly close to her. When he lay with her, she often struck him as absent, as if she were somewhere else in her thoughts.

On this day, two weeks after midsummer, Olaf had sailed out to the deeper waters off the coast with a fisherman friend of his, as he did nearly every day. Luck was with them: they happened across a school of mackerel that found its way into their net, which lay stretched between their two boats. Soon, they had lifted enough of the gray-blue fish with the black markings on their backs into their boats, and around midday—far sooner than usual—they returned home.

Olaf loaded his share of the catch into a handcart and pushed it up to his house in the hot sunshine. There, he shouted for Caitlin, brushing his hand across his sweaty hair. He was thirsty. He wanted his wife to bring him a jug of thinned ale before helping him gut the fish in preparation for smoking. When she didn't turn up, he went inside the house to look for her. She wasn't there. At a loss, he stood by his cart, wondering where she might have gone to.

A neighbor working in her vegetable garden straightened up and called over to him. "Caitlin took her boy to Hilda. Then she headed down the path to the charcoal pits. She carried a basket with her, said she was going to pick berries and mushrooms in the woods. She only left a short while ago."

Olaf thanked the helpful neighbor for the information and pushed the cart of fish into the shade by his house. He felt suspicion rising up in him—as far as he knew, Caitlin had never before gone to pick berries or mushrooms. Did she even know how to tell the difference between edible mushrooms and poisonous ones? With determined steps, he strode eastward, along the road paved with pounded clay, toward the charcoal pits. The track used to be merely a path, but the settlers had since made it wide enough for the horse-drawn carts that brought timber and charcoal from the woods to the village.

In the forest, it was pleasantly cool, and after a while, he reached the clearing where the charcoal was being made. Three pits were currently in use, evidenced by thin columns of smoke rising from them. Two huts had been erected at the clearing's edge. Olaf walked to the hut on the left and yanked open the door. Two servants sat at a table, one of them dropping his dice with fright. They both gave him a wide-eyed stare.

"Where is Caitlin?" he barked.

Both men shrugged, claiming they had not seen his wife. One of them, a lanky youth, seemed nervous. The seaman, who used to be in charge of ships and knew men well, only had to look into the boy's eyes to see that he was lying.

Olaf slammed shut the door and marched to the second hut. He had a hunch what awaited him behind its door, and blood thudded in his temples. When he pushed open the door, he saw that his inkling had been accurate. The thudding in his temples rose to a vicious hammering. His naked wife sat astride the loins of the undressed Irishman he knew by the name of Conor. Caitlin gaped at him with eyes wide. Her face turned white, as if her heart had sucked all the blood from her skin in shock. Conor sat up, aghast, staring at Olaf whose face was contorting with rage.

With two long strides, Olaf reached the bed, grasped his wife's full hair, and dragged her off Conor. Caitlin cried out in pain as she fell hard on the floor. Conor sprang to his feet to help his beloved, but before he could do anything, he was struck on the chin by a punch, followed by another to his stomach. Conor doubled over with pain, though it was just a mild beginning compared to the explosion in his groin when Olaf kicked him between the legs with his boot. Groaning, Conor sank to the ground. Overwhelmed by rage, Olaf kicked him repeatedly in the head and side, not stopping until Conor lay still.

As Caitlin, whimpering, crawled to her lover, shaking his lifeless body desperately and calling his name, the love Olaf had felt for her turned to pure hatred. Wildly determined to punish Caitlin for the shameful betrayal, Olaf snatched a brushwood broom and broke it in two.

"Get up," he snarled at his wife, his voice trembling with fury.

When she didn't react, still frantically searching for a sign of life from Conor, he lifted the head of the broom and swept the bundled twigs across her naked back. Caitlin screamed, trying to crawl away from her tormentor on all fours. Small beads of blood swelled from the cuts the brushwood had left on her skin.

"Get up!" he roared once more.

She obeyed. Trembling all over, she stood before him. As if Olaf were seeing her naked for the first time, she covered her breasts with her arms in shame.

"Run to the village! If you stop or stray from the path, you'll get another taste of this!" He waved the broom in front of her face. "Now go!"

Caitlin ran as if the devil were after her. Olaf followed her, cursing ferociously.

The charcoal servants stood outside their hut, gaping at the unusual show. Then, worried, they rushed over to Conor's hut to check on the friendly, calm Irishman who had become their friend.

The people in the fields paused their work to stare at the naked young woman who seemed to be running for her life along the road to the village. Behind her, Olaf was swinging the shortened broom. When she slowed, turning to her pursuer in the hope of mercy, he slapped the twigs on her back with a filthy curse on his lips. Screaming, she ran on.

Olaf chased her through the alleys of Woodhaven, cursing her as a whore, wench, and dirty harlot. More and more settlers emerged on the streets, startled by Caitlin's desperate cries and Olaf's angry shouting. Most of those following Olaf like the tail of a rat were women and children—some excited by the drama, while others pitied Caitlin. Olaf continued to drive his wife along mercilessly. When she tripped and fell, she immediately felt the broom's searing pain upon her naked backside. Quickly she scrambled to her feet and rushed on.

When Olaf spotted Thorolf outside the barn, he ordered Caitlin to stop and kneel. Gasping for breath, she sank to the ground. Olaf, too, was short of breath, drawing a few deep breaths before addressing Thorolf.

"This woman," ranted Olaf, "is a filthy whore. I caught her fornicating with that Irishman, Conor."

Thorolf nodded.

A crowd continued to grow in the village square. Evidently, no one wanted to miss this unusual spectacle.

Caitlin shuffled on her knees and folded her hands, stretching them out to Olaf as she whined for mercy. She desperately hoped to detect a glimmer of sympathy in the slits of his eyes, a small remainder of the love he used to show her. But all she saw was fury and hatred.

Cruelly he whacked the broom against her side. "Take down your damned hands. There will be no mercy for you."

When Olaf drew his knife, Caitlin looked around in panic. The settlers watched with a mixture of curiosity and discomfort. The faces of Asla, Stina, and Hilda, standing next to Thorolf, showed worry and sympathy. Asla hissed some words at Thorolf that Caitlin did not catch. Thorolf shook his head decisively and clutched Asla's arm hard, as if trying to prevent his wife from acting rashly. It dawned on Caitlin that she would not receive help from the settlers. No one would support a former slave woman who had broken the pledge she'd made to a free Northman.

Olaf grabbed Caitlin's hair and yanked back her head. She gave a hoarse cry of fear, believing the blade would touch her throat any moment now. But Olaf did not intend to take her life. Ignoring her whining, he sawed at her hair by its roots, paying no heed to the skin of her scalp. Soon he had removed all of Caitlin's magnificent hair. Contemptuously he dropped the thick blonde strands onto the ground beside her.

Caitlin cried without restraint. Blood flowed from the wounds on her stubbly scalp into her face, mixing with snot and tears and dripping onto the ground.

Olaf declared, "I curse you and cast you out," and he whipped her tortured body with the brushwood one last time. Then he turned and trudged off.

Hilda, Stina, and Asla rushed down to Caitlin, took the moaning young woman in their midst, and led her to the charcoal burner's house.

When Hilda offered her a stool, Caitlin slumped down heavily on it, burying her face in her hands. She barely felt the light blanket Hilda gently placed around her shoulders. The pain on her inside was far worse than the wounds Olaf had inflicted upon her. Worst of all was the shame of being chastised and humiliated, naked, in front of everybody. She only calmed herself when Stina fetched Caitlin's wailing son, placing him in her arms. Sobbing softly, she pushed a nipple into the hungry little mouth.

Caitlin was grateful to the women for their restraint, neither showering her with questions nor laying accusations at her feet. Stina held her hand in silence, while Hilda stoked the fire to boil water and Asla went home to fetch herbs for a healing brew.

At home, Asla found Thorolf sitting at the table, eating meat broth as if nothing had happened.

"Was that really necessary?" she asked her husband, her voice challenging. "Couldn't you command Olaf to stop?"

Thorolf looked at her blankly. "Castigating Caitlin and casting her out was his right. She betrayed him and committed adultery. Olaf acted according to the laws of our people."

"The laws of which people?" asked Asla pointedly. "According to the laws of our old people in the Northland, or according to those of our new community here on Catan?"

"Is there a difference?" asked Thorolf, frowning.

"Yes, a large one. Here on this island, we have the chance to throw old, dated traditions overboard and create better laws in their place. Especially for women."

Asla braced her arms on the table, bending her head forward until the tip of her nose almost touched his. Her voice sounded dangerously gentle when she asked him: "Do men not also commit adultery? Can you imagine in that large man skull of yours Caitlin chasing Olaf and beating him if he had betrayed her with another woman?"

Irked, Thorolf lowered the spoon he had raised to his mouth back into the bowl, returning her provocative stare. "No," he replied slowly, conscious of his words and his role as the settlers' chief. "Adultery committed by a woman weighs heavier. You women have your tasks in the house, while we take care of all things outside the house. We fight and ensure your safety; we toil in the fields and guarantee the daily bread for you and the children. In return, we expect you to loyally support us and not lie with other men. You should know all this, shouldn't you?"

Asla sat up. "So you, too, would chase me naked through the village if I betrayed you?"

Thorolf said nothing, which was enough of an answer for

Asla. Without another word, she snatched the satchel of herbs she needed to treat Caitlin's wounds and slammed the door shut on her way out. It would take some time for her anger to dissipate and for her to allow Thorolf to slip under her blankets again.

Toward the evening, Conor was able to stand up, thanks to the care of the two charcoal burner servants. Two armed settlers came to take him and brought him to Thorolf, who was outside his hall with Olaf, Yngvi, Hilda, and Godric. The Irishman looked pitiful. One eye was swollen shut, his narrow face was covered in cuts and bruises, and his brown hair matted with blood.

"Did you seduce Caitlin?" asked Thorolf harshly.

Conor croaked quietly, "No. It simply happened."

One of the blows must have struck the Irishman on the throat, thought Hilda. She felt sorry for the young man. Not only because Conor had been quick and clever at learning the trade of charcoal making, but also because of his upright, honest character and his friendly manner.

Olaf bestowed the Irishman with a hateful glare. "I demand that he be killed, or at least receive twenty lashes with the whip. He is a former slave and must pay for having touched the wife of a freeman."

Yngvi leaned over to Olaf and put a hand on his arm. "Calm yourself, Olaf. Conor is our guest and belongs to the community of the chain wielders. If we kill him, we provoke their wrath. Ryan paid for Conor's apprenticeship as a charcoal burner with ore and gold."

Annoyed, Olaf withdrew his arm. "The bastard abused our hospitality and forfeited his rights as a guest." Looking from one person to the next, he roared, "Do you want to let him get away unscathed?"

"Unscathed?" Thorolf gave a laugh. "You've already flayed the man alive. He can hardly walk after the beating you gave him."

Rising to his feet, he positioned himself before Conor. "You can choose: either you take ten lashes from the whip, which Olaf would be only too glad to execute, or you pay him a handful of gold as recompense for the adultery. Once your debt is paid—in whichever way—you will sail home on the next ship."

"What will happen to Caitlin?" whispered Conor, almost voicelessly.

"Your paramour has lost her rights as a free woman and belongs to me once more. You may take her, for all I care, if you pay me a handful of gold for her too."

"I don't own that much gold."

"Then your only choice is the whip, and Caitlin stays," Thorolf said with a shrug.

"I need to go home to collect the gold. I give you my word that you and Olaf shall receive it," Conor uttered painstakingly.

"I do not trust your word, Irishman."

Godric stood and addressed Thorolf in a firm voice. "I vouch for him. I give you my word—I will not leave Woodhaven until Conor has fulfilled his promise."

Thorolf trusted the young Anglo-Saxon from Ryan's people, whom Gregor was training as a priest, more than the Irishman, but was still undecided.

It was Yngvi who settled the matter. "I will vouch for Conor with my *Shieldmaiden* if you allow Caitlin to go with him. Should the Irishman fail to pay his debt within three moons, my knarr is yours."

"It's a deal, brother!" Thorolf laughed and brought down his hand on the Irishman's shoulder, causing the latter to wince.

"Then you might as well pack your things. The *Goldeagle* will set off for Ryan's village in the next few days."

Hilda gently touched Conor's arm. "You and Caitlin are welcome to stay at Gregor's and my home until the ship leaves."

While the Irishman nodded at her gratefully, Olaf quenched his thirst for revenge with images of holding a handful of gold soon. The yellow metal had become a sought-after means of trade, and it would make for a suitable bride-price should he wish to ask for the hand of the daughter of a freeman someday.

Three days later, Conor and Caitlin boarded the *Goldeagle*. Caitlin carried her little son in her arms. She hid her stubbly scalp, now covered in scabs, under a woolen hat Asla had given her.

When the knarr left the harbor, she thought of Yngvi, who had made it possible for her to leave this place of ill fortune and shame. This morning, she had thanked him and asked why he had spoken up for her. He had merely shrugged in response, a strange smile on his face.

When the images of her disgrace drifted past her mind's eye once again, tears rolled down her cheeks. Conor held her tight, and Caitlin gave him a grateful look. She hoped for a future among Ryan's people, a future with the man she'd fallen in love with the very first time they'd met.

CHAPTER 18
PARCHMENT

Yngvi stood next to Thorolf in the barn, wiping the sweat off his forehead. Four weeks had passed since midsummer, but even for this time of the year, it was extremely hot. The brothers' eyes rested contentedly on the large wooden tubs bulging with grain from their second harvest on Catan.

"That ought to be enough," observed Thorolf. "Don't you think?"

Yngvi nodded. "Then tell the people at the assembly tomorrow."

To avoid the heat of the day, Thorolf had asked the heads of households to meet on the village square early the following morning. More than forty men listened closely to the words of their leader when he described to them his plan for the division of the common goods henceforth: One-tenth he would set aside for their trade with Ryan, for Harald and Bran were in dire need of fresh supplies of high-quality ore from the chain wielders if they were to cover the demand for tools. Five-tenths Yngvi would divide fairly among the families, according to the number of heads in each family. The farmers and those who wished to become farmers would receive the remaining four-tenths for the next sowing.

Thorolf went on: "We are going to let the larger part of the fields that we work as a community grow into pasture for our cattle. The sheep, on the other hand, will remain in the delta. The ewes have lambed several times, and Yngvi is going to divide the herd up among our shepherds."

Thorolf paused for a moment. He enjoyed the eager expressions the settlers regarded him with. He heard no grumbling, and no one appeared to have any objections. "The pigs have bred well. Each of you may choose one tomorrow. The remaining pigs I will divide among three of my former servants. In the future, they will trade young animals ready to be butchered with you for grain or other goods."

"What about the cows?" one of the settlers asked.

"Unfortunately, the cows don't breed as quickly as the pigs," replied Thorolf. "For now they remain the property of all. We won't divide them until there are enough for each family to receive a cow for milking. We castrated some of the bull calves. Each farming family shall receive an ox for their field work eventually. Until they've grown, my brothers and I will continue to lend you our horses. The two bulls belong to all of us, and you can borrow them whenever you're in need." On cue, a rooster crowed. "I don't think we need to talk about the chickens," said Thorolf drily. "You've already divvied them up among you without my interference." Some of the men laughed.

Thorolf turned his gaze to the fishermen who stood together in a group. "You may continue to use my knarrs *Bride of the Winds* and *Wave Breaker,* as well as the dinghies, until Högni and his helpers have built sufficient smaller sailboats."

The men professed their support of their chieftain's plans

by stamping their feet and thumping their right fists against their chests.

Pleased with himself, Thorolf received the accolades with a proud smile. He loved it when the settlers showed appreciation for his deeds and looked up to him. In the fall, the headmen would elect him as their jarl. Who else should lead them? There was no better man than him.

The hot summer's day ended pleasantly. A gentle breeze from the mountains brought some welcome cool air. Yngvi sat outside his house, writing on parchment. With focused movements, he dipped the tip of the quill into the jar of soot ink, carefully draining the nib on the jar's rim to remove any surplus ink, and then added to a word he had started. Next to the parchment lay several wax tablets that he had covered in notes, as well as Cicero's *De re publica*.

He was about to dip his quill into the ink jar once more when his wife exclaimed in delight, "Yngvi, look! The boy placed the letters for the word 'arm' in the right order."

Carla was sitting at the other end of the long table with five boys and two girls between the ages of seven and twelve. On the table lay a wax tablet and the letter tiles Yngvi had whittled for Carla. Since she had mastered the alphabet, knew how to read, and was also becoming reasonably good at writing, Yngvi's wife had decided to instruct the children of their community in these skills. When Yngvi had asked her why she wanted to do so, she had simply replied, "Because I enjoy it—and so do the children."

The boy who had formed the word correctly beamed at the praise from his teacher. With reddened cheeks, he asked for another task. Yngvi knew the bright boy—it was Caven, Harald's bastard whom the smith did not acknowledge as his son.

Before Carla could do as Caven asked, the busily debating voices of Gregor and Godric announced their arrival. Yngvi had asked his friends here so they might exchange their ideas.

Carla carefully returned the letter tiles to their leather pouch and waved at her students to clear the benches. The children pulled disappointed faces, but then cheered happily when Carla cried, "Come, let's play ball!"

Impatiently, they jumped on the spot, hardly able to wait for their teacher to return from the house with the misshapen ball made of sewn-up rabbit furs and studded with yellow-beak feathers. Carla had told Yngvi that, when she was little, her parents had given her a similar ball, except it was made of leather. It had been her favorite toy in the world.

Before she left, Carla asked Gregor how little Johannes was doing—the boy Hilda had borne two moons prior.

The priest smiled a strained smile. "The boy is doing well. Whenever he is awake and not drinking, he cries. To be frank, I am glad to escape for a while and grant my ears some rest."

Yngvi, hoping his own offspring would be more considerate of him someday, called after Carla, "Look after yourself! Don't exert yourself too much."

She nodded in her carefree manner and rushed out to the peninsula with the children. On the former fields, grasses were sprouting, and after a few days of dry weather, they offered a suitable spot for playing ball. Yngvi's eyes followed Carla with concern. Her rounded belly showed clearly now. Asla said that his wife would give birth in three moons' time at the latest.

Gregor and Godric sat down opposite Yngvi. The young man from Ryan's village had settled well into the community. After more than half a year in Woodhaven, he spoke the Nordic tongue passably, and Gregor was pleased about his ward's improved Latin.

Gregor gestured at the parchment, which was half-filled with words. "You seem to make good progress."

Yngvi nodded contentedly. "Yes, I still have a few pages to go, but I should be finished before the election in the fall."

Leaning forward, Gregor gave Yngvi a serious look. "Have you spoken with Thorolf yet?"

"No, but I will soon."

Gregor had touched a sore point. Having read Cicero's *De re publica* several times and led many conversations with Gregor on the subject, Yngvi believed he finally grasped the work in its entirety, and he discussed with his learned friend the ideas of the Roman philosopher and politician. In his book, Cicero debated the advantages and disadvantages of monarchy, the rule of a few, and the rule of the people, which Gregor also called "democracy." Cicero reached the conclusion that a combination of the three was desirable, avoiding the downfalls of each of the three forms of government and uniting their advantages.

Thorolf wished for monarchy. His brother might call himself "jarl" instead of "king," but once he was chosen by his people, he would rule until the end of his days and pass down the title of jarl to his son. Yngvi considered Thorolf capable of ruling wisely and justly, but his heirs would not necessarily follow his brother's good example. No one would be able to stop them if they turned into cruel tyrants who brought death and perdition to their people. Yngvi himself had different ideas. Thorolf would not like them, but Yngvi would nonetheless have to come clean with his brother soon.

"Yngvi?" Gregor tore him from his thoughts. "We should talk about the new Bible."

Yngvi carefully placed the piece of parchment between two

linen cloths, where he kept the other pages on which he had noted down his thoughts concerning a better way of living together. Then he turned to the reason for their meeting.

He and Gregor had decided to make a copy of Gregor's Bible in the Nordic tongue. Then, later, Godric was to compose a copy in Anglo-Saxon. Latin, they agreed, had no future on Catan.

Gregor began thoughtfully, "Why don't we amend the Ten Commandments a little when we translate them? It isn't like the pope or some other dusty churchman looks over our shoulders here."

"How do you mean?" asked Yngvi, intrigued. Godric, too, eyed Gregor with interest.

Pensively, Gregor placed a finger on his chin. "As you know, the first commandment says: 'I am the Lord thy God. Thou shalt have no other gods before me.'" He paused for a moment, as if he were searching for the right words. "To me that sounds as if our Lord acknowledges that there are other gods, and as if he were a little jealous of them. The way I understand God, the first commandment ought to sound something like this: 'I am the one true God. Follow my commandments and I shall be with you.'"

They sat in silence for a while. Then Yngvi smiled. "What would the pope have done with you if you had told him of your suggestion?"

Gregor laughed unhappily. "He likely would have deposed me from all my offices and burned me at the stake as a heretic." His expression turned serious. "When I first contemplated the thought of changing the words of the Bible, I felt deeply uncomfortable. It was as if I were committing sacrilege. But, I told myself, what I was really trying to do was not to change God's commandments, but rather to dress them in fresh words, in words that convey his message more clearly. I appeased my conscience with the thought that I merely interpreted the Ten

Commandments Moses received from God a little differently from the Israelite prophet. Believe me—I fought a long and difficult battle with myself. But now I have made up my mind."

Godric appeared impressed by Gregor's musings. At the same time, he seemed to be shocked by the notion of changing God's written word. When he spoke up, his voice sounded anxious, almost as though he hoped Gregor would answer his next question with a definite no. "Do you wish to change anything else?"

The learned clergyman did not oblige. "Yes. In the ninth and tenth commandments, one ought to not desire one's neighbor's house, their wife, their servants, livestock, and anything else one's neighbor might possess. But people cannot prevent themselves from desiring. That would be like trying to stop the sun from rising above the horizon in the morning. I would have still desired Hilda even if her husband were still alive. But I never would have led her to commit adultery. That is the difference. God has given us a choice. If you curb your desire, you follow God's will. If you don't, you break commandments five, six, and seven: thou shalt not kill, commit adultery, or steal."

"Do you propose to blot out the ninth and tenth commandments?" asked Godric, stricken.

Yngvi couldn't stifle a grin at the horror in the young man's eyes. The future priest shuffled nervously on the bench. A large pimple glowed on the bridge of his nose, waxing increasingly red with agitation.

Gregor grasped his student's hand. "Calm yourself, Godric. I do not wish to blot out the two commandments. I'd like to merely summarize them and formulate them a little more clearly. We don't want people to believe that their thoughts alone are sins. Then how are they ever supposed to obtain God's grace?" He gave a subtle smile. "I would summarize the commandments as follows: 'Resist your desire for your neighbor's wife, house, and goods.'" He paused for a moment, frowning. "I feel like I have forgotten something."

Yngvi gave a quick laugh. "If I took your commandment literally," he said with a grin, "God would look the other way if a woman snatched her neighbor's husband."

Gregor's face lit up. "Of course! Equal commandments for men and women! It ought to read: 'Resist your desire for your neighbor's wife, husband, house, and goods.'"

Yngvi was impressed by Gregor's thoughts. With these new perspectives, he felt more prepared to accept God. "If you put the ninth and tenth commandments together, there are but nine commandments. Didn't you want to retain ten?"

Gregor nodded. "There is one more commandment that the Israelites did not adopt when Moses received God's word. In those days, keeping slaves was accepted by all and proved no conflict with their faith. Even the Christians in old Rome did not consider it wrong to keep slaves. But I ask you, can God as we know him truly approve of men robbing other men of their will and freedom?"

"No," said Yngvi. "The way I interpret the commandments, slavery contradicts the seventh commandment: thou shalt not steal. That is precisely what we are doing when we rob people of their freedom, forcing them to work for us."

Godric, listening to these ponderings, seemed less shocked now by the thought of tweaking the words of God that were written down by men. He nodded in agreement. "When I was a slave, I felt dishonored. I felt like I was being treated more like an animal than a man. I cannot imagine that God wishes for humans to be degraded to animals."

"Then we are agreed," observed Gregor with relief. "Our new tenth commandment shall read: 'Thou shalt not subjugate another person and rob them of their will and freedom.'" After a moment of silence, Gregor looked up at Yngvi. "You know what that means for yourself?"

"Yes. Carla and I will give our maid, Edna, her freedom. We were going to do so, regardless."

Not much would change, Yngvi guessed. Edna would be free to leave Carla's household, but she would hardly do so as long as no freeman was seeking her hand in marriage. For good reason—where else would Edna find a place to sleep as an unmarried woman, or receive food and clothing? His wife treated the gentle Anglo-Saxon like a member of the family. Edna took her meals together with Yngvi and Carla, and the two women were currently working on weaving a new tunic for the maid.

For a while, the three men sat in silence. They could hear Edna puttering around inside, preparing their evening meal.

"One more thing," said Yngvi. "Before we go our separate ways, we need more parchment for the two new Bibles. The bundle we purchased in Hedeby won't suffice—especially since I've already used a fair amount of it."

"I thought as much," said Gregor. "Do you know how to make parchment?"

Yngvi shook his head. "I only know that you need animal hides for it."

"Lucky I was forced to visit a tannery frequently as a young man, to fetch parchment for the pope's writing chambers. While I waited, I used to look around the workshop, and so I have at least an idea how to produce it."

"Excellent!" Yngvi looked at his friend with delight. "Then let us start tomorrow!"

Gregor crossed his arms on his paunch and smiled indulgently. "Manufacturing parchment is a lengthy process. Besides, we require milk of lime to remove the hair from the skins. Worst case, we could also use urine. But believe me, it's quicker with milk of lime and doesn't stink as bad."

"And where do we find milk of lime?"

"We don't. We have to make it from limestone. And first we must find the limestone."

Yngvi felt disappointed. Clearly, parchment did not fall from the sky. Weakly, he asked his friend: "And where do we find the limestone?"

"In the mountains, if we're lucky."

The men agreed to follow the Saltmarsh to the foot of the mountains the day after tomorrow.

Startled, Edvina clasped Ortwin by the arm. "Did you hear that?"

Ortwin stopped and listened. In the distance, he could make out an irregular *toc, toc*. "Sounds like someone is striking rock with a pickaxe. Come, let's take a closer look."

The louder the sound became, the more cautiously they moved through the dense underbrush. With one hand, Ortwin was balancing a thin log on his shoulder from whose ends dangled the rabbits and pigeons they had killed. With his other hand, he used a stick to probe the forest floor in front of him before taking the next step. But still he stepped on a branch concealed beneath the rotting leaves. The branch snapped with a loud crack. Terrified, the two outlaws held their breath until the pickaxe began striking rock once more. This time it sounded very close.

"Let's put our things down," whispered Edvina to her companion.

He nodded, sneaking after her to the underbrush of the

forest edge, taking great care not to produce any further sounds that would give them away. Cowering behind a wide tree trunk, they squinted against the brightness.

Scarcely thirty paces away, a young man with his upper body bared swung a pickaxe at a rock face, breaking light-gray chunks of rock out from it. He had his back turned to them and appeared to be alone. Then he set down his pick, wiped his eyes, and ran his hand through his red hair, looking to the side.

Edvina gasped in surprise, loudly enough for the stranger to hear something, for he turned his head in their direction.

"What are you doing?" hissed Ortwin when she walked out from the shadow of the tree, stepping into full view of the stranger.

The man stared at her in surprise. "Edvina," he muttered, and after gaping at her for a moment in disbelief, he ran toward her. Edvina rushed to meet him, tears running down her cheeks when her brother folded his arms around her.

Ortwin now left his hiding place, too. He guessed at the pair's connection—Edvina looked like a female twin of the stranger.

"Is that the brother you told me about?"

"Yes," said Edvina, sniveling happily. She gazed at the young man as if she were seeing him for the first time. "This is my little brother, Godric, who was seized with me from our parents' house by the Northmen. I thought he was dead."

"I thought the same of you," Godric said, his voice breaking. "But then I learned that you were involved in the murder of a freeman and forced to flee."

"Damn it," uttered Ortwin. "Your brother isn't alone!"

Edvina followed Ortwin's eyes and saw Yngvi and Gregor staring down at them with astonishment from the top of the rock face. "We must run," she gasped, frightened, and pulled away from her brother.

Godric grasped his sister's arm. "Stay! Those two won't harm you. They are my friends."

Edvina tried to pull herself free, but Godric held her arm in a tight grip, gazing deeply into her eyes. "Just think, sister! They have already seen you. Now I must persuade them to keep your secret to themselves so that Thorolf won't start searching for you again. I need your help for this."

Unexpectedly, Ortwin agreed with Godric. "Your brother is right, Edvina. Running will not help us. I know Yngvi and Gregor well—they are honorable men. They will listen to us before deciding our fate."

Edvina's body, taut in preparation for flight, relaxed. Resignedly she watched as Godric's companions climbed down the rocky slope. But contrary to her expectation, the chieftain's brother did not march toward them grim faced and with his sword drawn; he looked rather excited, intrigued. Nor did Gregor, the man of God following behind him, seem ill-disposed toward them.

Yngvi studied Edvina and Ortwin, who in their turn scrutinized him with suspicion. Yngvi thought their clothing looked worn, but they did not appear to suffer hunger.

He cut straight to the point. "Edvina, who killed Ansgar and how?"

The former maid jutted out her chin. "It was I. The drunk pig was going to rape me. Luke dragged him away from me, and so Ansgar beat him with his belt. When Dag tried to pacify the raving man, Ansgar started striking him with the buckle instead." Edvina's fascinating eyes turned into narrow slits, and they filled with hatred. "When that monster would not stop laying into Dag, I knocked him down with a jug." She looked Yngvi straight in the eye. "I don't regret killing the filthy bastard."

"Did you see proof of Ansgar's death?"

"No. Hedda said he was dead."

Yngvi nodded. It was just as he had thought. "You didn't kill Ansgar. The lump you gave him on his head was harmless. Hedda must have smashed in his skull after you escaped—and several times."

Edvina looked at him with surprise. The glimmer of hope in her eyes died as quickly as it arrived. "But that does not change our situation, does it?" she asked in a tone that suggested she already knew the answer.

"Sadly, no. Hedda would deny having killed her husband. And even if Thorolf were to believe you, you still would have attacked a freeman. At the very least, my brother would have you whipped."

Then Yngvi turned to Ortwin, speaking in a serious tone: "Your deed, however, weighs heavier."

Ortwin guiltily lowered his head. His crooked face was working. "I know," he replied slowly. "We only intended to fetch a rope and some grain for Edvina and her people from the barn—you would scarcely have noticed the loss. But then Harald caught us. He threatened us with severe punishments for the theft, and I saw only one way out."

"And then you struck down Harald, accepting the possibility that he might die. That mustn't go unpunished. You know that." Yngvi placed one hand on the pommel of his sword. "I will have to take you with me. I hope you won't make it difficult for me."

Ortwin shook his head. "I know I acted wrongly. I will follow you willingly. But on one condition only: tell Thorolf you found me alone."

Edvina cried out: "No! Ortwin saved Harald's life! Luba was going to kill the smith." She shook off her brother's arms and positioned herself in front of Ortwin, desperately fixing Yngvi with her ice-blue eyes. "Ortwin stopped Luba when she was about to kill the unconscious smith on the ground. She told me herself that she wanted to kill Harald to avoid having to flee."

Yngvi said nothing, his face unmoving. In despair, Edvina turned to Gregor, grabbing him by both arms. "What do you say? What says God?"

Gregor cleared his throat. "Ortwin doubtlessly loaded heavy guilt onto himself through the theft and the attack on Harald. On the other hand, he shows remorse for his deeds and is prepared to bear the consequences. If what you say is true, then he also saved Harald's life. I don't know how God would decide. But I, as God's priest, believe that our Lord would view condemning Ortwin to life as an outlaw to be sufficient punishment and would forgive his sin." Then he looked at Ortwin. "And if I tell you now, my boy, that Högni intended to give you your freedom at the next Yule fest, you will feel even greater remorse for having been cast out from our community."

Ortwin shrugged indifferently, but his face betrayed his true feelings. The news upset him.

In the course of the moons Godric had spent at Gregor's side, he had outgrown his initial timidness. Now the young man appealed to Yngvi in a firm voice, "Thorolf isn't going to believe that Ortwin was alone in the woods. He will torture him until he gives away his companions' hideout, and then innocent men like Dag and the other two servants will get punished, even though all they were trying to do was to make Ansgar see reason. Had they been free, their actions would not have borne consequences, and Hedda would never have had the opportunity to murder her husband. And then Ortwin would never have succumbed to the desire to help his friends." Godric paused a moment before asking the question that he knew would reach Yngvi's innermost core. "Are you not one of us—those who reject slavery and the oppression of men, Yngvi?"

"Well spoken, Godric," said Gregor, praising his student with a rewarding smile. "I couldn't have put it better myself. Come, Yngvi, can't you find it in your Nordic heart to help these people?"

Yngvi realized with astonishment just how deeply the traditions and laws of his people were still ingrained in him. Godric and Gregor were right: he needed to continue along the path of breaking open the encrusted structures of Northern society and replacing them with better ones. Exposing these outlaws to the danger of being executed or whipped—which was often tantamount to a death sentence—did not lie on this path.

Yngvi sheathed his sword. "Very well. Then let it be as if we never saw you. But stay away from Woodhaven, and don't even think about touching our livestock. Otherwise I might regret my decision."

Edvina swallowed back the unwise remark that they already stole several piglets and lambs. Relieved, she wrapped her arms around her brother and thanked him for his help. Godric stroked her back lovingly and kissed her forehead.

Ortwin stood there, his arms hanging down limply, feeling more like the spectator of an unreal event, rather than one of its participants. The fact that Edvina had defended him had impressed him deeply. Obviously she had forgiven him, and perhaps she cared more for him than she was willing to admit.

Shortly after their arrival at the outlaws' hidden valley, Ortwin had fallen in love with Luba—or at least he had believed it was love. The beautiful Slav seemed to be unaware of her effect on him, and no matter how hard he tried, she never responded to his advances. One evening, when he saw her sitting close to Dag in conversation, jealousy had swept over him hotly. He had grabbed his friend by his tunic and rammed his fist in Dag's face. Dag, who probably had no idea what it was about, had retaliated by breaking Ortwin's nose. Luke alone had managed to pull the two men apart.

Then Edvina had appeared, looking like a goddess of revenge with her fiery red hair, screaming at him contemptuously, "Don't you see that Luba doesn't want you? Nor does she want Dag! She wants neither of you. She doesn't like men—she prefers women. You can woo her until Judgment Day, and she still won't go to bed with you!"

By and by, he'd had to accept that Edvina seemed to be right. Luba, who appeared to have been unaware of his feelings for her, had turned tight-lipped and avoided both him and Dag whenever she could. Instead she sought the company of Bert, who in turn confessed to them that he wasn't drawn to women and that he loved men. Perhaps the two of them were connected by their experience of having lived in a society that forbade them to show their true feelings. Now they were finally able to speak about them, but in the valley of the outlaws, they were still unable to live them.

Dag turned his attentions to Nele, who did not refuse him. Once Ortwin was healed from his blind veneration of Luba, he found himself drawn to Edvina. He learned to appreciate her liveliness and her open, honest ways. But Edvina acted cold toward him. When he tried to touch and kiss her, she brushed him off with harsh words. "Many times I signaled to you that I like you. But you only had eyes for Luba, not seeing—or unwilling to see—my affection for you. And now that your beloved is unobtainable to you, I am supposed to serve as cheap seconds? Who do you think I am? Someone who will kiss your feet in gratitude for your attentions? Stick your prick wherever you want, Ortwin, but not inside me."

Ever since then, they had been distant around one another,

though without enmity. Ortwin's love for the proud, attractive woman had continued to grow, but he had not dared to touch her again.

"Ortwin? Are you dreaming?" Edvina's voice brought him back to the present.

"N-no," he stammered. "I thank you for defending me."

Edvina tilted her head with a mocking smile. "Don't flatter yourself. I merely meant to spare our tiny community the loss of a man who knows how to handle wood and produces many useful things for us."

Anyone who didn't know Edvina would find it difficult to discern emotions in her ice-blue eyes. But Ortwin had learned to read them, and he did not fail to notice the gleam of warmth in them that belied the cold mockery in her voice.

Yngvi took the pickaxe and set to work, breaking more lumps of limestone from the light-gray layer running at an angle through the rock.

Godric and Edvina sat together, taking turns telling each other about the time when they had lost sight of one another. Godric promised to bring his sister some of the items she and her companions needed most urgently.

"How do I find you?"

"You don't unless we want you to," said Edvina in jest. "Follow the Saltmarsh. After one day, you'll reach a rock that looks like a troll. Make camp there. Then, if you continue to follow the river the next morning, you will reach the entrance to a gorge. I will wait for you there in ten days' time."

Before they set off for home, Yngvi, Gregor, and Godric stowed the chunks of limestone in their sacks. Yngvi offered the outlaws a piece of advice. "Best keep away from this area. Our people will turn up here more often from now on to break limestone."

"What do you need the limestone for?" asked Edvina.

"Among other things, to work animal hides into leather," replied Yngvi.

Edvina's eyes looked at Godric with an unspoken question. He smiled. "As soon as I know more, I will share it with you."

One week later, Godric visited the smithy to pick up the fishing hooks, nails, and arrowheads he had ordered, paying Harald with a small lump of gold. Ever since Thorolf had divided up Ryan's host present among the families of Woodhaven, the yellow metal rose to popularity as a means of payment. Godric still had plenty of it, and he would only need to spend a few days in the Shannon's headwaters during his next visit at Ryan's village to fill his pouch at least halfway.

By the lakeshore, he saw Yngvi and Gregor engaged in debate. The two men were standing next to the ring-shaped wall, which was as tall as a man and which he had helped to build from loosely stacked rocks. The wall enclosed a space that was about four feet wide. On one side, there was a large opening with a short tunnel made of stones. Through this tunnel, they would feed a fire with logs.

In response to a question from Yngvi, Gregor wrinkled his forehead and said, "In the North, did you ever see a lime kiln?"

"No."

"Well, I did. In Rome. So do not question my choices," said Gregor, uncommonly harshly.

Godric, watching, had the impression that, in spite of the brisk speech, his teacher was not entirely certain of how the kiln worked.

When Godric joined the two men, Gregor handed him a

shovel. "I'm glad you're here. We must pile dirt around the kiln to stabilize the stones."

While Godric shoveled dirt, his eyes were caught by the pile of limestone they had brought back from their excursion. Later, they would layer these rocks inside the kiln and, with the help of fire, turn it into burnt lime. Then, Gregor had told him, if the burnt lime was mixed with water, the resulting concoction would help them remove hair from animal hides—an important step in the production of parchment as well as leather.

Under cover of prospecting for more limestone, Godric set off for his sister's hideout the following morning, carrying a sack and a pickaxe. As Edvina had predicted, he arrived at the entrance to the gorge on the morning of the next day, and it wasn't long before his sister emerged from the woods, happily waving at him. Chatting eagerly, they followed the river up to the lake at the gorge's end. There, they climbed atop the concealed raft, and Edvina paddled it across the water to the cave's entrance. She asked him to lie flat and help her direct the raft through the low gap with their hands. Godric was amazed how well-concealed the entrance to the outlaws' hiding place was.

His amazement grew when he stepped out of the cave and beheld the idyllic valley enclosed by rocky slopes. His sister and her companions could hardly have found a better home. The outlaws had cleared a fair amount of the forest which, Edvina told him, used to cover the entire valley. To his left and right, two small, simple wooden huts had been built against the rock wall. Their roofs were covered with turf and reached down to the ground, creating the illusion that they were but extensions of the meadow. An almost fully grown sheep was drinking from the stream that divided the meadow and ran merrily into the cave. Three slightly smaller sheep grazed peacefully nearby.

Between the meadow and the edge of the woods, stalks of grain were growing from dark-brown soil. Beyond, around two hundred paces away, three men swung axes to clear more space for fields and pasture. Godric recognized Ortwin by his dark head of hair. The other two men, blond, were Luke and Dag, his sister told him.

They stopped by the fireplace, around which nothing grew on the hardened ground. Edvina nodded toward a beautiful, dark-haired woman sitting outside one of the huts, grinding grain with quern stones and eyeing him with curiosity. "That is Luba." Quietly, she added, "I told you about her." Then, louder, she called out: "Luba, this is Godric, my brother."

Luba nodded at him with a thin smile. Carrying on with her work, she used one hand to pour more grain through the hole in the center of the upper stone while using her other hand to keep it turning against the bottom stone. The grain was ground into coarse flour with the sound of dull scratching and crunching.

"Ortwin made the quern," said Edvina proudly. "And he built three looms."

"The way you speak of Ortwin, you still seem to think highly of him."

His sister nodded. She had told him of the events leading to fisticuffs between Ortwin and Dag. "Yes, I like him very much. And by now, he only seems to have eyes for me. Still, I wish to be completely certain that I am more than just a replacement for Luba."

"How long have you let him dangle?"

"Almost three moons." Edvina smiled mischievously.

Godric laughed loudly, causing Luba to look up at them. That sounded just like his sister, he thought with amusement.

If she made up her mind about something, she would find the means to reach her goal.

"Don't be so hard on him," he said. "I can understand why this woman turned the heads of Ortwin and Dag. If I didn't know that Luba was out of bounds for men, I would probably fare no different." He gave her a cheeky grin. "But if you weren't my sister, I would still pick you in the end."

Edvina elbowed him in the ribs. "You old fawner. Some things never change. In the old days, if you wanted something from me, you'd butter me up until I could no longer say no. What do you want this time?" she asked jokingly.

Godric placed a finger to his mouth and pretended to think hard. "How about some delicious roast rabbit tonight? Prepared with this!" He produced a thick bundle of kitchen herbs from his sack, placing it in his sister's hand. "I'm sure you'll put them to good use. I remember well how you used to watch mother and her kitchen maid prepare our meals."

After removing his raincoat and a few other personal items from his carry sack, he turned it inside out. "And I also have this for you."

Bending down, Edvina excitedly and blissfully fingered the treasures that had tumbled to the ground. There was a pouch of salt, a roll of leather for new shoes, iron arrowheads, fishing hooks, two pots closed with skins, nails, and one round leather satchel.

"One pot contains honey that I bought from Digur," explained Godric. "And the other holds a healing ointment given to me by Asla. Hilda filled the satchel with seeds of kitchen herbs."

Visibly touched, Edvina rose to her feet and embraced him, whispering "thank you" in his ear. She was glad for the gifts he had brought, but gladder still for the gift from God that allowed her to be close to her brother, the last one living of her family—for having found in him a trusted friend with whom to share her innermost thoughts without any fear that he might someday use them against her.

Godric brushed his hand across her hair. "My pleasure." He remembered only one other occasion when he'd seen this much joy in his sister's eyes. It was the day their father gifted the then ten-year-old girl her own horse.

When they let go of each other after a while, he asked, "Aren't there seven of you? Two are missing, are they not?"

"Yes, Nele and Bert. The fat one is probably minding the pigs, letting them root for food in the woods. Two of them are almost fully grown, and we're hoping for offspring. Nele is probably in the woods also, digging for carrots and picking berries."

In the evening, by the fire, Godric told the outlaws of the progress in Woodhaven and in Ryan's village. Bert gave a satisfied grunt each time he took a bite of the roast rabbit, and the others, too, praised Edvina's clever use of the herbs and salt.

Godric patiently answered the outlaws' many questions. When they learned of his apprenticeship to the priesthood, Nele asked whether he, once he was ordained, would baptize Dag and bless their union in the name of God.

Dag looked at Nele with surprise. Somewhat irked, he asked, "Who says that I wish to become a Christian?"

"I want to become Christian," declared Luba, to everyone's surprise. "The gods of my homeland did not help me when I was enslaved. They are weak." She gazed at the siblings with her beautiful face. "But your God saved us and led us here. I would like to worship him in the future, and sacrifice to him." She looked Edvina straight in the eye. "Maybe then he will fulfill my heart's greatest desire."

Godric smiled. "You do not need to sacrifice to the Christian God, Luba. To him, it is enough if you follow his commandments and believe in him. And he does not interfere in matters of the heart."

Dag said, "I will think about it. It will take a while yet before you're an ordained priest."

Godric nodded.

When everyone had eaten their fill, Nele handed around a wooden bowl containing small black berries. Godric scooped up a handful of the tiny fruits and stuffed them into his mouth. He hadn't eaten berries or other fruit in a long while. "Those are delicious. Somewhat like the blueberries from back home. We don't have these by the coast."

"They seem to grow in higher regions, like our valley," said Nele. "The higher you climb into the mountains, the more of them you find."

Throughout the evening, Godric had noticed the furtive looks that Dag cast at Luba. Even if the handsome man had been forced to accept that Luba was out of reach for him, he evidently was not yet healed from his desire for her. He treated Nele, with whom he shared his bed and whose rounded belly showed she was with child, kindly enough, but more like a friend than a lover.

Ortwin, on the other hand, clearly showed no more interest in Luba. He was sitting next to Edvina, hanging on her every word and smiling at her when her eyes met his. And when he finally clasped her hand inside his, she did not withdraw it.

That night, a thunderstorm raged. Godric slept in the hut shared by Bert and Luke. The rain poured as if from buckets, and bright lightning flickered through the cracks in the timber walls. In between thunderclaps and over the pitter-patter of the rain, he could clearly make out the sounds of lovers from Edvina's hut. Godric smiled. His sister had achieved her goal.

"Can you bring more salt on your next visit?" asked Nele the following morning when Godric said farewell. "Unfortunately we don't have seawater we can boil. We used up our stores to smoke salmon, and the salt you brought us will not last for long."

Godric nodded. Ortwin whispered something into Edvina's ear.

"Ask him yourself," she replied with a laugh, gently nudging him with her elbow. "My little brother won't bite off your head."

"Well," began Ortwin awkwardly. "I . . . we badly need new axe-heads and hoes. Ours are worn and won't be usable for much longer. But we do not have anything to pay you with."

Godric studied Ortwin's crooked face. The brown eyes of his sister's chosen one gazed at him expectantly, radiating honesty and reliability. Ortwin was the right one for Edvina—of that he felt certain.

"Yes, you do have something with which you may reward me," Godric replied, speaking to everyone. "Look after my sister and make sure I find her unharmed when I return in two moons' time for my next visit. Then you may continue to count on my help."

"You can rely on us," said Ortwin, and the others nodded. Godric did not know whether they did so because they liked Edvina or because he was their only ally in Woodhaven able to supply them with valuable goods. But in the end, it mattered little.

Edvina kissed his cheek, whispering, "You do know that I am quite capable of looking after myself?"

Edvina accompanied her brother to the shore of the lake. Before they went their separate ways, Godric gave her a wide grin. "If my ears weren't mistaken last night, you finally took mercy on Ortwin?"

Edvina's face flushed pink. "Yes, and I do not regret it."

Three weeks later, two knarrs arrived in the harbor of Woodhaven. Hakon moored the *Goldeagle* by the jetty, while Liam anchored the *Freedom* in the bay.

Yngvi and Harald greeted the tall, athletic Irishman with friendly handshakes. Yngvi noted that, with Liam's blond hair and rakish face, covered in scars from fights, he would have made it far in the emir's bodyguard. But fate had decided otherwise. Now Liam, who was probably in his early twenties, acted as Ryan's right-hand man and was authorized to negotiate the price for the next shipment of ore.

Harald climbed into the *Goldeagle*'s cargo hold to inspect the lumps of ore in the solid wooden crates. It was the amount they had agreed on in exchange for the load of flax, barley, and wool Hakon had shipped to Ryan's village ten days prior.

"Good quality—as always," exclaimed the smith with a grin.

Without wasting another word, he hurried to his workshop. His iron stores had run out a few days ago, and he had desperately awaited fresh supplies. Harald ordered Bran and his servants to fetch the ore from the *Goldeagle*, prepare the bloomery—a type of kiln designed to extract iron from ore—and check the charcoal supplies. Tomorrow one of the servants would fill the bloomery through its chimney with alternating layers of coal and ore, while another servant would work the bellows to feed the flames. The heat would free the iron trapped in the rock. Once a servant had allowed some of the yellowish glowing liquid slag to run off from the bottom of the construction, he would smash the bloomery and search for the iron in the remaining slag.

Though Harald had watched this process many times, he was still gripped by awe every time. It was almost like witnessing a birth when they retrieved the lumps of still quite impure iron from the destroyed belly of the bloomery.

Harald looked around. His son Runar was supposed to be here to tidy up and sweep out the smithy. Where was the lazy good-for-nothing this time? Was he planning another one of his nasty pranks, like the one that nearly cost a maid her life the other day? Harald sighed. Even if he considered himself a good smith, capable of forging iron into any form desired, he doubted his abilities as a father. So far, he had failed to mold the boisterous and selfish character of his growing son for the better. Neither kind words nor a good thrashing seemed to work. He had a hunch that Runar would cause him plenty of grief in the future.

A storm arrived in the late afternoon, lightning flashing out from leaden, heavy clouds that brought with them an early dusk.

Hilda scurried the short way to Carla's and Yngvi's house. Heavy raindrops pattered onto her cloak, underneath which she carried baby Johannes. Gregor and Godric zigzagged after her, trying to avoid the large, muddy puddles that grew steadily, drenching their shoes. Hilda did not care. If she stepped into a pool of water, then so be it; anything to avoid falling and accidentally squashing her son.

Yngvi opened the door with a welcoming smile and helped them take off their cloaks. He had invited Liam to spend the night and asked his friends to come over for a shared meal.

Liam's generally serious face lit up when he spotted the priest. Gregor strode toward the Irishman and grasped him by the arms. "You look well, my friend. Especially with the new tunic. Suits you very well!"

The Irishman glanced helplessly at Carla, unable to understand Gregor's words. Godric was quicker, translating the priest's speech into Anglo-Saxon. On this evening, Godric and Carla would both have to translate many words yet.

"My wife sewed it. She is deft with a needle." Liam's voice was filled with pride.

"I can tell," said Hilda, nodding.

Gregor's eyes scanned the modest hall. In view of the mild winter, Yngvi, like most settlers, had cut a window into each long wall of the house. During foul weather, as tonight, the holes were covered with hides stretched across frames. The open hearth, enclosed with a stone wall, was in the center of the room. Cooking utensils hung on a wall, and a wooden shelf held pots, jugs, and cups. A table with two benches stood by the hearth, and beyond the table were chests holding Yngvi's and Carla's possessions. Next to them stood a loom and their bed. Edna's sleeping place was concealed behind a plain curtain.

It was a hall like many others. Unadorned, simple, nothing out of the ordinary. But it was cozy, and Gregor felt comfortable among these walls, sensing something that he could not place his finger on. Could it be the fact that Christians lived here? Perhaps, pondered Gregor. But then he changed his mind, for he had met Christians whose prayers were hypocritical and who did not deserve to speak the name of the Lord. Their greed, envy, and malice went against everything that Jesus taught, poisoning the atmosphere in their homes. This home of Yngvi, Carla, and Edna, in contrast, was infused with affection, mutual respect, and the readiness of its inhabitants to listen to and understand one another. Perhaps the walls of a house remembered what happened in their midst, revealing their secret knowledge to those sensitive enough to hear it.

Gregor was wrapped up in his musings, and the conversations around him were but dim murmurs to him. Only the delicious smell of cooked chicken woke him from his thoughts.

Carla was standing by the hearth, scattering herbs into a pot and stirring the broth with a large wooden spoon. The mistress of the house, who, compared to her delicate stature, carried a disproportionately large belly in front of her, gave her guests an encouraging nod. "Sit down already. There is enough food for everyone."

Gregor felt his mouth water. With a grateful smile at Carla, he sat down at the table. Edna brought a bowl for each of them, took the pot off the chain above the fire, and placed it on the table. Carla supplied her guests with cups and a jug of ale. Then they ate their chicken broth in silence.

Hilda dipped her finger into the soup and dripped a few drops onto her infant son's lips. He smacked his mouth softly, then cawed happily and opened his little mouth wide. "Even my Johannes likes your chicken broth, Carla. I couldn't do it better myself. Whoever taught you to cook like this?"

Carla placed a hand on Hilda's, gazing at her warmly. "I learned this from the best friend I ever had. She is a woman who cared for me as a mother when I was unwell, and I love her as a mother."

Gregor knew his Hilda, and, as he expected, her face flushed red with embarrassment. She squeezed Carla's hand and continued to drip-feed her little son as if there were no task more important on this evening.

When Carla made to fetch flatbreads and cheese, Edna sprang to her feet and gently pushed the heavily pregnant woman back down on the bench. "Let me," she said firmly, smiling at her former mistress.

Godric did not fail to notice Edna's gesture, and he felt touched. At first glance, the former maid might not have been as pretty as most of the other former slave women, but in time, one came to see her inner beauty.

After the meal, Hilda and Carla urged Liam to share news from his village. The Irishman obliged readily. Many women had given birth in recent months, and Enya was with child again following her miscarriage. Conor, he went on, had mastered the art of charcoal making, and the smith now rarely complained of too little coal. Caitlin, too, was doing well. She assisted her husband and was a great help to him. "That reminds me, Godric—Conor gave me something for you."

Liam reached into his carry sack and pulled out two fist-sized, heavily filled leather pouches, pushing them across the table. Godric took them and untied the strings, emptying their contents onto the table. Irregular lumps of gold rolled across the timber, gleaming yellow in the warm light of the tallow lamps.

"Those are the two handfuls of gold that we vouched for," observed Yngvi happily.

"Rather, four," joked Carla, picking up some lumps with her delicate hand.

Everyone laughed. The mood was light, and Godric felt relieved. Once he had paid Conor's gold to Olaf and Thorolf, he would be free to accompany Liam on his return to Ryan's village and there purchase the axe-heads and hoes for the outlaws. He had decided against purchasing the wares in Woodhaven—what would an aspiring priest want with several axes and hoes?

Yngvi raised his cup. "Let us drink to Conor, who kept his word."

They all raised their cups and, each according to their thirst, took a shorter or longer swig of ale in honor of the good charcoal burner.

Then Yngvi asked a question that seemed foremost on his mind, "How was it possible for Conor to accumulate this much gold within just a few weeks? He must have had his hands full with the charcoal business. Is there so much gold in the bed of your Shannon that a man merely needs to bend down to find a lump?"

"It's not quite that easy," replied Liam, amused. "Caitlin searched for several days to fill half a pouch. Conor borrowed the rest from us."

"And you just lent it to him?"

Liam nodded. "Conor is an honorable man, and we stick together. Each one of us chain wielders, man or woman, played a part in our liberation. We don't forget that."

Yngvi stroked his shaved chin pensively. "But surely you, too, have problems with people who do not abide by the laws and who damage your community. How does your leader deal with those?"

"Several weeks ago, Ryan had us elect a council of three men and one woman. They advise him in all important matters and lead trials when a crime is committed."

"You chose a council and a woman was elected?" asked Hilda with disbelief.

"Yes, though it wasn't without controversy," Liam admitted. "When Ryan declared that women were to receive the same rights as men, more than a few were appalled over this break with tradition. But Ryan listed good reasons for his decision. Without the help of our women, we'd never have freed ourselves. They fought just as bravely as we men did, and many of them died for our freedom. Why should they now be forced back into their role as the oppressed?"

The glaring flash of a lightning bolt lit up the skins in both windows, and the deafening thunderclap and low rumble that followed instantaneously caused the group around the table to shrink with fright.

Even though Liam, a battle-seasoned warrior, had looked death in the eye many a time, he feared the treacherous nature of thunderstorms, striking down man and beast at random and setting houses ablaze. He sipped his ale to steady his nerves before continuing. "We chain wielders are a ragtag collection of young men and women. We share no common homeland, no common traditions. We are united by the hope for something new, for a better future together. Like Ryan, I, too, believe that equal rights for men and women are a prerequisite for such a future."

Yngvi almost thought he heard himself speaking. Liam's and Ryan's thoughts matched his own almost exactly. "How great is the power of your council? Does Ryan accept its decisions?"

"If three of the four members make a decision," replied Liam, "then Ryan goes with it. Even if he himself is of different opinion, though this happens rarely. If the council cannot agree, then he decides."

There was a loud knock on the door, and Harald breezed in, along with a rainy gust of wind. "Thor is raging outside as if his beloved made a cuckold of him," he growled grumpily, peeling off his soaking cloak.

As if the weather god wished to support the smith's words with an angry fist, another lightning bolt struck nearby. The thunderclap booming almost in the same instant made everyone duck down for a moment before gazing upward—thankfully, the roof was intact.

A while later, Hilda, Gregor, Edna, and Carla withdrew to the back of the hall. The women wove flax while Gregor told stories from the Bible. They had left the table to Harald and Yngvi, who negotiated with Liam the price for the next load of ore. Godric had volunteered to translate.

Liam offered seven crates of iron ore for five pigs, seven sheep, and six sacks of rye. Harald, who considered this far too little ore, demanded twelve crates instead. The Irishman pulled his lips into a sneer, as if the smith had told a poor joke, dismissing his demand with a clear gesture.

Yngvi held back. Harald was more suited to bartering and haggling. The smith, usually quiet and solitary, seemed to come to life during negotiations. Just then the man jutted out his wide jaw, narrowed his eyes into slits, and practically spat his next offer at Liam. The latter jerked back, wiped his sleeve across his cheek, and waved dismissively once again. His face bright red, Harald uttered curses and maledictions that proved difficult for Godric to translate as he tried not to offend the Irishman. While Liam stuck with his current offer of nine crates of ore for the proffered wares from Woodhaven, Harald insisted on ten. The two men crossed their arms on their chests, glowering at each other in silence.

Negotiations had stalled, Yngvi realized with regret. When the two trade partners still showed no signs of relenting after a few more moments, he leaned forward to Liam. "Add a small pouch of gold to your offer. Then let the bargain be good."

The Irishman gave in to Yngvi's request, holding out his hand to Harald to seal the trade. The smith hesitated a brief moment before clasping Liam's hand with a gap-toothed grin.

Liam appeared relieved. "Send the *Goldeagle* in five weeks' time with the goods. By then, we'll have gathered enough ore."

What no one yet knew that night, and what became evident the following morning, was that the *Goldeagle* was no more. Parts of the jetty and the ropes with which the ship had been moored lay charred in the water. A mighty lightning bolt and the storm had sent the *Goldeagle* to a wet grave somewhere in the lake.

When Thorolf heard of the destruction of his beloved ship, he walked out of the house without saying a word, his face bitter.

Asla stayed behind, feeling sad. She did not grieve, however, for the knarr but for the love between her and Thorolf, which had become worn between the grinding millstones of life, turning to dust amid their frequent arguments. *When we were first together*, thought Asla wistfully, *he would have confided in me and shared his grief with me.*

CHAPTER 19
WOLFHOUNDS

Digur forced the plowshare deep into the ground, driving it through the soil with the help of his dun stallion. His servants Kilian and Enno worked behind him, hacking into the clods of dirt. These days, Digur especially enjoyed his work, for he no longer toiled on land belonging to everyone; instead, he now worked his own field—a field that he and his servants had wrested from the forest in hard labor. Between the new field and the village sprouted a wide, green belt of grass and weeds on the former common fields. In two weeks' time, they would fetch the cows from the delta and graze them on the new pastures.

For the end of summer, an uncommonly cool breeze swept down from the mountains, and the men were glad for the long trousers and leg wraps they had put on that morning.

From time to time, Enno glanced at the swineherd, a girl who stood leaning against the fence of the enclosure. The pigs were rooting the ground of a nearby field by the edge of the woods, which was supposed to be sowed in the next few days. Enno envied the former maid, who had married one of Thorolf's freed servants and had thereby become a free woman herself.

The small field her husband had cleared and the ten pigs Thorolf had given them would guarantee them a comfortable livelihood. Enno sighed. He would probably never experience the bliss of working his own land as a freeman. But perhaps Digur would show him some kindness and permit him to marry Kaja.

Late in the morning, Kaja came walking across the pasture. In one hand, she carried a reed basket of flatbreads, smoked fish, and wooden cups, and in the other, a pail of fresh water. Digur sat on the ground with his legs crossed, picked a cup from the basket, and scooped water from the bucket, draining his cup in one gulp. He gestured at his servants and maid to share the meal and water with him. In silence, they ate and quenched their thirst.

After a while, Enno gathered his courage. "Master, may I ask you something?"

Digur nodded, taking a bite of his bread.

Enno, knowing that long speeches and flowery words annoyed his master, cut straight to the point. "I ask you to give me Kaja's hand in marriage."

Digur wasn't surprised. Before the birth of her daughter, Kaja had been a fiery, imaginative lover, but after he declined to take her for his wife and acknowledge her daughter as his own, she had turned apathetic in bed, lying beneath him like a dry stick. In the end, he had lost interest and gave up asking her to share his bed. Enno must have noticed this, for the servant had been following the attractive Slavic woman around like a puppy for weeks now, paying her compliments and lending her a hand at work whenever possible. Kaja, evidently, welcomed his attentions.

Digur studied Enno, who had probably seen a little more than thirty winters, making him a few years older than Digur himself. The blond servant came from the land of the Frisians. The eyes in his narrow face stood close together, and he had a weak chin, giving him a sly look, but, in the course of the years,

Digur had learned to appreciate his servant's honest character and reliable service.

At last he released Enno from his anxious wait. "I am in agreement, if Kaja is, too. I know you will treat her and her child well."

Enno beamed with happiness. "I thank you, Master. I will honor my wife and be a good father to her daughter."

Digur looked at Kaja, who thanked him with a wistful smile. He said, "Build yourselves a hut next to my house. I've had enough of wailing children in my hall."

That ended the subject for him. He rose, picked up the bucket, held it out to his stallion, and let him drink.

When the horse had nearly emptied the bucket, his head suddenly jerked up with his ears pricked. The noontime peace was abruptly split asunder by a bloodcurdling scream from the swineherd.

Digur looked to the edge of the woods. The pigs were squealing shrilly, scattering across the field. One sow was headed in his direction. The swineherd ran after the pig, her face a mask of fear. Three huge gray dogs were hot on her heels. Four more dogs chased a boar and two sows with their piglets in another direction. Digur's stallion shrieked in panic and leaped forward. Dragging the plow behind, it galloped toward the village.

Digur swore, drew his dagger, and snatched up Kilian's hoe. Kaja stood with both hands clasped to her mouth, her eyes wide with fright. While Digur ran toward the fleeing swineherd, Enno grabbed his hoe and positioned himself in front of Kaja. Kilian drew the small knife he used to cut his food, not for the first time lamenting the fact that, as a servant, he wasn't permitted to own a larger one.

The first hound reached the screaming girl and knocked her to the ground. Digur couldn't get there in time. The beast sank its teeth into her neck and shook her until the young woman fell silent.

Furiously, Digur swung his weapon, slamming the heavy iron down on the dog's head. With a yowl, the huge beast collapsed atop the lifeless girl. Before Digur had a chance to swing the hoe again, the next hound leaped at him. Instinctively, Digur stepped back with one foot, bracing himself and thus preventing the large animal from toppling him. With his left, Digur slammed the hoe's handle side-on between the hound's opened jaws. With his right hand, he stabbed his dagger into the beast's neck. Meanwhile, the third dog had lodged its teeth in his leg wraps, trying to bring him down.

Enno rushed to his master's aid, hitting the hound on its hairy back with his hoe. The animal yelped and let go of Digur's calf, fleeing toward the edge of the woods.

"Where did they come from?" gasped Enno, horrified.

Digur shrugged, watching the dogs which, about a hundred paces away, were tearing chunks of flesh from dead pigs, hastily gulping them down. The farmers and their servants who had been plowing nearby banded together, the freemen drawing their daggers while the servants raised their hoes. Roaring curses, the men stamped toward the hounds, which eventually decided to flee. Two of the feral beasts managed to carry away a piglet each before vanishing in the underbrush.

Digur and Enno heaved the dead dog off the swineherd. Her throat was shredded. Gently, Digur closed her terrified eyes.

Kaja rushed to the village to inform Thorolf of the incident. Soon the rumor spread that Digur slayed two beasts no smaller than the mighty Fenrir wolf. Men and women, the free and the unfree, set down their work and, with their noisy children in tow, flocked across the meadow toward the edge of the woods.

Thorolf pushed his way through the crowd. His former

servant sat beside his dead wife, sobbing, holding her limp hand. Thorolf crouched down and placed a hand on the man's shoulder. The settlers, standing around them in a circle, fell silent. Their serious, somber mood infected the children, who ceased their bickering and arguing.

Thorolf inspected the two dead animals. They were large indeed, larger than any hound he had ever seen—measuring probably three feet at the shoulder. Bending over one of the dogs, he felt its gray fur. It was hard and bristly.

"Has anyone seen such beasts before?" he asked out loud.

An Irish maid stepped forward. "Yes, Lord, those are wolfhounds from my homeland. Our king owned several of them. He used them to hunt the wild boar, bears, and wolves."

"I, too, know them," said Hakon. "The Irish used them in the war. The chieftain on whose ship I sailed around Ireland many years ago received a wolfhound as a gift from an Irish jarl. The dog was of a gentle nature and soon became the favorite of all the crew. I'd never have thought, in a hundred moons, he might attack a person and mangle them like this poor woman."

Yngvi stepped forward, addressing Digur. "Did these animals seem to have any shred of respect or fear of humans?"

Digur shook his head. "They were hungry beasts, not normal dogs. They saw no difference between us and the swine. We were prey to them—they only respected our hoes."

"Then the beasts most likely belonged to a feral pack that has never encountered people before," concluded Yngvi.

"But how did they get here?" Thorolf wondered out loud. "They'll hardly have swum here from Ireland."

Yngvi scratched his stubbly chin. "Seafarers must have brought them here—though we don't know why or whether they still reside on Catan. But that is not the most pressing issue right now. What matters right now is that there are wolfhounds here, posing a risk to us. Moreover, the pack that attacked us is likely not the only one on the island."

"Then it is nothing short of a miracle that they've only just discovered us," said Thorolf slowly. "We've been here for more than a year now."

Yngvi shrugged. "Catan is big. Even if there are several packs, they have plenty of space to disperse in these expansive woods. This pack probably discovered us by chance." He prodded the fur of one of the slain animals with a stick. "Look, this animal was starving. It would seem the wolfhounds only just get by on birds, rabbits, and lizards—and now they've discovered our pigs, which fill their bellies properly." Raising his stick, he pointed at the forest edge. "Hunger will make them lie in wait there for an opportune moment to sink their fangs into our swine once more. Or into us, if we encounter them unarmed."

His younger brother was doubtlessly right. Gesturing at a few young men, Thorolf ordered them to arm themselves and join the swineherds.

The next morning, Thorolf appeared on the village square clad in his sword belt and his best tunic. Even though the air was mild, he had donned his bearskin. In a voice of determination, forbidding any objection from the beginning, Thorolf explained to the freemen what he intended to do against the danger of renewed attacks from the feral dogs.

Of uppermost importance was the defense of the livestock and the village, and Thorolf bestowed Hakon with the task of leading the defense. Every grown son of each freeman was to report to Hakon for duty. Further, Thorolf commanded each family to make one servant from their household available for the erection of new, taller pens for the animals. A freeman who'd learned the craft of carpentry with Högni was to oversee the construction.

The heads of the families of farmers and fishermen grumbled and groused that it would take them from their work on field and sea, but Thorolf decisively waved off any objection.

"I am your chief, and I'm telling you we cannot afford to lose our livestock to the wolfhounds." Determined to nip any further resistance in the bud, he placed his right hand on the hilt of his sword, staring grimly into the round. "Let he who disagrees step forward."

No one stirred.

Around noon, the young freemen and the servants gathered on the village square. Hakon's eyes scanned the two large groups contentedly—it was a promising start.

He divided the freemen armed with spears and bows into smaller groups. Half of them were to guard the livestock on the pasture and the servants at the building sites during the day, while the other half were to guard the village and the animals at night.

The wolfhounds attacked again two days later, this time at night. And this time, it wasn't just one pack that assaulted the livestock but two. The first killed several pigs that were still in one of the old pens by the edge of the woods, while the second pack hunted the sheep and calves that were still in the delta. Thanks to the men of the defense troops, the number of livestock lost was not excessive.

Those among the settlers who had criticized Thorolf's measures fell silent.

Following the first attack of the wolfhounds, Loki had failed to return from his daily hunt for rabbits.

When Asla waited in vain for the joyful barking of her loyal friend for the third evening in a row, her hunch grew into certainty: Loki must have fallen victim to the fangs of the hungry wolfhounds. Her eyes grew damp when she thought of the many evenings on which Loki presented her with a rabbit between his jaws, wagging his tail as he demanded to be stroked in payment. Tears ran down her cheeks as she imagined the bloodied, mangled body of her furry friend somewhere in the depths of the woods.

Ilka, noticing her mistress's grief, placed a comforting hand on her shoulder.

When Thorolf returned home late that evening, Asla still lay awake, telling him between sobs that Loki was most likely dead. He nodded, undressed, and lay down beside her. Soon he turned his back to her and started to snore.

Digur limped across his field, sowing rye grains onto the soil moistened from the previous night's rain. Kaja was walking to his right. Since he had loaned both his servants to the building of the pens, he had asked the maid to give him a hand with the sowing. Digur felt feeble that day, shivering despite the warm temperatures. His right lower leg throbbed painfully. He sensed that the wolfhound's teeth had left something evil inside his calf muscle, but he was determined to simply deal with it himself, just as he always dealt with everything. He stumbled and fell to his knees. He would have liked to rest a while, but Kaja's worried eyes on him, coupled with his fighting spirit, made him get back to his feet. He felt increasingly miserable, his aching leg barely carrying him now. When he fell for the second time, he stayed down. *Sleep*, he thought, *why not sleep for just a short while.*

Someone shook his shoulders and called his name. Digur

opened his heavy eyelids, turned his head, and saw Kaja gazing down at him in consternation. He felt a cool hand on his forehead.

"Digur, you are unwell. Get up! I'm taking you home."

Kaja pulled on his arm, trying to rouse him. Digur yanked free his arm and struggled to his feet. He felt dizzy, taking a few shaky steps across the field. Only when he stumbled once more did he allow his maid to brace him. A nearby servant spotted them and rushed over to help Kaja.

With great difficulty, they eventually managed to drag the large, heavy man to his house. There, he dropped exhaustedly onto his bedstead while Kaja asked the servant to fetch the healer.

Asla, who arrived in the company of her sister a short while later, carefully removed the leg wraps off Digur's injured calf and pulled up the trouser leg. She gave a start at the sight of the wound. The muscle was severely swollen and bluish-black. The wolfhound's teeth had gouged deep holes in the skin, which oozed foul-smelling pus. Gently she squeezed a blister beneath the skin. There was a crackling sound.

Asla turned to Stina and Kaja, standing behind her with worried faces, and whispered to them: "Kaja, fetch Thorolf and Yngvi. Tell them their brother is in a bad way. Tell Diara, too. And you, Stina, put some water over the fire and add the herbs for treating wounds. You know which ones."

Like Carla, Stina, too, had learned much from her sister's knowledge of healing. Pleased to be able to help, she opened Asla's carry sack with erratic movements. It upset her to see Digur—usually brimming with strength—feverish and weak on his bed, barely conscious. His closed eyelids twitched, and he tossed his head from side to side. During the brief moments that he was awake, he would open his eyes, which shone with fever, and mumble nonsense before drifting off again.

Thorolf and Yngvi, who happened to be in the village,

arrived first. They recoiled at the sight of their brother's nastily swollen, inflamed leg and at the repulsive stench emanating from it. Diara arrived soon after. She clasped her hands to her mouth with fright and glanced about helplessly when she beheld her eldest lying grievously ill on his bed. Her lips quivered when she sat down beside him and grasped his hand. Her voice shook as she spoke to him. Digur appeared not to hear her.

Asla led the brothers and Diara away from the sickbed, drawing them off to the side. "We must take off Digur's lower leg. If we don't, the rot will eat him up."

Diara gave a high-pitched, desperate cry.

Even though Asla had spoken quietly, Stina had heard her. Cold fear shot into her chest and stomach. She tried to ward off the gruesome image rising in her mind's eye: the tall, muscular man who danced in battle with his enemies, quick and nimble, stood one-legged, gazing at her sadly. Stina feared that, if he survived the wound rot, he would never get over the loss of his leg.

Asla went on in a low voice. "I have never done this before. I only watched once when the healer of our village sawed off a forearm. Can you think of anyone here who might know how to do this?"

Kaja had overheard the question. "Enno knows about such things. He told me that, before he was enslaved, he went to war with his people, the Frisians. Some older companion of his taught him to put broken bones in splints, sew up wounds, and take off limbs."

Yngvi nodded. "That's true. Enno used to care for the wounded warriors when he served Digur during times of war. I recall Digur mention one time that he was rather good at it."

Thorolf turned to the door. "I will fetch Enno. If I'm not mistaken, he is working on the new pens by the edge of the woods."

Diara touched Asla's arm with a pleading look in her eyes. "Is there anything I can do for him?"

Asla set a soothing hand on the tall woman's shoulder. "Place cold rags on his forehead and his good leg. We need to draw heat from his body. Hold his hand when he wakes up and is in pain. It will help him."

Diara swallowed hard. It wasn't much, but the little she could do for her son gave her a glimmer of hope.

When Stina went outside to relieve herself, Thorolf and Enno arrived at the hall. The servant carried a chisel and a fine-toothed saw which he had borrowed from Högni.

Upon Enno's advice, Thorolf and Yngvi tied their brother's healthy limbs and his mighty chest to his bedstead with thick ropes. They hoped it was enough to curb the great strength they thought Digur capable of even in his weakened state. Lifting his infected leg, they pushed a round log under his upper thigh and tied it in place with more rope. Then Enno tied another rope around the thigh with a wooden stick. During the surgery, he explained, he would twist the stick to tighten the rope and thus stem the blood flow.

Asla poured some wine into the patient's mouth, taken from Thorolf's last barrel from Coronium and laced with henbane. Digur was tall and strong, and she dosed him with a larger amount of the poisonous plant than she would give a smaller person. She hoped fervently that she had not chosen too high a dosage; only if she had calculated the henbane correctly would it help to deepen his sleep and ease his pain without killing him.

Diara placed a fresh cold cloth on Digur's forehead, then walked away when Kaja placed a sliver of wood between her master's teeth and grabbed hold of his head with both hands. Diara couldn't watch as her son was mutilated.

Enno gave Asla a baffled look when she asked him to wash

his hands in a bowl she had filled with the herb brew from the pot. "Just do it! I have fared well with this practice."

Upon Enno's request, Thorolf tied the chisel to a stick with its sharp end, placing the blunt end into the embers of the hearth where it soon began to glow red.

With the help of two wooden spoons, Asla fished the saw, a sharp knife, a sewing needle, and horsehairs from the hot water in the pot. Carefully she set down the objects on a clean cloth. Glancing at Enno, she noticed that his hands were shaking. She understood the servant's nervousness well. To him, there was probably a big difference between treating the wounds of some warrior after battle and sawing off half the leg of one's own master.

Asla placed a hand on his shoulder and gave him an intent look. "You are the only person who can save Digur now. Don't be afraid. If he survives, he will not bear you a grudge. Thorolf and I will make sure of it."

"He'll be grateful," said Yngvi in encouragement, even if his face betrayed his uncertainty in the matter.

The servant thanked them with a faint smile. Then he twisted the stick, tightening the rope around Digur's thigh. He asked Asla to hold the piece of wood. Then he picked up the knife.

Thorolf and Asla watched with serious faces as Enno placed the knife above the knee, pulled it downward through the skin, and finished the cut after curving to the opposite side. Only a little blood streamed from the wound. Then the servant separated the skin from the tissue beneath and folded the large, crescent-shaped flap of skin back to the point above the knee where he had started. There, he placed the knife once more. Small beads of sweat formed on Enno's forehead as he worked the knife through flesh and muscle down to the bone. When he had reached it, he picked up the saw.

At the other end of the room, Diara and Stina sat on a bench with their heads hung. It was obvious how perturbed they were by Digur's dire situation—Diara especially, whose fear and anxiety had turned barely visible wrinkles in her face into deep furrows, aging her by years. Yngvi, no less worried for his brother, walked over to them and sat between them. He picked up the women's hands and brought them together in his lap.

The saw's scraping and scratching filled the room. The monotonous sound reminded Asla of the laborious, rattling breathing of a dying old person. Reluctantly she stared at the blood-smeared teeth of the tool that ate its way slowly but steadily into the bone. She longed for the procedure to reach an end.

At last. Enno had successfully separated the sick lower leg from Digur's upper thigh. Asla thanked the gods that Digur was still in the clutches of a merciful sleep.

But when Enno pressed the glowing head of the chisel into the bloody flesh of the stump to seal the veins, Digur started to scream and pull at his bonds. Diara sobbed loudly, pressing her hands to her ears. Stina retched when she smelled the stench of burning flesh. A few unbearably long moments later, Digur fell silent.

Asla loosened the rope around the thigh a little. Only a small trickle of blood emerged from the stump. "You have burnt the wound well," said Asla appreciatively. "Go rest now. I can sew up the stump."

Thorolf seemed relieved at the—so far—successful surgery, patting Enno's shoulder. "You can be proud of praise from my wife." And, with a sarcastic note in his voice, he added, "She dispenses it exceedingly sparingly."

Asla heard Thorolf's snide remark. With a bitter frown, she threaded a horsehair on the needle and placed the first stitch by the edge of the flap of skin.

Everyone was glad about the successful amputation, but they

all knew it was only the first step. The life of their son, brother, and friend still hung in the balance.

Digur's mind hovered in gray nothingness, fighting eternal oblivion, an enemy that could not be vanquished with a blade. He dreamed heavily of fierce battles, slain warriors, and the blood-smeared face of a girl gazing at him accusingly from wide, innocent eyes. His spirit felt at peace when he hovered above a field of fertile, fragrant soil watching golden-yellow seeds of grain trickle through his fingers.

Then there was Asla, who prayed to her gods—Eir, in particular, the goddess of healing, begging her to give her hands the strength they needed to preserve the sick man's life. Carla spoke to her God, asking him to forgive her brother-in-law's sins, and, even if he was no Christian, to perform a miracle on him. Diara told Digur brief anecdotes from his childhood, pausing for ever longer intervals during which she cried without restraint.

The dull gray was broken by light when he heard the gentle voice of Stina. She did not pray for him—neither to the old gods nor to the lord of the Christians—and she did not unsettle him with desperate wailing. Instead, she would sing him a merry tune or tell him about the small tragedies of everyday life in the village: about the farmer's wife who had been unfaithful, about the two young freemen who had brawled over a maid, about the mishap of a young servant who struck his leg with an axe by accident, or about another attack by the wolfhounds, successfully deflected by the settlers. It wasn't the content of those meaningless tales Digur longed for, but her voice. The sound of her voice alone brought him comfort, and he longed for it deeply whenever it wasn't there.

When the world in which he dwelled turned black, his dreams and thoughts waxing more confounded and eventually disintegrating into disjointed fragments, Stina's voice reached him once more. This time, it sounded not gentle but demanding: "Fight, Digur! Fight for you and me! Fight for us!"

He could hear her sob, wanted to be with her and soothe her. But he did not succeed in wrestling down the dark wall that separated him from her. Digur steeled himself for the most important battle of his life.

Asla washed the stump of Digur's right leg with her infusion of herbs and smeared an ointment on it afterward. She gave her sister an encouraging look. "The stitches healed well, and his fever has gone down. Those are very good signs."

Stina allowed herself to hope. During the past seven days, Digur had been mostly unconscious. There had been a few brief phases during which he'd garbled unintelligible words, and Stina had used those moments to make him swallow a little herbal tea. The day before, when his fever reached another climax, they had feared Digur would not live through the night. She had picked up his hand and pleaded with him to not give up, urging him to fight for his life. When his fingers had jerked, she had felt certain that he heard her pleas.

Thorolf, who came to check on Digur, sighed with relief when Asla informed him that his brother was finally doing better. Since he was here, said Asla in her practical manner, he might as well help them wash their patient. Thorolf nodded readily and helped them turn his brother's heavy, muscular body, first to one side and then to the other, so that Asla and Stina were able to rub down Digur's entire body with wet cloths.

After Thorolf had taken his leave, Stina lingered by the sickbed, musing, her eyes resting on Digur's face. Even though his illness had left its mark on him, she could still see the strength of his character shine through with undiminished clarity. It was this strength, along with his respectful treatment of her and others, which she liked best in him and which drew her to him.

Once again, she touched the ring that, tied to a leather string, rested on his chest. It was the same ring she'd given him nearly two years ago out of gratitude for his support during her escape. It would seem he wore it hidden beneath his clothing all this time. Pensively, she stroked his wiry curls, leaned down, and kissed his forehead softly.

Digur unexpectedly opened his eyes. At first his gaze was dull, but then, stealthily, recognition entered his expression, and his lips formed a small smile.

"He is awake!" Stina shouted at her sister excitedly. Filled with happiness, she picked up Digur's calloused right hand and stroked it.

Asla, who had watched her sister, laughed out loud. "Your kiss appears to have healing powers."

"Thirsty," croaked Digur hoarsely.

Stina picked up the jug of water and poured a cup. When she made to lift his head and bring the cup to his lips, he shook his head. "Do it myself."

With great effort, he lifted his head and shoulders, propped his upper body on his elbow, and took the cup from her. *Typical Digur*, thought Stina. *No sooner does he rejoin the land of the living than he feels he must solve his problems without anyone's aid.*

When Digur had drained the cup, he sank back down, suppressing a groan that tried to escape him. "What happened?"

"You collapsed in the field," Asla explained. "The wolfhound's bite brought evil to your body and stole your consciousness."

The sisters exchanged an uneasy look. Eventually, Asla took courage. "We had to take off your lower leg in order to save your life."

Digur said nothing, staring at the rafters. Then he moved his right leg. Cold sweat formed on his forehead. He straightened up a little and pulled away the blanket. Shocked, he looked at the bandaged stump.

"Leave," he whispered, sinking back on the bed.

"You must eat something," said Stina imploringly. "You must regain your strength!"

"Leave!" he repeated, louder and sharper. "I can cope by myself."

The sisters exchanged another look. They both knew there was nothing else they could do for him right then.

On the afternoon of the following day, Digur sat dull-eyed upon his bedstead, eating without appetite the porridge sweetened with honey that Kaja had prepared for him. When the maid told him she and Enno had finished sowing his field and checked on his beehives—where all was in order—Digur showed no reaction. After the meal, he peed awkwardly into a jug, then lay down with his face to the wall.

That was how Stina found him when she visited him. She leaned two crutches against the wall and asked Kaja how he was doing.

The maid shrugged in reply, speaking in a low voice, "He doesn't talk, and he seems not to care what is going on outside. Even when his mother came to see him, he only stared at the wall. He only stirs when he needs to take a piss or shit in the pot."

When Kaja left the house, Stina was alone with the patient. She sat down on the edge of his bed.

"Digur?"

No reply.

"I know you can hear me. Talk to me!"

"Leave me alone," he grumbled.

But Stina did not oblige. "I know you cannot reconcile yourself with the loss of your leg. I understand. For a great warrior like yourself, it must be devastating to never again be able to fight like you used to. And you will probably no longer till your own fields, but you have Kaja and the servants for that."

Stina feverishly tried to think of something he would still be able to do with one leg. Hunting was out, and riding his horse would be difficult. Then she remembered his passion for his bees.

"No one knows bees the way you do. You can still grow your colony, even if you walk with crutches. You know how crazy the settlers are about your honey and wax."

When Digur did not react, her tone sharpened. "Turn around already and take a look at the crutches I brought you!" Then she went on in a gentler voice. "Gregor made them for you. He sends his regards and asked me to tell you that he would be very glad for a small pot of honey from you." That last part was a lie, but Digur was more likely to accept the crutches if he could pay something in return.

When still he did not stir, she shook him by his shoulder in despair, pleading with him. "Do you plan to lie here till the day the world ends?"

"Why not? What's it to you?" he muttered sullenly.

"Digur, it matters to me because you are important to me." She decided to gather all her courage. "I would like to be with you."

Digur turned with a sad look at her. "With me? That's

impossible. I never was good enough for you, and now more than ever."

"Why weren't you good enough for me?" she asked, genuinely surprised.

"I'm just not."

Digur stared at the wall again. Stina remained at his side in silence. She knew she mustn't push him now if she wished to learn more. It took some time before he murmured quietly: "I killed a girl once in a fight. She resembled you."

Stina wrinkled her brow. "I know that warriors sometimes kill the wives and children of their enemies in battle, but it does not strike me as something you would do."

"Maybe. But I did. I raided a village with my father and our men. I was facing two warriors at once when the girl appeared out of nowhere. She couldn't have been older than ten winters. I struck her with my sword."

"So you didn't kill her on purpose!"

Digur shook his head. "I did not aim for her. But in the heat of the fight, I accepted the possibility that I might strike her. In the end, it matters little. My sword killed the girl—she bled to death in my arms. Ever since that day, I see her large, sad eyes in my dreams." He fell silent, staring past her as if he could see the dying child now.

Stina dared not interrupt him now. She had the feeling that sharing his tale was good for him, and so she waited patiently for him to carry on.

Digur cleared his throat and looked up at her. "The little girl looked a lot like you. She was blonde with big green eyes, a snub nose, and freckles, like you. I was startled when I first met you. I almost believed the gods had played a nasty trick on me, bringing this girl back to life in the shape of you. Even though I feel drawn to you, I cannot be close to you. The girl looks at me through your eyes and won't allow it. I can't touch you with my bloodstained hands."

Digur faltered. It seemed as though the many words had exhausted him.

Stina had always sensed that there was more—much more—to him than a rough-hewn warrior, but she was astonished to learn that he was capable of such sensitive emotions and that he, usually so tight-lipped, knew how to put those emotions into words.

"Trust me, Digur, that girl is not inside me. She exists only in your head." She covered his hand with hers. "You are good enough for me. I am not as innocent as you believe me to be. I often feel envious of others, even of my sister, who knows how to do so many things and who always appears so dignified and queenly. Sometimes I feel like I'm nothing but a pale reflection of her. Also, I can be unjust when I'm upset over something and anger seethes inside me. Don't worry," she said with a smile. "This doesn't happen too often. Other times, I feel lazy. Then, I don't feel like doing anything at all and let others do the work for me."

Digur pulled his hand away and stared at the ceiling. "Even so. I am a cripple now. I won't be enough for you in the long run."

A stinging reply lay on Stina's tongue, but she swallowed it back. Without another word she stood and left the house. She realized that words alone wouldn't get her anywhere.

Long after night had fallen outside and Kaja had extinguished all but one tallow light, Digur lay awake. He was alone. Kaja slept with her daughter and Enno in a tent serving as their provisional abode until their hut was completed. Kilian was among the construction team in the delta. Countless thoughts buzzed through Digur's mind. He thought of all those battles he had survived without serious injury. None of his enemies ever defeated him. It seemed to him like a cruel jest from the gods that, of all creatures, a filthy dog succeeded in bringing him down with a bite.

The loss of his leg had seemed unreal to him at first—as if the Norns at the root of the sacred ash tree had woven his thread into the wrong place. But, he knew, the weavers of fate would not correct their mistake.

And now? With no leg? Images rose before his inner eye: he, galloping across the meadow on his stallion or hitching it to the plow; he, lithe, dancing with his sword in hand, teaching the art of combat to the young ones; he, going out to hunt down the beasts that attacked him. All those images were deceitful, showing him a future that no longer existed. Instead he saw himself staggering clumsily through Woodhaven on crutches, saw children pointing and laughing at him, and adults calling him a cripple in hushed tones. That was the fate he was condemned to from now on—a fate forcing him to accept the help of others. Or not, he thought grimly. Not if he decided to fall on his sword.

Unlike Thorolf, he did not believe that he would travel to Valhalla after death. Nor did he wish to wake up there, brawling and boozing with valiant warriors day in, day out until the end of time. His life as a warrior had ended the day the girl died by his hand. From then on, he'd traveled to sea with Thorolf and Yngvi. He had liked the change after life on the battlefields—it had been good for him. But it wasn't until he reached Catan that he found his true calling. Nothing in life had ever satisfied him as deeply as the work on his own field. But now those days were over.

Tomorrow, he decided, he would see his mother, Stina, his brothers, and their wives one last time, and then he would end his life. It was for the best—for Stina, too. He did not wish a life at the side of a one-legged man for her. With the thought of Stina's face, he finally drifted off to sleep.

Digur woke in the middle of the night. A hand was stroking his shoulder, and a warm, soft body pressed itself against his back. At first he thought it was Kaja, come to bring him comfort, but his maid smelled different. He turned around and, in the wan light of the tallow light, discerned Stina.

Careful not to touch his stump, she lay on top of him. Without uttering a word, she clasped his head between both hands and kissed his lips softly. Digur felt dumbstruck, and his first impulse was to throw her off him. But as her naked body rubbed against his, his arousal and his feelings for her won the upper hand. He returned her kiss, gently at first, then passionately, feeling his manhood grow. Stina sat up on his hips, reached for his penis, and guided it carefully into her moist vagina. Slowly, she lowered her pelvis until a brief moan of pain escaped her throat. But it did not stop her from continuing to move on him, up and down, cautiously first, and then, with growing excitement, faster and faster.

Filled with joy at this feeling of deep bonding, Digur caressed her face, her arms, her small firm breasts with their erect nipples, and, at last, he grasped her backside. Stina opened her mouth, moaning with pleasure, and threw back her head. When her chest slumped against his with a loud groan and he spilled his semen into her, he experienced almost deliriously how his longing for her became fulfilled. Wrapping his arms around her, he ran his fingers through her thick hair as they both caught their breath.

Unlike normally when he'd lie with a woman, Digur did not feel the need to be alone and send Stina away. He enjoyed holding her in his arms, listening to her breathing and feeling her body.

After a while, she began to drum her fingers on his breastbone. "Promise me something?"

"Depends," replied Digur good-humoredly.

"I move in with you and you give us a chance. If you still don't see a future for us in seven weeks' time, you may kill yourself."

Digur raised his eyebrows. "What makes you think I want to kill myself?"

"Everyone who knows you thinks you do. Your brothers and your mother believe you do. We are all terribly worried about you. Those who, like you, lose a leg, feel helpless, exposed, weak. Many find ways to cope with it—but not you. Half a Digur does not fit into your world. In your world, there can only be a whole Digur or none."

He said nothing. What could he say? She had hit the nail on the head.

"But you are strong and you will defeat your biggest enemy yet."

"Which is?"

"Your high expectations of yourself. You need to rethink those expectations and adjust them to your new situation. First you ought to learn to walk with your crutches. The way I know you, you'll soon be dancing with them." She smiled.

"You are a wise woman. I give us seven weeks." He squeezed her tight. "And then we'll see."

When the first light of day streamed through the small windows of his house, Digur sat up and positioned himself by the edge of his bed. He tried to move quietly, but Stina woke regardless.

She did not budge, watching him as he rose on his left leg

just to sit back down straight away. Evidently, he had felt dizzy. No wonder, after nearly ten days in bed. On the third attempt, he stayed up, bracing himself against the wall above her with his right arm. He took a small leap with his good leg, swayed from side to side, and paused for a while before risking another jump. She could have stood up to help him, but she wouldn't have been doing him a favor. Digur needed to accomplish the first few tasks he had set for himself on his own.

And he did. Once he reached the crutches, he stalked up and down the room a few times on them. Through half-open lids, Stina watched with joy how his grim, dogged expression relaxed a little more with each step. When he stopped by the bowl that Kaja had filled with fresh water the evening before, she thought she could glimpse a hint of hope in his face.

Digur put down one crutch, picked up a cloth, and washed half of his body. After swapping hands with the crutch, he cleaned the other side. He fished a clean shirt and a tunic from the chest, sat down on a bench, and pulled on the clothes. Then he sat unmoving for a while, seemingly in thought.

Stina stood, sat down beside him, and wrapped her arms around his neck. "How are you?"

"Better than yesterday," he grumbled, then cast a smiling glance at her naked breasts. "Are you trying to seduce me again?"

She laughed. "No, not right now." Mischief flashed in her eyes. "But better watch out for me this evening."

In that moment, Kaja opened the door and walked in. For a moment, she seemed startled to find Digur, bedbound and melancholy only the night before, dressed in fresh clothes and sitting upon a bench, but she quickly recovered. If she felt surprise at the sight of Stina naked, she knew how to hide it.

When Digur left the house, he was greeted by a warm, sunny morning. And yet this morning differed from every other morning of his life until then. This was his first morning of walking with crutches.

Gregor's house lay not far away, but the path was uneven, and every small rise and drop demanded Digur's full attention. Two children skipping toward him stopped in their tracks and stared at him with their mouths open. He limped past them, pretending not to notice. They would grow accustomed to the sight of him on crutches, just as he would perhaps learn to accept them in time.

Gregor worked under the roof he had built as a workshop next to his house. With a curved piece of iron, he was scraping an animal skin stretched inside a wooden frame to remove any remaining small hairs and uneven patches. Digur stopped outside the shelter and uttered a greeting.

Gregor broke off his work on the parchment and looked up with surprise. "You find me astonished and glad in equal measures at seeing you, Digur. I heard only yesterday you were still in your sickbed, refusing to leave it. How come you are visiting me, of all people, now?"

"I wished to thank you for the crutches. They fit. And I wanted to give you this." He asked the priest to hold one of his crutches while he pulled a small pot from his pocket. "Once I have more honey, I will thank you with a bigger pot."

Gregor beamed. "Thank you. Hilda, too, will be so pleased. But you must know that making the crutches for you was my pleasure and that you do not need to pay me for them." Gregor set the curved iron down on the table. "Come, let us sit on the bench."

For a while, they sat in silence in the shade outside Gregor's house, gazing out at the harbor where a knarr was leaving for the delta. Digur felt at ease in the presence of Gregor. The priest, who was a good two heads shorter than himself, radiated tranquility and assuredness. It seemed as if he lived in harmony with his life and the one God he believed in.

"Digur," said Gregor eventually. "I believe there is something on your mind that weighs you down—something you would like to discuss with me. In case you're afraid that I might share your secret with others, let me assure you. Even if you are not a Christian, I will keep everything you tell me to myself. I will not even share it with Hilda. That is my duty as a servant of God."

Digur read honesty and empathy in Gregor's eyes. He decided to confide in the priest and told him about the death of the girl, of his dreams, and of the astonishing similarity between her and Stina. Sometimes, he admitted to Gregor, he was unable to tell whether it was Stina gazing at him or the dead girl returned to this world.

"Stina wants to live with me, even though I'm a cripple. I'm not sure yet if I want this. But even if I did want it, there's still the dead girl between us. I want to be rid of her, but I do not know how. The gods of my people won't help me. On the contrary, I can hear them laugh at me and call me a weakling."

Gregor said nothing for a while, then asked, "What did you feel when you killed the girl?"

Digur thought about this. Slowly, he said, "I was in the middle of a fight. There was no time for feelings. Once I had defeated my opponents, I looked for the girl. I had cut open her side. She was bleeding to death, but still breathing. I couldn't just leave her lying on the ground like that, so I held her in my arms. She looked straight into my eyes and whispered something before she died."

"What did she say?"

"I think she asked, 'Why?'"

The stout priest rubbed his chin, watching Digur closely.

"What was it like when you fought? Did killing your enemies bring you satisfaction, pleasure?"

Digur shook his head. "They were all the same to me. I killed them before they killed me. I was only doing what I had been trained to do since I was a child. I was doing what my father praised me for. I feel pleasure when I look after my bees and plow my field." Digur's face turned bitter. "Which I am no longer able to do."

"Your reputation may be that of a great warrior, Digur," said Gregor gently. "But in your heart, you are a man who wishes to create and not destroy. Maybe you have always suspected as much, but you pushed the thought aside, suppressing it. The death of the girl opened your eyes—and with such clarity that the child's accusing look etched itself into your memory. To the same extent that you felt guilty for having taken the poor girl's life, you suddenly considered your life void of meaning."

Digur nodded slowly, contemplating the priest's words. "Perhaps. After that day, I left Halldor's army."

"The death of the girl touched you more deeply than you care to admit, Digur. You have no one to forgive you for your deed and free you from the burden of your guilt. That is why the girl appears in your dreams and plays tricks on you, making you believe she is looking at you through Stina's eyes."

Digur grumbled, "Forgiveness is for weaklings."

"I disagree. A weakling is a man who does not want to face the truth. Someone who would rather listen to other voices, instead of his own. You are no weakling, Digur. If you were a Christian, you could ask God for forgiveness."

"And what would your God ask in return?"

"He would expect for you to show genuine remorse for your deed, which you already have. And that you make amends to others for what you did to the girl."

Digur frowned distrustfully. "That is all—no punishment?"

"No," said Gregor with a smile. "But it isn't quite as easy as that. You would also need to live according to his commandments. If you want to learn more about the Christian faith, visit one of my services. I hold them at dawn each bath day."

Digur picked up his crutches and rose awkwardly. He wanted to be alone and ponder the priest's words.

"Hold on a moment," said Gregor.

Digur did as he asked, watching the little man scurry to his workshop on his short legs. Gregor returned with a wooden stick and a knife. He carefully pulled the trouser leg up over the bandaged stump. Then, leaning the stick against the stump, he cut a notch in the wood right at the spot where the stump ended.

"Why do you do that?" asked Digur.

"Oh, it's just an idea," said Gregor evasively. "Once you no longer need the bandage around the stump, come back here and bring some of your wax. Four big lumps, if you can, as large as your fist."

"That's a lot," said Digur, studying his large fist.

"Don't worry—you will get the wax back unharmed."

PART 7
THE ELECTION

(FALL, AD 861)

CHAPTER 20
THE FEUD

Sievert was unlucky with women. Most recently—almost a year ago now—Carla had rejected him. Following her rejection, he had almost buried his hopes of ever marrying a free woman and founding his own household. It wasn't down to his admittedly rather coarse features; Woodhaven simply had significantly fewer daughters of marriable age than sons. And Sören, his father, would first marry off Sievert's elder brothers to young women of respected families before it was his turn. He was the youngest.

At first, Sievert had not noticed her: Frauke, the tall, dark-haired young woman from Frankia who had been lent to his family as a maid by Thorolf. At first, the former slave woman had gone about her work shyly and quietly, but since she had given birth to a son a few moons ago and her mistress had welcomed the infant warmly into her household, Frauke was beginning to change back into the vivacious girl she used to be. With her sunny disposition and thoughtful nature, the family soon began to view her as a kindly spirit who had moved into their house, and Sievert, too, did not fail to notice the maid's transformation. Her high forehead and the dreamy look in her brown eyes, which gave her face an air of vulnerability, had roused his protective instincts and his interest.

Whenever there was an opportunity, he sought her out. Frauke had told him openly that she was the daughter of a tanner from Brema, and that she was raped and seized by Northmen who raided her hometown. The more familiar Frauke and Sievert became, the more talkative she grew, words pouring forth from her thin lips. Soon Sievert knew all the events, big and small, from Frauke's childhood and youth. This appealed to Sievert, who was more the quiet kind himself.

Aside from one kiss, which she tentatively returned, Sievert forbade himself to touch her. The surer he grew of his conviction that she was the right one for him, the more important it seemed to him to treat her as an honorable woman. She wasn't to blame for her little son. He would accept the infant and father his own sons with her.

When Sievert asked his father, Sören, for permission to marry Frauke, the older man replied with a hard no. "She is but a maid," he said. "She brings nothing to a marriage. Remember that, son!"

Sievert's mother, who had no reservations about having Frauke as her daughter-in-law, entreated her husband daily on the subject, always closing with her most persuasive argument: "You can't even find suitable brides for our two older sons. How is Sievert ever supposed to start his own family? Frauke is a good, hardworking woman—the best Sievert's going to find."

After three days, Sören was tired of arguing with his wife. "Very well," he told his youngest. "The maid is Thorolf's, though. If he agrees, you can marry her for all I care."

The following afternoon, Sievert went to the chieftain's house. Thorolf was sitting outside his house, listening to the worries and problems of the settlers. Sievert impatiently lined up.

When his turn finally arrived, he briefly presented his request. Thorolf did not think for long, agreeing to set Frauke free should she agree to the match.

Scarcely able to believe his luck, Sievert ran straight home. He would ask Frauke to be his wife this very day! But Frauke wasn't home. He was puzzled—normally, Frauke spun or wove with the second maid around this time.

Happily, he shared his news with his mother and inquired after Frauke's whereabouts. His mother, clearly pleased for him, said Frauke had taken a walk with her little boy since she hadn't had much time for him so far that day.

Sievert went out to search for the maid. It was around the time of the autumn moon; the days were becoming noticeably shorter, and dusk wasn't far away. When he had searched the village for her in vain, he rushed down to the lake. At last he spotted Frauke, sitting on the jetty with her son on her arm. But she wasn't alone.

Sievert's breath caught when he recognized the man who was placing an arm around her in a familiar gesture, kissing the spot where her neck met her shoulder. It was Einar, that coxcomb, acting as if he wanted to add Frauke to his long list of conquests.

Einar often bragged about how easy it was to bed the maids. He never considered taking them against their will—one look and one smile from him were all it took and the maid was his.

Sievert felt the blood rush to his head. He started running toward them. Frauke was holding her head tilted away from Einar as he nibbled on her ear. They only noticed Sievert once the wooden planks vibrated under his feet. Frauke started with fright when she saw her master's son storm toward her, his face twisted with anger. She tightened her hold on her child and anxiously scooted away from Einar. The latter rose and waited for his rival with a bored expression on his face.

Spittle flew from Sievert's lips as he roared at him. "Take your dirty fingers off my bride!"

Einar glanced calmly at his hands. "I see no dirt. But who knows where *your* fingers have been?" He gave Sievert a sneering smile. "Since Carla turned you down and not even the maids will open their hearts to you, there are always our cows."

Seething with rage, Sievert grabbed Einar by the collar with his left hand and raised his right. Einar, who would be at a disadvantage in a fight with this burly opponent, drew his dagger. But before he had a chance to use it, Sievert's fury-laden fist struck him in the middle of the face. Einar's nose cracked, and he went down, the world going black before his eyes.

Frauke cried out, and her infant son began to wail. Sievert walked off the jetty without as much as glancing at her. She ran after him, assailing him with words, wanting to know what he had meant by "bride." Sievert, however, trudged on, ignoring her.

Einar came to when he heard the fishermen laughing at him. The men were in the process of mooring the *Shieldmaiden* at the jetty, and evidently they had witnessed his humiliation.

"Must have kissed the wrong one," one of the fishermen jeered.

Another one joked, "Where is the anvil pretty Einar landed on?"

They all broke out in laughter again.

Only one of the men did not join in with the mirth. It was Einar's father, Fenrir, staring at him grimly. Einar felt deeply humiliated. His honor was smeared.

The morning sky gleamed an autumnal blue, promising a fair and mild day. A cool breeze blew from the mountains, carrying a foul stench to the men as they approached the pig enclosure. Later on, servants would shovel the stinking dung onto a cart and spread it on the fields as fertilizer.

The pig farmers pushed the oinking animals out of the pen and sorted them according to their brands. Soon each farmer led his small herd to a different spot by the edge of the woods, each accompanied by men armed with swords, bows, and spears.

Hakon did not speak much as he patrolled the area around the herd with Einar and Sievert. The farmer used the shaft of his spear to keep the rooting pigs close together. The men's eyes constantly scanned the sea of ferns and the maze of mossy tree trunks for any suspicious movements.

When the sun reached its highest point in the sky and there was no sign of any wolfhounds, they sat down on a fallen log in a small clearing and ate the food they'd brought. Hakon kept an eye on his two companions; decades of experience with men of many different crews had endowed him with a keen sense for trouble. And his sense did not deceive him now.

Einar touched his nose, bluish-green and crooked since Sievert's punch. Then he asked, "Hey, Sievert, have you ever even been between a woman's legs?"

Sievert stared at the last bit of cheese in his hand, ignoring Einar.

Feigning friendliness, Einar answered his own question in a gentle voice. "Hardly, you poor sod. With your face, even the chickens run away from you."

Hakon shot Einar a sharp look. "Shut your mouth!"

But Einar had different ideas. "I heard it was a troll who mounted the whore that is your mother and fathered you."

While Sievert had managed to ignore the mockery of his

appearance, his honor forbade him from suffering the insult to his mother. Rising to his feet, he slowly drew his sword.

Einar looked thrilled. With an arrogant sneer on his face, he, too, stood, unsheathing his own sword. "Better watch your feet, troll bastard. You don't want to trip over your blade."

Hakon leaped up and stepped between the young men with his hands raised, snarling at them with all the authority he could muster. "Quit your childish games! Sheath your swords and sit back down!"

Einar pointed his blade at Hakon's throat. "Keep out of this, old man! Our quarrel is none of your business."

Sievert agreed with his opponent. "I cannot ignore his serious insults. You know that, Hakon. Einar must pay for them, if not today, then tomorrow. So step aside!"

Hakon understood the young man. Ignoring Einar's defamation would cost Sievert the respect of the settlers—Einar would make sure of it. The farmer eagerly watching the events from the edge of the clearing would probably also report Sievert's cowardice and dishonor. Then, in the future, the villagers would call Sievert "troll bastard," and there would be nothing Sievert could do about it. Hakon accepted that he was powerless in the face of the impending disaster. He lowered his arms in resignation and cleared the space between the two young men.

Sievert and Einar circled each other watchfully. Each kept his eyes on both his opponent and the treacherous forest floor at the same time. The groundcover was mostly trodden down, but underneath the green leaves, there could easily lurk a branch or rock to trip them up.

Sievert attacked first.

When metal struck metal, all the pigeons in the vicinity ceased their cooing, and the mournful cawing of a raven also fell silent. Soon the only sounds nearby were the bright clanking and shrill whirring of blades meeting and scraping along each other, and the gasping breaths and angry shouts of the combatants.

Hakon had no choice but to watch the fight of the two young men. They weren't doing too badly, though Einar's style struck Hakon as more mature and superior to that of Sievert's. It was obvious that both had been attending the weekly combat lessons Thorolf had ordered among all freemen following Ryan's visit.

Sievert aimed a powerful blow at his opponent's head, but Einar blocked it with little difficulty. However, the poorly worked iron did not hold up to the blow and broke. Sievert's blade was slowed, but his blow still carried some force as it struck Einar's unprotected head. Einar dropped the hilt of his sword and groaned as he sank to the ground, blood streaming from the head wound.

Sievert paused for a moment, grappling with himself. But in the end, hatred and anger won, and Sievert thrust his sword deep into his opponent's chest.

For a while, there was perfect silence. Hakon only stirred when the pigeons resumed their cooing and the raven cawed as if nothing had happened. Without speaking, he picked up both pieces of the broken sword, placing the hilt in Einar's hand and arranging the snapped blade above it. Then he spoke a few traditional words, intended to accompany the fallen man on his journey to Valhalla.

Einar's body was burned by the lake. Thorolf watched the assembled crowd with concern. Many had come to pay their final respects to the dead boy. Apparently Sievert and his father, Sören, also viewed it as their duty to acknowledge with their presence the fair duel Einar and Sievert had fought and Einar's subsequent honorable death. A little off to the side stood Fenrir the Red with his two younger sons, the twins Finn and Lasse. The three men stared stony-faced at the flickering flames.

When the fire began to lose strength and the pyre collapsed amid a cloud of sparks, cracking loudly, Fenrir and his sons started to shout insults and death threats at Sievert, who listened to the abuse with a grim expression. Before the situation escalated, Thorolf broke up the gathering and asked his brothers as well as Sievert, Sören, and Fenrir to follow him to his house.

The men sat down in silence. Digur cursed, struggling with his crutches as he tried to lift his good leg over the bench. Yngvi tried to help him, but Digur snarled at him, "I don't need help."

Inconspicuous as ever, Ilka darted across the hall, carrying a jug of ale and cups to the table. Asla handed Jora, who was over a year old by now, to the maid and sat down beside her husband.

Thorolf looked the fisherman straight in the eye as he spoke. "Fenrir, I am sorry for the death of your son. I share your deep pain. But that does not give you the right to threaten Sievert with death. He defeated Einar honorably in combat."

The fisherman's face flushed deep red. He uttered a vile curse and slammed his fist onto the table. His pale-blue eyes blazed with hatred when he pointed a finger at Sievert and roared, "He attacked. For no reason. The fight was decided when Einar lay on the ground, bleeding. And yet this damned son of a whore gave him the death blow. He must pay for that." To underline his words, he thumped the table again, making the jug and the cups dance.

Thorolf admonished the fisherman sharply. "Moderate yourself! You are a guest in my house."

The silence that followed was broken when Yngvi addressed Fenrir. "Hakon told us your son insulted Sievert gravely, calling his mother a whore and claiming she had lain with a troll."

"So what?" intoned the fisherman in his deep voice. "That

was retribution for the broken nose the bastard had given him, and for the humiliation in front of the fishermen. I myself was there when they all laughed at Einar."

Thorolf tried to reason with Fenrir. "Do you really wish to start a blood feud with Sören's family? Do you believe Sören will simply accept it if you kill one of his sons? One of your twin boys would be next." Thorolf glanced at Sören, who nodded in agreement. "And then it would be your turn to take revenge again. And in the end, you will have wiped out your entire families. You know the bitter fates of families in our homeland who followed the rule of the blood feud."

When Thorolf thought the fisherman was beginning to think it over, he pressed on. "I know you are no fool, Fenrir. You won't soak the soil of our new home with the blood of your family and that of Sören's."

The fisherman said nothing.

Sören stood up, walked around the table, and stopped in front of Fenrir. The quiet, peaceable farmer placed a hand on the angry fisherman's shoulder. Fenrir let him. "Until yesterday, we were friends, Fenrir. We exchanged fish for grain and helped each other in times of need. Until our sons started their quarrel, we lived as good neighbors." Sören increased the pressure of his hand. "Let us not argue over which one of our sons has laden more guilt upon himself. I'll admit that Sievert had his part in this. Your son paid with his life. Now tell me—what is the punishment that would pay Sievert's debt in your eyes?"

Fenrir visibly fought with himself. Most likely, he wished to shout "Death!"—but Thorolf would never agree to that. Eventually he said from between clenched teeth, "I demand twenty lashes as payment. One bloody streak for each year of my son's life, on the back of his murderer." He looked at Sören. "And I want one of your servants to replace Einar's hands."

Thorolf thought for some time before pronouncing his judgment. "Twelve lashes shall be enough. Sievert might not survive twenty. Since Einar would have lived in your household for two more years at the most, let Sören give you his servant for that amount of time." He looked at both men in turns. "Agreed?"

Sören hesitated for a moment; then he agreed and returned to his seat. Fenrir looked at his feet, grinding his teeth. It seemed he could not bring himself to consent.

Suddenly, Sievert stood up. Until then, he had listened to the discussions over his fate in silence. Planting both fists upon the table, he leaned toward Fenrir. "I, too, do not wish for a feud between our families," he said in a calm, firm voice. "Least of all do I want to remain in your debt. I agree to the twenty lashes you demand."

Fenrir appeared surprised; his expression even betrayed a hint of respect. Then he gave Sievert a cynical smile. "We'll see if you still talk brave when my whip plows through your flesh." Turning to Thorolf, he growled, "I agree with your verdict."

"Then swear by the gods that you will not pursue a blood feud with Sören's family."

"I swear by the gods," muttered the fisherman, who rose and walked out of the house.

When, a while later, Sören and Sievert had also left, Asla sighed deeply. "I feel sorry for Sievert. I once watched when my father punished disobedience by a follower with twenty whiplashes. The warrior's wounded back became infected, and he died a few days later."

Yngvi sipped his mint water. "Sievert is going to need your

care afterward. And your ointment." He winked at Digur. "It worked a miracle for my big brother."

Digur merely nodded, reached for his crutches, and made to leave. Yngvi asked him to stay. "I have something important to tell you and Thorolf."

Asla rose, intending to leave the brothers alone, but Yngvi held her back by the arm. "I would like you to hear what I have to say."

Clearing his throat, Yngvi looked Thorolf straight in the eye. "You and Digur, you are my brothers. Together we've been through thick and thin. I love you both, and far be it from me to harm either of you. I hope you don't doubt this when I explain what's on my mind."

His curiosity aroused, Thorolf leaned forward encouragingly. "Out with it, little brother. Is there another maid you would like me to set free? Or do you perhaps wish me to release all maids and servants?" Amused by his own joke, Thorolf laughed. The tension that had been evident in his face during the conversation with Sören and Fenrir fell away from him, discharging in the form of pure mirth.

When his laughing fit subsided and he wiped the tears from his eyes, Yngvi asked, "Would you be willing, following the election, to forgo the title of jarl, instead introducing a form of rule that Gregor calls democracy?"

"Demo—what?"

Yngvi gave a small smile. "Democracy. You don't need to remember the word. It means that all heads of families vote men onto a council for a period of time. This council makes our laws and designates one among them who ensures that those laws are adhered to. That man can also make decisions by himself, provided they don't go against the laws and decisions from the council. You could be that man."

Thorolf was still grinning as he answered Yngvi good-naturedly, "You're crazy, little brother. The laws of our people have been tried and tested for centuries. A council like the one you propose sounds like a heap of bickering fishwives, unable to reach the right decisions. No. One man must rule and tell the people which way to go. And that man will be me."

Yngvi wasn't surprised at Thorolf's reply, even if he had hoped his brother would show a little more wisdom. "If that is the case, then you leave me no other choice. In the upcoming election of our future jarl, I will stand against you."

In the silence that followed, one could have heard a sewing needle drop on the dirt floor.

Thorolf jutted out his jaw, staring at his brother in disbelief. "You will . . . what? Become jarl? Have you lost your mind?" He scrutinized Yngvi as if seeing him for the first time. "You do not possess the authority required for the position. You are not a good swordsman. How do you intend to reprimand a rebellious farmer if he knows that you cannot defeat him in a fight? And besides, it was I who bought the livestock, the grain, and the tools and led the settlers here."

"Yes, but all that was only possible thanks to the whale oil. If I remember right, you said that we slew the whale together."

"And that is what gives you a claim to the title of jarl?" demanded Thorolf harshly.

"No. If I get elected, I will have the heads of households choose a council. Then I will relinquish the title."

In the back of the house, Jora began to wail. Asla called for Ilka, and the maid brought her the little girl, who calmed immediately when Asla put her to her breast. Yngvi thought it was unusual that his sister-in-law did not withdraw to nurse. Obviously Asla did not want to miss a word.

Yngvi waited for a reply from Thorolf, but the latter appeared to be at a loss for words. Yngvi reiterated that he would step down immediately following the election of the council. Still Thorolf said nothing, staring sourly at his cup while Ilka brought a wooden board with bread and cheese to the table.

Digur reached for a piece of bread and dipped it into the soft cheese. As he chewed, he turned to Yngvi. "Why should the council make laws? We already have laws."

Yngvi was pleased about Digur's question. His brother's interest was testament to his newly awakened will to live. "Today we witnessed where the laws of our old homeland lead us. Those laws do not forbid a man from repaying an insult with the sword. They allow the blood feud, which can wipe out entire families. I ask you—are those laws good laws? Are they suitable for a peaceful life in a land that provides us with plenty of food and promises wealth? Do you want bloody feuds to poison our future on Catan?" Yngvi did something he had never done before. He slammed his flat palm onto the table. "I say no!"

As Yngvi had intended, Thorolf lost interest in his cup and looked up at him with surprise. The furrow between Asla's brows, however, had not been intended. Jora, startled at the sudden noise, had choked on some milk.

Thorolf found his words. "Why do you not have faith in my ability to be a good chief to our people and rule them wisely?"

"I do have faith in your ability, brother. You are the best. But you could be struck down by disease tomorrow. Then who will be your successor? The strongest man? The best sword fighter? Or the loudest man, dazzling our people with big speeches? A man like Fenrir who would instantly set out to remove the chain wielders from the island, leading us into bloody battle?" Yngvi drank a sip from his cup, then paused for a few moments. "Yes, we need a man to lead us. But this man must not have unlimited powers. He must adhere to the laws and decisions of the men who were voted onto the council."

Asla handed Jora back to Ilka. The little girl was satisfied now, babbling happily. "I like your idea, Yngvi. But you only speak of men. There are women, too, who are the heads of their families, like Hedda or Gerhild, who lost their husbands. Should they not also have the right to vote on the members of the councils—or even to stand for council themselves?" She cast a defiant look at Thorolf. "And no man should be allowed to chase his wife naked through the village, chastising her."

Thorolf glowered at his wife. "You're sticking a knife into my back, too, like my brother?"

Asla tried to place an appeasing hand on her husband's, but he withdrew his hand, vexed. Yngvi regretted having worsened the tensions between Thorolf and Asla with his speech, but that was something he would have to accept if he wished to do away with the laws and customs of the old country. "I agree with you, sister-in-law. There needs to be a new law for the punishment of adultery, and women who lead a family ought to have the same rights as men."

Thorolf gave an artificial laugh. "Then I declare your endeavor doomed from the outset. The men will never accept women as their equal. And so they will vote for me."

"I would not be so certain, Thorolf," said Digur. "More than a few of the headmen are tired of the never-ending conflicts and blood feuds of the old country. They want a peaceful life on Catan, and they will welcome the establishment of a council. I daresay they would accept this concession to the women."

"You too?!" roared Thorolf, rising to his feet, his face flushed red with fury, and tossed his cup at Digur's mighty chest. Without another word, he stamped out the door and slammed it shut with a loud bang.

Jora, who had been playing quietly in the back of the house with wooden animals made for her by Thorolf, started to cry loudly. Ilka picked her up and hummed her a soothing lullaby.

"I feel like I have lived through a very similar moment before," mused Asla.

"You have," said Yngvi, remembering. "When our father, Ulrik, furious about your escape and the death of your brother, stormed out of his hall."

"True," said Asla. "And your mother predicted that Ulrik would soon calm himself."

"And so will Thorolf," said Digur. "He is becoming more like our father all the time."

Yngvi nodded. "The traditions of our people are deeply ingrained in him, and he spurns new ideas. If he could, he would board a ship in the blink of an eye and set out on trade voyages or to raid the monasteries and halls of Britain, just like Father."

Asla looked at the brothers. Her smile was soft, vulnerable. Even though Thorolf had changed, she still loved him.

Sievert's punishment was carried out on the village square. Many settlers had come to watch, forming a circle around Sievert and Fenrir.

Hungry for drama, most spectators waited for the first lash, curious to see whether Sievert would bear the pain like a man, though the faces of Sievert's family gazed with worry at their son and brother. Sievert was kneeling in front of Fenrir with his back bared, bracing himself with seemingly stoical calm on the hard ground. His teeth were clenched on a piece of wood. Thorolf stood next to Fenrir to see that the punishment was executed correctly. In his hand the fisherman held a whip, its tail made of leather that had been knotted in several places. Thorolf signaled for him to begin.

An evil smile played on Fenrir's thin lips as he raised his arm high and whacked the leather rope onto the naked back with all his strength. A low, suppressed moan escaped Sievert's chest when the very first lash tore open his skin in a bloody streak. The fifth lash still brought Fenrir enormous satisfaction. On the seventh lash, he started to ask himself with growing impatience when Sievert would finally drop the piece of wood and scream out his pain. When would his son's murderer finally whimper for mercy? Only then would his hatred become bearable. But Sievert did not oblige, responding to each whiplash with nothing more than an agonized moan. When Fenrir, his face a mask of grim determination, brought down the whip for the tenth time, blood splattered on him and Thorolf. More blood ran down Sievert's back in thin rivulets, saturating the soil. After the sixteenth lash, Sievert collapsed, unconscious. Only his mother's sobs could be heard in the silence that followed.

The eagerness had vanished from the faces of the crowd. Instead they gazed, partly upset, partly admiring, at the broken body of Sievert, who had borne the torture of his punishment valiantly. Vast areas of his back were reduced to a bloody mass.

The fisherman weighed the whip in his hand indecisively. Tormenting the unconscious youth further would not bring him satisfaction. Sievert would not even feel the pain. The murderer of his son had won the unequal fight. Against his will, Fenrir felt respect and esteem for the young man grow inside him. He lowered the whip. "That's enough."

Immediately, Sören and his two sons rushed over to Sievert, who was lying on his stomach, and carried him to their house.

Sievert awoke with a soft groan. Asla spoke soothingly to the injured man as she cleaned his maltreated back with a clean linen cloth which she had soaked in her warm herb concoction. Before she left, she gave instructions to Sievert's mother and to Frauke, the maid, as to the further treatment of the patient. She told them that he ought to spend the coming night on his stomach and move as little as possible. Handing a clay pot to the maid, Asla told her to apply the ointment as soon as the wounds had formed scabs. Asla would come back the next day to check on him.

Hesitantly, Frauke asked whether Sievert would recover.

Asla gave the worried young woman a look of encouragement. "If you apply the cream with clean hands, not too much and not too little, and if the wounds don't become infected, his chances are good."

The maid nodded gratefully and opened the door for Asla. Then, with a deep sigh, Frauke returned to Sievert and picked up his hand. He allowed it. She liked him. If he survived and if he'd still have her, she would make him a good and loyal wife.

CHAPTER 21

OX GALL

Asla was on her way home when Edna came running toward her. Breathing heavily, the former maid said between gasps, "Mistress, I searched for you everywhere. You have to come with me. Carla's child is coming."

"No rush, Edna. Children usually don't get born this quickly," said Asla with a smile. "Oh, and do call me by my name instead of 'Mistress.' I hear Yngvi has given you your freedom."

"Yes, though I don't even wish to be free," admitted Edna as they walked to Yngvi's house. "I am happy in Carla's household, much happier than I was with the master I served before the Northmen took me."

Asla laughed. "I hear you. If I were born unfree, I would choose Carla for my mistress."

The two women heard Carla's loud groans before they reached the house. When Asla opened the door, Yngvi rushed toward her, beside himself, shouting in a panicked voice: "Help her, she's dying!"

Asla grinned. Yngvi had most likely never witnessed a birth

and was unaware of the pain a woman suffered as her child strained to be born.

Gently, she pushed her brother-in-law to the door. "Women suffer when they give birth. It is normal. You know that, don't you?"

Yngvi nodded uncertainly. But when the next wave of labor pains gripped Carla, her shrill cries sounding as if a troll were ramming a knife into her guts, he made to rush back to his wife's side.

Asla stopped him decidedly. "Go away now and stop bothering me and Edna while we help Carla. Go to Gregor and Hilda's. Edna will fetch you as soon as your child is born."

Yngvi finally relented. Relieved, Asla closed the door behind him and prepared for the impending birth.

Gregor and Hilda welcomed the soon-to-be father with a warm embrace. Eager to put him at ease, they fetched some ale, inviting him to sit at the table outside their house. Gregor had recently completed a roof that jutted out from the house's front, providing pleasant shelter from the searing midday sun.

Hilda, bouncing babbling little Johannes on her knee, shared a tale of gossip, and then Gregor told him of a young free couple whom he had baptized the week before. Yngvi hardly listened to the meaningless chatter the two of them spouted in an attempt to distract him from his woes. His thoughts kept returning to Carla, willing Edna to appear and release him from the torment of uncertainty.

But time stretched mercilessly. He measured it in the sun's slow progress across the sky and in the number of ales he drank. Finally, after the fifth cup, Edna appeared with a happy smile that lit up her entire face.

Yngvi sprang to his feet. "So?"

"You have a healthy daughter. And before you ask: Carla is well."

Relieved to no end, Yngvi rushed to his house. The door stood open, and Asla received him with a forefinger pressed to her mouth. "Sssh, Carla is sleeping. The birth wasn't easy and cost her a lot of strength."

Yngvi sneaked to his wife's bed. The normally full, dark hair stuck to her sweaty skin. Her pale face and the tiny veins gleaming through the delicate skin of her eyelids made her appear ill and fragile. The newborn in her arms, on the other hand, looked healthy and contented, with its smooth, rosy skin. As if it were trying to yawn, it opened its little mouth wide, and a little fist found its way inside. Busily the infant began to suckle.

Yngvi bent over his wife, grasped her hand, and planted a gentle kiss on her forehead.

Carla's eyes opened, and she beamed at him blissfully. "Isn't she beautiful?"

"Yes, she is," he said, adding with a proud smile, "She takes after her mother."

As if his little daughter wished to prove him wrong, she dropped her fist from her mouth and scrunched up her tiny face, whining unhappily.

"What is it?" asked Yngvi.

"She's hungry," said Asla, amused. "What else?" She picked up her bag and headed for the door. "I'll leave you now. I'll come back to check on you tomorrow."

Carla smiled at her. "I thank you for being by my side. I couldn't have done this without you."

Asla was visibly pleased at her words. As she walked out, she drew Edna along. "Let's leave those two alone for a while."

In the silence that followed, Yngvi relished watching his wife nurse their little daughter. "What shall we name her?"

Carla thought for a moment. "Frida."

"Frida?" repeated Yngvi, astonished. "Why do you want to give our daughter her name?"

"I liked Frida very much. If she had not taken her life, I'm sure we would have become friends." Her dark eyes were full of tenderness. "You loved her, and I know that I must share a part of your heart with her."

"Yes, but—" said Yngvi, embarrassed.

Carla gently closed his lips with the forefinger of her free hand. "Don't say anything. I accept it. If we give her name to our daughter, then Frida becomes a part of us rather than standing between us."

Yngvi kissed her forehead for a second time. "Frida was the great love of my past. You, however, are my great love of now and always."

Yngvi had taken the *Shieldmaiden* out to sea. Despite the meager catch, he was in the best of spirits, for in the last two days, he had managed to draw three fishermen onto his side. Using all his powers of persuasion, he had reasoned with them, explaining the advantages of a council, and eventually convinced them to elect him as their jarl. Now he looked forward to seeing his little daughter, folding Carla into his arms, and sharing his success with her.

But it wasn't his wife welcoming him at the door this evening, but Asla, her face serious. "Quietly. Carla is asleep."

Yngvi looked at Carla, who was lying on their bed with her eyes closed. On the ground beside her, Edna was bending over little Frida, changing her diapers.

Asla shook her head in concern. "Your wife has a high fever. Edna says Carla was feeling weak around noontime, and that she was feeling sick and dizzy. Then she lay down and has been sleeping ever since."

Yngvi felt disquieted. "What is it? Is it something bad?" He hoped his sister-in-law would respond with an amused smile, telling him he was overanxious, reassuring him that he needn't worry.

But her face remained serious, her eyes taking on a sympathetic gleam. "If I'm not mistaken, Carla is suffering from childbed fever."

Yngvi felt as though someone was pulling the ground out from under his feet. He had heard of the treacherous illness which hardly any woman survived. Harald's maid had died from it recently. He could feel the blood drain from his face.

Asla took his arm and led him to the bench. "Sit down, Yngvi." She offered him a cup holding a bitter brew. "Drink. I gave some of this to Carla to strengthen her—it won't hurt you to take some of it, too."

Yngvi accepted the cup in an automatic gesture and drained it without batting an eyelid. After sitting in silence for a while, he looked up at Asla. "Is there anything you can do for her?"

Asla, knowing that her brother-in-law needed a tiny spark of hope, was willing to give it to him. "Oda, the wise woman who taught me so much, successfully cured two women from childbed fever."

Yngvi listened up. The color of his face took on a healthier tone. "Do you know how?"

"Yes, I know the recipe."

"But it did not work for Abena," he observed glumly.

"It doesn't always work. But when Abena lay ill, I was missing an important ingredient to make the medicine for childbed fever. And I'm still missing that ingredient today."

Yngvi felt a spark of hope. "What ingredient? I'll find it!"

"I need ox gall."

He gave her a confused look. "Ox gall? Won't gall of a normal cow do?"

Asla shrugged. "No idea. Oda always spoke of ox gall. I think we ought not to take any risks. Better to use the precise ingredient that worked for Oda."

Yngvi thought. Over a year ago, Thorolf castrated the first bull calves born on Catan so that they would grow into docile oxen for the farmers. By now the animals were almost grown. "I am going to ask my brother to let me have an ox."

Asla tilted her head skeptically. "Since Thorolf knows of your claim to the title of jarl, he is not well-disposed toward you."

Yngvi nodded. "I will persuade him."

Thorolf was cool and reserved when he received Yngvi. He did not ask his brother to sit. Instead, Asla offered her brother-in-law a seat at the table, asking Ilka to bring ale, bread, and cheese.

"What do you want?" asked Thorolf harshly.

Yngvi explained to his brother how sick Carla was. Then he asked him for an ox so that Asla might use its gall to produce the medicine.

Thorolf gave a jeering laugh. "You want me to slaughter a precious draft animal for a scrap of gall? For a potion that only works in my wife's imagination? Forget it."

Asla drew her eyebrows together, grooves of anger furrowing her forehead.

Not long ago, thought Yngvi, his brother had treated Asla with more respect. Not long ago, he wouldn't have mocked her healing skills thus. But Thorolf had changed. His conduct had waxed more selfish, imperious, and overbearing. Rarely these days did he relent in a discussion, unable to respect any opinion different from his own. He reveled in the role of the leader who decided everything, wisely steering the fortunes of his subjects while relishing their reverence.

Yngvi still believed in his brother's leadership skills, and he would have liked to see him as the foreman of a Catan council, but he knew that, to Thorolf, he was a traitor to his own flesh and blood, opposing him and challenging his sole leadership of the settlers. And a traitor—even if it was his own brother—couldn't expect leniency from Thorolf.

And so Yngvi did not even try to arouse Thorolf's empathy, asking soberly, "What do you want for the ox?"

Thorolf stared at him silently for a while, tugging on his earlobe, just like their father, Ulrik, used to do when he was thinking. Thorolf probably wondered whether he should deign to bargain with him. Yngvi did not believe his brother would ask him to abandon his claim to the title of jarl, for if he did, Thorolf would concede that Yngvi was a serious rival. Pride would forbid him any such move. But the cunning twinkle in his elder brother's eyes led Yngvi to believe that Thorolf was hatching something nasty.

"As you know, the storm in the summer took the *Goldeagle* from me. I need a replacement. Give me your *Shieldmaiden* and you can have your ox."

Yngvi moved no muscle in his face. He would not grant Thorolf the pleasure of seeing him shocked. A knarr was more valuable by far than an ox. Yngvi might not have been a passionate seaman, but the *Shieldmaiden* had carried him to Catan and enabled him to make a living from fishing. He had grown fond of his ship, and without it, he would struggle to feed his small family. And Thorolf knew all that. Yngvi briefly considered bartering with him, offering him shares in his catch or perhaps his two horses. But he thought he could tell, by his brother's look, that Thorolf would not accept a compromise.

If he weighed up the *Shieldmaiden*'s worth against the chance that Carla might live, as small as that chance might be, there was only one answer he could give: "Agreed."

Thorolf's eyebrows shot up. Evidently, he had expected Yngvi to haggle with him for the ox. If he had hoped to watch Yngvi squirm like a worm on a fishing hook to ease his anger, then his younger brother had denied him this.

Asla, who had listened to the brothers' negotiation, clearly felt ashamed at her husband's disgraceful demand. "Besides ox gall," she snapped at him, "I require some of your wine to make the medicine. What do you want for it? I do not own a knarr. I cannot promise you a son. In your eyes, what is an incapable healer like myself able to offer you so that she may try to save the life of a dear friend? Would our future great jarl like me to kiss his feet every day, or would you perhaps like to have your way with me twice in a row each night? I am prepared to pay this price."

Thorolf stared at his wife in disbelief. He had been made to feel her sharp tongue many times before, but never had she been this cold and hurtful. He clearly struggled to contain his seething fury.

"Take the wine and the damned ox. And you, *brother*," he said, turning to Yngvi, spitting the word "brother" with a mixture of mockery and contempt, "you can keep your *Shieldmaiden* if I am elected jarl. If not, she is mine. Your choice."

That night, Thorolf was unfaithful for the first time. He led the first maid he came across who seemed willing to the meadow beyond Woodhaven. She moaned with rapture as he thrust hard into her. Maybe she thought it was lust and pleasure spurring his performance, but in truth, it was the disappointment in his wife and anger at his brother that he vented on the warm female body beneath.

Högni and Diara had helped Asla butcher the ox and distribute the meat among their friends. Asla started work on the medicine the same day. For seven days, she explained to Yngvi, the various ingredients needed to rest in a copper pot before she would be able to give Carla the medicine.

When Yngvi sat down beside Carla in the evening, stroking her hair, she woke up. She was feeling a little better, she told him, and she even managed to eat something. Just a little porridge was all she had been able to force down, she admitted. She worried she would soon run out of milk for little Frida.

Yngvi held up a small clay jar. "Asla made this for you. Apparently, it's powerful enough to bring the dead back to life," he said jokingly, even though he didn't feel like it. Then, using a wooden spoon, he gave her a portion of the tonic.

"Tastes good," she said, eyeing the yellowish-brown mass. "What is it made of?"

"No idea," said Yngvi with a shrug. "Asla told me all the herbs and substances. But the only ingredient I remember is the honey Digur gave her. Apparently, it is a very special honey, but don't ask me what it is that makes it so special."

During the seven days, there were phases when Carla was awake and felt better. Then she would eat and drink a little. Usually, afterward, she would be sick, vomiting up the little she had consumed. Whenever Edna placed little Frida on Carla's chest, it was obvious how much the young mother loved stroking her daughter's soft, fluffy hair and feeding her the little milk she had left.

Digur and Stina came to visit, and Stina tried to cheer Carla by telling her funny tales from the village. But Stina was the only one who laughed.

Digur said nothing, merely taking Carla's dainty hand in his large paw and squeezing it gently. The message in his sympathetic blue eyes was clear: *Fight!* She returned the pressure of his hand, smiling at him gratefully.

Most of the time, however, Carla suffered from a high fever, only noticing at the edge of her consciousness when Edna or Yngvi cooled her hot limbs with wet cloths or washed her. When she felt Yngvi's arms around her at night and he whispered softly to her, words whose sense she scarcely discerned, then she felt safe, no longer fearing death, which was spreading its dark wings above her.

At last, the morning arrived when Asla's medicine was ready. Carla swallowed it obligingly and did so again in the afternoon. But still her condition worsened. Carla was rarely awake for longer periods now. Little Frida cried when Edna plucked her off her mother's chest. Carla's milk had dried up at last.

Like every evening, Hilda came to visit the patient. After she had taken the starved girl under her wing back in Hedeby, Carla had blossomed into a pretty young woman. But now, Hilda observed, with fright, Carla's physical state was reverting to its former pitiful condition. The girl's cheeks were sunken and her limbs bony. Her eyes shone with fever, gazing at Hilda sadly.

"I have no more milk for my daughter," Carla whispered with dry, cracked lips.

Only then did Hilda grow conscious of the wailing infant. Edna was sitting on a stool, using a wet cloth to drip water into the babe's mouth.

"Give her to me," she said in a tone that allowed no contradiction. "I have enough milk for two."

That night, the weather changed. Rain swept across Catan from the north. When Yngvi stepped outside his house in the morning, the gray, cloud-covered sky seemed to him like a mirror of his soul, gloomy and ominous.

Even though he did not really believe in the gods of his people, a small corner of his mind thought that perhaps they existed after all—and if so, he feared he might have made them envious over his bliss with Carla. Then he thought of the other God, the God of love and forgiveness, the God he had pledged himself to. This God would not be envious, Yngvi thought.

He stayed with Carla the entire day, and she continued to be feverish and delirious despite Asla's medicine. Hilda came by several times to nurse little Frida, and in the afternoon, Gregor came to sit with Carla.

Carla was pale and marked from the illness. Her eyes were closed. Her long, dark eyelashes twitched like the wings of a tiny bird, giving her face an air of lightness, as well as vulnerability. To Yngvi, it seemed as though Carla's soul was preparing to leave her body and float away on the breeze. He noticed her hand, clutching the wooden cross tightly, like it was the last anchor still tying her to life.

As if his gloomy thoughts had touched Carla somehow, she opened her eyes and recognized Gregor next to him.

"Will he help me?" she asked the priest in a thin voice.

Gregor covered her hand with his. "He is with you. You know it in your heart, and you can feel it in the cross. Whatever happens, God is not going to leave your side."

Carla nodded, pulling her dry lips into a brave, small smile. With a finger of his right hand, Gregor drew an invisible cross on Carla's forehead. "Let us pray."

Yngvi sat down next to Gregor and took Carla's free hand into his. He wanted to cry. Would he again have to suffer the loss of a beloved? Did the God he'd decided to follow wish to test his faith?

For his wife's sake, he pulled himself together, not permitting his lips to betray him with a twitch. Carla was aware of her dire state, and yet she still carried a spark of hope. And he did not want to take away that hope by spilling graveside tears before her eyes.

Gregor spoke the Paternoster together with Yngvi. Edna and Hilda, who sat on a stool with an infant at each breast, fell in with the prayer. Carla, too, whispered the first few words before falling asleep.

Yngvi remained alone by his wife's bed. Carla's breathing was quick and shallow. Her lids twitched as if she were dreaming heavily. Yngvi folded his hands and prayed to God. He thought of many things he could offer God in exchange for Carla's life: his ship, his house, his sword, his horses—for all those things would seem worthless to him if his wife died. He was prepared to attend Gregor's services regularly, trade smoked fish for sheep so that he could sacrifice the animals, or speak one hundred Paternosters every day. But Gregor had explained to him that the Lord did not bargain. And so he refrained from bartering with God the way he used to do with the gods of the North. Instead, he prayed quietly. "Lord, do not take my wife from me, and Frida's mother from her. Have mercy on us and show us a miracle."

No sooner had he finished speaking when he heard Gregor's voice in his mind, telling him that God did not interfere with the lives of people. If he followed God's path of love, then God would give him the strength to work the occasional miracle himself. Even though his friend had preached those words many times, Yngvi brushed them aside, stubbornly repeating his plea to God, begging him to spare Carla's life.

He was awakened in the middle of the night by his wife's groans. Fear tightened his chest. Was her life ending? Anxiously he leaned over her and saw that Carla had kicked the blanket off. Her shirt and her bare skin were wet with sweat.

"What is it?" he asked, hoping she might hear him.

"I'm hot," replied Carla sleepily and turned to the other side. Soon her regular breathing told Yngvi that she had gone back to sleep.

Carla's condition had changed. Yngvi wasn't certain whether sweating was a good sign, but he hoped it desperately. He lay awake for a long while, listening to Carla's breathing while he debated with God.

Carla woke him with a gentle nudge. "I'm hungry and thirsty."

Her eyes were no longer dulled from fever, now gazing at him with love and clarity. Yngvi did not know whether to laugh or cry with happiness.

Swiftly he rose and woke Edna. "Carla is hungry." He threw his hands in the air with joy. "I think the fever has broken!"

Edna quickly got up; it was obvious how pleased she felt for Yngvi and his wife.

After Carla had drunk some cold mint tea and eaten a small serving of porridge, she asked for her daughter. The infant suckled in vain on her breast and soon began to whine. Carla stroked her little girl's hair with sadness.

"Hilda will be here soon to nurse her," said Yngvi, trying to console his wife. "Little Frida won't have to go hungry."

Carla nodded in relief. "I would like to take a bath," she said eventually with longing, her bright voice sounding stronger than in the days before.

Yngvi felt so glad in that moment that he would have tried to fetch the moon from the sky for her, had she asked. Carefully he lifted Frida from her arms and nestled the child into her soft bed of furs. Then he wrapped his arms around Carla's body and lifted her off her bed. Edna smiled as she placed a piece of soap, a linen cloth, and a clean undergarment on Carla's belly. Barefoot and dressed only in a shirt, he carried her down to the lake. In his arms, Carla felt as light as a feather.

The horizon glowed in a warm orange light. A rooster greeted the nearing day with his confident crowing. Most inhabitants of Woodhaven still lay asleep, and Yngvi was pleased to avoid the villagers' inquisitive eyes.

He waded out into the crystal-clear waters. Slowly, he first dipped Carla's feet and then her legs into the cool lake. "Ready?" he asked, his voice filled with concern.

She nodded, tightening her grip around his neck.

Together with her, Yngvi dived under the water for a moment. Back above the surface, she sharply drew in the crisp morning air. The water was probably colder than she'd expected. But her face soon relaxed, and, smiling at him, she let go of him, rinsed out her mouth, and used her finger to clean her teeth. Yngvi helped her out of her shift, rubbing her hair and her naked upper body with the soap.

Holding onto his hand, Carla dived under once more, and when she reemerged, she was beaming with joy. "I feel like I've been born again."

"You have, in a way," he told her pensively. "Yesterday we, none of us, thought you would live through the night." He held her close, whispering in her ear: "You have no idea how desperate I felt, and how happy I am now that you're better."

She answered with a kiss on his cheek. "Take me back, please. I'm hungry again."

"Would you like to try to walk?"

She shook her head decisively, asking with mock indignation, "Are you trying to shirk the task of carrying your feeble wife?"

Yngvi laughed. "I will carry you to the end of the world! But only if I must," he jested.

On the lakeshore, he dried Carla lovingly and pulled the fresh undergarment over her head. When he picked her up and slowly strode up the path to the village, he felt profoundly grateful to God and Asla. He couldn't decide whether it was the Lord's mercy or the skills of his sister-in-law that brought Carla back to life. Perhaps it was some of both, and both went hand in hand.

CHAPTER 22
THE JARL

While Carla recovered, Yngvi continued to work on his vision for a new society. During the evenings, he set down on parchment progressive legislative treatises that he would present to the council following its inception, so that they might vote on them. During the day, when he wasn't fishing out at sea, he would visit the farmers working the fields or clearing the woods to expand their land. Yngvi would lend a hand and, whenever the opportunity arose, try to convince the farmers of his idea.

The older farmers reacted with skepticism, especially those who had owned land back in their Northern home. While they welcomed the notion of doing away with blood feuds, they took offense at Yngvi's intentions of giving more rights to women. Many of them told him that Thorolf was a good chieftain; he'd safely led them to Catan and ought to remain their leader.

Yngvi had little cause for hope of bringing more than one or two of the older men to his side, but things were different among the younger freemen and the former servants who had only received their freedom upon Catan. Most of them were open to Yngvi's ideas, promising him their vote at the election.

The shipyard lay near the waterfall, where several huts had been built by the lake's flat shore. One almost completed and two half-finished fishing boats were sitting on their keels, and one apprentice and two servants were busy attaching planks to the ribs of a fourth vessel. Sven and Tjure, Högni's eight- and nine-year-old sons, were smoothing boards that would later serve as planking. Högni, powerful as ever, was swinging an axe, turning a tree trunk into boards. The shipwright had much experience in cleaving the timber according to its natural growth, which would later give the planks high flexibility and prevent them from breaking.

When he saw Yngvi walk toward him, Högni set down his axe and greeted Yngvi with his deep, booming voice. "Have you come to inquire after the progress of your fishing boat, or are you angling for votes?"

"Both," said Yngvi with a grin.

Högni's laughter sounded almost like rolling thunder as he ran his hand through his shaggy blond hair, which was streaked with gray. "At least you're honest. Before you start explaining everything all over again, let me assure you that you have our vote."

"*Our* vote?" asked Yngvi.

"Diara belabored me until I threw up my hands and swore by the gods to vote for you as our jarl." Högni grinned. "You can't imagine the lengths that woman goes to in order to sway a man."

Right on cue, Diara emerged from one of the huts. She carried a basket in one hand and a jug in the other. When she spotted Yngvi, she smiled. Then she handed the jug of thinned ale to her husband, who drained half of it in one gulp before holding it out to Yngvi. "Want some?"

Yngvi took a long sip before gratefully accepting the piece of bread Diara had pulled from the basket.

"Have you seen my husband's garden?" With a mischievous twinkle in her eyes, she pointed at a patch of green on the far side of the track that led to the waterfall.

"Högni has a garden?" asked Yngvi, surprised. That did not sound at all like the dedicated ship builder, of whom some claimed in jest that he never went to bed without his axe. "All I see are weeds."

"Well, then. Let me show you!" The shipwright dragged him across the path by the arm, stopping in front of the area whose knee-high growth differed from the plants nearby. "Take a closer look, my friend. Perhaps you'll find you've seen my *weeds* before."

Yngvi crouched down and studied the leaves more closely. Then he called out with astonishment: "Those are oak leaves!" He took a few steps to the side. "And these are tiny beeches and ash trees! And those look like sprouts of apple trees." Yngvi laughed when he realized what kind of garden this was.

Högni grinned with pride. "I brought the seeds from our homeland. The little trees seem to like it here." He pointed at a small ash with healthy bright-green leaves that towered over the other seedlings by a good half foot. "This one here seems to like it particularly well. Next year, I'll dig her out and plant her in the middle of the village square. When she's bigger, we'll have a feast and dedicate her to Odin."

"A tree for the father of gods? Like the ash at Ulrik's assembly place? Thorolf will like that," said Yngvi, nodding at the shipbuilder.

Högni cast a wistful eye over his fosterlings. "One faraway day, I imagine them growing all over Catan, delighting future shipwrights with their straight growth and noble wood. Maybe," said Högni with a sigh, "I might still live to see the day on which we fell an ash and my sons cut the keel of the first knarr built upon Catan from it."

Yngvi gave Högni an encouraging slap on the shoulder. "Your wife will make sure you will."

Diara laughed. "I sure will!" she hooked her arm around Yngvi's as they slowly walked back. "You have no idea how glad I am that Carla has recovered. I have grown very fond of her—as have my boys." She glanced proudly at her sons, who were still busily smoothing a board. "They can hardly wait for her to teach them again."

"I can see why," said Yngvi with a smile. "She is skilled at teaching the letters to her students. To the children, the lessons seem more like a game."

"I reckon the brats are just trying to shirk their chores," said Högni sullenly. "What use is reading and writing going to be to them? I build my ship with an axe, not with a feather."

Diara placed a hand on her husband's shoulder. "Come, you old grouch. Allow your sons this one pleasure. They do enough for you. Maybe one day, they'll write about how artfully you build your ships, thereby honoring their father."

The thought seemed to appeal to Högni, and he said no more on the subject. "By the way, Yngvi knows that I will vote for him at the election. He also knows that this is in no small part down to you," he grumbled good-naturedly.

Diara winked at Yngvi. "Yes, my poor husband was fed meager meals, his ale became thinner and thinner . . ." she said with exaggerated pity, "there seemed to be no one to wash his dirty laundry and empty his chamber pot." Batting her lashes innocently, she caressed Högni's cheek. "Then, at some point, he recognized the worth of a woman."

"Nonsense," objected Högni with a sour tone, "you know how much I value you." Then he paused for a moment, as if he found it difficult to utter the next words in Yngvi's presence. "And how much I love you. I am open to new ideas, or else I wouldn't have sailed here with you. Your lack of care and our countless discussions merely sped up my decision." Högni picked up his axe, weighing it in his hands. "The quarrel between Sievert and Einar opened my eyes, when it started to look like it was going to turn into a bloody feud. I realized that we brought the old laws with us like a viper in our carry sacks when we settled this island, which is loved by the gods." He swung the axe and brought it down hard on a wooden block beside him. "And if we don't cut off the viper's head now, it will poison this land and us."

Chewing on his bottom lip, he looked straight at Yngvi. "That is my honest opinion, but I struggled with the idea of giving women who lead their families the right to attend assemblies, raising them to the same level as men. That was the reason I was reluctant at first. But by now . . ." Högni paused, then glanced at his wife, who peered at him distrustfully. "But by now, I've made my peace with it."

Yngvi stifled a grin. Högni had narrowly avoided angering his wife once more. Diara gave Yngvi a wide smile in farewell and strolled down to her sons.

"So? How's my fishing boat?" asked Yngvi.

"Nearly done. All that's missing is the mast—and a sail. Diara and her maid are weaving it. You'll only have to wait two more weeks."

Yngvi nodded contentedly. He would need this boat, which he would name *Carla*, if he won the vote and relinquished the *Shieldmaiden* to Thorolf.

Stina and Digur had been living together for almost seven weeks, and their life had found a rhythm. During the day, Stina helped her sister with the preparation of creams and tinctures and with caring for the sick, or else she relieved Hilda with the supervision of the charcoal servants and with teaching a young freeman who had shown an interest in the trade and who was proving useful.

Meanwhile, Digur would first tend to his bees with the help of Kaja before checking on his fields with Kilian and Enno, instructing the servants to do this job or that. Sometimes the servants had a hard time keeping up with their master when he sped along the paths between the fields on his crutches.

Every bath day, Digur attended Gregor's service. Ever since his conversation with the short, burly man, he felt drawn to the Christian God, a God who offered people a prospect of love and forgiveness and who was completely different from the Northern gods. The priest was gifted at bringing this God nearer to Digur—and not just to him. When Gregor stood before his congregation, preaching God's commandments in words that were easy to understand, telling them stories from the Bible in his powerful voice and explaining those stories with intelligent and understandable comments, he seemed truthful to the people. In those moments he appeared to grow, turning into an esteemed and respected man, into their priest, from whose lips they received God's word, comfort, and hope.

In the beginning, Digur had attended the services by himself, but when, following his first few visits, he came home less melancholy, more open and even talkative, Stina's curiosity was aroused. The next time he went, she accompanied him to the meeting of the Christians. She sensed that it was good for Digur to share what he heard with her and to discuss his thoughts about God.

During the nights, they made love or lay together, talking. So, too, they did on this night.

Nestling her head on Digur's wide chest, Stina asked quietly, "Do you want me to leave tomorrow? Our seven weeks are up."

Digur stroked her hair. His answer wasn't quite what she had hoped for. "You are a free woman. If you want to leave, I won't stop you."

Stina propped up her upper body and looked him in the eyes, which gleamed blueish-green in the light of the tallow lamp. "Would you try to stop me if you weren't a cripple?" She didn't mean to insult him, but she knew Digur liked plain words; with him, she'd get nowhere beating around the bush.

Digur said nothing, which she took to mean yes.

"And what if I expected your child? Would you then try to stop me?"

Now Digur straightened up too. "You're with child?"

"Yes," said Stina in a whisper. "I haven't bled, and in the last few days, I've been feeling ill in the mornings. Asla, too, is certain that I'm with child."

Digur sank back down, trying to capture and sort his galloping thoughts. He loved Stina—more than he'd ever thought possible. Leaving her in the lurch with a child who would have to get through life as a fatherless bastard was more than he saw himself capable of. There was only one way out of this dilemma, cripple or no. "Then we marry."

"Who says I want to marry you?" retorted Stina flippantly, while on the inside she rejoiced. The Digur who was responsible and capable of love had vanquished the crippled and proud Digur who had railed against his fate.

Digur said nothing. He drew her close and kissed her.

Gregor's congregation had grown steadily in the last few months. In the beginning, it had consisted mainly of servants and maids captured from Christian countries, but now more and more freemen and women came to the services. The small yard outside Gregor's workshop was growing too tight for the many people who regularly attended.

Digur and Stina waited in the very same yard after the end of the service until they were alone with the priest.

"Would you like to join us for our evening meal?" asked Gregor, who appeared to sense that the two of them wished to discuss something.

Digur wasted no time. "We wish to marry. As Christians."

Gregor did not seem surprised. "I know your reasons, Digur. I am pleased for you that you wish to walk the path of your life alongside God from here on." He turned to Stina. "And you? Why do you wish to adopt the Christian faith?"

Stina leaned her blonde head against Digur's upper arm. "If God is good for Digur, then he is good for me, too."

Gregor gave a laugh. "I've never heard a profession of faith like this before. But if you are serious about following God, then we have much to discuss. Won't you come in and eat with us after all?"

Stina carried a yellow lump in one hand and a clay jar covered with a thin piece of hide in the other when she entered the house. "Hello, dear sister. I bring the wax and the honey you asked for. Digur says to tell you that both are of the best quality."

Asla set aside the bowl in which she had been grinding dried herbs with a clay pestle, and asked Stina to put the wax and the honey on the table she used to prepare her creams and tinctures.

Then she reached into the pouch on her belt to retrieve a small lump of gold from it.

Stina grasped Asla's wrist. "Leave it! Or do you wish to insult Digur? He would never allow you to pay for his honey. He is glad to pay off his debt to you—after all, you and Enno saved his life."

Asla nodded. "Very well. Then deliver my thanks and tell him I would love to return the favor if there's ever an opportunity."

"Will do. But I'm also here for another reason."

Asla raised her eyebrows inquisitively.

"Digur and I are getting married next bath day. Gregor baptized us yesterday, and he's going to marry us at the end of his service. I'm sure Thorolf won't want to come to the Christian ceremony, but you are more than welcome at our small feast afterward."

Asla wasn't surprised. To her, it had been obvious that the two of them were going to marry. "I'm pleased for you. I look forward to it, and I'll gladly come to Gregor's service, too. But you'll have to ask Thorolf yourself. I can't speak for him," she said feebly.

"You don't look overjoyed, sister. Is everything all right? Are you unwell?"

Asla sat. A tear rolled down her cheek. "He is cheating on me. With a maid. Has been for weeks," she burst out.

Visibly appalled, Stina lowered herself onto the bench next to her. "Are you sure?"

"Sören's wife was here with her daughter this morning. The woman kept giving me these pitying looks while I sewed up a wound on her little girl. And then she said that Thorolf had been carrying on with her maid. And since he isn't even trying to keep it a secret, folks are beginning to talk." Asla rubbed her eyes. "Now I know why he barely shows me any interest and why he falls asleep the moment he comes to bed."

Stina picked up her hand. "I am sorry." Then, after a few moments of silence, she added, "But she is only a maid. You are his wife. I'm sure he will soon recall his love for you."

"I am not certain that this is still what I want," confessed Asla huskily. "It's not just the maid. Thorolf has changed. He barely listens anymore when I speak and cuts me short when I disagree with his decisions. He no longer respects me like he used to, often treating me no better than a maid."

Stina thought for a while. Then she said, "You are a strong woman who contradicts him from time to time and speaks her mind openly. The way I know Thorolf, he can't handle that. He wants to be admired and expects you to look up to him. He probably wishes that you adore him as if you considered him akin to the father of gods."

Asla shook her head and folded her hands in her lap. "That I cannot give him. I would despise myself and feel even more miserable than I do now." Raising her voice, she said angrily, "Then let him go to his whore! I bet she gazes at him—the big chieftain—admiringly and submissively when he mounts her."

"Do you still love him?" asked her sister.

"I think so," replied Asla softly. "If I didn't, I wouldn't feel so hurt."

"And what are you going to do now?"

"I will make up a bed for myself in Ilka's chamber and ignore him. If I'm still important to him, he will come to me. If not, then I will leave him."

Stina squeezed her hand. "Should it come to that, you are welcome at my and Digur's house."

Stina and Digur kept their wedding celebration small. The weather was wet, forcing the newlyweds and their guests inside the house.

When Thorolf sat down, he was shocked to see Kaja, Enno, and Kilian sit down at the other end of the table. Averting their eyes with embarrassment, they did not dare to look at him. Thorolf turned to Digur, puzzled. "Your maid and your servants are sitting with us?" Then he nodded in the direction of Carla and Hilda, who were standing by the hearth, turning a piglet on a spit and frying flatbread in a large pan. "And you allow free women to prepare food for unfree folk, even *serving* them? Have all the gods deserted you?"

"Indeed they have, brother," replied Digur, unfazed. "I renounced the gods. I have been a Christian for a few days now, and since then, Kaja, Enno, and Kilian are free. They are our guests this evening."

Thorolf didn't seem to understand. "What does your pathetic god have to do with freeing your servants?"

Gregor replied in a calm voice. "As Christians, we must obey God's commandments. One of his commandments asks us to refrain from oppressing our brothers and sisters and from taking away their freedom."

"'Brothers and sisters,'" parroted Thorolf, his voice dripping with mockery. "I only have two brothers here. And it would seem your blather has shrouded their senses." Leaning forward, he gave Digur a jeering smile. "Then how are you going to cope as a one-legged man in the future? Who is going to work your fields and clear the woods for new fields and pasture? I'm afraid you've lost your mind along with your leg!"

Stina, sitting next to Digur and looking radiant with flowers braided into her hair, leaned forward and lifted her chin feistily. "Digur isn't alone, brother. All of us here, except for you, perhaps, stand by him. Kaja, Enno, and Kilian won't leave us for now, but we will pay them for their work from our earnings. That will be the only difference."

Thorolf glared at her disapprovingly before turning back to his brothers. "You are trampling all over our traditions. Heimdall himself, son of Odin and father of mankind, created the classes of thralls, freemen, and jarls with his seed. If you deny the class of the unfree, then you disregard the gods and the order intended by them." He raised a warning finger. "And for that, believe me, Odin will have his revenge. He will send messengers of doom."

"Then why did Thor send a lightning bolt that sank the *Goldeagle* to you, of all people—you who honor the gods like nobody else?" asked Yngvi pointedly.

Thorolf looked at a loss for a moment but recovered quickly. "Maybe," he growled, vexed, "because the gods wished to warn me? Because they were sending me a clear message to remind my subjects to honor them and to win their favor through sacrifice?"

Yngvi took notice. "*Your subjects*? So you already are the jarl? And should you become the jarl, then will you make bonded men of all freemen, forcing them to submit to your will?"

"If it is in their best interest, I will demand obedience!" Thorolf was talking himself into a rage. "Was it not I who led the settlers here and brought them wealth?" He stood and slammed his right hand against his chest repeatedly. "It is *I* who knows what is best for Woodhaven and our growing tribe." Thorolf pointed his finger around the room. "You Christians insult the gods and damage our community. By the father of gods, I ought to drive you all into the sea!"

In his growing anger, the words had slipped out and now his pride prevented him from taking them back.

Asla had turned as white as chalk. She gave her husband

a saddened look. "If that is your will, then you must drive me into the ocean too, for I have decided to follow your brothers and my sister on their path of Christianity."

Thorolf looked down at her grimly, coldness in his eyes. Then he turned to Digur and dropped a small pouch of gold on the table. "My wedding gift."

With those words, he left the house, slamming the door shut so that it quivered in its hinges like an evil omen.

The guests exchanged appalled looks. Asla covered her eyes with one hand, trying to hold back her tears.

Yngvi tried to break the silence with sarcasm. "Any Christians among us who do not know how to swim better learn it soon."

"After that display, I am well and truly certain that our people are better off in the hands of Yngvi," said Högni quietly to his wife.

"Thorolf has grown so . . ." Diara waved her hand as if she could make the missing words magically appear on her tongue that way. "So overbearing and hard."

Stina rose, clapping her hands together. "Enough of the gloomy faces! Today we celebrate the union of Digur and me. Let us enjoy the piglet Yngvi and Carla have brought us, and let us drink of Hilda's delicious ale." With a loving glance at Digur, she caressed his broad neck. "And when we've all eaten our fill, then we will taste the mead my husband brewed from the honey of his bees."

Despite Thorolf's unhappy demeanor at the beginning of the evening, the mood soon improved. Following the meal with plenty of ale and mead, they conversed eagerly, laughed at Yngvi's jokes, and smiled at Gregor's observations. Asla alone barely uttered a word. She seemed to be in the clutches of profound melancholy. No one dared to bother her with shallow words of encouragement. They all understood the reason for her somber mood, and they all knew that no one would be able to help her on this evening.

"I still have a gift for you," said Gregor to the brand-new husband. Unaccustomed to the mead, he seemed a little unsteady on his feet as he walked to a corner and returned with an object wrapped up in a skin.

Digur watched with interest as Gregor unpacked the object. It was a solid wooden stick that widened into a bowl on one end and thickened into some kind of hoof at the other end. From opposite edges of the bowl protruded two battens. Slits had been cut into one of the two battens, and fastened through those slits were two leather belts.

With flushed cheeks, Gregor placed the gift into the big man's hands.

"It's a peg leg," observed Digur with amazement. He had heard of such a replacement for a lower leg before but had never seen one. "That's why you took a wax print of my stump!"

Gregor nodded. "I filled the hollow space with clay, and once it dried, I had an exact replica of your stump. The bowl should be a good fit."

"Where did you learn that?" asked Digur.

"I didn't." Gregor grinned. "A friend at the pope's court moved about on a peg leg. I once had the opportunity to inspect it, but other than that, I improvised."

Yngvi stood. "Let's find out if you can walk with it."

Digur turned around on the bench.

"Hold on." Hilda walked around the table and placed a small linen cushion stuffed with feathers inside the bowl. Then, she wrapped a long strip of sheepskin around the stump and fastened it with two cloak pins. Then, Gregor pushed the bowl over the stump, and Hilda drew the belts around the second batten, fastening them in the grooves that had been carved for them. Digur felt the wide battens tighten snugly against his cushioned thigh. He lifted it tentatively—the peg leg followed.

"Now you have a stiff leg, just like Hakon," observed Yngvi. "With a little practice, you should be able to walk without crutches."

Digur gave his brother a look first of disbelief, then of hope. "I'm going to try!"

Yngvi and Hilda helped him up. Like a father trying to entice his little boy to walk, Gregor waved Digur toward him. Yngvi tightened his grip on his mighty brother's arm, as if fearing Digur might fall and crush the much smaller Gregor.

They all watched the hulking man excitedly as he shifted his weight onto the peg leg and risked a step with his good leg. Then he dragged the stick leg forward and attempted another step. The realization that he would henceforth be able to move about on two feet brought a wide smile to his lips and an adventurous sparkle to his eyes.

Stina thought she had never seen her husband this happy. In his mind's eye, he probably saw himself plowing his fields already.

Encouraged by the enthusiastic cheers of Stina and his guests, Digur limped two laps around the table without Yngvi's help. At last he stopped in front of Gregor, and, deeply moved, said, "Thank you."

With his left, he pressed the short man's head against his chest, and with his other hand, he patted Gregor's back. Digur was grateful to him for so much more than just the peg leg.

Gregor started to wave his arms and shift his legs restlessly, but Digur appeared deep in thought and seemed to have no intentions of letting go of the priest.

"Don't squeeze your benefactor to death, brother dear," called out Yngvi with a laugh.

Everyone else joined in with the laughter, and even Asla couldn't help but smile.

Digur unclasped his arms. Gregor staggered backward and drew a deep breath, feeling his nose, which had been compressed against the strong man's hard chest. Then he blew his nose and grinned. "He who has you for a friend need not fear his enemies."

During the weeks leading up to the day Thorolf had set as the date of the election, the people of Woodhaven had argued passionately over the better candidate. It was as if a rift had opened up in the village, dividing it in two. The rift did not discriminate, splitting families, threatening friendships, and provoking the occasional fight.

On bath day, the families brought their older children to the village square with them. Everyone was clad in their best garments, and the leading men proudly carried their swords on their belts, designating them as freemen. The heavy clouds that moved low across the country seemed to turn the world gray, stealing the color from the cloaks and tunics flapping in the wind. All the more colorful were the discussions, which, like waves, rose and fell, heated one moment and subdued the next.

"Silence!" roared Högni. Thorolf and Yngvi had asked him to oversee the vote, and now he tried his best to fulfill his duty. The wind tugged at his wild head of hair as if it were a scrappy flag while the stocky shipbuilder tried to make his powerful voice heard. At last the babble of voices ebbed off, and Högni directed those men permitted to vote to one side of the square while banishing their families to its edge. He motioned for Yngvi and Thorolf to stand in the free space in front of the barn. He told the brothers to speak.

Thorolf jutted out his pronounced chin and pressed his lips into a determined line. Then he spoke. "Men, you know me. It was me the gods led to this fertile island. I was the one who ensured you had grain, livestock, and tools. Thanks to me, you are far better off than you were in the old country. With me as your jarl, that will not change. This I swear in the presence of our gods!" Thorolf paused for a few heartbeats, registering both excited and skeptical faces. "Have faith in Odin and Thor! I am near to them, and I am the only one who can secure their favor for a golden future upon this island." He raised his eyes to the fast-moving clouds and held out his right fist toward them. His expression was solemn, as if he had just glimpsed the face of Odin, and he hammered his fist into the air, pointing his other arm at Yngvi. "My brother wants to break with our traditions, and he denies our gods! Odin will punish him harshly for his wickedness." Thorolf's left arm swiveled toward the leading men, and his voice almost broke when he shouted at them. "And equally he will punish every one of you who votes for my brother!"

Thorolf's supporters cried their support and stamped their feet.

Yngvi waited for the crowd to quiet down. Slowly, he also lifted his right hand. But instead of clenching his fist like his brother, he pointed a finger at the sky. His voice wasn't as powerful as that of Thorolf's, but it nonetheless filled the square loud and clear. "Listen to me, gods! If you exist, then punish me now for doing you wrong and for that which I intend to do. If not, then stay silent for good." Yngvi cast a challenging look at the dull, gloomy sky. "Thor, where is the lightning bolt that strikes me down? Odin, why don't you send your ravens down from the heavens to peck out my eyes?"

Some of the women clasped their hands to their mouths

with fright, peering expectantly at the dark clouds. They seemed heavy enough to be thunderclouds, but Thor sent no blinding bolt of light to the earth, nor did a raven swoop down on black wings to attack Yngvi.

Respect showed on the faces of many as they saw Yngvi stand firm in his place, untouched by the wrath of the gods. Fearlessly, he continued to point his finger at the sky, challenging the gods, but they did not send a reply.

Yngvi lowered his arm. "I have spoken with each of you. You know what to expect if you elect me: nothing less than the freedom to determine our own future on Catan! As you have seen, the gods do not condemn me. You have nothing to fear from them if you vote for me." Yngvi, who was now a firm believer in the Christian faith, would rather have avoided the following sentence, but he forced himself to say it. "The Northern gods as well as the Christian God are with me, and therefore they will be with you, too, if you give me your vote."

While Yngvi spoke, Thorolf gazed at each man grimly. Many who noticed his glare looked uncomfortable. Under their chieftain's piercing, glowering stare, the applause for Yngvi turned out rather muted.

Högni asked Thorolf to stand by the barn's left corner, while he sent Yngvi to the right. "Now, men, walk up to the man you wish to have as your jarl!"

Each male head of household marched toward one or the other of the brothers. Thorolf gave a bitter sneer when he saw Digur limp to Yngvi. All the servants that he'd freed for their services also went to Yngvi's side.

Högni was visibly nervous when he counted the men of each group. He counted for a second time, and still reached the same result. He started to perspire despite the cool weather, small beads of sweat forming on his forehead. He had hoped for a clear result—a result that would have spared him offending Thorolf. But there were twenty men on each side, and he was forced to make his choice as the last leading man. With a sigh in view of the unavoidable, he walked over to Yngvi's side. As he had expected, Thorolf bestowed him with a look that was, in equal parts, disappointed and furious.

Then Högni announced the result in a firm voice. "Yngvi has received one more vote than Thorolf and wins the election."

Yngvi's followers began to cheer instantly. The men who had voted for him slapped his shoulder and repeatedly gave three cheers for him. Their wives danced merrily on the spot, lifting their arms and clapping their hands. Carla, Hilda, and Stina could no longer wait by the edge of the square; their faces flushed with excitement, they ran toward the group around Yngvi, and other women soon followed them. Everyone wished to congratulate the newly elected jarl.

Asla remained standing where she was, her expression unmoved, her chest filled with conflicting feelings. On the one hand, she was pleased for Yngvi and for the women her brother-in-law planned to give more rights to; but on the other hand, she knew exactly how Thorolf felt. It was tough for him to see his dream shattered, his dream of shaping the settlers' future as their beloved and venerated jarl. Part of her was tempted to rush to his side, to embrace him and console him. But her legs wouldn't budge. They felt leaden, as if filled with all the misery that had taken place between her and Thorolf during the last few moons.

From amid his disappointed followers, Thorolf bitterly watched the hubbub around the victor. He spat on the ground to rid himself of the stale taste in his mouth. In his thoughts, he cursed his brother's talent for wrapping folk around his finger with clever words. That was the only reason Yngvi had managed to steal the rule over the settlers from him. Of that, Thorolf felt certain. The hot anger that had been simmering inside Thorolf turned into cold, calculating rage.

Thorolf stepped away from his group of followers, beckoning at two strong young men, who rushed toward him. They were farmers' sons who had shown themselves particularly deft at the sword exercises and who were loyal to him. They were the first two men of his retinue, and they would make for a worthy frame to the scene he was planning.

Once the din from his well-wishers subsided and only a few people surrounded him, Yngvi heard his brother calling for him. His feet planted firmly apart and his arms crossed on his chest, Thorolf stood in the middle of the square and stared at him. Yngvi vaguely knew the two sword-bearing young men behind him, looking as if they were Thorolf's bodyguards. Yngvi slowly approached him.

Thorolf jeered, "I congratulate you on being elected jarl. Would you like me to bend the knee?"

Yngvi found no trace of warmth in Thorolf's voice. The coldness and scorn that met him made him shudder. The man standing in front of him and regarding him frostily wasn't the brother he loved and for whom he would lay down his life. Standing before him was a stranger, someone he didn't know how to gauge and who was glaring at him as if he were a poisonous adder that needed to be stamped out.

Yngvi held his brother's gaze. "No one will bend their knee

to me. As soon as the council has been elected, there will be no more jarl. You know that."

"But for now you are still jarl," replied Thorolf with a wolfish grin. "And you know the laws of our people, don't you?"

Yngvi preferred to say nothing.

"The rule of the strongest man," replied Thorolf in his stead. "Only the strongest man is worthy of leading a tribe. You are weak, preferring to fight your enemies with treacherous words rather than openly with the sword. You are not worthy to hold the title of jarl."

He had spoken loudly, and those among the crowd who had started to walk home returned, forming a half-circle around the brothers. Lightning flashed in the distance, announcing a thunderstorm. A powerful wind gust billowed the cloaks of the onlookers.

Yngvi couldn't think of anything to say other than repeating his words. "I will give up the title of jarl as soon as the council is chosen."

"But still you are jarl," Thorolf said once more, drawing his sword and pointing it at his brother's chest. "Draw your sword and fight! Defend your title, your stupid council, your pathetic god and everything else haunting your crazed mind!"

Yngvi swallowed hard. Behind him, he could hear the villagers gasp, and he thought he heard Carla stifle a scream. He would never have thought possible what was happening right now: Thorolf was pointing a weapon at him, prepared to spill his own brother's blood to achieve his goal. Yngvi gazed intently into Thorolf's eyes, begging him silently to end this unbearable scene, but all he saw there was implacable resentment.

Yngvi knew he stood no chance against experienced, battle-hardened Thorolf, who was an outstanding swordsman. But even if he had been his brother's equal in combat, he would have declined to fight him. Yngvi grasped Thorolf's blade with one hand and pushed it aside. "I will not fight my brother."

Thorolf gave a hateful laugh. "Because you are a coward, a pathetic worm who values his life higher than glory at Valhalla."

"And you," replied Yngvi calmly, "are neither brave nor valiant, for you know perfectly well that I am no match for you in a sword fight. It is you who is pathetic and cowardly. Pathetic because you place your own benefit and your lust for power above the well-being of others, and cowardly because you fear anything new and are unwilling to try out a better way of living together. If you want to become jarl, then why don't you just run me through with your sword?"

Thorolf narrowed his eyes. He shifted his sword to his left hand, raised his right hand, and slapped Yngvi's cheek hard. The slap echoed across the village square, and most of Thorolf's followers cheered and laughed. There were shouts that called Yngvi a cowardly dog and a frightened girl.

To Carla, the events unfolding before her appeared unreal. Bottomless, helpless fear for her husband opened up beneath her. She wanted to run over to Yngvi and place herself between him and Thorolf, but Asla managed to catch her by the arm, yanking her back.

"Thorolf isn't going to kill his brother," Asla said, pleading with Carla. "I know him. Believe me, he won't go that far. If you get involved now, you will not help Yngvi. He would only look even weaker in the eyes of the men, which would suit Thorolf."

Carla gave in, hoping fervently that Asla was right.

Even though Yngvi's head ached viciously, and there was a whistling in his ear and his jaw throbbed, he did not lift his hand to touch his cheek. Unmoved, he stood before his brother. He wasn't prepared to give Thorolf the satisfaction of reveling in his pain.

Thorolf laughed. "Well, jarl? Don't you want to obey your god? Doesn't he expect of you to turn the other cheek now?"

In the laughter of his followers, Thorolf failed to hear the dragging sound approaching him from behind. He looked surprised when Digur appeared, positioning himself in front of Yngvi and tilting his head to one side. In his deep voice, he demanded, "Go on, brother. If you hit the one brother, you must also strike the other."

A ghostly silence descended over the village square. The settlers, seeing Digur's hand resting on the pommel of his sword, held their breath.

Thorolf's rage collapsed like a burning house whose pillars could no longer support the roof. He could tell that he had overstepped a mark and that he was now running the risk of having to fight his older brother—even of having to kill him, for Digur would fight unto his dying breath. In the end, he would have battled a cripple and yet lost. Then, after already having killed Hilmar, the best friend from his youth, he would also have murdered his brother, the man he had looked up to for as long as he could remember. But he could not see a way to defuse the situation without losing face.

Diara's voice rang out shrilly. "Stop it, Thorolf! Do you wish to become a brother-slayer?"

Högni wrapped both arms around his wife's chest to stop her from running to Digur. "What do you think you'll do? Scratch out Thorolf's eyes? The brothers must settle this among themselves."

Meanwhile, Stina ran over to her husband with tears in her eyes and grasped his right hand, desperately trying to pull it away from the pommel of his sword, but Digur's hand wrapped itself around the hilt and held it in an iron grip. "Don't do this," she begged him. "You don't stand a chance against Thorolf with your leg. He is going to kill you!"

When Digur did not react, she threw herself against his chest, crying, trying to push him away from Thorolf, but her husband gently forced her aside with his left arm, standing like a rock and gazing at Thorolf with an unmoved and strangely unperturbed expression.

Lightning flashed and thunder followed just a few moments later. As if the clouds had only waited for this signal, they suddenly released their heavy burden. But the people were unconcerned by the rain, fixing their eyes on the drama unfolding between the brothers.

Yngvi stepped up next to Digur. He sensed what was going on inside Thorolf, had a hunch that he was trapped in this situation, neither seeing any way forward nor back. Yngvi feared the tension between his brothers might end at any moment with a bitter tragedy. With a heavy heart, he made his decision.

Turning to the settlers, he declared in a clear voice, "I decline the vote. Thorolf is your new jarl!"

There was silence. Even Thorolf's most loyal followers refrained from breaking out in cheers.

Yngvi loosened Digur's hand from the hilt of his sword, and his older brother allowed it. Then Yngvi placed his right hand on Digur's shoulder, and the two brothers looked at each other in silence. They needed no words to understand.

Stina wiped the tears from her eyes and threw her arms around Yngvi. "Thank you," she whispered in his ear and breathed a kiss on his sore cheek.

Thorolf sheathed his sword. His brothers and Stina walked away without another look in his direction. Pensively, his eyes followed them. He had asserted his will and become jarl of the people of Woodhaven, but unlike how he'd pictured it. He wasn't filled with joy. His victory had cost him dearly; he had paid with the closeness and affection of his brothers.

"Thorolf?" Asla stood in front of him, her arms hanging at her sides. The rain pouring in heavy drops ran down her beautiful face, which gazed up at him sadly and yet filled with determination. She blinked and wiped some drops from her eyes. When she spoke, her voice wasn't hostile but resigned. "I am leaving you. I cannot live with you any longer." She handed him the golden choker he had gifted her at Jora's birth. "Take it and give it to your next wife. Perhaps it will bring her more luck than it brought me. May she give you many healthy sons."

Thorolf was not surprised. Still, he asked, "Why?"

"Because you are no longer the man I once loved. Your greed for power has spoiled you—even drove you to the verge of enacting your brother's death. You no longer respect my wishes and betray me with a cheap maid. The whole village is talking about it."

Thorolf accepted her explanation. "Where will you go?"

"Jora and I are welcome in the house of my sister. Maybe Digur and his former servants will build a hut for us. I'll earn my living with my skills as a healer."

Asla did not wait for another reply. She turned around and left him standing in the rain.

Thorolf lingered alone on the village square for a while. He wasn't bothered by the heavy rain that had long drenched his clothes and streamed down his body in small rivers. The final loss of Asla and the break with his brothers pained him. He wondered how it could have come this far. Had he done anything wrong? Thorolf shook his head. His brothers were to blame for their quarrel—they had gone against his leadership, betraying him. Asla had supported them in this, questioning his authority as a husband and as a chieftain time and again. And that was what, in the end, had smothered his love for her.

He tried to focus on his future, and gradually the bitter expression on his face softened. He would choose another wife—the daughter of a freeman, an agreeable girl, someone who admired him, instead of contradicting him, and who would bear him many sons. He would demand tributes from the families and build a large, three-aisled hall at least as big as the one of his father, Ulrik. There he would hold court and steer the settlers' fortunes. They would honor him and praise his wisdom. Suddenly, all that he had won seemed to weigh heavier than the loss he had suffered.

A smile on his lips, Thorolf left the village square.

The following day, the thick clouds had gone, and the sun reigned in a bright-blue sky. But the light on this beautiful fall day wasn't strong enough to dispel the shadows that darkened the hearts of many settlers. Many among them were saddened by the defeat of Yngvi, whose visions had touched them, and even some of Thorolf's followers weren't happy with the way he had conducted himself.

The events from the previous night were still playing in Digur's mind, too, and so, in the evening, he rapped on Yngvi's door accompanied by Stina and Asla, who had moved in with them together with Jora. Yngvi greeted him with a heartfelt embrace, asking him and his sisters-in-law to enter. Digur nodded at Carla, Edna, and Hilda, who sat nursing. Carla served a simple meal and a jug of thinned ale.

They discussed the events of the previous day, grieving over the unhappy transformation of the man who had once been a treasured brother, beloved husband, and valued brother-in-law. Then, after a moment of silence, Yngvi shared his decision with his guests—a decision that he and Carla had reached during the morning in the presence of Edna and Hilda. "Carla and I are going to leave Woodhaven."

Digur raised an eyebrow, and Stina choked on her ale. Asla thumped her coughing sister's back and gave Yngvi a questioning look.

He smiled tiredly. "Why did you leave Thorolf?"

Asla thought for a moment before replying. "Because I couldn't bear it any longer. I struggled to breathe in his house."

Yngvi nodded. "That is how I feel, too. Only, it isn't his house that I struggle to breathe in but all of Woodhaven. After my confrontation with Thorolf, this place makes me feel low. I see no future here, and no home for Carla, Frida, and myself."

Asla's face fell. "I'm going to miss you."

Stina had recovered from her coughing fit. "I will miss you, too," she said sadly. "And what about you?" she asked Edna. "Will you stay here?"

"I'm going with them," replied the former maid with a small smile.

"Where will you go?" asked Digur, even though he knew the answer.

"Ryan's," replied Yngvi. "We get on well. I'm sure he will take us in."

A few days later, Yngvi, Carla, and Edna stowed their belongings in the bow and stern of the sailing boat Högni had completed.

Yngvi's new boat, which he paid with his house and his two horses, was seaworthy, possessed two pairs of oars, and offered room for eight people. Carla, going against her husband's wish to name the boat after her, had christened it *Hope*.

Shortly before his departure, Yngvi sought out Thorolf to arrange the handover of the *Shieldmaiden* with him. They spoke coldly and formally with each other, only discussing the bare necessities. Yngvi sensed that Thorolf was relieved at his departure—evidently, his brother had also reached the conclusion that Woodhaven was too small for the both of them.

When Yngvi asked his brother whether he would add a pregnant cow to the bargain, Thorolf nodded without hesitation. Yngvi suspected Thorolf felt a need to make good some of what had happened and to ease some of the bitterness between them. Thorolf promised to have the animal loaded onto the next ship traveling to Ryan's village. Yngvi nodded and left without a word of farewell.

On the way to the harbor, he ran into Gregor and Hilda, who would join him on the journey. Hilda, who had grown very fond of little Frida, wished to nurse the babe for a few weeks longer, until the girl could better stomach cow's milk and start to eat more solid food. This suited Gregor fine. He hadn't visited his congregation in Ryan's village for a while and suspected his flock longed to hear the word of God, be married by Gregor, and confess their sins. And there were bound to be a few newborns waiting to be christened by now.

Despite the cool morning, Gregor was sweating, staggering awkwardly down the path to the water under the weight of a heavy sack while his wife strode happily alongside him, carrying their little son in her arms.

Yngvi couldn't help but smile. He guessed the sack was filled with all sorts of items which Hilda had deemed indispensable for their journey, while Gregor wouldn't for a moment have thought them necessary. Taking pity on his friend, Yngvi took the sack off him and was rewarded with a look of gratitude from the red-faced, heavily breathing priest.

Waiting next to Carla on the jetty were Digur, Stina, Diara, Högni, and Asla; Edna had already climbed aboard with little Frida. The time had come to say farewell. Not forever, surely, but for a long while. Yngvi and Carla folded each person into their arms. These were the people they had grown close to during their voyage and during the time that followed, and they would miss them dearly.

Their friends waved when the *Hope* set off. Yngvi and Hilda pulled at the oars, while Carla held the tiller.

As they moved farther and farther away from the village, Yngvi gazed wistfully back at Woodhaven, which had been his home for almost one and a half years. The houses sat dotted along the gentle slope. Behind them, the rich green grass of the meadows and the golden-yellow ears of the fields swayed in the warm light of the morning sun. The settlement had developed well, and the families of farmers and fishermen pursued many different useful occupations. They produced baskets, pottery, fabric, and a variety of other everyday items, supplying their community with everything they needed.

Yngvi hoped Thorolf would rule Woodhaven wisely and justly, placing his own needs behind those of his people. But he had his doubts when he thought of the large, three-aisled longhouse Thorolf intended to build. His brother's first act of office had been to determine the amount of tribute the settlers were obliged to pay him each year and to organize a building crew for the erection of his new domicile.

When they reached the delta, Yngvi raised the sail. He looked over at Carla, who was sitting at the steering oar as if she was born to it, smiling at him. Her eyes radiated a confidence that infected Yngvi, dispelling his melancholy. They would have to begin anew in Ryan's village, and it would not be easy. But they were young, and they were strong. And they loved each other.

AFTERWORD

About the Game

Catan is an island. Not only in this novel, but also in the board game by the same name, which I developed during the early 1990s and which was published by Kosmos in 1995.

At the beginning of a round of Catan, we place nineteen hexagonal terrain tiles at random and soon behold an untouched island. There, among pastures, forests, and mountains, we build our first settlements, receive resources from adjacent terrains, and expand. Often, we lack the required resources for a project—like a road, for example, which we could use to cut off our opponents' access to a profitable settlement site. Perhaps another player has the resource we seek? We haggle and barter until we get what we need: "I offer ore for grain!" "Two wool for just one lumber!" or "Bricks! Bricks! Who will give me bricks?" shout the players excitedly across the island, which rests peacefully on the table and which we, competing fiercely and yet in friendship, gradually make our own. Even though only one of us will carry away the wreath of victory, the rest of us are left contented, proud of the land we made our own with roads, settlements, and cities.

I often get asked what gave me the idea for the game. Can I even call it an idea? No. It was a desire that lodged itself in the back of my mind after reading a book about the exploratory journeys of the Vikings. There were warriors among those people who, during the early Middle Ages, plundered the coasts of European countries. But there were also those who created a flourishing exchange of goods between north and south as merchants, helping to fill the vacuum left by the collapse of the Western Roman Empire.

Over time I acquired more books on these seemingly fearless seafaring people who inhabited the Scandinavia of the early Middle Ages. I learned that the term "Vikings" was erroneously used as a blanket term for the early Norwegians, Swedes, and Danes. The majority of those belonging to these groups were farmers and livestock herders who worked their land and grazed their animals. The term "Viking" only applied to the wealthy farmers and jarls who preferred to raid with their warriors rather than trade, and who took their ships on viking trips—raiding voyages.

Then there were the later-born sons of free farmers whose futures looked anything but rosy, since there wasn't enough arable land and pastures for everyone. Forced by hardship, they searched the expanse of the sea lapping at their shores for new, kinder land. They sailed their oceangoing vessels bravely across the open seas, discovering foreign climes—among others Iceland, then uninhabited. During the ninth century, an interglacial period determined Europe's weather patterns, and the south of Iceland profited from this. The women and men landing on the island's southwestern shore would have been welcomed by the sight of lush pastures, fertile plains, and expansive birch forests.

I imagined how those people of the North disembarked from their ships, filled with awe and hope at once as they set foot on this untouched land, their new home. With their sharpened axes, they felled trees and used the timber to build houses as shelter from the forces of nature. They let their sheep graze freely and without fear on the rich pastures, because there were no wolves on Iceland. Nor was there any game for them to hunt, and so the cultivation of fields must have been the settlers' uppermost priority.

In my—admittedly quite romantic—imagination, three sentiments came together upon arriving at a new land: the purity of nature, the simplicity of a natural life, and the sense of excited anticipation. The desire in the back of my mind throbbed ever more intensely, wishing to experience at least a hint of these emotions as part of a settler in a game. The throbbing erupted at last, giving birth to Catan, the game.

About the Book

Sometimes, when I played Catan, my imagination would run away with me. I would see men and women scuttling about busily in the settlement, cutting wood in the forest, tending sheep in the pastures, or plowing the soil of their fields. I would wonder what the settlers looked like, what they experienced together, and what dramatic circumstances had brought them to this island in the middle of a tumultuous Atlantic Ocean.

Whenever an idea came to me that would answer some of my questions, I noted it down. By and by, the initially faceless settlers took on form, and from the basis of the Northern culture of the Viking age grew—in fragments, at first—the tale of the women and men who, following a long and dangerous journey, arrived on Catan and settled there. I was filled with a growing urge to bring my notes together and set them down on paper as one tale. If I wanted to tell everything that was buzzing around my mind, I estimated that I would need around two thousand pages. Too much for one book, and so I decided on a trilogy, the first volume of which you, dear reader, now hold in your hands.

My tale about the settlement of Catan is historical fiction, but not fantasy. "Hang on," I can hear some of you shout, "Catan doesn't exist! It's fantasy." I would reply, however, that Catan might have existed if the central Atlantic mountain range in the area of the Azores had risen a little higher over the millennia, forming, instead of the many small islands, one larger one in their middle.

The line between fantasy and fiction is thin. If I had populated Catan with mammals like bears, wolves, wild boar, or horses, I would definitely have slipped into the realm of fantasy, because those animals would never have managed to swim for hundreds of miles from the European mainland to the isle of Catan or the Azores, respectively. How come the settlers on Catan encounter rabbits and Irish wolfhounds? That is a mystery I will solve in the second volume.

Not only its fauna, but also the original flora of the Azores differs significantly from the European continent due to their isolation. Prior to the arrival of the Portuguese explorers at the beginning of the fifteenth century, there were no beech, oak, or ash trees in the primeval forest covering much of the islands. Most of the growth were bushes like tree heath, Azores laurel, or Azores juniper, the seeds of which birds had carried to the islands in their droppings in ancient times. Thanks to the moist subtropical oceanic climate and the absence of human interference and that of larger herbivores, those bushes grew into imposing, treelike structures.

The protagonists of this novel are entirely fictitious, but they could have existed—especially Halldor, a made-up representative of the jarls, who, during the early Middle Ages, wrestled for the crown of the western Northland. Harald Fairhair was the first to unite large parts of what is modern-day Norway under his rule around AD 900.

Not made up are the viking voyages from the years AD 844 and 850, which set sail with huge fleets for the Iberian Peninsula, plundering and laying waste to settlements along the shores and rivers of Galicia and Asturias, in the north, and the Cordovan emirate in the south. In the end, they were stopped by the fleet the emir sent to meet them.

Iceland, which was mostly settled by people from what is now Norway in the years around AD 900, acted as an inspiration in many ways during the creation of my fictitious island and its history. For one thing, it was a good model geographically, because like Catan, the island in the North Atlantic lies remotely in the ocean and remained uninhabited until the arrival of its first settlers. For another, Iceland provided sociopolitical inspiration: from AD 930 onward, the leaders of Iceland, the *goðar*, met annually with the freemen of age of their territories in an assembly called Althing. There they settled arguments, reaching and declaring verdicts. Many view the Althing as the first parliament of northern Europe. There were similar forms of assemblies at other territories conquered by the Northmen, like the Faeroe Islands and the Isle of Man. The striving of my character Yngvi for a better system of society has its roots in, among other things, this history of the early Icelandic settlers who turned away from the rule of one and instead decided to govern their own commonwealth.

It is possible that some of my readers will find some of the topics I decided to discuss in my story, like equality between the sexes and the respect of human dignity, as premature for the early Middle Ages and therefore implausible. But why shouldn't a colorful mix of young people who—like the chain wielders in my novel—shared a difficult experience be able to free themselves from traditional values and make a stand for a fairer, more humane community in a new land?

Building settlements, exploiting resources, and trading are obvious parallels between the game and the book. But the topic of human rights also relates to the board game. At the gaming table, everyone is equal: origin, skin color, gender, sexual orientation, religion, and age do not matter. Everyone holds the same rights within the framework of the rules. While we play, we meet each other with respect. During the course of a game, we learn that we are more successful if we communicate, approach one another, and cooperate. War is not an option as a solution to conflict—neither in the game nor in the book.

ACKNOWLEDGMENTS

To everyone who stood by my side while I wrote.

My former colleague and friend Hans Lange sailed a small yacht across the Atlantic years ago and described to me his experiences in handling tall breakers in a stormy sea. I am deeply grateful to him, my only seafaring experience stemming from a cruise ship on my way to Iceland and the Azores. Like Olaf in my novel, Hans, too, has experienced the force of a white squall, which he and his friends thankfully survived unharmed.

I did not know much about bees and their keeping in the early Middle Ages when I first started to write. Andreas Göbel, a beekeeping friend of mine, filled my large knowledge gaps and provided me with extensive articles on beekeeping in the Middle Ages.

My wife, Claudia, as well as my two sons, Benjamin and Guido, read my manuscript, and their helpful comments led me to revise several points in the text.

Thank you at this point also to Gavin Allister, who pointed out the occasional inconsistency.

My friend Peter Neugebauer, who is a trained theologist,

advised me in religious matters. I was enormously relieved when he raised no objections to the reformulation of the Ten Commandments as Gregor suggests it in the book.

Peter Gustav Bartschat, bookseller, author of historical crime novels, and one of my two long-standing advisors in the development of the Catan card game for two, checked my manuscript for mistakes in historical matters and provided me with one or two helpful hints.

Juliane Voorgang was in charge of the design and production of my novel. Two years prior, she edited my book *Mein Weg nach Catan* very sensitively. Like then, working with her once again brought me much pleasure.

My special thanks to my editor, Kristina Wengorz, who not only corrected linguistic errors but also tracked down any last remaining contradictions in my story, lending me competent advice on the development of several of my characters, as well as to Lisa Reinhardt, who, in the course of her translation of my novel into English, prompted me to deepen my female protagonists.

Klaus Teuber, January 2022